The Traveller

John Katzenbach has been the criminal court reporter for the *Miami Herald* and also for the *Miami News*. His work has appeared in many other newspapers, including *The New York Times, Washington Post, Chicago Daily News* and *Philadelphia Enquirer*. His novel *In the Heat of the Summer* was a final nominee for the Mystery Writers of America's Edgar Award for the best first novel and was made into the film *The Mean Season*. He is also the author of the highly praised true crime story *First Born*.

John Katzenbach

The Traveller

Pan Books
in association with Macmillan

First published in the UK 1987 by Macmillan London Ltd
This edition published 1988 by Pan Books Ltd,
Cavaye Place, London SW10 9PG
in association with Macmillan
9 8 7 6 5 4 3 2 1

© John Katzenbach 1987
ISBN 0 330 30332 5

Printed and bound in Great Britain by
Richard Clay Ltd, Bungay, Suffolk

For Maddy

'Well, I never heard of the dev — of your claiming American citizenship,' said Dan'l Webster with surprise.

'And who with better right?' said the stranger with one of his terrible smiles. 'When the first wrong was done to the first Indian, I was there. When the first slaver put out for the Congo, I stood on her deck. Am I not in your books and stories and beliefs, from the first settlements on? Am I not spoken of still in every church in New England? 'Tis true the North claims me for a Southerner, and the South for a Northerner, but I am neither. I am merely an honest American like yourself – and of the best descent – for, to tell the truth, Mr. Webster, though I don't like to boast of it, my name is older in this country than yours . . .'

STEPHEN VINCENT BENÉT
The Devil and Daniel Webster

1 The reasons behind Detective Barren's obsession

1

She dreamt uneasily.

She could see a boat adrift, first in the distance, then suddenly closer until she realized that she was on the boat and surrounded by water. Her first thought was panic, to search about her and find someone to tell the important news that she was unable to swim. But each time she turned to look, her perch on the edge of the boat grew more precarious, and the wave action would sweep the small craft upward, balancing momentarily on wave edge, then falling away, sickeningly, bouncing her about, out of control. In her dream she looked for something solid to hold on to. As she seized the mast of the boat and clutched it with all the strength she could muster, an alarm went off, ringing, horrible, and she knew that it was the sound made when the boat sprung a leak and that she was moments from finding seawater lapping at her feet, tickling her with terror. The alarm continued to blare and she opened her mouth wide, ready to call or shout in fear for help, struggling as the boat rocked around her. In the dream the deck pitched abruptly and she cried out, as if to her sleeping self, Wake up! Wake up! Save yourself!

And she did.

She gasped wildly, spinning from sleep-state to wakefulness, sitting up suddenly in her bed, her right arm shooting out and seizing the bedstand, something solid amidst the vaporous fears of the dream. She realized then the telephone was ringing.

She cursed to herself, rubbed her eyes, and found the

telephone on the floor by the bed. She cleared her throat as she answered:

'Detective Barren here. What is it?'

She had not had time to assess the situation. She lived alone, without husband, without children, her own parents long since passed away, and so the idea that her telephone would ring in the midst of the night did not hold any particular terror for her, as it would have for so many people who are unaccustomed to late-night calls and who instantly would have foreseen the telephone ringing in the darkness for precisely what it was: terrible news. And, being a detective by trade, it was not unusual for her to be summoned at night, police work by necessity often taking place beyond banking hours. That was what she fully expected, that for some procedural reason her capabilities as a crime-scene technician were needed.

'Merce? Are you awake?'

'Yes. I'm fine. Who is it?'

'Merce, it's Robert Wills in homicide, I . . .' He let his voice trail off. Detective Barren waited.

'How can I help you?' she asked.

'Merce, I'm sorry to be the one to tell you this . . .'

She had a sudden mind's eye picture of Bob Wills sitting at his desk at the homicide office. It was a hard, harsh, open office, illuminated with unforgiving fluorescent light that was always on, filled with metal file cabinets and desks that were colored orange and to her mind seemed stained with all the horrors that had passed so casually in confession and conversation over the desktops.

'What?'

For an instant she felt a rush of excitement, a kind of delicious fear, far different from the dream-panic in which she had been immersed. Then, as her caller paused, an emptiness formed in her stomach, a kind of vacuum sensation, that was instantly replaced by a rush of anxiety. 'What is it?' she asked, aware that there was a touch of this new sense in her voice.

'Merce, you have a niece . . .'

'Yes, dammit. Her name is Susan Lewis. She's a student at the university. What is it? Has she been in an accident?'

But then the realization struck her: Bob Wills in homicide. Homicide. Homicide. And she knew then what the nature of the call was.

'I'm sorry,' he was saying, but his voice seemed very distant and for an instant she wished she were back in her dream.

Detective Mercedes Barren dressed swiftly and headed across Miami's licorice late summer night toward the address she'd written in a hand she thought was possessed with someone else's emotions; she'd felt her own heart racing, but seen her hand steady, scratching numbers and words on a pad. It had seemed to her that it was someone else who had finished the conversation with the homicide detective. She had heard her own voice hard and flat requesting available information, current status, names of officers in charge, facts about the crime already known, options being pursued by detectives. Witnesses. Evidence. Statements. She persisted, trying not to be put off by Detective Wills' evasions and excuses, recognizing that he wasn't in charge, but knew what she wanted to know, and all the time thinking that she was screaming inside, filled to explosion with some beast emotion that wanted to twist her into a single sob-shout of agony.

She would not allow herself to think of her niece.

Once, as she steered the car up on to the interstate that cuts through the center of the city, blinded for an instant by the headlights of a semi-tractor trailer truck that had pulled in horrifyingly close, air horn sounding raucously, she had fought off the sudden fear of a crash and discovered that she'd replaced the sensation with a picture of herself and her niece some two weeks beforehand. They had been sunning by the pool in the small beachside apartment building where Detective Barren lived and Susan had spotted her service revolver sticking awkwardly out of a beach bag, silly and incongruous amidst towels, suntan lotion, a frisbee, and a paperback novel. Detective Barren thought of the teenager's response: she'd called the revolver 'gross', which was, to the detective's mind, an absolutely apt description.

'Why do you have to carry it, anyway?'

'Because technically we're never off duty. If I were to spot a crime, I would have to react like a policewoman.'

'But I didn't think you had to do that anymore, not since . . .'

'Right. Not since the shooting. No, I'm a pretty tame policewoman now. By the time I get to a crime everything is pretty much over.'

'Yuck. Dead bodies, right?'

'Right. Yuck is right, too.'

They'd laughed.

'It would be funny,' Susan had said.

'What would be funny?'

'To get arrested by a policeperson wearing a bikini.'

They'd laughed again. Detective Barren had watched her niece rise and dive into the opaque blue pool water. She'd watched as Susan had effortlessly swum submerged to the far end, then, without rising for air, pivoted and snaked back to the edge. For one instant Detective Barren had felt a twinge of lost youth jealousy, then let it pass, thinking, Well, you're not in such bad shape yourself.

The younger woman hung on the edge and asked her aunt: 'Merce, why is it that you live next to the ocean and can't swim a lick?'

'Part of my mystery,' she replied.

'Seems silly to me,' Susan had said, slipping from the pool, the water glistening, flooding from her thin body. She continued: 'Did I tell you I've decided to major this fall in oceanographic studies? Slimy fish for sure.' She'd laughed. 'Spiny crustaceans. Massive mammals. Jacques Cousteau, move over.'

'That's excellent,' said the detective. 'You've always loved the water.'

'Right.' She sang, 'Oh for a life of the sun, the sand, the deep blue sea and fish guts for me.'

They'd laughed again.

She was always laughing, thought the detective, and she accelerated through the night. The explosive whiteness of the downtown night lights burst beside her, illuminating the edges of the great buildings as they rose up in the Southern sky. Then Detective Barren felt a great rush of heat in her heart, choking her, and she forced herself to concentrate on her driving, trying to wipe her mind free of memory, thinking, Let's see, let's find out, trying not to connect the scene she was heading toward with the memories in her brain.

Detective Barren turned off Route 1 and drove through a residential area. It was late, well past midnight and closing rapidly on dawn; there was little traffic and she had hurried, filled with the emergency sense of speed that accompanies any violent death. But a few miles short of her destination she slowed precipitously, until her nondescript sedan was barely crawling down the empty streets. She searched the rows of trim, upper-class houses for signs of life. The streets were dark, as were the homes. She tried to envision the lives that slept behind the ordered suburban darkness. Occasionally she would spot a light burning in one room and she wondered what book or television show or argument or worry kept the occupant up. She had an overwhelming urge to stop, to knock on the door to one of these houses with their meager sign of life, to stop and say, Is there some trouble that keeps you awake? Something that probes at the memory and heart and prevents sleep? Let me share.

She turned the car onto Old Cutler Road and knew the distance to the park's entrance was only a few hundred yards ahead. The nighttime seemed to permeate the foliage; great melaleuca trees and willows hid blackness in their leaves and branches, stretching over the road like enveloping arms. She had the eerie sense that she was entirely alone in the world, that she was a sole survivor heading nowhere in the midst of an endless night. She could barely make out the faded white lettering on the small park entrance sign. She was startled when an opposum ran in front of the wheels of her car, and she slammed on her brakes, shuddering with fear for an instant, breathing out harshly when she realized that the animal had avoided the tires. She rolled down the window and could smell the salt air; the trees around her had shrunk in stature, the giant palms that rode the edge of the highway replaced by the tangled and gnarled branches of waterfront mangroves. The road curved sharply, and she knew she would be able to see the wide expanse of Biscayne Bay when she emerged.

She thought at first that it was moonlight glistening on the bay waters.

It was not.

She stopped the car suddenly, and stared out at the scene before her. She became aware first of the mechanical noise of powerful generators. Their steady rhythmic thumping powered three banks of high-intensity lights. The flood-lights delineated a stage cut from the darkness at the edge of the park's parking lot, peopled with dozens of uniformed police officers and detectives, moving gingerly through the unnatural brightness. A row of police cruisers, an ambulance, white and green crime-scene search wagons were lined up on the fringe of the stage, their blue and red emergency lights throwing sudden strobes of color onto the people working within the parameters of the floodlights.

She took a deep breath and headed toward the light.

She parked her car on the rim of activity and started to walk to the center, where she spotted a group of men gathered. They were staring down at something that was obscured from her vision. She knew what it was, but this was an appreciation of experience, not of emotion. The entire area had been encircled with a three-inch-wide strip of yellow tape. Every ten feet or so a small white sign had been hung from the tape: POLICE CRIME SCENE DO NOT ENTER. She lifted the barrier and slipped underneath. The motion caught the eye of a uniformed officer, who swiftly moved to intersect her path, holding out his hands.

'Hey,' he said. 'Ma'am, you can't go in there.'

She stared at him and he stopped. His hands dropped. Exaggerating her movement by pacing it slowly, she opened her purse and produced her gold shield. He glanced quickly at it, then backed off rapidly, muttering an apology. But her arrival had been noted by the men in the center of the scene, and one of them quickly broke from the crowd and moved to block her.

'Merce, for Christ's sake. Didn't Wills tell you not to come down here?'

'Yes,' she replied.

'There's nothing here for you.'

'How the hell would you know?'

'Merce, I'm sorry. This must be . . .'

She interrupted him furiously.

'Must be what? Hard? Sad? Difficult? Tragic? What do you think it must be!'

'Calm down. Look, you know what's going on here, can you just hang on for a couple of minutes? Here, let me get you a cup of coffee.' He tried to take her by the elbow and lead her away. She shrugged off his grip swiftly.

'Don't try to steer me away, goddammit!'

'Just a couple of minutes, then I'll give you a complete briefing . . .'

'I don't want a goddamn briefing. I want to see for myself.'

'Merce . . .' The detective spread his arms wide, still blocking her vision. 'Give me a break.'

She took a deep breath and closed her eyes. She spoke in a clipped, deliberate fashion.

'Peter. Lieutenant Burns. Two things. One, that is my niece lying there. Two, I am a professional policewoman. I want to see for myself. Myself!'

The lieutenant stopped. He looked at her.

'All right. It will only be a few minutes now before the medical examiner completes his initial inspection. When they put her on a stretcher, you can come over. You can perform the official identification then if you want.'

'Not a few minutes. Not on a stretcher. I want to see what happened to her.'

'Merce. For Christ's sake . . .'

'I want to see.'

'Why? It will just make it harder.'

'How the hell would you know? How the hell could it make anything harder?'

A sudden flash of light burst behind the lieutenant. He turned and Detective Barren saw a police photographer moving in and out of position. 'Now,' she said. 'I want to see now.'

'All right,' said the lieutenant, stepping aside. 'It's your nightmare.'

She marched past him quickly.

Then she stopped.

She took a deep breath.

She closed her eyes once, picturing her niece's smile.

She took another deep breath and carefully approached the body. She thought: Remember everything! Fix it in your mind. She forced her eyes to scan the ground around the shape she could not yet look at. Sandy dirt and leaves. Nothing that would produce a solid shoeprint. With a practiced eye, she estimated the distance between the parking lot and the location of the shape – she couldn't, in her mind, speak body. Twenty yards. A good dumping distance. She tried to think analytically: There was a problem. It was always easier if the – again her thoughts were staggered and mentally she hesitated – victims were discovered in the location where the homicide took place. Invariably there would be some physical evidence. She continued to scan the ground, hearing the lieutenant's voice behind her: 'Merce, we searched the area very carefully, you don't have to . . .' But she ignored him, knelt, and felt the consistency of the dirt. She thought: If some of this stuck to the shoes, we could make a match. Without turning to see if he was still there, she spoke out loud, 'Take earth samples from the entire area.' After a momentary pause, she heard a grunt of assent. She continued, thinking, strength, strength, until she was next to the shape. All right, she said to herself. Look at Susan. Memorize what happened to her this night. Look at her. Look at every part of her. Don't miss anything.

And she raised her eyes to the shape.

'Susan,' she said out loud, but softly.

She was aware of the other people moving about her, but only in a peripheral sense. That they had faces, that they were people she knew, colleagues, friends, she was aware, but only in the most subliminal fashion. Later, she would try to remember who was there, at the scene, and be unable.

'Susan,' she said again.

'Is that your niece, Susan Lewis?' It was the lieutenant's voice.

'Yes.'

She hesitated.

'It was.'

She felt suddenly overcome by heat, as if one of the spotlights had singled her out, covering her with a solid beam of intense brightness. She gulped a great breath of air, then another, fighting a dizzying sensation. She remembered the moment years earlier when she'd realized that she was shot, that the warmth she felt was the lifeblood flowing from her, and she fought with the same intensity to prevent her eyes from rolling back, as if giving into the blackness of unconsciousness would be as fatal now as it would have been then.

'Merce?'

She heard a voice.

'Are you all right?'

She was rooted.

'Somebody get fire-rescue!'

Then she managed to shake her head.

'No,' she said. 'I'm going to be okay.'

What a silly thing to say, she thought.

'You sure? You want to sit down?'

She did not know who she was talking to. She shook her head again.

'I'm okay.'

Someone was holding her arm. She snatched it loose.

'Check her fingernails,' she said. 'She would have fought hard. We may have a scratched-up suspect.'

She saw the medical examiner bend over the body, gingerly lift each hand, and, using a small scalpel, gently

15

scrape the contents under each nail into small plastic evidence bags. 'Not much there,' he said.

'She would have fought like a tiger,' Detective Barren insisted.

'Perhaps he didn't give her a chance. There's severe trauma to the back of the head. Blunt instrument. She was probably unconscious when he did this.' The doctor motioned at the pantyhose that were wrapped tightly around Susan's throat. Detective Barren stared for a moment at the bluish cast to the skin.

'Check the knot,' she said.

'I already looked,' said the doctor. 'Simple square knot. Page one of the Boy Scout Handbook.'

Detective Barren stared at the pantyhose. She desperately wanted to loosen it, to put her niece at rest, as if by making her look as if she were only sleeping it would be true. She remembered a moment when she was growing up. She had been very young, no more than five or six, and the family dog had been hit by a car and killed. 'Why is Lady dead?' she'd asked her father. 'Because her bones were broken,' he replied. 'But when I broke my wrist the doctor put a cast on it and now it is better,' she had said. 'Let's put a cast on Lady.' 'But she lost all her blood, too,' said her father. 'Well,' the child in her memory said with insistence grown of despair, 'let's put the blood back in.' 'Oh, my poor little child,' said her father, 'I wish we could. I wish it were so simple.' And he'd wrapped big arms around her as she sobbed through the longest of childhood nighttimes.

She stared at Susan's body and longed for those arms again.

'How about the wrists?' she asked. 'Any signs of restraints?'

'No,' said the doctor. 'That tells us something.'

'Yeah,' said a voice from the side. Detective Barren didn't turn to see who was speaking. 'It tells us this creep conked her before he had his fun. She probably never knew what hit her.'

Detective Barren's eyes scanned down from the neck.

'Is that a bite mark on the shoulder?'

'Probably,' said the medical examiner. 'Got to check microscopically.'

She fixed her eyes for an instant on her niece's torn blouse. Susan's breasts were exposed, and she wanted to cover them. 'Swab the neck for saliva,' she said.

'Did it,' said the doctor. 'Genital swabs, too. I'll do it again when we get to the morgue.'

Detective Barren's eyes slid down the body, inch by inch. One leg was flung over the other, almost coyly, as if even in death her niece was modest.

'Was there any sign of laceration to the genitals?'

'Not visible out here.'

Detective Barren paused, trying to take it all in.

'Merce,' said the doctor gently, 'it's pretty much like the other four. Mode of death. Positioning of the body. Dumping ground.'

Detective Barren looked up sharply.

'Others? Other four?'

'Didn't Lieutenant Burns tell you? They think it's this guy the papers are calling the Campus Killer. I thought they'd told you . . .'

'No . . .' she said. 'No one told me.'

She took a deep breath.

'But it makes perfectly good sense. It fits . . .' And her voice trailed off.

She heard the lieutenant's voice next.

'Probably his first of the semester. I mean, nothing is certain, but the general pattern is the same. We're going to assign the case to him so the task force can work it – I think that's best, Merce?'

'Right.'

'Seen enough now? Will you come over here and let me tell you what we've got and what we haven't got?'

She nodded. She closed her eyes and turned away from the body. She hoped that they would move Susan soon, as if by pulling her out of the underbrush and dirt that it would start to restore some humanity to her, lessen somehow the violation, diminish somehow the totality of her death.

She waited patiently next to the cars belonging to the crime-scene search specialists and the evidence technicians. They were all people she knew well, the night shift in the same office she worked. Individually, they all broke off from their duties within the yellow tape area and spoke to her, or touched her shoulder or grasped her hand, before going back to processing the scene. In a few moments Lieutenant Burns returned with two cups of coffee. She wrapped her hands around the Styrofoam cup he held out to her, suddenly chilled, though the tropical night was oppressively warm. He looked up at the sky, just starting to fade from dark, creeping gray light marking the edges of morning.

'Do you want to know?' he asked. 'It might be better, all around, if you just . . .'

She interrupted quickly. 'I want to know. Everything.'

'Well,' he started slowly. She knew he was trying to assess in his own mind whether sharing information with her would hinder the investigation. She knew he was wondering whether he was dealing with a policewoman or with a half-crazed relative. The trouble, she thought, was that he was dealing with both.

'Lieutenant,' she said, 'I merely want to help. I have a good deal of expertise, as you know. I want to make myself available. But, if you think I'll be in the way, I'll back off . . .'

'No, no, no,' he replied quickly.

How simple, she thought. She knew that by offering to not ask questions she would get permission to ask every one.

'Look,' the lieutenant continued, 'things are pretty sketchy so far. Apparently she and some friends went out to a bar on the campus. There were a lot of people around, a lot of different guys hanging about. She danced with a number of different guys, too. About 10 p.m. she went outside to get some air. She went alone. Didn't come back in. It wasn't until a couple of hours later, just about midnight, that her friends got worried and called the campus cops.

'Just about the same time a couple of fruits down here in the park just getting it on in the bushes over there stumbled on the body . . .' He held up his hand. 'No. They didn't see or hear anything. Literally stumbled, too. One of the guys fell right over it . . .'

The body, she thought. It. She bit her lip.

'Girl disappears from campus. Body gets discovered in a park a couple of miles away. It wasn't hard to put one and one together. And we've been here since. Her purse had your name in it. That's why you were called. Your sister's kid?'

Detective Barren nodded.

'You want to make that call?'

Oh, God, she thought.

'I will. When we clear here.'

'There's a pay phone over there. I wouldn't want to make them wait. And it's likely to be awhile before we finish . . .'

She became aware of the growing dawn light. The area was steadily losing its nighttime blackness, shapes taking form, becoming distinct as the darkness faded.

'All right,' she said.

She thought how utterly mundane and hopelessly banal the act of telephoning her sister and brother-in-law was. For a second she hoped that she did not have a quarter to put in the pay phone's slot, then hoped that the telephone would be out of order. It was not. The operator answered with routine brightness, as if immune to the hour of the day. Detective Barren charged the call to her office. The operator asked her when someone would be there to confirm accepting the charges. Detective Barren told her someone was always there. Then she heard the electronic clicking of the number being dialed, and suddenly, before she was ready with the right words, the phone was ringing at her sister's house. Think! Detective Barren thought. Find words! And she heard her sister's voice, slightly groggy with sleep, on the other end of the line:

'Yes, hello . . .'

'Annie, it's Merce.' She bit her lip.

'Merce! How are you? What's . . .'

'Annie. Listen carefully: It's Susan. There's been a . . .' she fumbled. Accident? Incident? She just barreled on, oblivious, trying to keep her voice a professionally calm, even, flat tone. 'Please sit down and ask Ben to get on the line . . .'

She heard her sister gasp and then call to her husband.

In a moment, he joined the line. 'Merce, what is it?' His voice was steady. Ben was an accountant. She hoped he would be as solid as numbers. She took a deep breath.

'I don't know any way of telling you this to make it easier, so I'll just tell you. Susan is dead. She was killed last night. Murdered. I'm sorry.'

Detective Barren suddenly saw her sister, some eighteen years earlier, immense with pregnancy, a week from delivery, moving uncomfortably through the oppressive July heat that hung unforgiving in the dry Delaware Valley summer to sit at her side. Detective Barren had tenaciously clutched the flag the honor guard captain had bestowed on her, her own mind black, empty, reverberating with the chaplain's words, blending with the crisp sound of the rifle volley fired over the grave. She'd had no words for any of the family or friends who'd sidled up self-consciously, wordless at the incongruity of someone as vigorous and young as John Barren dying, even in battle. Annie had settled herself onto the couch next to Detective Barren and when no one was watching, or at least when she thought no one was watching, had taken her sister's hand and placed it on her great stomach and said with heartbreaking simplicity, 'God took him unfairly, but here's new life and you shouldn't leave your love in the grave with him, but give it to this child instead.'

The child had been Susan.

For a moment, Detective Barren smiled at the memory, thinking: The baby saved my life.

And then, suddenly, swirling back into reality, she heard her sister's first sob of broken mother's anguish.

*

Ben had wanted to take the first flight to Miami, but she was able to dissuade him from that course. It would be simpler, she told them, if she made the arrangements with a funeral home to ship the body when the medical examiner finished the autopsy. She would accompany Susan's body back on the airplane. Ben had said he would call a local funeral home to co-ordinate plans. Detective Barren told them that they would probably hear from the newspapers, perhaps even the television. She recommended that they co-operate; it was much easier, she said, and the reporters would be less likely to get in the way. She explained that preliminary indications were that Susan was the victim of a killer who had prowled the campuses of Miami's various colleges the past year and that there was a task force of detectives assigned to the cases. Those detectives, she said, would be in touch. Ben had asked if she was sure about that killer, and she said nothing was certain but that it appeared to be the same. Ben had started to bluster, angry, but after spitting out a few words of rage, he'd stopped, lapsing into a continual stunned acquiescence. Annie said nothing. Detective Barren guessed that they were in different rooms, and that it would not be until they hung up and turned to face each other that full despair would hit them.

'That's all I can tell you for now,' Detective Barren said. 'I'll call later when I know more.'

'Merce?' It was her sister.

'Yes, Annie.'

'Are you sure?'

'Oh, Annie . . .'

'I mean, you checked, didn't you? You're certain?'

'Annie. I saw her. I looked. It's Susan.'

'Thank you. I just needed to know for sure.'

'I'm sorry.'

'Yes. Yes. Of course. We'll talk later.'

'Ben?'

'Yes, Merce. I'm still here. We'll talk later.'

'All right.'

'Oh, God, Merce . . .'

'Annie?'

'Oh, God.'

'Annie, be strong. You'll have to be strong.'

'Merce, please help me. I feel like if I hang up the telephone with you now, it will be like killing her. Oh, God. What is going on? Please. I don't understand.'

'I don't understand either, Annie.'

'Oh, Merce, Merce, Merce . . .'

Detective Barren heard her name fading. She knew that her sister had let the telephone slip from her hand to the bed. She could hear tears and it was like listening to a heart break. She remembered in high school watching a football practice; as she stood on the sidelines, one of the players had been struck awkwardly. The sound of the leg snapping had risen above the noise of bodies thumping together. She'd seen one of the other players get sick as the coaches and trainer rushed to the stricken boy. For an instant she expected to hear the same cracking sound. She held the telephone in her hand momentarily, then, gently, as if trying not to disturb a sleeping child, replaced the receiver on the hook. She stood still, listening to her own heart. She swallowed deeply, then flexed her arm muscles once, twice. Then her legs. She could feel the skin, muscle, and tendons stretch and contract. I'm strong, she thought. Be stronger still.

2

It was midmorning before Susan's body was finally removed.

Detective Barren had remained on the fringe of the crime scene, watching the orderly collection of evidence. Uniformed policemen kept a steadily growing crowd of the curious far back, for which she was grateful. The Miami news media had arrived early, ubiquitously insinuating themselves into the scene. The television cameramen had photographed the activity while the reporters had busied themselves questioning Lieutenant Burns and some of the other detectives. She knew it was inevitable that one of the reporters would eventually hear of her connection to the body, and that it would become prominent in the retelling. She decided to simply wait for the questions.

She had turned away when two medical examiner's office technicians had gingerly slipped Susan's body into a black bag. She walked over to where Lieutenant Burns was standing, speaking with a pair of nattily dressed detectives in three-piece suits who seemed oblivious to the gathering muggy day's heat. When he saw her approach, he turned and performed the introductions.

'Merce. Detective Barren. I don't know if you know detectives Moore and Perry from county homicide. They head up this Campus Killer investigation.'

'Only by reputation.'

'Likewise,' said Detective Perry.

They all shook hands and stood awkwardly.

'I'm sorry to meet under these circumstances,' Detective Perry said. 'I've been a fan of your work. Especially on that multiple-rape case.'

'Thank you,' said Detective Barren. She had a brief vision of a pockmarked face and misshapen nose. She remembered poring over some two dozen case files again and again until coming up with the link that had led to the arrest. The heavily muscled rapist always wore a stocking mask. Almost every victim said she was aware he suffered from severe acne on his back. A dermatologist had told her that people with acne on their back are generally scarred on the face as well. But she had thought the mask was to hide something else. She'd begun hanging out at the local gymnasiums and health clubs. More a hunch than a probable cause. At the 5th Street Gym on Miami Beach, a place where aspiring boxers' dreams mingled freely with the sound of speed bags thumping, she'd spotted a short, powerfully built lightweight, heavily pockmarked on the back and face, with a badly broken nose and a distinctive red scar that twisted down his cheek.

'Never underestimate intuition,' said Detective Perry.

'Except it doesn't do much with a judge when you need a search warrant.'

They all smiled hesitantly.

'So how can we help you?' Detective Perry said.

'Was there anything discovered underneath the body?'

'Nothing of obvious value. There was one odd piece of paper.'

'What was it?'

'Actually a fragment. It looks like the top part of the type of tag they put on your luggage handle when you check your bags at the airport, only considerably larger. Some kind of tag, anyway.' He held up his hand. 'No, there were no markings on it. It was just the top quarter, the rest was torn away. Also, there was no way of telling how long it was there. She could have been put on top of it. Just a piece of trash, I think.'

She thought of her niece lying amidst the refuse. She shook her head, trying to clear the thought.

'What are you going to do now?' Detective Barren asked.

'We're going to work the nightclub, see if we can find anyone who noticed someone talking with her, following her . . .' The detective looked at Detective Barren. 'It'll take some time.'

'Time is not relevant.'

'I understand.'

He paused.

'Look, detective. This must be impossible for you. I know that if it was one of my sisters I'd be going crazy. I'd want to blow the guy away myself. So, as far as I'm concerned, you can know whatever you want about the investigation, as long as you don't try to get in the way or do our job for us. Is that fair?'

Detective Barren nodded.

'One other thing,' Detective Perry added. 'If you get ideas, bring them to me directly.'

'No problem,' Detective Barren said. She wondered if she were lying. She thought for a moment. 'One question. This is the fifth, right? What's the status of the others? Can you make somebody on an earlier case?'

The detectives hesitated, looking at each other.

'Good question. We got some leads. A couple of good

ones. You come in in a couple of days, we'll talk, okay? After you get a little settled, huh?'

Condescending bastard, she thought.

'That's fine,' she said.

She left the men still conversing and walked back to the evidence trucks. A thin, ascetic-looking man was checking the numbers written in black Magic Marker on plastic bags against a master list on a clipboard in his hand. 'Hello, Teddy,' she said.

The man turned to her. He had large bony hands that seemed to flap about. 'Oh, Merce. I thought you'd gone. You don't have to be here, you know.'

'I know. Why does everyone keep telling me that?'

'I'm sorry. It's just that, well, no one really knows how to react. I guess you make everyone nervous. We're not accustomed to being affected by death, you know, and this, well, seeing you, makes it less a job, more a reality. Does that make any sense?'

'Yes.' She smiled at him.

'Merce. I can't tell you how badly everyone feels for you. Everyone has worked real hard on the scene. I just hope there's something here that will lead us to the creep.'

'Thanks, Teddy. What have you collected?'

'There's not too much. Here's the list.'

He handed her the clipboard and her eyes scanned the page:

1. Blood sample area of v's head
2. Blood sample area of v's crotch (see diagram)
3. Saliva sample v's shoulder
4. Swabs v's genitals
5. Swabs v's shoulder (bite mark see diagram)
6. Dirt sample A (see diagram)
7. Dirt sample B (see diagram)
8. Dirt sample C (see diagram)
9. Fingernail sample v right hand (see diagram)
10. Same, left hand (see diagram)
11. Unknown substance/leaf
12. Possible clothing sample
13. Trace blood on leaf

25

14. Cigarette butt (see diagram)
15. Cigarette butt (see diagram)
16. Used condom
17. Used condom
18. Unused condom in foil (Ramses brand)
19. Beer can (Budweiser)
20. Coca-Cola can
21. Perrier bottle (6 oz)
22. Unknown substance in tin foil wrapping
23. Unknown substance in plastic bag
24. Film box Kodacolor Instamatic film
25. Film box Kodacolor Instamatic film
26. Box end Kodak 400 black/white film for negatives
27. Used Cutter Lotion 5½ oz
28. Sea and Ski lotion 12 oz
29. Crushed package (empty) Marlboro cigarettes
30. Woman's handbag (contents listed separately)
31. Woman's wallet (victim)
32. Woman's earring
33. Tag end paper color yellow origin unknown (under body)

'What about the condoms?' she asked.

He shook his head. 'Merce, look at this stuff. It's the kind of stuff you find in any picnic area. The unknown stuff appears to be like tuna fish. And the condoms seem old, probably several days, just guessing. And look at the diagrams. Except for the skin and blood samples, all this junk was collected at least a couple of feet away. It's the kind of stuff you might bring along for a little time in the sun – not a killing in the middle of the night.'

She nodded.

'Is this painful? Do you want to . . .'

'Yes.'

'That's what I figured. Anyway, until we really get the stuff into the lab we won't know, but it seems to me and just about everyone else that she was dropped here. Probably the creep pulled his car up and just dumped her a little ways away. When we get the guy's car, that's where we'll put him away. There's got to be blood, skin, the works inside it. Can't hide that stuff. But workable evidence from this scene? We can hope, but I wouldn't count on it.'

She nodded again.

'I'm not saying anything you don't know.'

'That's right.'

She handed the list back to him and stared at the rows of plastic bags, carefully lined up in the back of the wagon. She didn't really know what she was looking for.

'What's that?' she asked, pointing at one bag.

'That's the last item on the list. Some kind of yellow tag. It was found under the body.'

He handed it to her. She searched through the clear plastic, turning the frayed piece of paper back and forth beneath her scrutiny. What are you? she wondered. What do you mean? What are you trying to tell me? Who put you there? She had the sudden urge to shake the small piece of paper viciously, as if she could force it to talk back to her. I will remember you, she said to the paper. She looked up at all the collected items. I will remember all of you.

She was overcome with how crazy she was. She put the plastic bag into the back of the wagon.

She thought she seemed silly. She knew that it would take come time to process the scene, knew the likelihood of some relevant piece of evidence was minimal. She flushed suddenly, turning around. She saw the detectives getting into an unmarked car. A police photographer was in the distance, taking long shots. The medical examiner's truck was pulling out of the rear of the lot; she saw the television cameramen lined up, getting a picture of the exit. She was overcome with a sense of helplessness, as if the carefully constructed police-veneer that had guarded her throughout the long morning was slipping away, as the crowd of technicians, detectives, and curious began to dissipate. She felt a sudden vulnerability, as if all she would be left with was her emotions. She caught a gasp forming in her chest, working its way up her throat. Breathing hard, she turned away and walked back to her own car, feeling the blast of built-up heat flood out as she opened the door. She quickly slid behind the wheel and closed the door. She sat in the broiling interior, letting the warmth penetrate her resolve.

She thought of Susan. She thought of her dream. She wanted to scream to herself, as she had in the last moments of sleep. Wake up! Save yourself!

But she could not.

The lady in the flower store had eyed Detective Barren oddly and finally asked, 'Is there some special occasion or event that these would be for?' Detective Barren had hesitated before replying, and the lady had continued, blithely, 'I mean, if these are for a co-worker or secretary, then I might recommend one of these floral arrangements. Are they for a shut-in or an invalid? A bouquet like this would look nice. Someone in the hospital perhaps? We find that hospital patients love to receive small plants – you see, they enjoy watching the plants root and grow . . .'

'They're for my lover,' said Detective Barren.

'Oh,' said the woman, slightly taken aback.

'Is there something wrong?'

'No, it's just unusual. Usually, you see, it's the men who come in for flowers, roses generally, for their, uh, companions. This is a change.' She laughed. 'Some things never change in the world no matter how modern we get. Men buy flowers for their women friends and wives. Not the other way around. They come into the store and stand rather self-consciously in front of the refrigerated display, staring for all the world at the flowers as if hoping there would be a sign, a something, that said: Buy me for your wife. Or girlfriend. And not young men, either. Young men today don't seem to understand the value of proper flowers. Sometimes I think we have grown too – I don't know – scientific. I mean, I expect they'll want to send computer-written Valentine's cards soon enough. But it's always men, dear, not women. No, I don't believe I've ever had a woman come in and . . .'

Detective Barren looked at the woman, who stopped speaking in mid-sentence, hesitated, then continued.

'Oh, dear,' said the woman. 'I'm making rather a fool of myself, aren't I?'

'A little,' Detective Barren replied.

'Oh, dear,' the woman said again.

'It's all right,' Detective Barren said.

'You're kind,' said the woman. The detective watched as she brushed a strand of gray hair off her forehead and composed herself. 'I'll try again,' said the woman. 'How may I help you?'

'I'd like to buy some flowers,' said Detective Barren.

'For someone special?'

'Of course.'

'Ah, let me suggest roses. They are perhaps the least original selection, but the most trustworthy. And always loved, which, of course, is what we are buying flowers for.'

'I think that would be nice,' said Detective Barren.

'A dozen?'

'Excellent.'

'I have red, white, and pink?' This was a question. The detective thought for a moment.

'Red and white, I think.'

'Excellent. And some Baby's Breath to set them off, I would imagine.'

'They look lovely.'

'Thank you.'

Detective Barren paid and the woman handed her the box. 'I get a little crazy,' said the woman.

'I beg your pardon?' replied the detective.

'You see, I end up spending most of the day talking to the flowers and plants. Sometimes I forget how to talk with people. I'm sure your, uh, friend will enjoy those.'

'My lover,' said the detective.

She clutched the flower box under her arm and tried to remember how many years had passed since she'd been to John Barren's grave.

The early September air had not even the slightest intimation of fall. Instead it hung heavy with residual summer heat, liar's blue sky broken with a few huge white clouds; a day for lazing about in August memories, ignoring the January inevitability of the Delaware Valley, with its snow, cold wind off the river, ice, and frequent visitations of what

29

the natives called slush storms, an unfortunate mingling of ice, sleet, snow, and rain together in an impenetrable, chilling, slippery impossibility. One of those storms, thought Detective Barren with a small smile. She had been caught outside, battery dead, boots soaked. When she finally returned to her home, empty, cold, alone, she had vowed to start over somewhere warm. Miami.

She placed the flowers on the passenger seat of the rental car and drove out of Lambertville, across the bridge over the river to New Hope. The town, filled with the quaint, the precious and the upscale, stretched out on either side of the river; in a few moments she had left it behind, travelling slowly through the warm afternoon, down a shaded road, toward the cemetery. She wondered for a moment why the family had ever moved closer to Philadelphia when it was so pretty in the country. She had a sudden picture of her father, learning of his appointment at the University of Pennsylvania, swinging her mother like some buckaroo at a square dance. He had taught mathematical theory and quantum mechanics; his intelligence daunting, his worldliness absent. She smiled. He would not have understood for an instant why she was a policewoman. He would have admired some of the deductive reasoning, some of the investigative tactics, some of the apparent precision of police work, but he would have been confused and dismayed by the truths of the profession and the ever-present rubbing up against evil. He certainly would not have understood why his daughter loved it so, though he would have admired the basic simplicity of her devotion: that it was the easiest way to achieve some good in a world filled with – in her mind she hesitated, as she had so often over the past few days – filled with creeps who kill eighteen-year-old girls suffused with life and promise and future and goodness. Detective Barren drove on, the warm memory of her father sliding away in the shadows, replaced by a sketchpad in her mind, and her imagination trying to draw in the features of a killer. She almost missed the entrance to the cemetery.

Someone had placed a small American flag on John

Barren's grave, and for a moment she wasn't sure that she wanted it there. Then she relented, thinking, If this gives the local VFW some satisfaction, who am I to refuse it? That was what gravesites and memorials are for, she thought, the living. She could not look at the headstone and the parched grass that covered the plot and envision John below in a coffin. She caught her breath suddenly at a memory:

Remains nonviewable.

The coffin had a tag on one handle. It was probably supposed to be removed before she saw it, but she had seen.

In her unruly grief she had puzzled at the tag.

Remains nonviewable.

She had thought first, strangely, that it meant that John was naked, and that the Army, in a silly, foolish, masculine way, was trying to protect everyone from embarrassment. She had wanted to say to the men surrounding the coffin. Don't be so stupid. Of course we saw each other naked. We delighted in those moments. We were lovers in high school, in college, on the night he was drafted and in the hours before he took the bus to basic training, and constantly in the two short weeks of leave before he went overseas. In the summer, down at the Jersey Shore, we would sneak out after our parents had gone to bed and meet in the moonlight and roll naked in the sand dunes.

Remains nonviewable.

She'd considered those two strange words. Remains – well, that was John. Nonviewable – well, that meant she couldn't see him. She wondered why. What had they done to him? She tried to ask, but discovered that a young dead man's bride didn't get straight answers. She'd been hugged instead and told that it was all for the better, and told it was God's Will and war was hell and any number of things that, to her mind, didn't seem to have a great deal of relevance to the issue. She had begun to grow impatient and increasingly distraught, which only made the military men and family men all the more frustrating in their denial. Finally, as her voice had started to rise and her demands grew more strident, she'd felt a hand clamp her arm tightly. It had been the funeral director; a man she'd never seen before. He'd looked at her intensely, then, to the surprise of her family, led her into a side office. He had sat her down, businesslike, in a chair across from his desk. For a moment he'd shuffled papers, while she sat, waiting. Finally he discovered what he was searching for. 'They didn't tell you, did they?' he asked.

'No,' she said. She hadn't known what he was talking about.

'They just told you he was dead, right?'

That was true. She nodded her head.

'Well,' he said brusquely, then suddenly slowing, 'you sure you want to know?'

Know what? she wondered, but she nodded again.

'All right,' he said. Sadness crawled into his voice. 'Corporal Barren was killed while on routine patrol in the Quang Tri province. The man next to him stepped on a land mine. A big one. It killed your husband and two others.'

'But why can't I . . .'

'Because there wasn't enough of him left to look at.'

'Oh.'

Silence filled the room. She didn't know what to say.

'Kennedy would've got us out,' the funeral director said. 'But we had to kill him. I think he was our only shot. My boy's there now. God, I'm scared. It seems like I bury another boy each week. I'm so sorry for you.'

'You must love your boy,' she said.

'Yes. A great deal.'

'He wasn't clumsy, you know.'

'I beg your pardon?'

'John. He was graceful. He was a beautiful athlete. He scored touchdowns and he made baskets and home runs. He would never have stepped on a mine.'

She thought of the old children's rhyme: Step on a crack, break your mother's back. Step on a mine, break my heart for all time.

Remains nonviewable.

32

'Hello, lover,' she said. She took the flowers out of the box.

Detective Barren sat on the gravesite, with her back against the headstone, obscuring her husband's name and the dates of his life. Her eyes were lifted toward the sky; she watched the clouds meander across the great blue expanse with what she thought was an admirable purposelessness. She played the children's game of trying to guess what each cloud's shape was like; she thought of elephants and whales and rhinoceroses. She thought that Susan would have seen only fish and aquatic mammals. She allowed herself a pleasurable fantasy, that there was a heaven up beyond the clouds and that John was waiting there for Susan. The idea comforted her some, but she felt tears forming in the corners of her eyes. She wiped them away swiftly. She was alone in the cemetery. She thought that she was fortunate, that her behavior was decidedly ungrave. She felt a small wind that cut an edge off the heat, rustling in the trees. She laughed, not in humor but in sadness, and spoke out loud:

'Oh, Johnny. I'm almost forty and you've been dead eighteen years, and I still miss the hell out of you.

'I guess it was Susan, you see. You were dead and she got born and she was so tiny and helpless and sick. Boy. Colic and then respiratory problems and God knows what else. It just overwhelmed Annie, you see. And Ben, well, his business was just starting and he worked all the time. And so I just got caught up in it. Sitting up all night so that Annie could get a few hours' sleep. Rocking her. Walking her. Back and forth, back and forth. All those little baby tears, you see, all the pain and hurt she was feeling, well, I was feeling too. It was as if the two of us could cry together and feel a little better and I think if it hadn't been for her, I don't think I would have made it. You big creep! You had no right to get yourself killed!'

She stopped.

She remembered a night, crammed together in a small bed in his dormitory room when he told her that he had refused to submit his request for a student deferment from the draft. It wasn't fair, he'd said. All the farm boys and ghetto kids were getting slaughtered while the lawyers' sons went to Ivy League schools in safety. The system was unfair and inequitable and evil and he wouldn't participate in the evil. If he got drafted, so be it. If he passed his physical, so be it. Don't worry, he'd said. The Army won't want me. Troublemaker. Anarchist. Rabble-rouser. I'd make a lousy soldier. They'd yell charge and I'd ask where and why, and how come, and why not over there and let's take a vote. They had laughed at the improbable picture of John Barren leading a group discussion on whether to charge the enemy or not, arguing pros and cons. But her laughter hid a great misshapen fear, and when the letter that began with greetings from the president arrived, she'd insisted they get married, thinking only that she had to have his name, that it was important.

'Susan got better,' Detective Barren said. 'It seemed to take forever, but she got better. And suddenly she was a little girl and Annie was a little older and less scared of everything and Ben's job wasn't so hard and I guess it was okay, then, just to become Auntie Merce because she was going to live, and I guess I knew I was too.'

Detective Barren suddenly choked on her thoughts.

'Oh, God, Johnny, and now someone's gone and killed her! My baby. She was so much like you. You'd have loved her, too. She was like the baby we'd have had. Doesn't that sound trite? Don't laugh at me for being a sentimentalist. I know you, you were worse than me. You were the one that always cried in movies. Remember *Tunes of Glory*? At the Alec Guinness festival? First we saw *The Ladykillers* and you insisted we stay for the second feature. Remember? After John Mills had shot himself and Guinness goes a little crazy and begins to do a slow death march in front of the other men of the mess? The bagpipes were faint and you were sitting there in the theater with tears just streaming down your face, so don't call me the emotional one. And in high school, remember, when Tommy O'Connor couldn't shoot against St Brendan's and he threw you the ball and you went straight up, the whole place screaming or holding

34

their breath, championship on the line, thirty feet from the basket? Nothing but net, you said, but every time I brought that up, you started crying, you old schmooze. You won and it made you cry. I guess Susan would have cried, too. She cried over sick whales that beached themselves and seals that didn't have the sense to flee from hunters and seabirds covered with oil. Those are the things you would have cried over, too.'

Detective Barren took a deep breath.

I'm crazy, she thought.

Talking to a dead husband about a dead niece.

But they've killed my love, she said to herself.

All of it.

Detective Barren showed her badge to a uniformed officer sitting at a desk, monitoring all the visitors to the Dade County Sheriff's Office. She took the elevator to the third floor and followed her memory to the homicide division. There was a secretary there who made her wait on an uncomfortable plastic couch. She looked about her, noting the same blend of old and new office equipment. There was something about police work, she thought. Even when things are new, they lose their shine almost instantly. She wondered if there was some connection between the grime of the job and the never-clean atmosphere of police offices. Her eyes strayed to three pictures on the wall: the President, the Sheriff, and a third man she didn't recognize. She stood and approached the unfamiliar picture. There was a small plaque beneath the portrait of a smiling, slightly overweight man with an American flag in the lapel on his jacket. The plaque was tarnished bronze. It had the man's name and the inscription KILLED IN THE LINE OF DUTY and a date two years earlier.

She remembered the case; he had been making a routine arrest, following a domestic that had been a homicide. A drunken father and son in Little Havana. A subject murder, the easiest of homicides: the father was standing over the body, sobbing, when the police arrived. He was so distraught that the uniforms simply sat him in a chair, without handcuffs. No one had suspected that he would explode when they tried to take him out, that he would seize a gun from a policeman's holster and turn it on them. Detective Barren remembered the funeral, thinking of the full-dress uniforms, folded flag, and rifle salute, so much like the one she had known earlier. But what a silly way to die, she thought. Then, thinking again, she wondered what was a useful way to die. She turned away swiftly when Detective Perry entered the room.

'Sorry to keep you waiting,' he said. 'Let's go to my office.'

She followed him down a corridor.

'Cubicle, really. Work space. We don't really get a real office with doors anymore. This is progress, I guess.'

She smiled and he motioned her toward a chair.

'So?' he asked.

'That's my question,' she replied.

'Okay,' he said. 'Here's something.' He tossed a sheet of paper across his desk to her. She took it and stared at a composite picture of a curly-haired, dark-complexioned man, not bad-looking except for a pair of deeply recessed eyes that gave him a slightly cadaverous look. But not enough so to throw one off, she thought.

'Is this . . .'

'Best we can do,' he interrupted. 'It's been distributed all over the city and all the campuses. It was on the television stations while you were at the funeral.'

'Response?'

'The usual. Everybody thinks it looks exactly like their landlord, or the neighbor who happens to owe them money, or the guy that's dating their daughter. But we're checking them out slowly. Maybe we'll get lucky.'

'What else?'

'Well, each of the killings has some distinctive features, but when you get everything settled they are pretty much the same. The girls have all been picked up at a mixer or a bar or a student union or a campus movie. Picked up isn't right. Followed out is more likely. No one has seen the guy actually snatch his victim . . .'

'But . . .'

'Well, no buts. We're interviewing people. We're doing background checks on all sorts of people – gardeners, students, hangers-on – trying to find some guy who has experience on all the campuses and is young and with-it enough to blend in.'

'That could take a while.'

'We've got a dozen guys working on it.'

Detective Barren thought for an instant. She wasn't exactly getting the runaround, but nor was she getting the entire picture. And she perceived a sense of confidence in Detective Perry that didn't blend with a portrait of legwork, long hours, and frustration. She had the sensation of being humored. She also knew that she had to come up with the right question to open the right door. She thought for a moment. Then it struck her.

'What about assaults?'

'I beg your pardon?' Detective Perry said.

'So what you've been saying is that you've got a little bit of this, a little bit of that, but no makeable case out of the homicides. What about an assault? If this guy has been at this for, how long? A year or more, I'd guess, then he has to have had a few near-misses. Screwed up. Been surprised by another student when he tried to snatch a victim. Something like that, huh? You tell me.'

'Well,' Perry replied, drawing the word out. 'That's an interesting idea . . .'

'Which I'm not the only person to think of.'

'Well . . .' He hesitated.

'Don't bullshit me.'

'I don't want to.'

'Then answer.'

He looked uncomfortable. He shuffled some papers. He looked around for help. 'I wasn't supposed to be that candid,' he admitted.

'I didn't think so.'

'Can you back off? I mean . . .'

'Forget it,' Detective Barren said. 'I want to know.'

'Okay, but I'm not gonna get too specific.'

She nodded.

'Twice.'

She nodded again.

'Twice the creep screwed up. Last time was the night before your niece got it. We got a partial license plate and a make.'

'Have you got a name?'

'Can't tell you.'

Detective Barren stood up.

'I'll go to your boss. I'll go to mine. I'll go to the papers . . .'

He motioned her to sit back down.

'We got a name. And he's got a tail. And when we got enough for a warrant, we'll let you know.'

'You sure?'

'Nothing's certain. Look, the papers have been all over this thing and a lot of details have been in the press. So we're moving slowly, we want to make certain that we make this guy on a murder-one charge, not attempted assault. Hell, we want to make him on all five. That's taking some time.'

'Do it right,' she said.

Detective Perry smiled, relieved.

'That's what I figured you'd say.'

She looked at him.

'Well,' he said, 'that's what I hoped you'd say.' He stood up. 'I want this creep to understand boxes. The first box is the one I'm putting together for him. Everywhere he turns, I'm gonna have an answer. No way he can crawl out. The second box is gonna be a nine-by-eleven on the Raiford Riviera . . .'

Death row, thought Detective Barren. She nodded.

'And you can guess what the last box will be.'

She felt a momentary rush of satisfaction.

Detective Barren stood up. 'Thank you,' she said.

'You want to be in on it when it goes down?'

'Wouldn't miss it.'

'All right. I'll call.'

'I'll be waiting.'

They shook hands and she walked out, for the first time in several days feeling hungry.

When she returned to her own office, two days later, after a hot, dirty day doing an inventory of car parts uncovered at a chop shop in the warehouse district, she found two memos on her desk. The first was from her own commander, listing a disposition of evidence gathered at the site where Susan's body had been recovered. The second was an autopsy memo from the medical examiner's officer. She read them carefully.

TO: Det. Mercedes Barren
FROM: Lt. Ted March

MERCE: That was a bite mark. But it was too ragged to make a distinct mold and is therefore not of high evidentiary value. Saliva breakdown from swab of the area shows normal enzyme values, but trace alcohol rendered it difficult if not impossible to come up with blood type. Guy must have had a drink or two. Booze always screws things up. Even just a beer or two. Anyway, I've sent the entire sample back over to the lab again and told them to try again. The two prophylactics recovered at the scene contained different sperm samples. Both had deteriorated considerably. Still, one was Type A/Positive, the other O/Positive. Further breakdowns are underway. No workable prints on anything so far, but they're going to try that laser evaluator on the soda cans. I'll let you know. Pretty much a total wash so far. Sorry. But we're going to keep trying.

TO: Detective Mercedes Barren
FROM: Assistant ME Arthur Vaughn

DETECTIVE: Cause of death of deceased white female, age eighteen, identified positive as Susan Lewis of Bryn Mawr Pennsylvania, is massive trauma to the right rear portion of the occipital bone coupled with asphyxiation due to strangulation by nylon ligature around neck. (See autopsy protocol for precise cause.) Genital swabs negative. Acid phosphase test negative.

Detective: she was unconscious from the head blow when she was assaulted. She probably never regained consciousness when he strangled her. Sex act was premortem, however. But there were no signs of ejaculation. This could have been due to prophylactic device.

I'm terribly sorry about all of this. The autopsy protocol should answer any questions you have, but if it doesn't don't hesitate to call.

Detective Barren put the two reports in her pocketbook. She glanced at the autopsy protocol, with its schematic diagram and pages of verbatim description of her niece's body, transcribed from the medical examiner's tape recorder. Height. Weight. Brain: 1220 grams. Heart: 230 grams. Well-developed, post-adolescent female American. No abnormalities noted. Life reduced to so many facts and figures. No way to measure youth, enthusiasm, and future. Detective Barren felt queasy and was thankful that the medical examiner in his compulsive thoroughness had neglected to send the autopsy slides.

On her way home from the office that night, Detective Barren stopped at a small bookstore. The clerk was a beady-eyed man who rubbed his hands together frequently, punctuating his voice with body motion. Detective Barren thought him a perfect reincarnation of Uriah Heep.

'Something to escape in? A novel, I suppose, an adventure, or a gothic horror story. A romance, or a mystery. What shall it be?'

'Real escape,' said Detective Barren, 'is substituting one reality for another.'

The clerk thought for a moment.

'You're a nonfiction type, huh?'

'No. Maybe. I just don't feel romantic. But I want something distracting.'

She left with two books. A history of the British campaign in the Falkland Islands and a new translation of Aeschylus' *Oresteia*. There was a gourmet shop down the street, and she indulged herself in a pasta salad and a bottle of what the counterman assured her was an excellent Californian Chardonnay. She would eat well, she thought, read a bit. There was a football game on the television that night which she could watch until she fell sleep. This was a secret passion. She smiled to herself; she hid her enthusiasm from her co-workers. They were threatened enough by her female competence. If she tried to usurp their game as well . . . So she enjoyed in private. Buying single game tickets, sitting in the Orange Bowl end zone, or staying home and plopping down in front of her television by herself, her concession to her own gender represented perhaps by the glass of white wine in a cut-glass long-stemmed goblet rather than the can of light beer. But, she thought, she did dress for the occasion. If the Dolphins were playing, she would break out her aqua and orange tee-shirt and watch sweaty-palmed as any man. She recognized a level of foolishness in her behavior, but thought it harmed no one and she was comfortable with it. She thought of Susan, coming over one Sunday a year earlier and watching in almost open-mouthed amazement as Detective Barren, swearing frequently, unable to sit still, stalked around the living room of her apartment in obvious agony, relieved only by a forty-nine-yard field goal by the Dolphins' kicker in the waning seconds of the game. Detective Barren smiled at the memory.

'If only they knew . . .' Susan had said.

'Shh. Secrecy,' her aunt replied. 'Tell no one.'

'Oh, Aunt Merce,' Susan had said finally, 'why is it I never know what to make of you?' And then they'd embraced. 'But why football? Why sports?' the niece persisted.

'Because we all need victories in our lives,' Detective Barren replied.

3

Several times over the next few days Detective Barren fought off the urge to telephone the county homicide detectives. As she went about her own business, processing other crimes, working evidence, she envisioned what was happening. She saw the tail working the killer, silently mirroring his movements while other detectives ran down his whereabouts, started showing his picture to witnesses, putting together all the minor pieces of a criminal case.

Some ten days after Susan's murder, Detective Barren

was on the witness stand in a murder case; from the locations that shell casings had been discovered inside the house where a drug dealer and his girlfriend had been murdered, Detective Barren had reconstructed the entire crime. Her testimony was important, not crucial; consequently her cross-examination by the contract killer's high-priced attorney was more of a badgering than a blistering. She knew that she could not be shaken on facts; she was working hard, however, not to let the attorney so confuse the jury that the impact of what she had to say was lost.

She heard the attorney drone another question.

'So, because the shell casings were located here, you concluded that the killer stood where?'

'If you will refer to the diagram, marked into evidence as state's exhibit twelve, counsel, you will see that casings were discovered some twenty-four inches from the doorway to the bedroom. A Browning Nine-Millimeter ejects casings at a constant rate. Consequently, it is possible with a degree of scientific certainty to say precisely where the shooter was standing.'

'They couldn't roll?'

'The rug in that portion of the room is a two-inch shag carpet, counsel.'

'Did you measure it?'

'Yes.'

The attorney turned toward his notes. Detective Barren fixed her eyes on the defendant. He was a wiry, small Colombian immigrant, uneducated save in methods and modes of death. He would be convicted, she thought, and within thirty seconds another would get off the next Avianca flight to take his place. Killers were the Kleenex of the drug industry; they were used a few times and then discarded unceremoniously.

Her eyes drifted up past the defendant, and she saw Lieutenant Burns enter the back of the courtroom. For a moment she connected him with the killer on trial. Then she saw him surreptitiously give her a thumbs-up sign.

Her imagination leaped.

She watched the lieutenant stride down the center aisle

of the courtroom and bend over the barrier to whisper a few words into a bored-looking prosecutor's ear. He sat up straight, swiveled, and then rose to his feet.

Detective Barren looked at the lieutenant, who smiled at her, but only a small smile, just the slightest upturning at the corners of the mouth.

'Your honor,' the young prosecutor said, 'may we come to side-bar?'

'Is it important?' asked the judge.

'I believe so,' replied the prosecutor.

The defense attorney, the court stenographer, and the prosecutor all walked around to the judge's side, where the jury could not hear them. There was a moment of conversation, then the three returned to their seats. The judge turned to the jury.

'We're going to take a brief recess now, then the state will continue with another witness.' He looked at Detective Barren. 'Detective, apparently your services are needed elsewhere. You are subject to recall, so please remember that you are under oath at all times.'

Detective Barren nodded. She swallowed.

The judge frowned. 'Detective, the stenographer cannot record a nod of the head.'

'Yes, your honor. Under oath. I understand.'

Detective Barren and the lieutenant hurried from the courtroom. As they passed through a sally port entrance and then through a metal detector, the lieutenant said, 'They whacked the fucker about ninety minutes ago. He's at county homicide being questioned. They're doing his house and car now. Search warrant got issued this morning. Hell, you probably passed it on the way into court. We tried to reach you, but you were on the stand. So I decided to come get you myself.'

Detective Barren nodded.

The two hurried outside. It was Florida fall, a subtle lessening of the oppressive heat of summer. A mild breeze caused the flags outside the courthouse to buffet about.

'Why'd they move on him?' she asked.

'The tail watched the creep buy two pairs of women's

43

pantyhose last night at an all-night drugstore. He stashed them in a locker at the University of Miami, along with a ball-peen hammer.'

'Who is he?'

'A weirdo and a foreigner. He's some sort of Arab. Kind of a professional student, from what I've heard. Took courses all over the place. Registered with a bunch of different names, too. We'll know more soon.' The lieutenant paused at the door of an unmarked cruiser. 'You want to watch the questioning or the search of his place?'

She thought for a moment.

'Let's swing by his house, then go over to county.'

'You got it.'

The city washed past the windshield as they drove to the suspect's house. The lieutenant drove swiftly, not speaking. Detective Barren tried to fix a picture of the suspect in her head and was unable. She chided herself; good police work required one to draw suspicions and conclusions on the basis of fact. She knew nothing about this man, she thought. Wait. Absorb. Collect. That was how she would come to know him. The lieutenant slowed the car and took an exit for the airport. A few blocks shy of the airport, he turned onto a nondescript street. It was a place of small cinder-block houses, with mostly Latin and black families. Many homes had chainlink fences surrounding them and large dogs patrolling within. This was an urban normality; the largest of dogs lived in the fringe areas, the working-class neighborhoods that were so vulnerable to robbery, where both husband and wife went off to work each day. The houses were set back slightly from the street, but without foliage. The street was devoid of trees, even the palms that seemed everywhere in the city. Detective Barren thought it was a singularly uninviting place; in the summer the heat probably turned the entire street into a single hot, insistently dusty place where tensions and angers bred with the same intensity that bacteria did.

At the end of the street she saw police cars lined up around the last of the small brown houses. There was a truck from the dog pound. The lieutenant motioned at it.

'Seems the guy had one loyal Doberman. One of the SWAT guys had to blow it away.' An airplane, wheels and flaps down, passed frighteningly close overhead, drowning out in a huge flood of noise anything else the lieutenant was going to add. Detective Barren thought that if she had to listen to that sound with any frequency, she would have become a killer as well.

They parked the car and pushed through a small crowd of curious people who were watching the proceedings silently. Detective Barren saw a pair of homicide men she knew working the neighbors, making certain that they obtained any workable leads before the press was all over them. She nodded at the head of the team that was processing the house. He was a former street cop, not unlike herself, who had worked undercover a few too many times. In one of his last cases there had been a rather singular question about some drug money seized in a raid. A hundred thousand dollars in twenties and hundreds had been turned in to the property office, along with a kilo of cocaine. The defendants were two college students from the Northeast; they had told internal affairs that they had had more than a quarter million in cash when the raid went down, leaving some one hundred fifty thousand unaccounted for. A sticky situation that had resulted in the policeman being transferred and the two students receiving greatly diminished charges. The money was never recovered. Like many cops, Detective Barren had steadfastly refused to draw the obvious conclusion, preferring to believe that someone had lied and hoping that it wasn't the policeman. Still, she thought as she approached him, he was an extremely competent detective, and she was in an odd way relieved.

'How ya doing, Fred?' she said.

'Good, Merce. And you?'

'Okay, I guess.'

'I'm real sorry for the reason you're here.'

'Thanks, Fred. I appreciate your saying so.'

'This is the creep, Merce. Stone cold solid. Just walk inside and you can feel it.'

'I hope so.'

He held the door open for her. It was cool inside the small house. She could hear the air conditioner blasting. Probably the detectives turned it up, she thought. Still, for an instant she shivered, wondering whether it was the sudden change in the temperature.

At first glance the house seemed typical for a student. The bookcases were made from gray cinderblocks and pine boards, and rows of paperbacks vied for space. The furniture seemed threadbare and modest, a couch with a faded Indian print covering it thrown over it to conceal a rend in the fabric, a pair of sitting chairs covered in plastic, a worn brown wood table scarred with cigarette burns. On the walls there were travel posters for Switzerland, Ireland, and Canada, all showing bucolic lush green settings. Detective Barren swept it all into her head, thinking so far it added up to nothing.

'Pretty ordinary, huh?'

She turned to the voice.

'Fred, show me something interesting.'

'You just got to look a little closer. Check out the typewriter.'

There was a typewriter on the brown table with a sheet of paper in the platen. She stood over it and read what had been written:

unclean unclean unclean unclean unclean unclean unclean
unclean unclean unclean unclean unclean unclean unclean
God God God God God God God God God God God God God
God
Kill
I must wash the earth

'We also found his trophy box.'

'His what?'

'Trophy box.'

'I don't . . .'

'Forgive me, Merce, I forgot your connection.' The detective paused. 'Apparently he kept something from his victims. Or at least something from some of them. In the

46

closet was a shoebox with a bunch of clippings about the killings, right up through the murder of your niece. There were some earrings and a ring or two also. Let's see, a woman's shoe and a pair of panties with a bloodstain on them.'

He hesistated.

'It was the kind of box that guys like us always pray for on one of these. I don't know if there's something there that will link him positively to every one of the killings, but there's enough there to link him to some. And that means the sucker's nailed, solid.'

She looked at him.

'I hope so.'

'Believe it. No doubt about it. The damn thing is, I'll bet there's a couple of crimes this creep's done we didn't even know about.'

He put his arm around her and started to lead her out.

'Don't worry. The search is legal. The evidence is there. The guy's probably copping out now. All there is to worry about is that weird note. He's probably whacko. Why don't you go see for yourself.'

'Thanks, Fred.'

'Think nothing of it. Don't hesitate to call, anytime, if you need to know something.'

'I appreciate that. I feel better already.'

'Great.'

But she didn't.

She turned to Lieutenant Burns, who was waiting for her outside. 'I want to see this guy. In the flesh.'

She did not look back at the house as they pulled away.

At the county homicide office, she and Lieutenant Burns were escorted into a darkened room which had a two-way mirror which overlooked a second room. She shook hands with several other policemen who were assembled watching the questioning in the adjacent area. One man was operating a tape recorder in a corner. No one spoke. For an instant she was reminded of hundreds of movies and television shows she had seen. Someone offered her a chair and whispered, 'He's still denying everything, and he seems strong. They've been at him for two hours. I give him maybe another five minutes, maybe another five hours. Hard to tell.'

'Did he ask for an attorney?' she wondered.

'Not yet. So far, so good.'

She thought of the typewritten note.

'Is he straight?' she asked the voice while looking at the suspect for the first time. He was a short, wiry-muscled man, powerfully built, like a lightweight wrestler or boxer, with wavy black hair and bright blue eyes, a combination that was oddly unsettling to Detective Barren. He wore jeans and an orange tee-shirt that celebrated the University of Miami's national football championship. To the detective, he seemd coiled; she watched the muscles on his arm flex. She thought how powerful that small arm was, and suddenly envisioned the short, chopping stroke of the hammer, an instant white flash of pain exploding into darkened nothingness.

'He's weird. Quoted the Koran a minute ago. Listen.'

She concentrated on the three men in the interview room. Detective Moore was doing the questioning while Detective Perry sat, taking a few notes, but mostly fixing the suspect with an unwavering harsh glance, his eyes following each motion the suspect made, narrowing as the subject pontificated, equivocated, or evaded, narrowing evilly and threateningly as if angered to the point of violence by the lack of truth. Each time the detective shifted in his chair, the suspect moved uneasily. Detective Barren thought it a masterful performance.

'Tell me why you bought the pantyhose.'

'It was a present.'

'For whom?'

'Someone at home.'

'Where's home?'

'Lebanon.'

'What about the hammer?'

'It was to fix my car.'

'Where were you the night of September eighth?'

'I was at home.'

48

'Did anyone see you?'

'I live alone.'

'Why did you kill all those girls?'

'I have killed nobody.'

'So how come we found an earring belonging to a young lady named Lisa Williams at your house? And what about a pair of bloody pink panties just like the pair Andrea Thomas was wearing when some creep snatched her off the Miami-Dade campus? I suppose those were a present, too? And you've been a busy boy with the clippings, huh? Like to clip stories out of the newspaper, huh?'

'Those are my things! My special things! You had no right to my things! I demand their return!'

'Whoa, motherfucker. You ain't demanding nothing.'

'You are a devil.'

'Yeah, maybe, 'cause then I'll see your ass in hell.'

'Never! I am a true believer.'

'What? A believer in murder?'

'There are unclean people in the world.'

'Young women?'

'Young women especially.'

'Why are young women unclean?'

'Hah! You know.'

'Tell me anyway.'

'No. You too are unclean. Infidel!'

'Just me or all cops?'

'Policemen, all policemen.'

'You'd like to take a shot at me, huh?'

'You are an infidel. The Book tells me that it is holy to kill an infidel. The Prophet says it is a passageway to heaven.'

'Yeah, well, where you're going, fella, ain't much like heaven.'

'It means nothing. It is only flesh.'

'Tell me about the flesh.'

'The flesh is evil. Purity comes from thoughts.'

'What must you do with evil flesh?'

'Destroy it.'

'How many times did you do that?'

'In my heart, many times.'

'How about with your hands?'

'This is between me and my master.'

'Who is that?'

'We have but one master who resides in the garden.'

'How do you know?'

'He speaks with me.'

'Frequently?'

'When he commands, I listen.'

'What does he say?'

'Educate yourself in the ways of the infidel. Learn her customs. Prepare for the holy war.'

'When does the holy war begin?'

The suspect laughed greatly, pitching back in his chair, opening his mouth wide, letting the snorts and whines of his voice flood the small room. Tears started to roll down his cheeks. He continued laughing for several minutes, uninterrupted by the detectives. Detective Barren listened to the sound and felt it rend her heart. Finally the suspect calmed, until only an occasional giggle slipped from his lips. He stared directly at Detective Perry, then spoke in an even, dreadful voice:

'It has begun already.'

Perry suddenly pushed himself out of his chair and smashed both of his fists down hard on the table separating him and the suspect. The sound was like a shot and Detective Barren saw the men in the room with her stiffen.

'War on little girls, huh? Was fucking them part of the battle plan?'

The suspect stared frozen at the detective.

There was a silence.

When he spoke it was deliberate, awful.

'I know nothing about your unclean women.'

He pointed a finger at the detective.

'I will not speak more to you.'

The finger suddenly slapped down on a piece of paper in front of the suspect. Detective Barren knew it was a constitutional rights form. The suspect started to drum his fingers on the page.

'I do not have to speak to you . . .'

The finger drumming sounded like small-caliber pistol fire.

'I would like an attorney present . . .'

The rapping sound increased in intensity.

'Appoint one for me . . .'

The fingers curled into a fist and slammed on the table.

'I know my rights. I know my rights. I know my rights. I know my rights. I know my rights.'

The two detectives stood, staring malevolently at the prisoner.

'You do not scare me,' he said. 'God is with me, and I fear none of your infidel justice. Bring me my attorney so that I may enjoy my rights! So I may delight in my rights! Do you hear? Sadegh Rhotzbadegh requires counsel, hah!'

The two detectives exited the room.

'I am a true believer!' he shouted. 'A true believer!'

The suspect watched them go. Then he turned to the mirror and raised his middle finger. The tape recorder rolling silently in the corner captured another long, raucous burst of laughter before being switched off by a policeman who swore under his voice. Detective Barren stood up and sighed. At least, she noted, the man who killed Susan is easy to hate! And she took some comfort from that thought.

Time slid around Detective Barren's emotions.

She resumed her day-to-day routine, forcing the arrest of the Lebanese student into a location of diminished prominence. There was a difficult day when she went to Susan's dormitory room and packed all the books and clothes and papers away to send to her sister. She had come across a half-finished love letter to a boy named Jimmy, whom she had never met, that was filled with the mixed gushings of a young woman leaving her childhood behind so rapidly. She had read the words and connected them to a tall, gawky boy who'd stood self-consciously to the rear of the church during the service, and just to the side at the gravesite, unsure what his position was in the midst of the grief; embarassed, the detective thought, as she herself had once been, at the idea of being alive, and horrified at the awkward sense of relief that speaks inside youth at moments of death, saying: At least my life goes on. Detective Barren read: ' . . . I cannot wait for the year to get going. In midterm we are going on a week-long laboratory in the Bahamas. We take the research boat down and spend a week underwater. I wish you could be there to share it with me. I think about those last few nights and what we shared . . .' Detective Barren smiled. What had they shared? For an odd moment she hoped that her niece had known real passion and abandonment, given into desire completely. It would mitigate somewhat the violation of her last moments.

Then she had put the letter away. Reading it, she thought, was somehow unfair. But she had experienced a momentary pleasure, as if Susan had, if not been resurrected, at least for the barest of instants been restored. This made the detective feel a great sense of guilt, and she had occupied herself with the packing, setting aside the letter and a few others like it for forwarding to the gawky boy.

Keep busy, she told herself.

Ten days after the arrest of Sadegh Rhotzbadegh she called Detective Perry at county homicide. It was late in the afternoon on a Tuesday, the day the grand jury usually met. He came to the telephone swiftly, apologetically.

'Jesus, Merce, I'm sorry I haven't called, it's just been so goddamn busy . . .'

'That's all right,' she replied. 'Did you go to the grand jury today?'

'Well, yes and no.'

'Explain that to me.'

'Well, yes we went to the grand jury and yes, we're expecting first-degree murder indictments today. But not on Susan's case and one other.'

'I don't get it.'

'Look, the MO was the same on all five homicides in Dade and one in Broward County at the community college there. He was taking a course up there in electrical engineering. Anyway, he had newspaper clippings of all six killings in his house. His blood type matches the blood from one of the semen samples found near Susan's body – but not the other. And there's the question of age on the sample that matches. He is a very common blood type and it was not possible to type it down much further. The best the lab could do was to get him into a twenty-five-percentile category.'

'They couldn't eliminate further?'

'No. Same thing in the Broward case.'

'So?'

'On one of the other Dade cases there's nothing, just the newspaper clipping.'

'So?'

'Well, the bottom line is, we link him through jewelry, through the lingerie discovered at his house, through a shoe, which for some ungodly reason he kept, to three of the six homicides. Link isn't the right word. Nailed is more like it. So what it amounts to is this: we're clearing all the cases. But we're only going for three indictments. Now, we may introduce evidence of the others if it gets to a death-penalty phase of a trial – but that's down the line.'

Detective Barren sat silently, thinking.

'Merce, I'm sorry. The point is, the guy's going to go away. Maybe the death penalty. Isn't that what counts?'

'Don't give up,' she said.

'What?'

'What about his car?'

'It was clean except for an earring.'

Detective Barren started to speak but was cut off.

' . . . No – I know what you're thinking. It belonged to one of the other girls. We haven't matched the earring found at Susan's body. If we could, well, bingo.'

'Don't give up.'

'Merce, we won't. We'll keep at it. But you know how these things work. I have to justify manpower and time to my superiors. They've cleared the case. We're going to get a conviction. The guy's history. My bureaucracy isn't any damn different from yours.'

'Damn,' she said.

'I don't blame you.'

'I feel cheated.'

'Don't look at it that way. Think of the people who commit murders and skate. C'mon, Merce, you know how unusual it is for us to make a case on some random killer like this creep. You got to be satisfied with seeing him do hard time for the cases we can lock.'

'He never copped out?'

'Nah. He's too crazy smart for that. You know, one of his courses at the university was in constitutional law.'

'He's not . . .'

'Not a chance. I mean, I'm sure they'll give the old insanity plea a ride, and I got to admit the guy's not playing with a full deck. Actually, it's more like he's shuffled a couple of decks together. I mean he's definitely not all there. But even if Allah was whispering in his ear to kill those girls, he as sure as hell wasn't telling our boy also to rape them. That's not how Allah works, even on his bad days. And it sure isn't how some paranoid schizophrenic operates, either.'

They were silent for a moment.

Detective Barren felt uncomfortable, as if the room had suddenly grown hot. She heard Detective Perry's voice on the line.

'Look, Merce, don't hesitate to call. If we get anything else I'll let you know.'

She thanked him and hung up the telephone.

It was, she thought, completely unfair and unreasonable and precisely how the system of justice operates. She hated herself for being so familiar with the trade-offs and corner cutting that marks the legal system. That what had happened to Susan's murder was completely understandable from the policeman's point of view made her angrier. She was outraged with herself for understanding.

She could not sleep that night. She watched all the late-night talk shows and finally read Aeschylus until dawn, when, as the first few lights of morning crept into her apartment, she changed to reading the opening stanzas of the *Odyssey*, but even the classics could not settle her. She went to work early that day and stayed late, working fever-ishly on paperwork, redoing reports, analyses, and crime-scene workups, rendering her output as perfect as she could make it, until, finally, well into the evening darkness again, she went home and after stripping to her underwear and a tee-shirt, she put her pillow and a blanket on the floor and slept on the hardwood, thinking all the time that she wanted to know no comfort.

Liquid time enveloped her. She felt as if all her feelings had somehow been placed on hold while she waited for some sort of resolution to Susan's death. After the indict-ment for three first-degree murder counts was announced, Detective Barren went to the chief of homicide prosecution at the state attorney's office, reminding him, through her presence, that though uncharged with Susan's death, the Lebanese student still was responsible for it. She attended every court hearing, every meeting by the two young pros-ecutors assigned to the cases. She reviewed the assembly of evidence, considered it, then went and reviewed it again. She tried to anticipate areas of weakness that could be exploited by the public defenders that were charged with defending Sadegh Rhotzbadegh. She sent memos to the prosecutors with her every consideration, then followed up the memos with either a visit or, at the least, a telephone call, until convinced that the perceived gap in the case was closed. She knew that they found her behavior infuriating, especially in the pedantic way she would go over every aspect of the case. But she had also seen too many cases lost by lack of vigor on the part of the prosecution, lack of anticipation, and she was determined that this would not happen.

And when she had exhausted her mind and memory in constant review of evidence, she would go to the county jail, where the Lebanese student occupied a single cell in the highest-security wing. Past the electronic locking systems, down corridors gray with the crimes of men, through metal detectors and past a sign that declared: UNAUTHORIZED ENTRY TO WEST WING IS PUNISHABLE BY PROS-

ECUTION. She would draw up a chair in the corridor outside the cell where the Lebanese student lived and simply watch him. The first time she did that, he'd laughed and shouted obscenities in her direction. When that failed to change her visage, he'd exposed himself. Once he grabbed the bars of the cell, spitting, raging, trying to reach through at her. Finally, however, he cowered, removing himself to a spot behind the toilet, occasionally peeking over the top to see if the detective was still there. She was careful never to speak to him, nor really listen to anything he might say. She let the force of her silence fill him, she hoped, with dread.

She told no one of those clandestine visits. And the jail personnel, fully aware of the reasons behind her attention, never logged her entry or departure on any official form. It was, the captain of the security unit told her in passing, the least they could do.

She attended the evidentiary hearing, when the defense tried to suppress the items seized at the student's house. She sat in the front row, eyes pouring onto the back of the student. She knew he could feel her gaze, and it was with great satisfaction that she noticed him wiggle in his seat and occasionally turn and meet the detective's glance. The evidence was not suppressed. She whispered, 'Good going,' to her friend Fred, the county detective, after he finished his testimony. 'Piece of cake,' he whispered back, striding out of the courtroom.

She attended a mental competency hearing for Sadegh Rhotzbadegh. She heard the defense attorneys argue that their client was decompensating under great stress, which, she was glad to note, the judge said was a normal state for someone facing the death penalty.

Months passed. Miami's winter arrived. The daytime light seemed to gain a new clarity, unburdened by harsh tropical heat. At night Detective Barren would sit on her porch and let the cool air wash her like a bath. She thought of little save the upcoming trial; her only pleasure or release from the concentration on the case came when she would go to the old Orange Bowl, her end-zone ticket in hand,

and stomp and cheer and wave a white handkerchief at the enemy as the Dolphins cruised through their schedule. When they lost the conference championship game on a bleak, New England sort of day, wet, steady drizzle and wind blowing in the open end of the stadium, chilling the shirt-sleeved crowd so unaccustomed to any weather other than warm, she felt an awful coldness inside. A fan's death, she thought. Losses are inevitable, yet terrible. To follow the game was always, ultimately, to know the wretchedness of defeat. That night she consumed almost an entire bottle of wine before sleeping. She awakened with a headache, and thought that the team from Los Angeles was filled with Lebanese football players.

In the evening, a week before the trial date, she received a call from Detective Perry. He sounded excited.

'Merce,' he said, 'it's going down tomorrow.'

'What?'

'It's guilty-plea time.'

'No trial?'

'No. He's going to cop to the three cases.'

'What's the deal.'

'He gets to live. That's all.'

'How much time?'

'The max on each. He does a mandatory twenty-five calendar, straight time, hard time, no gain time, no good time. All consecutive. Seventy-five years straight. Also he's gonna cop to some assaults, so the judge is going to add on some more time. He'll score a hundred easy. We can go up to Raiford Prison and dig his grave, 'cause that's where he's gonna die. He'll never get out.'

'He should get the death penalty.'

'Merce, Merce. He's in front of Judge Rule. The old bastard's had a dozen first-degree murder cases before him, including that biker-torture case, and he still hasn't fried anyone. You remember that case, Merce?'

'I remember.'

'Cattle prods, Merce. Zippo lighters.'

'I remember, dammit.'

'Those guys are just doing twenty-fives.'

'It still . . .'

He interrupted her.

'Sure, it pisses you off. It pisses off the other victims' families, too. But they're going along. Everyone's a little wary of the guy's insanity defense, too.'

'Bullshit! The guy may be screwed a little tight . . .'

He interrupted her again.

'I know, I know. But those two guys defending him walked that guy who cut up his girlfriend with a hacksaw into a mental hospital last year.'

'Yeah, but . . .'

'No buts. You want to take the chance?'

She thought hard for a moment. Before she responded, Detective Perry cut into her thoughts.

'And don't think for a minute that you could do the creep yourself. I know about all those jailhouse visits, Merce. Don't think it.'

'He deserves to die.'

'He is going to die, Merce.'

'That's right,' she said. 'We're all going to die.'

'Merce,' Detective Perry said. His voice had softened. 'Merce. Give it a rest. The guy's going away. He's history. It's over, understand? Don't make me make this speech. Hell, you probably know it by heart. You've probably given it a few times yourself. It's over. Over, Got it?'

'Over.'

'Right.'

'Over.'

'Will be, at nine in the morning.'

'See you there,' she said, hanging up the phone.

Sadegh Rhotzbadegh seemed mouselike, timid, shivering, though the press of people jammed into the courtroom made the air thick, hot, and stifling. When he spotted Detective Barren sitting in her customary front-row seat he shrank close to the side of one of his public defenders, who turned and glowered at the detective. There was a stiffening in the courtroom as the judge swept in. An elderly man with a shock of white hair that gave him a slightly demented look, the judge surveyed the courtroom quickly, noting the lineup of victims' families and television and newspaper reporters, filling all the chairs and pressed up against the walls. It was an old courtroom, with pictures of distinguished judges staring down, now in utter anonymity, from dark walls.

'We'll take Mr Rhotzbadegh first,' he said. 'There is, I believe, a plea.'

'Yes, your honor.' One of the young prosecutors had risen. 'Simply put, in return for a guilty plea to all outstanding charges, the state will waive its pursuit of the death penalty. It is our understanding that Mr Rhotzbadegh will then receive maximum terms on all counts, running consecutively. That would be a total of one hundred and eleven years.'

He sat down. The judge looked at the defense table.

'That is correct,' said one of the defense attorneys.

The judge looked at the defendant. The Lebanese student rose.

'Mr Rhotzbadegh, have your attorneys explained what is happening to you?'

'Yes, your honor.'

'And do you agree with the terms of the plea?'

'Yes, your honor.'

'You haven't been coerced or forced to make this plea?'

'No, your honor.'

'It is of your own free will?'

'Yes, your honor.'

'You know that your attorneys had prepared a defense and that you had the right to confront your accusers before a jury of your peers and force the state to prove beyond and to the exclusion of any reasonable doubt these allegations against you?'

'I understand that, your honor. They were prepared to argue that I was insane. I am not.'

'Do you have anything you wish to add?'

'I did what I did because it was written and commanded of me to do. This is what I am guilty of. In the eyes of the Prophet, I am blameless. I will welcome the day that he gathers me to his bosom and we walk together in the gardens.'

Detective Barren heard the sound of reporters taking notes, trying to get all of the suspect's words. The judge broke in.

'That is fine, and I'm glad that your religious beliefs are a comfort to you . . .'

'They are indeed, your honor.'

'Good. Thank you.'

The judge made a small hand motion and the Lebanese student sat down. The judge looked out over the crowded courtroom.

'Are the relatives of the victims here?'

The room remained silent. Then an elderly couple sitting to the right of Detective Barren stood up. She saw another couple stand, followed by an entire family. She stood, too. The courtroom continued in fragile quiet and she noticed that Sadegh Rhotzbadegh's shoulders were twitching. Fear, she thought. He kept his eyes resolutely forward.

'Would any of you care to say anything for the record?'

There was a moment's confusion. Detective Barren's imagination flooded with words, about Susan, about what she meant, about what she would have become. Emotion gagged her and she sat down. But one of the others who had stood, a tall and thin, distinguished-seeming man wearing a well-cut blue pinstripe suit, strode forward. His eyes were red. For an instant he stared down at the defense table with a glance that seemed to suck the heat from the room. Then he turned to the judge.

'Your honor. Morton Davies, father of Angela Davies, victim . . .'

He hesitated.

'We have agreed to this plea because we understand that the system would sooner cheat us, who have suffered such loss, than it would this . . .' He stumbled, searching for a word.

' . . . this refuse.'

He paused.

'Our loss, your honor, our loss . . .'

And then he stopped.

His last word hung in the courtroom air, echoing in the sudden silence.

Detective Barren knew instantly why he'd stopped. Everyone did, she thought. How could one put words to the loss? She felt her own throat closing, and for an instant felt a kind of panic-sense that she wouldn't be able to breathe much more, certainly not at all, if he tried to continue.

He did not. He turned on his heel and walked through the room, through the doors to the rear, out to the corridor. There was a sudden flash of light as the television cameramen staked out in the hallway captured his grief. Detective Barren turned again to the front. Sadegh Rhotzbadegh had risen, his attorneys on either side. He was being fingerprinted and the judge was intoning the sentence, reading the counts off and pronouncing the maximum term. The years were adding up swiftly and suddenly the judge concluded and the two defense attorneys stepped aside, replaced instantly by two immense prison guards who firmly and deliberately began to lead Sadegh Rhotzbadegh from the courtroom. She heard the judge declare a recess and disappear, black robe blurring, through a side door. The reporters were on their feet around her, and there were questions and answers flooding the air. One family pushed by, shaking their heads. Another stopped to inveigh against the system. Detective Barren saw the prosecutors shaking hands with a grinning Detective Perry. Then she stepped forward and watched the Lebanese student. He was almost to the prisoner's exit when he stopped and turned, eyes searching. They met with Detective Barren's, and they locked together for an instant. For the first time his eyes seemed, not scared, but filled with sadness. The two people looked at each other. He shook his head vigorously, as if trying to insist, trying to pass some negative of importance. She saw him mouth a word or two but wasn't sure what they were.

And then he disappeared. Swallowed up. She heard the door slam shut and lock.

She felt, then, a complete emptiness.

*

At first she did everything to excess. Accustomed to an easy two-mile run on the beach in the mornings, she upped it to five miles in forty-five minutes, aching and panting with lost breath in the aftermath. At work she pursued every aspect of each of her cases two or three times, precision and exactitude a comfort to her. She began to drink more, too, finding sleep elusive unless aided. A friend offered her Valium, but she used what she thought ruefully was the remainder of her good sense to turn down the drugs. She recognized that she was behaving exotically, desperately, and knew also that she was in trouble. Her dreams, when she could sleep, were fitful, filled with the Lebanese student, or Susan, or her own dead husband. Sometimes she saw the face of the man who'd shot her, sometimes her father, who looked at her curiously, tearfully, as if saddened, even in death.

She hated the idea that it was over.

She knew the procedure. Sadegh Rhotzbadegh would be sent to the classification center in mid-Florida, where he would get his physical and mental examinations. Then, in due course, he would be shipped up to the maximum-security unit at Raiford, to begin his prison life, begin living out his days.

That he lived dismayed her.

In her mind's eye she replayed over and again the small shrug that had passed between them, trying to decipher, amidst the confusion and terror and madness, what he'd meant with that final shaking of the head.

She would lie in bed at night, thinking.

She would slow it, like fancy television camerawork, trying to separate each motion into a whole. His head bent first to the right, then the left, his mouth opening, words formed, but evaporating in the noise.

She took to spending time each weekend on the police range. It gave her some satisfaction to sharpen her skills with the standard issue .38 Police Special. The sensation as the weapon bucked and thrust in her hand was sensual, relaxing. She purchased a Browning 9-millimeter semiautomatic, a large, violent gun, and grew proficient with that, too. She went to Lieutenant Burns and requested a transfer out of crime-scene analysis and back to the street.

'I'd like to go back on patrol duty.'

'What?'

'Take a regular shift. Maybe a beat.'

'No chance.'

'This is an official request.'

'So? I should let you go out there and blow some purse snatcher away? You think I'm crazy? Request denied. If you want to go above my head, fine. If you want to go to the union, fine, but the bottom line's gonna stay the same.'

'I want out.'

'No, you don't. You want peace. I can't give you that. Only time can.'

But she knew none.

She called Detective Perry.

'You know, Merce, we were damn close at the end to indicting him for Susan's murder. We had the newspaper clipping found at his house, and after the guy's picture ran in the newspaper a couple of students who were at the bar with Susan the night of the killing made him. They would have testified that they saw him there that night. Trouble was, they didn't see him with her, or follow her out, and one of the students distinctly remembers seeing the creep after Susan had to have disappeared. So we were close, but . . .'

'Can I have their names?'

'Sure.'

She scribbled them down. She intended to visit them.

She thought often of the Lebanese student's head shaking. What, she thought repeatedly. What was he saying?

She lay in bed feeling blackness surround her. It was weeks after the sentencing; the tropical springtime with its great rush of growth and lushness had enveloped the city. Even the darkness seemed alive with resurgence. Suppose, she thought, he was trying to say, No, I didn't kill Susan. Don't be ridiculous. He hated you, she thought. He was mad as a March hare. Allah this and Allah that, he was seeking some kind of forgiveness. From her? He was too scared and too arrogant, an impossible combination. Then what was he saying? He shook his head, that's all. Forget it. How?

And then she was filled with an odd, disquieting fear, as if there were something very obvious that she had forgotten. For a moment her head spun and then she turned on the light. It rended the nighttime. She padded across the bedroom to a small desk, where she kept all the copies of reports, evidence and notes from the investigation and solution of Susan's murder. Slowly she spread them about her. Then, carefully, thinking to herself, Be a goddamn detective, stop acting like a grief-stricken puppy, she began to search through them. Look, she said to herself. Find it, whatever it is. Something is there.

And there was. A small something.

It was in the evidence-disposition report from her boss. *Trace alcohol.*

She read: ' . . . Guy must have had a drink or two. Booze always screws everything up . . .'

'Oh, God,' she said out loud to no one.

She ran to a bookshelf in the living room, pulled out a dictionary, and looked up 'Shiite Moslem,' but it wasn't enough of a help. She spotted a course catalog from the university that Susan had once left behind. She seized it and tore it open. She found Middle Eastern Studies on page 154. She underlined the department chairman's name and grabbed a telephone book. He was listed.

She looked at the clock. Three a.m.

She sat motionless for three hours, trying to blank out her fear.

Sorry, she thought, as the clock turned 6 a.m. She dialed the number.

'Harley Trench, please.'

'God,' said a voice clouded with sleep. 'You've got him. No damn extensions, I told you all in class.'

'Professor Trench, this is Detective Mercedes Barren of the City of Miami Police. This is a police matter.'

'Ohmigosh, I'm sorry. It's usually students. They know I'm an early riser and they take advantage of me . . .'

She heard him collect himself.

'How can I help?' he asked.

'We have a suspect in an important case who is of Middle Eastern extraction. He claims to be a Shiite Moslem.'

'Oh, like that horrid fellow who killed the young girls.'

'Very similar.'

'Well, yes, go on . . .'

'We need to know, well, we can exclude this fellow as a suspect in a case if we can show that he took a drink.'

'You mean, like some alcoholic beverage.'

'Right.'

'A beer, or a glass of wine or a gin and tonic.'

'Right.'

'Well, that's a simple question, detective. If he's a sincere Shiite, like that poor crazed fellow said he was, not a chance.'

'I beg your pardon?'

'A mortal sin, detective. No alcohol at all. Not through their lips. Not any time. It's a pretty widespread tenet of the fanatic Moslems and the reformists. A true conservative Moslem wouldn't touch a drop. Probably think the ayatollah himself would come after him. Now we're not talking about a Saudi, here, or a North African Moslem. But a real eye-rolling hostage-taking Shiite? No chance. Does that answer your question, detective?'

Detective Barren was silent.

'Detective?'

'Yes. Sorry. Just thinking. Thank you, it does.'

Trace alcohol, she thought.

She felt dizzy.

She hung up the telephone and stared at the words before her. *Trace alcohol*.

Oh, God, she thought.

She saw the head as if in slow motion, shaking back and forth, insistent.

She raced to the bedroom and rifled through the papers

until she came to an inventory of everything at Sadegh Rhotzbadegh's house. no liquor.

But he was at the bar, she thought. They saw him there.

But did they see him drink?

Oh, God, she thought again.

She got to her feet and walked into the bathroom. For a moment she stared at herself in the mirror. She saw her own eyes open in fear and horror. Then she was overcome by nausea, bent over the toilet and became violently ill. She wiped herself clean and looked back in the mirror.

'Oh, God,' she said to her reflection. 'He's still out there. I think he's still out there. Maybe, maybe, maybe, oh, God, maybe. Oh, Susan, oh, my God, I'm sorry, but he still may be out there. Oh, Susan, I'm so goddamn sorry. Oh, Susan.'

A sob filled her throat. It burst from her lips like an explosion.

'Oh, Susan, Susan, Susan,' she said.

And then, for the first time since the first phone call so many months earlier, she gave in to her sorrow, capitulating to all the resonances of her heart that she'd suppressed so successfully and was suddenly, completely, utterly taken over by tears.

2 An English Lit major

4

The glare off the highway filled the windshield, blinding him for a single second, and he pictured the way he'd stared across the table at his brother as his brother had said, 'You know, I wish we'd been closer, growing up . . .'

He remembered his reply, quick, flip, but accurate: 'Oh, we're closer than you think. Much closer.'

Douglas Jeffers drove south thinking of the wan light of the hospital cafeteria that had caught his brother's face and made it lose its edge. The light, he thought, I always remember the light. He pushed down on the accelerator and watched as the scrub pines and bushes on the side of the highway seemed to pick up speed, rushing toward him.

America in a blur, he thought.

He spoke out loud to himself: 'Ninety-five. Ninety-five on Ninety-five,' and he goosed the accelerator again. He felt the surge of the car and he watched with some delight as the scenery fled past beyond the windows. He had the odd sensation that he was standing still and that the world was careening past him. He gripped the wheel tightly as the car shuddered, swooping past a tandem-semi-trailer truck, caught for an instant in the conflicting velocities of the two vehicles. He felt the wheel beneath his fingers twitch, as if registering a mild complaint or warning. But the engine seemed to him to be roaring in excitement, basso profundo, as it swept up the miles. He looked down at the speedometer and when the needle touched ninety-five, he abruptly took his foot off the gas until the car had slowed to a modest sixty-five miles per hour. He fiddled for a moment with the radio dial until he got a clear signal out of Florence, Georgia, country and western twangy-thump, thump. The deejay was drawling a request, a tune 'for all those striking school bus drivers in Florence, listening out on the picket line . . .' And he cued up Johnny Paycheck singing, ' . . . now you can take this job and shove it, I ain't working here no more . . .'

Jeffers joined in the refrain and thought about the meeting two days earlier with his brother.

He waited patiently at a small table in a corner of the hospital cafeteria until Marty finished morning rounds and entered. 'I'm sorry I kept you waiting,' the younger brother started, but Douglas cut him short with a quick shrug of dismissal. They made small talk for a few minutes, ignoring the clatter of dishes and the voices that surrounded them. Fluorescent lighting filled the room, giving both brothers a pale and sickly appearance.

'The light here makes everyone look pre-psychotic,' Douglas Jeffers said.

Martin Jeffers laughed.

'How long has it been?' he asked.

'A couple of years. Maybe three,' Douglas Jeffers replied.

'It doesn't seem that long.'

'No, not really.'

'Busy?'

'Both busy.'

'True enough.'

Douglas Jeffers thought of his younger brother's laugh and how rarely he'd heard it. His younger brother, he thought, was prone to a quiet seriousness. Then, that was what one would expect from a psychiatrist, even one that spent his days surrounded by the clanging noises and abrupt, disjointed screams of a large state mental hospital.

'Why do you stay here?' he asked.

Martin Jeffers shrugged. 'I don't exactly know. I'm comfortable here, the pay is good, there is the thought that I'm actually doing something good for society . . . a lot of factors.'

Penance, Douglas Jeffers thought.

But he failed to speak the word out loud.

My brother, he thought, sees too much. And, consequently, sees little.

When his brother drank coffee, his little finger extended from the cup, like some dowager aunt daintily drinking tea. His brother had busy hands. He was forever plucking at the name tag he wore on his white hospital coat, or seizing a pen from his pocket, chewing the end for a few moments, then slipping it back out of sight. When he was considering a question, he would often slip his hand behind his head and twirl his finger around a strand of hair. When the strand tightened sufficiently, he would reply.

'So, how's the shrinking business? Keeping up?' Douglas Jeffers asked.

'A growth industry,' Martin Jeffers replied. 'But only in numbers. It's always the same stories, over and over again, told in different tones and different language, but the same, only individualized. That's what makes it interesting. Sometimes, though, I envy the variety you have . . .'

The older brother frowned.

'It's not that different,' he said. 'In a way, for me, too, the stories are always the same. Does it really make a difference if it's Jonestown or Salvador or the Miami riots or the barrio in East LA? The misery is the same, whether it's a 727 crash in New Orleans or the boat people in the Philippines. One after the other. A tragedy a week. A disaster a day. That's all I do, really. I follow on the heels of evil, trying to catch a little glimpse of it before it heads off to some new location.'

He smiled. He liked that description.

His brother, of course, shook his head.

'When you put it that way,' Martin Jeffers said, 'it sounds . . . unattractive. More than that, really, it sounds exhausting.'

'Not really.'

'You don't tire of it? I mean, I get angry with my patients . . .'

'No. I love the hunt.'

His brother did not reply.

Douglas Jeffers looked ahead down the roadway and saw the

two-lane blacktop shimmering with heat. The sun reflected harshly off the hood of the car, spinning light into his eyes. The road was empty ahead and he let his eyes wander, registering the colors and shapes of the Georgia countryside. Tall pine trees leaped up a hundred yards back from the breakdown lane, throwing cool shadows onto the earth. The shade looked inviting, and for a moment he longed to stop and sit beneath a tree. It would be pleasant, he thought, to do something simple and childlike. Then he shook his head and stared straight down the road, measuring the miles between his car and the dark hump on the highway ahead of him. A minute passed. Then another and he came on the rear of a station wagon. It was a large American wagon, filled with children, suitcases, the family dog, and parents. A tarp that covered the bags tied to the roof flapped in the wind. Douglas Jeffers' eyes met those of a young boy, who was sitting in the rearmost seat, his back to the front, as if ostracized by the rest of the family. The boy lifted his hand in a tentative way to Jeffers, and Jeffers waved back, smiling. Then he pulled out into the left-hand lane and accelerated past.

'Do you remember,' his brother asked him, 'the books we read when we were young?'

'Of course,' Douglas Jeffers replied. '*The Wizard of Oz. Robinson Crusoe. Captains Courageous. Ivanhoe. The Hobbit* and *The Lord of the Rings* . . .'

'*The Wind in the Willows. The Wonder Clock. Treasure Island* . . .'

'*Peter Pan.* Just think happy thoughts . . .'

'And you can fly.'

They laughed.

'That's what I call them,' Martin Jeffers said.

'Who?'

'The men in my program. It's a hospital in-joke. The men in the sex-offenders program. We call them the Lost Boys.'

'Do they know?'

Martin Jeffers shrugged. 'They feel special enough.'

'True,' said Douglas Jeffers. 'They aren't your ordinary types.'

'No, not at all.'

They were silent for a moment.

'Tell me something,' his brother asked. 'What is it that you like the best about photography?'

Douglas Jeffers considered the question carefully before replying. 'I like the idea that a picture is indelible, with a pristine quality. Almost a sanctity. It does not, it cannot, lie. It captures time and events perfectly. When you need to remember, in your business, you need to delve into the past that is knotted by emotions, anxieties, tangled memories. Not me. I need to see the past, I can flip to a file, pick out a picture. Clear. Unencumbered. Truth.'

'Can't be that easy.'

But it is, Douglas Jeffers thought.

'I'll tell you what I don't like,' he said. 'It always seems that your best work is in the rejection pile. Photo editors always look for the best illustration of events. It is rarely the best photo. Every photographer has his private gallery, his secret stash of pictures. His own recollections of truth.'

They were quiet again. Douglas Jeffers knew exactly what his brother was going to ask next. He wondered how he had held back so long.

'So why now?' Martin Jeffers said. 'Why come visit?'

'I'm going on a little trip. I want to leave the key to my place with you. That all right?'

'Yes, but – where are you heading?'

'Oh, here and there. Back to some memories. I thought I'd revisit some past experiences.'

'Can you stay for a bit? We could talk over old times.'

'You will recall that our old times weren't so damn fine.'

His brother nodded.

'Okay. But where exactly are you going?'

Douglas Jeffers remained silent.

'You won't say or you can't say?'

'Let me put it this way,' he finally replied. 'It's a sentimental journey.' He mock-crooned the words. 'To disclose the route would remove some of the, well, adventure.'

Martin Jeffers looked perturbed.

'I don't get it.'

'You will.' Douglas laughed harshly. Heads turned at the sound. 'Look, I just wanted to say goodbye. Is that so mysterious?'

'No, but . . .'

The elder interrupted. 'Indulge me.'

'Of course,' replied the younger instantly. The two men walked down a hospital corridor in silence together. Light from a bank of plate-glass windows reflected off the white walls of the hospital, giving the two men a luminescent glow. They reached the hospital's main entrance and paused. 'When will I see you again?' Martin asked.

'When you see me.'

'You'll stay in touch?'

'In my own way.'

Douglas Jeffers could see his brother was on the verge of asking more questions, but instead he bit back the query, keeping his mouth shut.

'Maybe you'll hear from me,' Douglas Jeffers said.

The younger nodded.

'Maybe you'll hear about me.'

'I don't get it.'

But the elder shook his head and gave his brother a fake punch on the chin instead. Then he turned and started through the exit. But before walking through the doors, he turned, expertly seizing the camera from his shoulder bag and raising it to his eye in one fluid motion. He crouched, framing his brother quickly, then snapping off a series of shots. Douglas Jeffers lowered the camera and waved jauntily. Martin Jeffers tried to smile, and tentatively, awkwardly, lifted his arm in half-salute.

That's how he had left him. Douglas Jeffers laughed out loud remembering the look on his brother's face. 'My brother,' he spoke to himself, 'sees but cannot see, hears but cannot hear.'

For an instant he slid into sadness. Goodbye, Marty. Goodbye for good. When the time comes, take the apartment key and learn, if you can. Goodbye.

His attention was suddenly swept away by the sight of a police cruiser parked adjacent to a stand of trees. He quickly looked down at the speedometer. He was doing sixty-three. Then he thought. What difference does it make?

After Tallahassee, he warned himself, he would have to pay much more attention. The idea that his trip would be cut short by the accidental encounter with a police officer made him slow further. However, he thought a slow car draws as much attention as a speeder. Stick to the median. He reached down under the seat of the car and felt for the leather case he'd stuck in the hollow. It was where he'd left it. He pictured the short-barreled gun. Not as accurate as the 9-millimeter packed away in his suitcase, nor as well tooled as the Ruger semiautomatic 30-caliber rifle in a case in the trunk. But at close range it was very efficient. And it fitted nicely into the pocket of his jacket, and that was an important consideration. It would not do to wander about the campus with a gun bulging beneath his coat.

He passed a sign. The Florida border was ten miles ahead. Closing in, he thought.

He felt a delightful rush of excitement, like awakening on the first morning of summer vacation. He rolled down the window and let the hot insistent Southern air blow through the car. The heat swirled around him, and into him, filling his bones with lassitude. He felt sweat start to form in his armpits and he rolled up the window again, letting the air conditioner take over.

He drove on, leaving the memory of his brother behind, concentrating on the highway, turning off the interstate and cruising through the Panhandle on his way to the state capital. The trees, he thought, looked less stately, shorter, as if beaten by the heat, shrunken by the sun.

He found a motel about ten miles out of town. It was a run-down, forgettable place called the Happy Nites Inn. He started to remark on the spelling to the tired woman with stringy gray hair behind the counter of the small office building, but then thought otherwise. He signed with a false name, ready to provide proper identification, but she didn't ask for it. He paid in advance for five nights and took the key to the furthermost bungalow in the rear of the motel. He suspected that he would not be bothered there. No need even to ask. The rooms cost $18 a night and he got what he paid for. The bed was shaky, sagging, with gray sheets and a threadbare blanket. But for the most part, the room was clean, and, he thought, perfectly isolated. He slipped the weapons beneath the mattress, showered, and turned on the television, but he wasn't interested and within a few minutes decided to sleep.

As he lay in bed, however, indecision pummeled him.

He went over all the arguments that had filled his imagination for weeks. Once again he considered a history major. One of them would provide context, he thought, a sense of continuity, able to fit the actions into the larger scheme of things. But could they write? Would they have the necessary quick-wittedness to stay alert, instantly prepared to document what he had in mind? He hesitated. Perhaps a sociology major. They would have a better concept of trends and would see the statement in proper social perspective. But again he paused, concerned more about individual flexibility. He dismissed a psychology major out of hand; he would be forced to perform with a kind of clinical exactitude that he did not care for. It was easy to rule out the sciences and government. They would be dogmatic and probably uninformed. And he certainly didn't want to spend his free time talking politics. He knew, too, he didn't want a mathematician, or, for that matter, a musician or a linguist. They would be too wrapped up in their own particular specialities to appreciate the events.

His first instincts were probably the right ones: that he would seek either a literature major or a journalism major. Someone with an interest in journalism would be helpful; he would be able to discuss the many stories he'd covered, and in that way deflect some of the natural fear and anxiety. But, in the same respect, he reflected, a budding journalist might not understand the full picture, settling for an unfortuante recounting, producing a single-minded narrative of the events and missing some of the subtleties that he envisioned. What I'm going to do, he thought, could fill a book, so it is a book-child I must get. Someone from the English Department, he decided. He felt a surge of pleasure at having made the decision, recognizing, too, that his first feelings, after careful review and analysis, had been correct. But he hesitated again, cautioning himself, Be patient: a lonely, reclusive type would be disastrous. But someone too popular will be too easily missed. No bookworms, no cheerleaders. Choose carefully, he warned himself.

He felt a quietness sweep over him. Outside he could hear night sounds of bugs bumping against a window screen and far in the distance the high-speed wail of big trucks on the highway.

Stick to the plan, he thought. The plan is good.

He felt satisfied and within moments slipped into sleep.

Bright lights flooded through the windows of the McDonald's on the edge of Florida State University campus in Tallahassee. He put his hand to the glass and felt warmth building on the outside. He was aware of the noise of the air-conditioning system, battling with the exterior, fighting against the heat rising from the bank of frying machines and the sizzling rows of hamburgers, lined up in military precision on the stove. Though it was morning, the restaurant was already crowded with students. He sipped his coffee and pored over the campus map, checking locations against a class schedule easily obtained from the university library before breakfast.

By his third coffee he had managed to isolate several promising courses in suitable locations. He packed the map and course catalog away in his briefcase. He checked his appearance in the mirror in the men's room before leaving. He straightened his tie and brushed his hair back. He wore a blue seersucker sportscoat and khaki slacks. No one would think twice about the dark sunglasses, he thought. Everyone on a campus in Florida wears sunglasses. He arranged the pens sticking from his shirt pocket and rumpled his jacket slightly, then took a paperback copy of John Fowles' *The Collector* from his briefcase and stuck it in his coat pocket, so the bookjacket title would protrude. He had purchased the book that morning and had carefully dog-eared the pages and bent the spine to make it appear well-read. He should have had the sense to bring his own copy, he thought. In the other pocket he stuck a sheaf of papers. He stared at himself, pleased. A graduate teaching assistant, he thought. Perhaps a young assistant professor, slightly befuddled by academia, greatly worried about tenure, but still friendly, outgoing, a little handsome and, most of all, harmless.

He set off for the campus. Confident. Excited. Pleased with his appearance, pleased with his plan.

But first, he thought, a spiritual stop.

He walked down a quiet, tree-lined street, passing an occasional knot of students, smiling, nodding to them as they swept past, searching for the address. He expected a sign out front, the way other sorority and fraternity houses were marked. It was an exceptional day; warm but not yet overwhelming, a relief from Florida's usual summertime. In its own way, he thought, the typical summer day in Florida is much like the dead of winter in the Northeast: in Florida, the heat creates the same oppressiveness, the same shut-in quality that the bitter cold does in the North. It is equally difficult, on the worst days, to travel abroad. In Florida one hides behind the air conditioning. He looked up at the sun, cutting across a cloudless sky, shading his eyes. He thought of Jack London and extrapolated: No, a man can't walk alone in Florida when the temperature rises . . .

Douglas Jeffers smiled to himself and paused beneath the dark branches of a tall oak tree. He stared across a green lawn at a white two-story wooden house, set back twenty yards from the sidewalk. Two teenage girls exited the wide front door as he watched, and he averted his glance, turning to look across the street until they passed. They were laughing together, and he doubted if they realized he was there. He looked back at the white house, studying the front. The house had many windows and a side exit. On the front lawn was a sign with two Greek letters. He read the letters twice to himself, then smiled inwardly.

Chi Omega.

Here we are, he thought. Here's where it happened.

His mind's eye envisioned the picture with professional swiftness.

76

Straight-on, he thought. Catch the light as it hits the left front quadrant. Simply a scrapbook shot, make it quick. Don't get noticed. He would have liked to wait for someone to walk down the path, or come through the door, which would have given the building a size perspective in the shot. But the person might notice, and that would be difficult. He framed the shot visually, so that a large oak tree on the edge of the closely cropped green lawn would provide a vertical measurement on one side. He moved a few feet to put himself slightly on angle. Quickly he checked up and down the sidewalk. Then he bent to one knee, as if tying his shoe, opened his briefcase, and grabbed the camera. He adjusted the speed and the aperture before removing the camera. Then, in a single, fluid, quick movement, he brought the camera up to his eye, pivoting toward the sorority house, focusing as he turned. He twisted the lens and snapped off a shot. The motordrive whirred and he punched the trigger again. Then again. Then, satisfied, he slid the camera back into the briefcase, actually tied his shoe, and stood up. He glanced about to make certain that no one had seen him and paced quickly down the street.

He walked swiftly for a dozen blocks, onto the campus, not stopping until he spied an empty bench beneath a tree. He settled on the bench, realizing suddenly that he was breathing hard, which he recognized came from excitement, not exertion.

'Did you get the shot?' he asked himself. In his imagination, his voice had the edge-of-desperation sound of a harried editor.

'I always get the shot,' he answered himself.

'But did you get this shot?'

'Have I ever failed you?'

'Please, just tell me, did you get the shot?'

'No sweat.'

He laughed out loud.

What a tourist, he thought. While everyone else who comes to Florida heads to Disney World or Epcot Center or treks to the Keys, you visit the site where . . . where what? He considered. Most people would look at a picture of the

Chi Omega House on the campus of Florida State University and think of it as the location where two young women had been brutally murdered as they slept in their beds and a third badly injured. For a moment Jeffers considered the phrase: brutally murdered. It was journalese, a language with only the slightest connection to English. Murders were always brutal. So were beatings, except when they were savage. The clichés of the newspaper world created a type of safe shorthand – readers could absorb the words 'brutally murdered' and not have to know that the killer was in such a frenzy that he'd severed one girl's nipple with a bite and clubbed another with an oaken branch like some berserk prehistoric man. Douglas Jeffers thought of the young women he'd seen walking from the house, laughing. He wondered for an instant whether at night she and her sorority sisters double-locked their doors, throwing solid deadbolts on memory. Jeffers pictured the house. He thought: They think of it as a place to stay, camaraderie for four years of college, but it's more, it's really a monument to something much more important: it marks the site where a prolific murderer started really to lose control and bring on his own end.

Jeffers remembered the short, wavy-brown-haired man he'd first seen on assignment in a Miami courtroom many months after the terrible night at the sorority house.

Idiot! he thought.

His mind segmented the memory into pictures. Click! The killer turned. Click! The killer eyed him. Click! They stared at each other, locking eyes. Jeffers wondered if the man could see past his own little stage-show. Click! The killer's mouth opened as he started to voice a word which evaporated into a slightly skewed, wry smile. Click! The killer turned back, smirking, glibly commenting on the trial work in front of him, angering the judge, alienating the jury, ensuring the inevitability of the result. Click! Jeffers caught that smirk, that dark edge of madness and fury, just before it was covered with sarcasm and arrogance. That was the picture he'd kept for his own file.

What a fool! he thought again.

Jeffers' stomach twisted with the memory. The papers had called him intelligent!

Jeffers shook his head sharply back and forth. What kind of intelligence can't control his own passions? Where was the self-discipline? Where was the thoughtfulness, the planning, the invention, in bursting in the dead of night into a crowded sorority house and savaging the occupants? Out of control. Enthralled by desire. Weakness, Jeffers thought. Silly, schoolboy indulgence born of conceit.

He remembered his own inner fury when his colleagues on newspapers and television had breathlessly marveled at the incongruity of an articulate, educated man who was a mass murderer. He looked like one of us. He talked like one of us. He acted like one of us. How could he be what the police said he was?

Jeffers spat, angry.

The truth was, Jeffers thought, he wasn't.

How simplistic. How foolish. So he was bright. So he was likeable.

Well, does he like death row?

He deserves it, Jeffers thought.

First Degree Stupidity.

He rose from his seat, aware again of the increasing heat of the day. He decided to go over to the student union to eat some lunch before making his final reconnoiter and executing his plans.

The cafeteria was crowded, noisy, anonymous. Jeffers took his tray to a corner table and ate slowly, his map and course list spread before him, occasionally daring to look up and survey the melee of students. He thought that there was a nice symmetry in his behavior; he remembered the few months that he'd spent in college before dropping out to begin his career as a photographer. His time had been spent in much the same way as he was spending his time now. Alone. Quiet. Keeping to himself, watching, rather than joining. Listening rather than speaking. He remembered the awkwardness he'd felt, alone in his dormitory, separate from the easygoing welcome of the college community. It had been winter in the North, a frozen, regrettable day, gray-pitched and damp with the threat of snow, when he'd thrown his few clothes into a duffle bag, loaded his cameras, and stepped out to the edge of the campus, saluting freedom with his thumb, hitchhiking west across the nation. The memory of that trip made him smile: He'd sold his first photograph a week after starting out. He remembered sitting at a table in a soup kitchen in downtown Cleveland. He was alone, as always; one old derelict had tried to sit next to him, rubbing a knee against his beneath the table while spooning great gobs of greasy stew into his mouth and trying to behave with an ancient, encrusted nonchalance. Jeffers had hooked the man's leg beneath the table with his own feet and pulled suddenly back and to the side, twisting the derelict's brittle knee angrily. The leg creaked as the man grasped the table, about to shout out in pain, but stilled by Jeffers' quiet warning: 'Say a word, scream, shout, anything, and I'll break it and you'll die out there this winter, huh?'

The man had swiftly crabbed away when Jeffers released him. A few moments later, just as he was sopping the last of his stew with a piece of doughy white bread, Jeffers had heard sirens, many of them, swoop down the street and come to a stop a block away. He'd grabbed his camera bag and jogged down to the scene of a two-alarm in a tenement. The families were passing children out the window to firemen, screaming, panicked, and Jeffers had shot all of it. But it was a picture of a fireman, icicles hanging from his coat and hat, clutching a terrified six-year-old in a blanket and carrying her to safety that he'd sold. The photo editor of the *Plain Dealer* had been skeptical, but had allowed Jeffers to use the darkroom. It had been a slow news day and he was anxious for a piece of art for the local break page. Jeffers remembered how careful he'd been, locked alone in the darkroom, mixing his chemicals with an abundance of caution, slowly souping the print until the image began to form. It had been the eyes that sold the picture, Jeffers thought, the benign mixture of exhaustion and exhilaration in the look on the rescuer's face in counterpoint to the accumulated terror in the child's. It was a very powerful picture and the photo editor logged it for the front page.

'Helluva shot,' the photo editor said. 'Fifty bucks. Where do we send the check?'

'I'm just passing through.'

'No address?'

'The Y.'

'Where are you going?'

'California.'

'Everyone wants to go to lotus land.' He sighed. 'Free speech, free love, orgies and drugs, Haight-Ashbury and acid rock.' He laughed. 'Hell, doesn't sound so damn bad.'

The editor pulled out his own wallet and handed over two twenties and two fives. 'Why don'tcha stick around a little bit, take some more shots for us? I'll pay.'

'How much?'

'Ninety a week.'

He thought. Cleveland's cold. So he said it.

'Cleveland's cold.'

'So's Detroit and Chicago. New York's a bitch and Boston is out of the question. Kid, you want warmth, head for Miami or LA. You want to work, give it a ride right here. Hell, it's winter. Tell you what, I'll make it ninety-five and I'll buy you a parka and some long johns.'

'What'll I be shooting?'

'No flower shows. No Chamber of Commerce meetings. Just more of what you did already.'

'I'll give it a try,' Jeffers said.

'Great, kid. One thing, though.'

'What's that?'

'I'm gambling. This picture today, well, it turns out to be a lucky shot – I mean, I don't get more of the same – and well, bingo, you're back on your way to California. Catch my drift?'

'In other words, show me.'

'You got it. You willing, still?'

'Sure. Why not?'

'Kid, with that attitude you'll go far in this business. And one other thing. Cleveland's a blue-collar town. Get your hair cut.'

He spent eleven short-haired months in Cleveland.

He remembered. An antiwar protester clubbed over the back by a hardhat carrying a two-by-four. Shot at 1/250, f-16, with a telephoto, from a block away. The grainy quality had accentuated the violence. A mob funeral, with a bodyguard exploding in rage at the collected bank of photographers and cameramen. He'd shot fast, ducking at the last minute, catching the black-suited muscleman swinging, teeth bared, 1/1000 at f-2.4 with high-speed film. Another funeral, flag-draped, a flyer who'd taken too much flak over Haiphong and nursed his f-16 all the way back to the *Oriskany* and safety in the Gulf of Tonkin, only to lose power on his approach and die in the warm choppy waters before rescue could scramble to his side. The family had seemed resigned, Jeffers thought; there had been few tears. He'd caught them in a line, staring down into the grave, as if on parade, 1/15 at f-22, leaving the print a little long in the mix so as to bring out the grayness of the sky. He remembered, too, the stiffened, frozen body of a junkie, warmth found from a needle, who'd braved a February night outdoors and simply died. It had been by the waterfront; his shot had grabbed light from the Cuyahoga, reflecting an icebound world, 1/500 at f-5.6. But, as always, when he remembered Cleveland, he thought of the girl.

He had been in the darkroom, a small transistor radio that he'd purchased with his first paycheck playing in the corner, filling the room with Doors' harsh lyrics and sound. Every time he switched on the radio 'Light My Fire' had flowed out. He had spent two blistering summer days walking an early beat with one of the city's last foot patrolmen. He'd found the photos routine, too filled with softness. The policeman was popular, outgoing. Everywhere he went he was greeted, applauded, welcomed. Jeffers had snarled at the pictures. Where was the edge? Where was the tension? He wanted someone to take a shot at the cop. He prayed for it, and decided to spend another day on the street. Lost in the music, the darkness, and his plans, he'd barely been aware of the voice of the photo editor yelling for him.

'Jeffers, you lazy slug, get out of there!'

He'd carefully put his things down, moving deliberately. Jim Morrison was singing, 'I know that it would be untrue . . .' The photo editor, he had swiftly learned, existed in two states: boredom and panic.

'What?' he'd asked, stepping from the cubicle.

'A body, Jeffers, one hundred per cent dead, right in the middle of the Heights. A nice white teenage girl in a rich neighborhood very goddamn dead. Go, go, go. Meet Buchanan at the scene. Go!'

He had paced, oddly nervous, on the edge of the police perimeter, standing apart from the other newsmen and television cameramen who were waiting in a knot, joking, trying to learn a little, but mostly willing to wait until a spokesman or a detective came over to brief them *en masse*. Where's the shot? he'd demanded to himself. Moving right, then left, in and out of afternoon shadows, finally, when no one would notice, swinging up into a large tree, trying to get some clear vision. Stretched out like a sniper on a tree limb, he'd fixed a telephoto lens to his camera and peered down at the policemen working meticulously around the body of the young girl. He swallowed hard at the first sight of a naked leg, tossed haphazardly aside by the killer. Jeffers had strained to see, feverish, snapping off pictures, pulling the camera tightly on the victim. He needed to see her breasts, her hair, her crotch; he adjusted angle and focus and continued to fire the camera like a weapon, twisting it, manipulating it, caressing it to bring him closer to the body. He wiped sweat from his forehead and fingered the trigger again, swearing every time a detective moved into his line of sight, the motor-drive whirring every time he had a clear shot.

He'd kept those pictures for himself.

The paper had run three others: a shot of fire-rescue personnel bringing the body-bagged-wrapped victim out on a stretcher, a ground-level long-lens shot of the detectives kneeling over the body, which was obscured by their position save for a striking thin young arm, flung back from the torso, gently held by one of the policemen, and a picture of a tittering gaggle of teenage girls, drawn by fear and curiosity to the edge of the crime scene, staring out in tears and surprise as the body was carried out from the underbrush. He had liked the last shot the best, carefully approached the girls to get their names, sweet-talking the information out of them easily. The shot, he thought, spoke of crime's effect. One girl's eyes were wide in semishock, while the girl next to her had thrust her hands to her face, the eyes just peering over the edge of fingers stiffened with fright. A third girl's mouth hung wide, while a fourth was turning away from the vision. It was, the photo editor said, the best of the bunch. It ran outside, page one. 'There might be a bonus,' the photo editor said, but Jeffers, still suffused with excitement, thought that his real bonus remained developing in chemicals back in the darkroom, and, as soon as he'd seen the crop and the layout, he'd hastened back to his solitude.

He smiled.

He still had those pictures, almost twenty years later.

He would always have those pictures.

He heard laughter and turned toward a group of students sitting close by. They were teasing one of their own, who was taking it all good-naturedly. Jeffers could catch only snatches of the conversation, but it was about a term paper that the student had turned in, nothing of great import, a small, typical moment. Jeffers looked at his schedule and his map and decided it was time to start.

He cut rapidly across campus; it was just before 1 p.m. and he wanted to be in his seat before 'Social Awareness in Nineteenth Century Literature' started. He bounced up the short flight of stairs to the classroom building, sliding his sunglasses off as he entered the darkened hall, striding purposefully into Lecture Room 101 with a steady stream of students, some marching in singly, others in pairs. The lecture hall was filling rapidly; he quickly found a seat on the aisle, near the back. He smiled at the young woman sitting next to him. She smiled back, not breaking her conversation with a boy next to her. He looked about swiftly; there were a dozen or so conversations such as the one he was next to, just enough noise to crack the silence of the hall. To his right he spied a student reading a newspaper, another flipping through the pages of a paperback. Others arranged notepads in front of them. He did the same, trying to read something into some piece of behavior, a small movement that displayed an attitude which would signal to him a person's candidacy.

He spotted one girl, sitting alone, across the aisle and several rows down. She was reading Ambrose Bierce, bending head down over *In the Midst of Life*. Jeffers felt his eyebrows rise, thinking, What an extraordinary combination: the writer who may have sold his soul and a nineteen-year-old girl. Interesting, he thought. He determined to watch her during the lecture.

Sitting a few chairs away was another young woman. She was sketching lazily on a pad. Jeffers could just make out the skilled shapes that were forming beneath her pencil. He thought for a moment, excited, about the intriguing possibility of the sketch artist. He wondered if she could sketch with words. He thought: Someone who can recreate reality in art – perhaps a good selection. He decided to watch her as well.

At a single minute past one the professor entered.

Jeffers frowned. The man was in his mid-thirties, his own age, and glib. He started the hour with a joke about David Copperfield's narration of his own birth, as if that were some quirk of Dickens', some archaic piece of silliness. Jeffers suddenly wanted to rise and scream. Instead, he kept his seat, searching the auditorium for someone who failed to laugh at the professor's witticisms.

There was one who caught his attention.

She was sitting just off to his left. She raised her hand.

'Yes, Miss . . . uh . . .'

'Hampton,' said the young woman.

'Miss Hampton. You have a question?'

'Do you mean to imply that because Dickens was writing for serial consumption that he tailored his ideas and his style to fit the weekly newspaper form? Don't you think the reverse is true, that Dickens understood implicitly the points that he wished to make, and, using his considerable skill, fitted them into manageable segments?'

Jeffers felt his heart slow, his mind concentrate.

'Well, Miss Hampton, we know that the form was important to Dickens . . .'

'Form, sir, over substance?'

Jeffers wrote that down in capital letters and underlined it: FORM OVER SUBSTANCE?

'Miss Hampton, you misunderstand . . .'

Like hell, thought Jeffers.

' . . . Dickens was, of course, preoccupied with the political and social impact of his work. But because of the necessities of form, we can now see limitations. Don't you wonder what his characters and stories would have been like if he had not been forced into the pamphleteer's role?'

'No, sir, I can't say that I have.'

'That was my point, Miss, uh, Hampton.'

Not much of one, at that, thought Jeffers.

He watched the young woman bend her head back to her notepad, scribbling some words on the page rapidly. She had dirty-blond hair which fell haphazardly about her face, obscuring what Jeffers thought was considerable natural beauty. He noted, then, that she sat with an empty seat on either side.

He felt his body quiver involuntarily.

He breathed in deeply and exhaled slowly.

Again, he thought, drawing in a great draught of air and letting it loose carefully, as if it were valuable. He surreptitiously placed his hand over his chest, speaking to himself: Be calm. You did not expect to find a biographer in the first class you visited. Caution, caution. Always caution. She has potential. Wait. Watch. He forced himself to study the other two young women he'd noticed earlier. He had a sudden image of himself as some small, dark, coiled beast, waiting, anticipating, curled in obscurity beneath a loose rock on a well-traveled path. He smiled, thinking with pleasure to himself: Progress.

3 Boswell

5

Afternoon sun filtered weakly through the library window. It struck the notepad open on Anne Hampton's table, making the blue-ruled lines disappear, washed away in the glare. She looked down at the words she had been writing, staring so hard that the edges of the letters blurred and grew indistinct, the entire page becoming a floating, vaporous field. It made her think of snowfields in winter, back home in Colorado. She envisioned herself poised at the top of some long run, the sunlight exploding off the open expanse of snow, uncut as yet by skiers' trails. It would be early morning, the sun would hold no promise of warmth, just a single cold light flooding the white. She thought to herself about the way the reflection seemed to reach up, tangible, blending with the freezing air and wind, creating a world without edges, depth, or height, a solitary great white hole in the world, waiting for her to suppress that momentary hesitation that is the border of fear, and then plunge outward, down, dizzyingly thrust forward, feeling the cold sensation of flying snow bursting like shells around her as she cut through the deep powder.

She laughed out loud. Then, remembering where she was, clapped her hand across her face in mock embarrassment and sat back in her chair, looking out the window across the quadrangle toward a stand of palms that rippled gently as she watched. The palms, she thought, can find a breath of breeze even when there isn't one. They clatter their leaves together as if in greeting, feeling the slightest sway in the air, welcoming it, enjoying it, she thought with an odd jealousy, even when she was unable to detect the meagerest motion of relief in the summer's heat.

She looked back at the books spread about her. It must be easy to spot the literature majors, she thought. She separated her stack of books into two separate piles: Conrad, Camus, Dostoevsky and Melville on one side of her notepad, Dickens and Twain on the other. Darkness and light, she thought. She shook her head. She wasn't even reading half of the books and did not really understand why it was so important for her to tote them around in her backpack. But she did, packing them in every day, next to current assignments, as if the weight of great words resting on her back would somehow permeate her vision and motivate her behavior. She wondered if she had some unconscious time limit for carrying once-read works. She imagined that she could develop a rating system for literature; books that she carried about more than a month after completion were true classics. Three weeks meant a lasting greatness. Two weeks, probably should be hauled about for their themes, if not their execution. A week reflected perhaps a great character, but not a great book. Less than a week? Pretenders.

But, she thought, there is an odd comfort in knowing great words are close.

She sometimes wondered whether books were alive; whether, after shutting the covers, the characters and the places and the situations didn't change, argue, debate somehow, only to return to place at the moment the cover was flipped open. It would be fitting. She started at the Camus, lying atop her dark pile. Perhaps, she thought, Sisyphus rests when the pages are closed. He sits, breathing hard, his back slumped up against his rock, wondering whether this time the rock will teeter at the top and then, miraculously, stick. Then, feeling the pages of the book open about him, he climbs to his feet, puts his shoulder to the rock, and, feeling the comforting coolness of the hard surface, flexes his muscles, gathers his strength, and shoves hard.

She was suddenly tempted to reach out and snatch open the book, to see if she could catch Sisyphus resting.

She smiled again.

She looked up and her eyes momentarily caught those of a man sitting across the room. He had been reading; she couldn't make out the title. He had looked up, it seemed, at the same moment. He smiled. She smiled back. A young professor, she thought. She looked away, out the window, for an instant. Then she let her eyes return to the man. He had returned to his reading.

She looked at her books. She looked at her notes. She looked out the window again. She looked back at the man, but he had disappeared.

She thought suddenly of her mother's complaint: 'But you won't know *anybody* in Florida!'

And her reply: 'But I don't *need* to know anybody.'

'But we'll miss you . . . and Florida is so far away.'

'I'll miss you. But I need time to get away.'

'But it's hot all the time.'

'Mother.'

'All right. If it's what you want.'

'It's what I want.'

It wasn't hot all the time, she thought. Her mother had been wrong. In the winter there was an inevitable freeze, some wayward mass of cold Canadian air, lost in its pursuit of Massachusetts, tumbling down the mid-section of the nation and landing squat and awkwardly on the Florida panhandle. It was a wretched cold, without any of the beauty or terrifying stillness of the Colorado mountains. It was simply irritatingly cold; the palms seemed to buckle, the buildings, lacking much in the way of insulation, seemed tenaciously to hold in the cold air. It was sweaters and overcoats underneath a sky that seemed to speak properly only of beaches. She thought it ironic that she had been far colder on a January day in Tallahassee than she ever had been at home.

She looked at the sunlight hitting her desk. Thank God for the summer heat, she thought. She was struck with the odd observation that in three and one half years she had failed to make a close friend, despite the warmth, despite the familiarity that it bred.

Pizza friends, she thought.

Beer friends. Beach friends. What-did-you-get-on-the-test friends. Did-you-read-the-extra-assignment friends. Will-you-go-to-bed-with-me friends.

Not too many of those, she laughed to herself.

But not for lack of people trying.

She pulled her notepad toward her and wrote: *Face it, you're a cold fish* in the margin. She was pleased. It was an easy association: cold fish and Camus.

She settled into her chair and continued reading.

It was dusk when Anne Hampton left the library and began to walk slowly across the campus. In the west the setting sun had turned the sky an astonishing purple, illuminating massive, stately cloud formations somewhere over the Gulf of Mexico. She thought how she loved to walk at that hour; the residual daylight seemed tenacious, seeking out form and shape and trying, against the oncoming dark, to give solidity to the world before acquiescing to the night.

Dying time, she thought.

She remembered the way it seemed that the last few fragments of sunlight caught on the diver's regulator when he emerged through the hole in the ice at her grandfather's pond, carrying her brother's form. The light had tumbled down from the bright aluminum apparatus of this odd marine creature, just hitting the little boy's encrusted features. Then she had lost sight; Tommy was surrounded instantly by firemen and rescue personnel, and all she could see was a dark mass being rushed up the hillside toward a pulsating red light. She saw his skates, the laces sliced, tossed aside. She pulled out from her grandfather's agonized grip and retrieved them.

Of course, she thought, as she walked along, he didn't actually die then; it was not until two hours later, amidst all the hum and buzz and beep of modern medical apparatus that he technically expired. The hospital's intensive-care unit was a wonder of lights, she thought; everywhere she had looked there was another light, filling every angle, probing every corner. It was as if by refusing to allow any darkness into the rooms, they could somehow stave off death.

She had caught sight of a physician's chart. It had an entry for Time of Death and the nurse had scribbled in 6:42 p.m. She had thought that inaccurate. When did Tommy die? He was dead when I heard the little spiderwebs growing in the ice surface below my feet. He died when I called out to him and he waved his arm at me in little-boy irritation and over-confidence. He died as he hit the water. She remembered thinking how undramatic it had been: one instant he was sliding along, arms pumping, the next, swallowed by this dark hole that had materialized beneath him, dying as the black cold enveloped him. His head did not bob to the surface even once. She had a sudden memory of the numb-cold pain in her feet as she ran, after stripping her own skates off, for her grandfather's house. Each step had seemed colder, harder, the snow deeper, more treacherous. She had fallen a half-dozen times, sobbing. She thought: I was only a little girl. And he was already dead then.

A warm breeze plucked at her shirt and she ran a hand through her hair. The sunlight had almost vanished; with it a sense of purpose and enthusiasm, replaced by a summertime lassitude amidst the evening heat.

No thin ice in Florida, she thought.

Not ever.

She cut through the campus, past knots of students making their way to meals, parties, studies, or whatever, and turned down Raymond Street, heading for her apartment. She filled her mind with the mundane, envisioning the stash of yogurt, cottage cheese, and fruit in her refrigerator, briefly considering stopping for a cheeseburger, then discarding the idea. Eat nuts and berries, she said to herself, laughing. She visualized her parents; both had a tendency to *size*, she thought. She hated the meals of mashed potatoes and steaks that inevitably hit the table before her on her rare visits home. They must think I'm anorexic, she thought. I'm not. I'm selectively anorexic.

She cut under the mercury vapor light at the corner of Raymond and Bond streets, marveling, as always, at the way the light turned her clothes and skin into a fluorescent purple. She had a brief vision of herself as the star of some 1950s horror flick; accidently exposed to a unique dose of radiation, now she would turn into . . . into what, she wondered. The Incredible Wallflower? The Fantastic Grind? The Phenomenal Serious Student? She heard raucous laughter pour suddenly from an open window, blending with a quick resonating chord from a stereo with the volume cranked up. Summer session, she thought, is the least serious of all the semesters. She preferred it, she realized; it made her own work stand out amidst all the people making up one failure or another.

She continued walking along, now humming a nameless snatch of music borrowed from the blasting stereo, until she turned onto Francis Street. She was two blocks from her apartment and she did not see the man until she was almost on top of him.

'Excuse me,' he said. 'Can you help me? I think I'm lost.'

She started. The man was standing at the edge of a shadow, next to the open door of his car.

'Did I frighten you?' he asked.

'No, no, not at all . . .'

'I'm sorry if I did . . .'

'No, it's okay. I was just thinking.'

'Your thoughts were elsewhere?'

'Right.'

'I know the feeling,' he said, striding forward. 'One thought leads to another, then another, and before you know it you're in the midst of some tiny reverie. Sorry to intrude.'

'Reality,' she said, 'always intrudes.'

He laughed.

She looked at him closely in the meager light from a

lamp a half block away. 'Didn't I see you earlier today, in the library?' she asked. He smiled.

'Yes, I was there, catching up on some reading . . .'

She saw him study her own face.

'Aren't you the girl – I'm sorry, woman – with all the books? I thought you'd never get to leave if you had to read all those.'

She smiled. 'Some. Not all. Some were read already.'

'You must be an English major.'

'Bingo'

'Not that hard to tell, really.'

'No, I suppose not,' she said. 'It's funny. I was just thinking that, earlier.'

'See,' he replied, 'good instincts.'

She smiled at him and he grinned in response.

They were silent for a moment. She thought the man handsome; he was tall, well built, with a sort of easy scruffiness about him. Probably just the seersucker jacket, she thought to herself. It adds a bit of rumpled familiarity to almost every man.

'Are you a professor?'

'Of sorts,' the man said.

'But not from around here?'

'No. First visit. And I can't seem to find Garden Street. I've looked all over the place . . .' The man turned, first pointing up one way, then peering down the other. She thought for an instant that he was searching for something as his gaze lingered in each direction before turning back toward her.

'Garden Street is pretty easy,' she said. 'Two turns. Left at the corner, two blocks, then right. Garden Street intersects that street a couple of blocks down. I forget what it's called, but it's not very far.'

'I've got a little map, not a good one,' the man said. 'Would you mind just showing me where I am exactly?' He smiled. 'That of course is really a philosophical question, but this once I'd settle for the topographical.'

She laughed. 'Sure,' she said.

She stepped next to him as he spread the map out on

the roof of the car. He reached into his pocket for a pencil, talking to himself, really: ' . . . now here is where I think I am . . .' And then a sudden 'Dammit! Don't move!'

'What is it?'

'I dropped my room key.'

He bent down. 'Got to be here somewhere . . .' She started to bend down to help him look, but he waved her off. 'See if you can't pinpoint for me where I am on that map.' She stepped forward to the edge of the car and looked at the map. For an instant she was confused: it wasn't Tallahassee, but Trenton, New Jersey.

'This is the wrong map . . .'

She didn't have time to finish.

For one instant she looked down. She saw the man had a small rectangular device in his hand.

'Good night, Miss Hampton,' he said.

Before she could move, he jerked her leg toward him and thrust the device up against her thigh. There was a crackling sound; an immense pain fled through her body; it felt as if someone had reached inside her and seized her heart and twisted it savagely. How does he know my name? she thought. Then she could feel her eyes rolling back and blackness sweeping over her. The crackling sound stopped and she thought: The ice broke.

And then she entered the darkness.

6

Her first thought upon reawakening was that death was not as she had expected it. Then, as her faculties came slowly into focus, she recognized that she was alive. Next she realized the pain; it felt as if every bone and muscle in her body had been straightened to its limit then hit or twisted. Her head throbbed and her thigh burned where she had been struck. She moaned slowly, trying to open her eyes against the pain.

She heard his voice, close but disembodied.

'Don't try to move. Don't struggle. Just try to relax.'

She moaned again.

She blinked her eyes open, thinking that she must not panic, though fear was quickly overcoming the sensation of pain and covering her like a shroud. She gasped in air, hyperventilating. She heard the voice again.

'Try to remain calm. I know that seems difficult. But try. It's important. Think of it this way: If you remain calm, you extend your life. If you panic . . . I know you're about to be hysterical . . . well, that would be hard for both of us. Take a deep breath and stay in control.'

She did as she was told.

She opened her eyes and tried to assess her situation. There was only a small light, in a corner; the room was mostly dark. She could not see the man, but she could hear his breathing. She became aware, slowly, that she couldn't move; she was lying on her back on a bed, her hands roped together and fastened to the headboard, her feet tied to the baseboard. There was a little play in the bonds; she shifted about as much as they would allow, trying to see where she was.

'Ah, curiosity. Good. That shows you're thinking.'

She was suddenly overcome by two swift emotions, one following the other without hesitation. First she felt an abrupt absorbing despair at her vulnerability, and she sobbed once. It was as if she had fallen from some great height and was tumbling downward faster and faster. Then, as quickly as this sensation came, it retreated and she felt a burst of anger. I will live, she thought. I will not die.

Then, as this internal declaration suffused her, it was broken by the man's cold, even voice.

'There are many kinds of pains in the world. I am familiar with most of them. Don't test my skills.'

She could not stifle the sob. She felt tears welling up in her eyes. She started to wonder what was about to happen, but managed to stop herself, thinking: Nothing good. But the words came out of her mouth as if spoken by someone else, some lost child.

'Please. Please let me go. I'll do whatever you want. Just let me go.'

There was a silence. She knew he was not considering her request.

'Please,' she said again. She was struck by how useless the very sound of the word was.

'Tell me what you want from me,' she pleaded. Her mind raced over the possibilities, but she refused to put words to visions. She heard the man breath out slowly. It was an awful sound.

'You are a student,' he said. 'You will have to learn.'

She felt for an instant as if her heart had stopped.

The man hovered for the first time into view, just stepping past the shadows into the periphery of her vision. She craned her neck to see him. He had changed his clothes, replacing the seersucker jacket and khaki slacks with dark jeans and a black sportshirt. It disoriented her, and she had to look twice to make certain it was the same man. His face, too, seemed different; gone was the easygoing loose grin. He suddenly seemed to be all edges and angles. His eyes grabbed hers and she had the sensation of being tugged forward, helpless, by the rigidity of his gaze. She swallowed hard.

'Don't fight things,' he said.

He paused.

'If you fight it only prolongs things. It's smarter to go along with the program.'

'Please,' she said. 'Don't hurt me.' She listened to herself speak. The words simply emerged, unbidden, plaintive, impotent. 'I'll do whatever you want.'

'Of course you will.'

He did not take his eyes from hers. The absolute certainty of his words struck her a blow.

'Whatever I want.'

He hesitated again.

'But that is a learned response. Conditioned. And the lesson has just begun.'

He held up the small rectangular device so that she could see it. She twitched involuntarily, shrinking from the man. He pressed a button on the side of the device and she saw an electrical current jump from one pole to another. 'You're already familiar with this,' he said. She was suddenly acutely aware of the pain in her body. She let out a half-groan, half-sob. 'Do you know that you can buy a stun gun without a license in the states of Georgia, Alabama, Missouri, Montana, and New Mexico and at least a half-dozen others? They are also available through mail order, but that is more easily traced. Now, what reason would anyone have for one of these?'

He answered his own question.

'Except for inflicting pain.'

She felt her lower lip trembling, and the quaver in her voice was new.

'Please, I'll do anything, please.'

He put the device down.

'It would hardly be fair,' he said again, 'after letting you experience it once, to use it again.'

She sobbed, almost thankful.

Then she gasped as he thrust his face down close to hers.

He hissed: 'But imagine. It was on its lowest setting when I hit you with it before. Imagine. Imagine how it would feel if I turned it up. Consider that pain. Did it feel like someone had reached for your soul and torn it from your body? Think of it.'

She had a sudden vision of black agony. It swept over her. She heard the little-girl reply:

'Yes, yes, yes,' she said. 'Please, God.'

'Don't pray,' he said quickly.

'No, no, I won't. Whatever you say. Please.'

'Don't plead.'

'Yes, yes, of course. Yes.'

'Just think.'

'Yes, yes, yes.' She nodded vigorously.

'Good. But remember. It's never far away.'

'I'll remember, I'll remember.'

His voice changed suddenly. He was solicitous.

'Are you thirsty?'

The word made her realize her throat was parched. She nodded. He disappeared from her sight. She heard a water tap running. He returned to her side with a dampened

97

towel. He began to caress her lips with it. She sucked at the moisture.

'Isn't it fascinating how we can get so much relief from such a simple thing: a towel doused with water . . .'

She nodded.

. . . 'But that the same thing which gives us relief can terrify us?'

As he spoke the last word, he suddenly pushed the towel down over her mouth and nose. She choked and gasped, trying to scream out, stifled by the wet towel. Oh, God! she thought. I'm dying! I can't breathe! She realized she was drowning and she had a sudden vision of her brother waving across the ice toward her. Her lungs felt as if they were being ripped from her chest. Her eyes rolled back and she twitched against the bonds, as her mind became a single black sheet of panic.

Then he released her.

She struggled for breath, filling her lungs desperately.

'Now relief,' he said. He used the towel to dampen her forehead. She sobbed again.

'What are you going to do to me?'

'If I told you it would remove the mystery.'

Sobs took over her body and she cried freely.

'Why?'

He ignored her, letting her cry for a moment.

The tears stopped and she looked at him.

'More questions?' he asked.

'Yes. No. I can't . . .'

'It's all right,' he said gently. 'I expected you to be curious.'

He thought for a minute. Time seemed to hesitate with him.

'Have you ever read a story in the newspaper, a crime story, that suggests that maybe this thing or that thing happened to someone, but that it isn't quite clear, and your imagination has to filter through the euphemisms and analogies in order to come to an understanding? Have you?'

'Yes. No. I guess so. Please, whatever you want.'

He looked at her angrily.

'Well, that's what's happened to you. You're caught up in one of those stories. You're a news event . . .' He laughed. 'Only it isn't all written yet. And the headline remains to be invented. Do you understand that? Do you understand what I'm saying?'

She shook her head.

'It means you have a chance to live.'

She sobbed. She did not know whether to be grateful.

Then he slapped her hard across the mouth and the room spun. She fought unconsciousness. She could taste blood on her gums and one tooth seemed to be loose.

'But it also means you might not. Keep that in mind.'

He waited for a moment, watching the effect of the words on her face. She knew she could not hide the terror she felt. Her lip quivered.

'I don't like that,' he said matter-of-factly.

Then he struck her again. His hand moved as if in slow motion toward her face. She was surprised that she felt the pain. She relaxed, wondering how she was able, and then this time she gave in to all the agony and passed out.

When she emerged from the nighttime of unconsciousness she was cautious to bite back the sound of hurt that was her involuntary response to the return of her faculties. She could feel how swollen her lip was and taste dried blood. She was still bound, and the pain in her joints and muscles had returned less sharp but with a throbbing energy that she feared.

She could not hear the man, but she knew he was close.

She breathed in slowly, fighting the pain, and forced herself to assess the surroundings. Without moving her head, she let her eyes scan the ceiling. There was a single overhead lamp with an exposed bulb, but it was out. She could tell that the room was small and she guessed that she was in a small apartment or motel room. Rocking her head slightly from side to side, she could see a few tacky furnishings and a window with its shade drawn. There seemed to be a small corridor just beyond the scope of her vision, and she thought that was probably the entranceway.

She could not see where the meager light in the room came from, but guessed that there was an adjoining bathroom and that he'd left the light on. She could not tell what time it was or how long she'd been unconscious.

She realized with a sudden pang of despair that she could not remember the day or date, and she quickly tried to recall. I was working, she thought, on a Tuesday in the library. It is July. It is the end of July. The last week. There are only three more weeks in the semester.

Or is it four? She bit her lip and felt tears well up in her eyes. Remember! she screamed to herself. She could feel her mind spinning in agony over her inability to recollect the date.

How long have I been here? she cried to herself.

And then, as if he had been listening to her thoughts, the man answered: 'I control time from now on.'

His voice seemed to carry a blackened finality to it and she could not fight off her tears. One sob slipped from her mouth, then another, until finally her entire body shook with despair.

He let her continue. She did not know how long she cried, whether it was minutes or hours. When she stopped, she heard him sigh and he said, 'Good. Now we can continue.'

Her body stiffened reflexively.

Out of the range of her vision she heard him rustling through a bag.

'What are you going to do?' she asked.

Immediately he was at her side.

'No questions!' he whispered savagely.

He slapped her.

'No questions!'

He slapped her again.

'No questions!'

He slapped her a third time.

It had happened so quickly that the pain and surprise seemed to meld together. 'No, no, no, I'm sorry . . .' she said.

He looked at her.

'Any questions?' he asked.

She shook her head quickly.

He laughed briefly.

'I didn't think so,' he said.

Again she felt her heart plummet with despair. She fought against a sudden rush of hysteria.

She heard a small clicking sound and craned to see what it was.

'It's exposure time,' he said.

He held up a pair of surgical steel scissors.

The sensation of the blunt metal was cold against her skin. She shuddered, then listened. Then she moaned, thinking it had to be, Oh, God, I knew it. He was gently but steadily slicing through the denim of her jeans.

He cut first up one leg from ankle to waist, then the other. He carefully folded the pants back, exposing her legs. She shivered. She felt his hand reaching underneath her, pushing up on the small of her back, lifting her buttock off the bed, then releasing her as he removed the jeans. She heard him toss the tattered pants into a corner. She closed her eyes and felt the scissors working with a terrible steady precision on her shirt. She felt her bra being removed and then the sensation of steel on her hips as he cut off her panties.

Again she sobbed.

In her mind she was filled with agony and embarrassment, exposed, trussed, and lost. The inevitability of what was about to happen to her seemed too dull, so obvious, so unavoidable; it was almost without fear for her. She thought, Just do it, please, get it over with.

She waited for him to cover her.

Seconds rolled into minutes and she became aware that she was cold. She shivered, her eyes still closed.

She could hear nothing except his breathing close by.

She was aware that the minutes were building.

She had a terrifying thought: My God! Suppose he can't? Suppose his frustration . . . then she bit her thoughts off and opened her eyes slowly. He was simply sitting next to her. When he saw that her eyes were open, he let his track down her body.

'You realize, of course, that I could do what I want?'

She nodded.

'Spread your legs.'

She pushed her legs apart as far as the bonds would allow.

She heard the whirring sound of a camera motordrive, and behind her squeezed eyes the world suddenly went red as a flash exploded. There was another explosion, then a third. She opened her eyes slowly.

'All right,' he said. He was returning his camera to a bag.

She tried to pull her legs back close, nervously.

'Are you going to . . .' she started, but her words were lost in the sound of another slap across the face.

'I thought we had learned that already,' he said.

He hit her again.

She could not help the tears.

'I'm sorry, sorry, sorry,' she said. 'Please don't hit me again.'

He simply looked at her.

'All right. You may ask your question.'

She sobbed.

'Ask!'

'Are you, are you, are you going to rape me?'

He was silent.

'Do I have to?' he replied.

He put his hand on her crotch. She felt her skin shrink beneath his fingers.

Then he slapped her again. She gasped.

'I asked you a question. Don't keep me waiting.'

'Oh, God, no, yes, I don't know, whatever you want, please.'

'Good,' he said.

He stood up and moved to the foot of the bed. She lifted her head off the pillow to watch him. He held up something small and it reflected the little light.

'Do you see what this is?'

She groaned. Her mind darkened.

'I have always,' he said, 'been fascinated by the simple razor blade. It could cut your throat with such subtlety that your first awareness of its work would be the lifeblood gurgling in your gullet.'

Her eyes opened wide in fear.

His glance met hers. Then he slowly, carefully lowered the blade and ran it along the tough skin of her big toe.

'Please,' she started, but stopped when his eyes flashed at her. He moved to her side and touched the edge of the blade to her hip. She could not feel anything, but saw a small line of blood an inch or two long appear on her skin.

'Think of me as a razor blade,' he said.

He moved up her body and slid the blade along her forearm, just on the edge of her peripheral vision. She could just make out the sight of another streak of blood. She felt herself spinning dizzily, trying to keep alert, in control, to scream, to do anything. Suddenly he was next to her face, and she could see the blade in his fingers. He slammed one hand down over her nose and mouth as he hissed:

'Shall I rearrange your face?'

And she spun into oblivion.

Anne Hampton woke gently, thinking to herself that she would make herself a slow breakfast, and a large one, indulging in eggs and toast and bacon, coffee, perhaps a Danish roll, and a leisurely reading of the morning newspaper. She thought that food and hard news would serve well to rid her of the nightmare that had plagued her, a dream vision of razors and madness. In half-sleep, she tried to roll from the bed, only to feel again the limit of the restraints that bound her. For a moment she felt confused, as if she could shake the sleep from her eyes and be done with this vaporous intrusion of nightmare on the solidity of day-to-day life. Then the tension in her wrists and ankles became real, and she realized that the thoughts of morning were the dream and she sobbed once in admission and defeat.

And then she thought of her face.

Her hand involuntarily shot toward her eyes, only to be stopped by the bonds. She tried to bend toward her hands: I need to feel! she screamed to herself. What has he done?

She felt an unruly, uncontrolled terror. Am I still me? her mind roared. She craned to look at the razor's cut on her forearm. To her immense fear, she couldn't feel a thing, though she could see where the blood had clotted into a thin brown scab. No pain, no sensation whatsoever. My face! What has he done to my face? She tried to segment her visage into parts: She twitched her nose, and it seemed to respond normally. She arched her eyebrows slowly, trying to feel the telltale hesitation in the flesh that might mean parted skin. She pushed her jaw forward, stretching the skin over her chin and lower lip. She was unsure, her lip was still swollen. She ordered her mouth into a smile, then a wide grin, feeling the flesh on her cheeks tighten and contract. She tried to wrinkle her forehead at the same time. Then she held this grotesque position, searching as if from behind, in the dark, like the blind man in a familiar room, aware suddenly that someone has shifted all the furniture from the positions he has so carefully and painstakingly memorized.

She was unable to be certain, and that frightened her as much as anything. She closed her eyes, praying silently that just this once she could open them and find herself back in her own room, surrounded by her own things. She squeezed her eyes tight and tried to remember her bedroom. She thought of the pictures that lined her bureau top: her parents, her grandparents, her drowned brother, the family's old sheep dog. She had a small box, an antique wooden hand-carved jewelry box, in the center between the photographs, where she kept earrings and rings and necklaces that were all worth considerably less than the box itself. She tried to picture the Christmas morning when she had unwrapped it and the hug and kiss she had bestowed on her parents in return. She tried to remember the smooth, satisfying texture of the polished wood. The scroll-like carving on the lid was especially fine and subtle, and she struggled to form the memory of the sensation in her fingertips when she ran her hand across the top.

But it seemed distant, as if something recollected from a wayward dream, and for the first time she wondered if anything that had existed so few hours earlier had ever been real.

She shivered, but not from the cold.

Where is he? she wondered.

She could not hear his breathing, but that told her nothing; she knew he was close by. She lifted her head to take in her surroundings in the same wan light that insinuated itself into the room. She did not see the man, but what she did see pitched her mind wildly and crashed into her heart with terror.

She slammed her head back down on the pillow and let sobs thunder through her body. It was then, for the first time, that she knew real violation.

He had dressed her.

She was wearing underpants, pants, a new bra and a tee-shirt.

She thought: I am a child.

And she cried out of control.

It was not for several minutes that she realized that the man was sitting in a chair just behind her head. As her tears slowed, he touched her lips again with a dampened washcloth. Then he carefully, gently started to wash her face for her. He kept this up as she gained a grip on her fears; she concentrated on the sensation of the cloth against her skin, trying to be aware of any hesitation or pain that might signal his handiwork with the razor blade. There was none, and she allowed herself an inward sigh. She felt her muscles relax, and fought to maintain a rigidity, thinking that she must be prepared for anything. She became aware then that the discipline of her mind over her body had surrendered, that she no longer could order her limbs to perform, that somehow in the past hours, in the fear and tension, she had given up a part of her self-control.

He started to speak then, softly, smoothly. She hated the sound of his voice but was unable to oppose its effect.

'Right,' he said. 'Relax. Breath in and out slowly.'

He was quiet.

'Close your eyes and find your strength.'

She thought: He does not mean that. He means for me to lose it.

'Listen to your own heartbeat,' he said. 'You are still alive. You've made it this far. You've made progress.'

She thought of a hundred questions and bit each back.

'Just be quiet,' he said.

She felt her breathing had stilled and that her heart had slowed. She hid behind her closed eyes, aware that he had stepped away from her side. She could hear him shuffling about a few feet away, then, just as quickly, he returned to her side.

'That's right. Keep your eyes closed,' he said. His voice had a gentle lilt to it.

He stroked her forehead gently.

'Do you think I would hurt you?' he asked softly.

'No,' she replied slowly. Her eyes remained shut.

'But you're wrong,' he said, in his mild voice.

Light seemed to explode behind her closed eyes as he struck her. The sound of his hand on her cheek was sharp and awful, and she gasped back in mixed surprise and pain. Her eyes flashed open and she saw his hand drawn back for another blow, the only steady thing amidst a wildly spinning room.

She squeezed her eyes shut and tried to shrink into the pillow. 'No, no, no, no, not again, please,' she said.

And there was a silence.

In the darkness behind her closed eyes, Anne Hampton's mind spun wildly. For the first time she could think of nothing but pain, hating it, fearing it, longing to be free of it.

After a moment he spoke.

'I owe you another blow,' he said. 'Consider that.'

And she heard him step away from the side of the bed, somewhere into what she was beginning to understand as the vast darkness of the little room. She remained behind her closed eyes, feeling abandoned completely, save for constant hurt.

She was no longer completely cognizant whether she was asleep or awake. The distinctions between fantasy and reality, between dream and alertness, had evaporated. She wondered momentarily whether the same barrier between life and death was becoming equally blurred.

The thought frightened her and she tried to encourage herself, thinking: But I am still alive. If he means to kill me, he would have already. He would have done it right at the start. He wouldn't keep me alive, keep up the pain, just to kill me in the end. No, he needs me. That need spells life.

And then, just as swiftly, the darkness of her mood returned, and she imagined that perhaps she was wrong. Perhaps he needed her only for what she had provided, a trussed victim. Perhaps he was simply building toward a climax, and once reached, she would be, what? Dispensable? She tried to sweep the thought into a pile and deposit it in some closed container of the mind, but once envisioned, it grew until it came to dominate her imagination. She saw scenes as if from the evening news on television: a gaggle of cameramen, a squad of detectives, a milling mass of curiosity seekers all gathered around her naked form. In this vision she was trying to scream out to the crowd that she was alive, that she breathed and cried and thought, but she was ignored. To the mass of people, she was dead, despite her loud insistence to the contrary, and in this waking nightmare she saw herself loaded, frozen with fear, onto a gurney to be taken to a morgue. It was as if her screams of life were silent, soundless, disappearing unheard into the sky.

The man moved into the reverie and she saw that he was holding a revolver.

'I have other weapons,' he said in his even tone.

For a moment she had difficulty determining whether it was the vision or reality. Then, slowly, she became aware of the dim light, the beige walls, the straps that held her, and she returned from the *demi-monde* into the motel room.

'Pick up your hips,' he said.

She did as she was told.

He put the gun down and as she held herself up, he pulled down the pants and panties that he had put on her, exposing her.

'A gun is an extremely cold thing,' he said.

He placed the gun on her flat stomach. She could feel the weight and the chill of the metal. He let it remain there for a moment.

He picked up the gun. She watched him look at her, then at the weapon.

'If you wanted to destroy your identity, wouldn't you start by shooting yourself in the crotch?' he said.

He pointed the weapon between her legs.

'Oh, God, no!' she cried.

She heard the hammer click as he drew it back. She watched as he sighted down the barrel. She twisted on the bed wildly, fighting against the bonds as the man slowly took aim. She started to make small animal-like whimpers of protest, staring up at the black round hole of the revolver. It seemed to be gigantic, about to swallow her whole. She pulled hard one last time against the bond holding her, then slumped back in defeated acquiescence on the bed. She did not close her eyes; they remained fixed on the barrel of the gun. For a moment she thought she could envision the bullet coming out.

The man looked down at her, hesitated one moment, then pulled the trigger.

The hammer came down with a click.

'Empty,' said the man. He pulled the trigger again. The gun clicked on another empty cylinder.

The breath fled suddenly from her body and she felt as if she had been pounded on the back. She gasped for air.

He watched her intently. Then he pulled from his pocket a handful of live cartridges and slowly began feeding them into the pistol chamber.

She felt a wave of nausea overcome her.

'Please,' she said, 'I'm going to be sick . . .'

He moved swiftly to her head. The gun was tossed aside and she felt his hand beneath her neck, supporting her. He was holding a small plastic waste container. She gagged, but nothing came up. He put her head back slowly and quickly began to stroke her lips with the moist washcloth. She licked at the dampness and sobbed again.

'Pick up your hips.'

Again she did as she was told.

He swiftly hiked the pants and underpants back up, fastening them deftly. He picked up the gun and showed it to her. 'I am an expert at this as well,' he said. 'But you knew that, didn't you?'

She nodded.

'In fact,' he continued, 'in modes and styles of death I am extremely well versed. Experienced. But again, I didn't have to tell you that for you to know it, did I?'

She shook her head.

'You are learning.'

He looked down at her, pausing before continuing.

'You've read your Dostoyevsky, haven't you?'

She nodded. 'Some . . .'

'*Crime and Punishment*? *The Brothers*? *Notes*?'

'Yes. And *The Idiot* as well.'

'When?'

'Last year, in junior-year seminar.'

'Good. Well, you remember what happened to the celebrated author before he was shipped off to the work camp in Siberia?'

She shook her head.

'He and the other condemned men were lined up against a wall before the Tsar's firing squad. Ready, yelled the captain, as the men stood trembling. Aim, he continued, as the men swiftly said their last prayers and stared out helplessly at their executioners. The captain's sword was raised, but before he could slice it down and yell the command to fire, a horseman thundered up, wildly waving a paper. It was the Tsar's pardon. Men fell to their knees in gratitude. Some babbled in instantaneous madness, their minds lost in that quick moment where they saw death. Several died anyway, their hearts too weak. And they were all shipped off to the camps. How did you survive in the camps?'

It took her a second to realize she'd been asked a question. Her mind fled back to the small room where she and nine other students had gathered to talk over the Russian's novels. In her memory she could see the sunshine reflecting off the flat green of the blackboard.

'By obedience,' she replied.

'Good. Do you think the same is true here?'

She nodded.

He hesitated, looking carefully at her.

'Tell me, of all that has happened to you, what is the worst? What frightens you the most? What is giving you the greatest pain?'

He sat on the edge of the bed, waiting for her answer.

She was suffused with a wave of emotions and memories, thrown into despair by the question. She thought of the pistol he'd pointed at her crotch and fought against the bitter taste of bile in her mouth; of the electric savagery of the stun-gun; of the razor poised above her face; the drowning sensation that overcame her when he'd forced the towel down over her mouth and nose; or the arbitrary and capricious beatings he'd administered. Everything hurt, she screamed to herself. Everything terrifies me. And then she asked herself: Why does he want to know? Out of kindness – what kindness is that? She could not force herself to think carefully and rationally; the idea that she somehow held some power, some ability to affect the situation, dismayed her. And then she was swept with a new terror: Perhaps he wants to know because he will eliminate the others, leaving only the worst. Oh, God, she thought, how can I tell?

'Come on,' he said with a small note of impatience. 'What's the worst?'

She hesitated. Please, she prayed to herself.

'Well?'

'The razor.' She started to cry. Tears flowed unchecked down her cheeks.

'The razor?' he replied. He stood up as she continued sobbing. He went out of her sight momentarily, then returned, holding the razor blade in his hand. 'This razor?' he asked.

'Yes, yes, yes, please, God, please.'

He held it closer to her face.

'This is what gets to you the most?'

'Please, please, please . . .'

He put the razor inches above her nose.

'Can't handle it, huh?'

She simply sobbed, her mind wasted with fear.

'Okay,' he said simply.

She looked at him through the tears.

'Okay. I won't use the razor anymore.' He paused. 'Except to shave myself.' He laughed. He looked at her and said, 'You can smile. That was a joke.'

She cried on. He said nothing as she sobbed minute after minute. Finally, when she started to regain some control over herself, he looked at her carefully and said, 'Would you like to go to the bathroom?'

She was stunned again at the simplicity of the offer.

She nodded.

'All right,' he said. He swiftly loosened her bonds. Before untying her wrists, however, he looked at her closely. 'Do I need to explain the rules or do you think you already understand them?'

She was confused again. She did not know what he was talking about.

'No,' he said. 'I think you know how to behave. The bathroom is right there, around the corner. There is, of course, a small window, which will present you with a choice. To some, an open window might signify freedom. But let me assure you the opposite is true. There is only one way you will find freedom from me, and that is when I say you may have it. You should understand that by now. Still, the window is there. So the choice is yours.'

He untied her wrists. She swung her legs to the side of

the bed and tried to stand, but the blood rushed from her head and she was suddenly overcome with dizziness. She gripped hard on the bedstand, steadying herself.

'Take your time. Don't fall.'

He had remained seated, not moving.

She stood slowly and felt the muscles throughout her body contract in pain. She took a small step, followed by another.

'Baby steps,' he said. 'Good.'

She steadied herself against the wall with one hand, then the other. Using the wall as her guide, she stepped into the small corridor, then maneuvered into the bathroom. The light hurt her eyes and she shaded them. Her first thought was the mirror, and she forced her eyes open, the pain of it merely joining all the others that coursed through her body. She thrust her face up to the mirror and searched for wreckage. The lip is swollen, she thought, but that I expected. There was a bruise on her forehead which she could not recall receiving. Her jaw, too, was red and blemished from where he had hit her. But otherwise she was intact. She let out a sob of gratitude. Her hands shook as she ran water into the sink and splashed it on her face, washing some of the hurt away. She was suddenly aware of a huge thirst and she began to paw water into her mouth until she started to feel ill. She felt a wave of nausea, and she bent over the toilet and was violently sick. When she had finished, she reached back up and steadied herself on the sink. Again, she cleaned herself.

Then she looked up and saw the window.

It was open, as he had said it would be.

She allowed herself one brief fantasy of flight, then realized that he would be waiting on the other side. She knew this with absolute certainty. Still, she went to the window and placed her hand on it, as if hoping some of the slight cool in the summer night air would comfort her. She looked out at the blackness. He's there, she thought. She saw his shape moving, just on the periphery of her vision. She saw tree branches bend in the wind, but knew he was there, waiting. He would kill me, she thought, though the word kill did not form in her mind as much as a blackness of pain and hurt.

She suddenly thought: I'm taking too long! He'll be angry! She moved back swiftly to the sink, and, as quickly as she could, splashed another handful of water onto her face, then another into her mouth. Hurry! Just do what he wants!

She grabbed the wall again and staggered out into the motel room.

'I'm waiting,' she heard him say.

She spun through the room to the bed. Without being bidden she slid back on to it, stretching her hands up to where he could bind them easily. She did the same with her legs, feeling the ropes tighten.

'Better now?' he asked.

She nodded.

'Do you want to sleep or would you like me to answer questions?'

She felt suddenly suffused with exhaustion, as if the trip to the bathroom had been some impossibly difficult peak to climb.

'Sleep, then,' she heard him say.

She felt her eyes roll back.

He was sitting at the foot of the bed when she awoke. 'How long was I . . .' she started to ask, but he interrupted her.

'Five minutes. Five hours. Five days. It makes no difference.'

She nodded, thinking that he was right.

'Can I ask questions now?'

'Yes. This would be a good time.'

'Are you going to kill me?' she asked. As soon as the ords were out of her mouth, she regretted them.

'Not unless you make me,' he replied. 'You see, that hasn't changed. You still control your fate.'

She did not believe that.

'Why are you doing these things to me? I don't understand.'

'I have a job for you and I need to be certain that you will do it. I need to be confident in you. Comfortable, too.'

'I'll do whatever you want. Just ask . . .'

'No,' he said. 'Thank you for your offer, but I need to know beyond your verbal assurance. You have to know the length of my reach. You need to know just how close you are to death.'

He stood up and untied her hands from the bedstand, retying them together in front of her.

'I have to go out now. I will be back shortly. I don't have to remind you what is required of you.'

He stepped away and started toward the door.

'Please,' she said. 'Don't leave me alone.' She was surprised at the sound of her voice, and more surprised at the words that had blurted out.

'I'll be back shortly,' he said. 'You'll be fine.'

She cried again as he went through the door. She saw a brief moment of darkness outdoors and she thought: It must still be night.

Alone in the room, she looked about her. Everything was as it had been earlier, but, with the man absent, it suddenly seemed more frightening to her. She shivered. She thought: This is crazy. He's the one doing these things to you. Then she grew more afraid, thinking, He didn't lock the door. Anyone could break in here and find me. She was suddenly scared that someone else would come in and rape her and it would be for nothing; it would anger the man, he would think of her as damaged goods and dispense with her like so much trash. She kept arguing inwardly, warring between two selves, one screaming at her for the wrongheadedness of her thoughts. He's the one! Get the gun! Kill him! Now's your chance!

But she remained rooted where she was.

Untie yourself! she heard herself say. Run!

Run where?

Where am I? Where can I go?

He'll kill me, she thought. He hasn't yet, but he will if I try to run. He's right outside the door, waiting. I won't make it ten feet.

No, run! Don't run!

She cried again to herself and tried to think of school, her family, her friends, her life. But they seemed terrifically distant, ephemeral. The only thing that is real, she thought, is this room.

She tried to comfort herself and found herself singing softly a memory from childhood: 'Lavender's blue, dilly, dilly, lavender's green; When I am king, dilly, dilly, you shall be queen . . .' She remembered how she would sing the song to her younger brother and he would fall asleep. She felt tears welling up inside her. But he's dead, she thought. Oh, God, he died.

She put her head down on the pillow and waited for the man to return. She tried to make her mind a blank, but thoughts and fears kept intruding. She realized that she could no longer gauge time as it flowed around her, as if the man had somehow eliminated her ability to measure the moments that passed. Had he been gone an hour? Or five minutes? The silence around her was pervasive, the darkness, angry and threatening. She forced herself to listen for the noise of his returning, but she could pick no recognizable sound out of the blackness of the room. She raised her hands and covered her eyes, squeezing her eyelids tightly shut, thinking that she could at least retreat into her own darkness and perhaps find something solid there to hold on to. She tried again to think of something small, routine, and common, some item she owned that spoke of her existence, some memory that would remind her of her past and give her something concrete on which to struggle for her future. She thought of her parents back home in Colorado, but they seemed suddenly ghostlike. She forced herself to concentrate on her mother's face; in her mind's eye she built the features as one would paint a portrait. She fixed in her head the eyes, the mouth, the smile that should have been so familiar. Then she wondered whether the memory was all a dream, and she slowly opened her eyes.

She started suddenly, gasping.

The man was hovering over her.

'I didn't hear you come in,' she said.

She saw his face set. He simply stared hard at her for a moment. 'This is reality now,' he said. Then he struck her with his open hand, hard. 'Do you believe?'

'Yes, please,' she replied.

He hit her again. She felt her body cloud with pain.

'Do you want to live?'

He hit her. She nodded furiously.

'I don't believe you,' he said.

He hit her a third time.

'Yes, yes,' she pleaded.

A fourth blow slapped her face.

Then a fifth, sixth, and seventh, in rapid succession, until the man was raining blows, using both hands, as if stoking the fire of her hysteria. She tried sobbing out 'please' in the seconds between the blows, but finally, as his fists flew out of the darkness at her, she quit, raising her bound hands in supplication, letting her tears speak for her. He stopped only when he finally grew short of breath from exertion.

He sat on the side of the bed, resting as she cried quietly to herself. He spoke after a few seconds, his voice seeming distant, coming from someplace far on the other side of her pain and tears.

'You frustrate me,' he said.

She felt his hands on her pants and suddenly he pulled them down, as he had before, exposing her.

'Are you listening to me?' he asked.

'Yes, yes,' she said, opening her eyes and looking up at him. She saw he had the revolver in his hand.

'You're too much of a problem,' he said, in his solid, matter-of-fact tone. 'I had hopes for you. But I see you won't learn. So I'm just going to fuck you and kill you, which is what I should have done in the first place.'

The words crashed through her agony and she rushed from her isolation to the moment. 'Please, no, no, no, no, no, I'll do anything, give me a chance, just tell me what you want, what you need, I'll do anything, please, please, whatever you want, anything, please, no, no, no, please,

please, give me a chance again, I won't be bad, I'll do what it is, anything, you just say it, please, I didn't realize, please anything, anything, anything . . .'

He stood by the bed, sighting down the pistol at her.

'Oh, God, please, please,' she sobbed. She wanted to think of something different, to spend her last moment somewhere else, but all she could see was the terrifying barrel of the gun. She moaned as the seconds passed.

'Anything?' he finally asked.

'Oh, yes, yes, yes, please, anything . . .'

'All right,' he said. 'We'll see.'

He stepped out of her sight for a moment, then returned. He was holding the electric stun-gun. He put it into her hand. 'Hurt yourself,' he said. He pointed to her crotch. 'Right there.'

It seemed to her then, suddenly, that all the pains she had endured to that point were insignificant. Her mind flooded with terror. She felt it choking her, as if, finally, all the things he'd done to her had fallen on her at once. But in the midst of this jumble of agony, she had one clear thought: Don't hesitate, she said to herself.

And she plunged the gun down against herself, trying in the same flashing instant to harden herself against the pain she knew was letting loose within her.

But there was none.

She looked up in confusion.

'Disconnected,' he said.

He took the gun from her hand.

'A reprieve,' he said. He laughed. 'From the Tsar.'

She started to cry for what seemed to her to be the millionth time in the past few minutes.

'There's hope for you.'

He waited a second.

'I mean that literally.'

He stepped back into the shadows and let her cry on unchecked.

Anne Hampton's first thought upon completing her tears was that something had changed. She was unsure precisely what it was, but she felt like some climber who had slipped on the glacier ice and spun wildly down into a crevasse until abruptly checked by a safety rope. She had the distinct sensation that she was spinning like a spent yo-yo on the end of a tether, aware that she was still in peril but safe for the moment. For the first time she allowed herself the thought that through compliance she might have a chance to live. She tried to picture herself, but could not. She remembered that she had had dreams and aspirations once, but she could no longer recall what they were. She allowed herself the recognition that she might be able to recollect them someday and in the same thought resolved to do whatever was required to remain alive. She looked up and saw the man staring at her face. He nodded as if signaling her that she was correct.

'We won't need these for a while, will we?' he said.

He undid the lines that had trapped her to the bed.

'Take off your clothes,' he said.

She complied. She felt nothing as he searched up and down her body.

'Why don't you take a shower. You'll feel better,' he said.

She nodded and started hesitantly toward the bathroom. When she reached the door, she turned back to look at the man, but he was sitting, absorbed, reading a road map in the dim light.

Hot water cascaded over her, and she thought of nothing save the sensation of soapsuds and warmth. She had not realized how cold she'd been. For the first time her mind seemed refreshed, empty, and at ease. She glanced at the open window, but only to see wan gray dawn light slowly slicing away the darkness.

She felt an odd sadness as she shut off the water, as if she had washed away something old and familiar. She dried quickly, wrapping one towel about her head in a turban, another around her midsection. She tried to hurry, but grew dizzy and had to grab the doorframe to steady herself. She saw the man look up. 'Be careful,' he said. 'Don't slip. It'll be some time before you get all your strength back.'

She sat down on the bed.

'It's almost morning,' she said. 'How long have I been here?'

'Forever,' the man said. He stood and approached her. 'Take this,' he said. He held out a pill and a cup of water.

She started to ask what it was, then stopped herself. She swallowed the pill swiftly. He knew her thoughts.

'Just painkiller. Codeine, actually. It'll help you sleep.'

'Thank you,' she replied. She glanced over at the map. 'When are we leaving?'

He smiled. 'This evening. It is important that I get some rest as well.'

'Of course,' she said. She lay down on the bed.

He rummaged for a moment in the duffle bag that contained his weapons. He pulled out a pair of handcuffs. 'These will be more comfortable than the ropes,' he said. 'Sit up.' She complied. He cuffed one of her wrists, then fastened the other cuff to his own. 'Lie down,' he said. She rested her head back. He put himself next to her.

'Sweet dreams,' he said.

Like spent lovers, they both reached out for sleep.

Anne Hampton awakened to the sound of the shower running. She realized quickly that she was handcuffed to the bedstand again. She curled up, as best she could, into the fetal position and waited. The towel she had wrapped around her midsection was gone and she was naked. For a moment she wondered whether the man would rape her when he came out, but the thought swiftly faded from her mind, replaced with a dull acquiescence.

She heard the shower stop and after a few moments the man emerged, drying himself. He was naked.

'I'm sorry,' he said. 'I had to take your towel. This is a cheap place; they're stingy with the linen.'

She waited.

'No' he said, after pausing. 'Time to get a move on.'

She nodded.

'Good,' he said.

She watched him pull on underwear, jeans, and a sweatshirt. She idly noted that he seemed extremely fit. He combed his hair swiftly, then sat on the edge of the bed and slipped on sweatsocks and running shoes. She waited for a command, as the man collected his things. She saw him thrust the stun-gun and the revolver into a small duffle bag. He pulled a small suitcase out from beneath the bed and she caught a glimpse of the seersucker jacket folded and put away.

'Back in a minute,' he said. She watched him walk out the door. It was night. He returned in a moment. He carried a medium-sized red duffle bag that had several zippered compartments. 'I'm sorry,' he said briskly, 'but I had to guess at colors and sizes. But I'm usually pretty good at this sort of thing.' He uncuffed her completely and stood back, eyeing her.

The duffle was filled with clothes. There were khakis, jeans, a pair of shorts, a windbreaker, a sweater, and a sweatshirt. There were also two silk blouses, one a bright floral design, and a matching skirt. There was also a silk dress with a designer label. In one compartment there was a tangle of undergarments, in another, stockings and socks.

'Wear jeans,' the man said. 'Or the khakis if you prefer.' He turned and handed her two shoe boxes. She did not see where he had been keeping them. There was a pair of dress sandals and a pair of running shoes. 'Pack the dressy ones,' he said.

He watched as she dressed.

'You're pretty,' he said when she stood before him.

'Thank you,' she replied. It seemed to her that it was someone else's voice that was speaking. She wondered for an odd moment who could have joined them, until realizing that it was herself.

He handed her a paper bag with the name of a pharmacy on it. She opened it and saw toothbrush, toothpaste, some makeup, a pair of sunglasses and a box of Tampax. She picked up the blue box and stared at it oddly. A disquieting fear moved through her slowly, triggered somehow by the box.

'I'm not having my . . .' She stopped.

'But you might, before we're finished,' he said.

She wanted to cry then but realized she should not. Instead she bit her lip and nodded.

'Straighten yourself up and then we're going,' he said.

She moved gingerly into the bathroom and started using the toiletries. First she brushed her teeth. Then she dabbed a bit of makeup on her face, trying to cover the bruises. He stood in the doorway, watching her.

'They'll fade in a day or so.'

She said nothing.

'Ready?' he asked.

She nodded.

'First use the toilet. We're going to be on the road awhile.'

She wondered where her modesty had disappeared. Again she had the sensation that it was someone else that was sitting on the toilet as the man watched, not herself. Some child, perhaps.

'Carry your own bag,' he said.

She placed the toothbrush and other articles into one of the compartments. Then she hefted the bag up. It had a shoulder strap, which she placed over her arm. 'I can carry something else,' she said.

'Here. But be careful.'

He handed her a battered photographer's bag and held the door open for her.

Anne Hampton stepped out into the night and felt the evening Florida warmth overtake her, crawling into her muscles and bones. She felt dizzy and hesitated. The man placed a hand on her shoulder and pointed her toward a dark-blue Chevrolet Camaro, parked in front of the small motel unit. She looked up for a moment and saw the sky filled with stars; she picked out the Big Dipper and the Little Dipper and then Orion. She felt a sudden warmth, as if she were somehow at the center of all the sky lights, her own brightness melding with theirs. She fastened on one star, one amidst the uncountable mass, suspended in the dark void of space, and thought to herself that she was that star and that it was her: alone, unconnected, hanging in the night.

'Come along,' said the man. He had walked to the side of the car and was holding the door for her.

She stepped to his side.

'It's a beautiful night,' she said.

'It's a beautiful night, Doug,' he corrected her.

She looked at him quizzically.

'Say it.'

'It's a beautiful night, Doug,' she said.

'Good. Call me Doug.'

'All right.'

'It is my name. Douglas Jeffers.'

'All right. All right, Doug. Douglas. Douglas.'

He smiled. 'I like that. Actually, I prefer Douglas to Doug, but you can use whichever you are comfortable with.'

She must have looked odd, because he smiled and added, 'It is my real name. It's important for you to realize that I will not tell you any lies. No falsehoods. Everything will be the truth. Or what passes for it.'

She nodded. She did not for one instant doubt him. She wondered idly why not, but then shook the thought loose from her imagination.

'There is one problem,' Douglas Jeffers said. His voice had a sudden dark edge which frightened her.

'No, no, no, no problems,' she said quickly.

He looked up at the sky. She thought he seemed to be thinking hard.

'I think you need a new name,' he said. 'I don't like your old one. It comes from before and you need something for now and from now on.'

She nodded. She was surprised that she thought this a reasonable idea.

He motioned to the car and she sat in her seat.

'Seat belt,' he said.

She complied.

'You're going to be a biographer,' he said.

'A biographer?'

'That's right. You'll find steno pads and pens in the glove compartment. They're for you. Make sure you always have enough to get down what I say.'

'I don't understand exactly,' she said.

'I'll explain as we go along.'

He looked down at her. Then he smiled.

'From now on you're Boswell,' he said.

'Boswell?'

'Right.' He smiled. 'A little literary joke, if you will.'

He closed her door, walked around the car, and climbed into the driver's seat. She watched him fasten his own belt and turn on the ignition. 'Try your door handle,' he said to her. She put her hand on the latch and pulled. The latch moved freely, but the door didn't open. 'One of the nicer aspects of the design of the Chevrolet Camaro is that the door latches are remarkably easy to disconnect. So, whenever we stop, you wait for me to walk around and let you out. Got it?'

She nodded.

'I learned that in Cleveland, covering the trial of a football player who liked to pick up hookers, then expose himself. When they tried to get out, no go. That was what gave him the real kick.'

Douglas Jeffers looked at her.

'You see, that's the sort of thing you need to get down.'

He nodded toward the glove compartment.

She felt a momentary panic and reached out swiftly.

He stopped her. 'It's okay. Just giving you an example.'

He looked at her.

'Boswell, you see, takes down everything.'

She nodded.

'Good,' he said. 'Boswell.'

Then he put the car into drive and gently accelerated, slowly entering the darkness of the nighttime highway. She turned and looked back up at the stars. She thought suddenly of the childhood rhyme and spoke it to herself: Star light, star bright, first star I see tonight, I wish I may, I wish I might, have the wish I wish tonight.

To live, she thought.

4 A regular session
  of the Lost Boys

7

Obscenities crashed in the air around him, but he paid no attention. Instead, he pictured his brother sitting in the hospital cafeteria, grinning with an insouciance that he thought more properly belonged on an adolescent, but which on his brother's adult face had an oddly disquieting property. He tried to remember the regimen of his thoughts, but fixated only on the moment when he'd spoken in a foolishly heartfelt way, 'You know, I wish we'd been closer, growing up . . .'

And his brother's cruel, cryptic, unfathomable reply:

'Oh, we are. We're closer than you think.'

How close do I think? wondered Martin Jeffers.

To his right, two of the men's voices had steadily gained in volume, swiftly escalating in tone and content, reaching to the edge of rage. Jeffers turned and eyed the men, trying to assess the nature and quality of the dispute, wary, cautious, realizing that confrontation was an integral element of the therapy, but equally that these were violent men, and that he wanted no part of the savagery he believed them capable of inflicting on each other. He had the unusual thought that they were like some angry gaggle of old women, arguing less over some idea or real conflict than for the actual enjoyment of dispute. He decided to intercede.

'I don't think you're saying what you mean.'

This was one of his usual comments. He knew that the men were frustrated by his olique postures; for the most part, they were men of concrete ideas and sentiments. It was his desire to make them think, then feel, in the abstract. Once they could empathize, he thought, then they can be treated.

He remembered a professor in medical school standing before an assembled class, saying, 'Think of the experience of disease. Consider how it controls our senses, feelings, emotions. And then remember, no matter how capable a physician you think yourself, you're only as good as your last correct diagnosis.' To which, a decade later, Martin Jeffers thought he would have added: And treatment, too.

Jeffers eyed the two men who were arguing.

'Fuck you, Jeffers,' said the first, dismissing him with a half-hearted wave of the hand.

'Fuck yourself first,' interceded the second. 'And you'd better enjoy it, because you ain't gonna be fucking anything else for a real long time . . .'

'Look who's talking.'

'That's right, you better look at who's talking, little man.'

'Whoa. I'm shaking. Look at my hands. They're fucking shaking with terror.'

Jeffers watched the two men carefully. He checked each for signs that the argument would prompt them from their seats. He was not terribly concerned about this particular argument: Bryan and Senderling went at it frequently. As long as they were trading insults, it was likely to remain verbal. Under different circumstances, Jeffers guessed, they would probably be considered friends. It was silence that worried him. Sometimes, Jeffers thought, they stop talking. It's not the silence of not knowing what to say, or being bored, or waiting for someone to say something. It was a silence forced by anger. Then it can be the eyes narrowing and fixing on the opposition that signals an attack, or sometimes just a subtle tensing of the muscles. Jeffers thought that he often spent his time looking for white knuckles on the fingers gripping the arm rests of the day-room chairs. There was once one man in the group, Jeffers remembered, who always sat on the front edge of a chair with his legs crossed in an X beneath him. When one morning the man unfolded his legs, Jeffers was already on his feet, moving to intercept the explosion that had arrived seconds later. Jeffers realized, as the months slid past, that he came to know each man in the group not only as a collection of memories and experiences, but with a recognizable physical posture as well. That there were twelve dossiers crammed with entries back in his office was to be expected; one did not qualify easily for the Lost Boys. It took two things: depravity and the misfortune to be caught engaged in it.

'Fuck you!'

'Fuck you right back!'

Obscenities were the currency of the group, scattered about like so many coins of small denomination. He wondered idly how often he heard the word 'fuck' each day. A hundred times? Surely more. A thousand, perhaps. The word no longer had any correlation with the sexual act for him. Instead it was used as punctuation for the group. Some men used 'fucking' as others would use commas. He thought of the famous Lenny Bruce routine where the comedian started out by staring at the audience and querying, 'I wonder how many niggers are here tonight,' before moving on to spics, micks, kikes, wops, limeys, whatever, and ultimately by commonizing the insults so profoundly that they were rendered harmless and meaningless. Jeffers imagined that much the same process went on in the day room. The men used the word 'fuck' with such frequency that it no longer carried any weight. It certainly had little to do with the crimes which they had pleaded guilty to, although each man was a sexual offender.

'Ahhh, the hell with you,' said one of the men. It was Bryan. He turned to Jeffers. 'Hey, doc, can't you straighten this dumb son of a bitch out? He still don't realize why he's here.'

'Look, asshole,' Senderling replied, 'I know why we're here. I also know that we ain't going anyplace real quick. And when we do, it's gonna be over to the state pen to serve some real time.'

Another man chimed in, first forming his mouth into a kiss, then smacking loudly enough to gain the room's attention. Jeffers looked and saw that it was Steele, who sat across the room and particularly liked to bait Bryan and Senderling. 'And you know, sweethearts, how much guys like you are appreciated over there . . .'

The three men glared at each other, then turned to Jeffers. He realized that they expected some sort of response from him. He wished he'd been paying closer attention.

'You all know the arrangement here.'

He was met with sullen silence.

The first lesson of psychiatric residency, he thought. When in doubt, say nothing.

So a benign silence filled the room. Jeffers tried to meet each man's eyes; some glared back at him, others turned away. Some seemed bored, distracted, minds elsewhere, some were poised, anticipating, eager. Jeffers momentarily considered the mystery of the group dynamic: there were twelve members of the Lost Boys, each man unique in the mode of his offense, typical in the nature of it. Jeffers was struck with the thought that the men all suffered from the same thing: once upon a time, in each man's childhood, they had been lost. Abandoned, perhaps, was a better term. The rocky shoals of childhood, he thought. The darkness and cruelty of youth. Most people rise and grow and leave it behind, carrying their scars internally, forever, learning to adjust. The Lost Boys did not.

And the punishment they had wreaked upon the adult world was sorry indeed.

Twelve men. Probably close to a hundred reported crimes shared among them. Easily twice that number hidden, unreported, unsolved, unattributed, ranging from vandalism and petty theft to a rape, or two or a half-dozen, a dozen, a score or more. There were three killers in the Lost Boys as well – men who in the peculiar weighting system of the criminal justice system had managed to take lives that somehow were less valuable and therefore required less punishment, though Jeffers was hard pressed, sometimes, to understand the distinctions between a manslaughter and a first-degree murder, especially when viewed from the corpse's point of view.

The silence in the day room persisted and Jeffers thought again of his brother. It had been so typical of Doug, Jeffers thought. Call one instant, show up the next. Three years between visits, months between even casual telephone conversation, acting as if nothing were out of the ordinary. Drop his apartment key off with the usual impenetrable instructions. Typical.

What was he doing? Jeffers wondered. He returned to the meeting in his mind. But first he thought: What was typical of Doug? and felt a mild uneasiness at his lack of a ready answer.

He pictured his brother sitting across from him, sunlight caught in his shock of sandy hair. Doug, he thought, has this loose, flush, good-looking appearance, easygoing, relaxed, the kind of good looks that stemmed not from any striking physical feature but from a devil-may-care approach to life. For a moment he envied his brother the blue-jeans-and-running-shoes informality that accompanied the job of the professional photographer, resenting, momentarily, the quiet formality of his own profession. I am stiff, he thought. He envied his brother's out-of-doors life, surrounded by things that were actually happening instead of merely being talked about. Sometimes I cannot stand the constancy of small rooms and closed doors, suggestive comments and observations, and quiet, meaningful looks that make up my profession, he thought.

Then he shook his head, inwardly, and said to himself: Of course you can stand it. Not only that, you love it.

For a moment, though, he wondered idly what it was like to see life through a lens.

'Oh, we're closer than you think. Much closer.'

Is it that different? he thought suddenly. Surely. He sees with an immediacy defined by the event, the moment. I hear the story told long after the fact.

He was dismayed by the quick realization that he could not remember his brother's first camera. It seemed that Doug had always had one, from grade school on. He wondered where and how Doug had acquired the first; surely not from their parents.

The only thing they gave out in substance was misery, Martin Jeffers thought.

The two brothers had never disagreed about that.

He suddenly remembered the night they'd been taken in,

and wondered instantly why it had been so long since he had thought of it. He thought of the wild rain that had been driving against the police station windows rattling in the summer storm's wind. Night had surrounded the building, but the hard wooden bench that he'd sat upon, gripping tightly to his brother's hand, had been awash in artificial light. It had been late at night and they had been very young; not filled with Christmas Eve excitement over staying up late, but filled instead with a complete dread, aware somehow that they had been caught in some adult mystery that had taken place when their own little boys' eyes properly should have been closed and their minds captured by sleep; seeing something not meant for them to see at an hour not meant for them to be awake. His stomach tightened at the memory of looking up through the light at his first view of his cousin, face set, rigid and unwelcoming, remembering her first words: 'Your mom's gone, which is as we expected for some time. You're to be with us now. Follow me.' And the sight of that small, bent back, turning and leading them out into the storm. I was four, he thought, and Doug was six.

He tried to shake the memory loose, wondering why it was that they'd never talked about their real mother. He stared out the day-room window and tried to recall the features of her face, but could not. He remembered only that she'd lacked tenderness and seemed forever angry. She'd not been that much different from the cousin who'd become their mother. He saw her easily, wispy brown hair pulled back in a severe bun, contradicting wide lips covered in bright lipstick that never creaked into a smile. In the car, in the rain, the wipers making a dirgelike drumming sound, this new woman-mother had turned to them and said, 'We're your parents now. I'm mom. He's dad. There won't be no talk about any other.'

He remembered his own therapist asking once, 'But what did happen to your real mother?'

And of his reply: 'But I never really learned.'

The therapist had been silent. A classic doubting silence; he'd used it himself a thousand times.

What did happen? he asked himself.

It was simple: She was gone. Dead. Run away. What difference did it make? They both had to work in their parents' drugstore. He had to clean the medicine bottles and keep the stacks of prescription drugs arranged neatly on the shelves, and he'd become a doctor. Doug's job had been to sweep out the darkroom and then mix the chemicals for the film-developing service and finally to do the developing himself, when he got older, so he became a photographer. It was simple.

We turned out fine, he said to himself.

But what did we become?

Nothing is simple.

He knew that. It was the first thing he'd learned in his residency. Things of the mind may seem clear-cut and direct, but they rarely stayed that way. If the formulations of psychiatry made sense – the theories and diagnoses and treatment plans – the realities of behavior always seemed to him strangely inexplicable. He understood why the Lost Boys were sex offenders, in a clear-cut clinical way, but he felt defeated by some greater why that eluded him. He could picture the physical strength it took to seize a victim by the arm and force her, but could not imagine the power of will that it also took.

He shook his head.

Doug understands realities, he thought. I understand theories.

He thought of his own life. I survived, he thought. Hell, we both did. We've done well. Damn well. Then he considered how extraordinary it is that one can acquire all the education and experience of human frailties and suffering and fail to be able to apply any of that knowledge to oneself.

He laughed at himself: You're a liar, he thought.

And not a good one.

He wondered why it was that his brother's visit stirred so many memories, then thought how silly a question that was; of course his brother's visit would prompt introspection.

He felt hot and realized that sunlight was slipping through

the window and hitting his chest. He shifted in his chair, unsatisfactorily, then moved his chair slightly.

'You know what I hate the most,' said one of the Lost Boys. 'It's being treated like we're some kind of freaks in a sideshow, huh.'

Jeffers looked up to see who was talking. His eyes caught a glimpse of Simon, the hospital orderly assigned to keeping order among the Lost Boys. Simon seemed to be dozing in the sunlight, unaffected by the conversation. He was an immense black man whose build was well concealed by the loose-fitting white smock the orderlies wore. Jeffers knew, too, that he possessed a black belt in karate and had fought professionally as a kick-boxer. Simon's presence was the ultimate deterrent to violence.

'Freaks, freaks, freaks, that's what we are.'

It was Meriwether speaking. This was one of the small man's favorite topics. Meriwether was a slight, sallow, middle-aged man who had owned a meager accounting business and who had pleaded guilty to the rape of a neighbor's daughter. It was only after entering the Lost Boys that Jeffers uncovered a compulsive affection for youth in the man. Meriwether was on the doubtful list: Jeffers doubted that the crime he was condemned for was his sole one, and he doubted that the program could do anything for him. Someday, Jeffers thought, he will cruise down some street and pick up some teenage boy who is more than he can handle and will get his throat cut for his pocket change. Jeffers refused to be ashamed by his unscientific guesswork.

'I can't stand the way they look at us,' Meriwether said.

'At you,' said Miller, sitting across the circle. Miller was a bona fide criminal in addition to being a rapist. He had twice killed men in barroom brawls, three times served prison terms for assault, robbery, and extortion. Jeffers particularly liked him for his straightforward approach to the therapy sessions: Miller hated them. He was, however, not on the doubtful list; Jeffers thought it possible that the man could learn not to be a rapist. What would remain, however, was a regular full-time criminal.

'You see, little man, they can sense something about you.

131

Something slimy just beneath the surface. We all can, little man. We all can. Makes you think, don't it?'

Meriwether didn't hesitate: 'Well, maybe they can sense something about me, but all they got to do is take one look at your face and they know, you know what I mean? They *know*.'

Miller growled, then laughed. Jeffers appreciated the fact that Miller was unbaitable, although he wondered what force of restraint the man would have with a drink in him.

The other men sitting in the loose day-room circle laughed or smiled as well. Wright; Weingarten; Bloom, who seemed to prefer boys; Wasserman, who was the youngest at nineteen and had raped a prom queen who refused him a dance; Pope, at forty-two, the oldest, intractable, malevolent, gray-haired, with trucker's muscles and tattoos. Jeffers believed that he had committed far more crimes than the police suspected. He remained silent, mostly, leading the doubtful list. Parker and Knight completed the Lost Boys. They were a matched pair, acned, angry, in their mid-twenties, both college dropouts. One had been a computer programmer and the other a part-time social worker. They sneered at much, but, Jeffers thought, would eventually come to realize that they had a chance at a life.

The laughter faded and Meriwether jumped into the quiet.

'I still don't like it.'

'Like what, little man?'

'We're not crazy. What are we doing here?'

Several voices jumped in quickly:

'We're here to get fixed . . .'

'We're here for the program . . .'

'We're here, you dumb fuck, because we were all sentenced under the state's sex-offenders act. That clear enough for you, slime?'

'Man, maybe you don't know what you're doing here, but I sure do . . .'

The last comment gained laughter. It subsided after a moment and Jeffers watched Meriwether wait until he had clear silence.

'You guys are stupider than I thought . . .' he started. There were hoots and meager catcalls. Again Meriwether waited. Jeffers noted the wry grin that the little man wore, clearly enjoying being the center of the group's attention.

'Think about it for a minute, freaks. Here we are in a loony bin, but are any of us really crazy? If we were really criminals, don't you think they'd just lock us up? Instead they got us here in this carrot-and-stick world. Do the program, they say, learn to love right. Learn to hate what you were. Then we'll straighten you out and head back to the world . . .'

He paused, watching for effect.

'You know what gets to me? Every time I walk through one of the psych wards everyone steps out of the way. For me! It's enough to make you laugh, isn't it, Miller, you tough guy? But they know, don't they? They know.'

He laughed.

'All of us here, inside, huh, way inside where we figure the shrink can't see, figures we're gonna beat this. We just hang on long enough and say the right things . . . well, we're gonna walk. They aren't going to be able to change me!'

He turned to Jeffers.

'Screw your aversion therapies. Screw your peer-group pressures. I'm smarter than all that.'

'Is that what you think?' Jeffers replied.

Meriwether laughed.

'What a wishywashy question. Can't you see it's what all of us think deep inside . . .'

He thought. 'Way inside. Way, way inside. Where you can't touch it.'

Miller growled. 'Speak for yourself, asshole.'

'I do,' said Meriwether.

The two men stared at each other and Jeffers thought again of his brother. He remembered how surprised he had been when he learned that Doug routinely robbed the drugstore's register for pocket money. He had thought that wrong, he realized, not because it was wrong to steal but because the consequences would be so severe if discovered.

133

He recalled his brother's easy laughter and insistence that the money was only partially the reason.

'Don't you understand, Marty? Every time I take something I feel like I'm getting back at him. His precious money. A little here, a little there. It makes me feel like I'm not just his victim.'

Doug had been thirteen. And he had been wrong. We were his victims.

He beat Doug, Jeffers thought. Why not me? He supposed it was his brother's insistent, obvious rebelliousness. Then he shook his head, thinking that was probably only partially true. Certainly Doug had been irrepressible, but there was something else, something further that their father had seen, which had catapulted him into red-faced anger and savagery.

'Little man,' said Miller, 'you piss me off.'

'The truth,' replied Meriwether, 'always hurts.'

'Tell me what you think is the truth,' Miller said. 'You know so much, you squirrelly little numbers runner, you tell me what you know about my life!'

Meriwether laughed.

'Let me think,' he said. He eyed Miller like an appraiser looking over a cracked piece of goods.

'Well,' he started slowly, aware that he had the entire group's attention, 'you probably hated your mother . . .'

Everyone laughed except Miller.

'She loved everyone except you . . .'

Meriwether smiled at his audience and continued.

'And now, unable to punish her . . .'

The room laughed at the truism.

'You punish others.'

Meriwether hesitated. then, smiling to the audience, said, 'Tah-dah! Basic truths illuminated!'

Miller did not smile. Jeffers found himself again trying to picture his own mother's face, but unable. When he spoke the word 'mother' to himself, all he pictured was the druggist's wife, their cousin-mother, who would sit in the afternoons in a corner of the house, fanning herself, drinking tea, regardless of whether it was summer or winter.

'Keep going, hot shit. You're in a world of trouble already, might as well shoot the moon,' Miller said.

Jeffers wondered briefly whether Miller would explode, then doubted it. He was too con-wise. If he feels he needs revenge, he'll take it at his convenience. He'll wait and bide his time; all cons knew that what they had in abundance was time, and the savoring of revenge could be as much enjoyment as the homemade shiv firmly wedged between the ribs itself. Jeffers scribbled a note on the daily session log to watch out for conflict between the two men.

'Well,' said Meriwether, 'how old was that last chick? The one you beat up and robbed in addition to, how shall we put it? Delicately, of course, ah, enjoyed. . . . Could she have been twenty? No, perhaps more. Thirty, then? No, still a mite shy. Well, forty? Lord, no, not close . . . fifty? Sixty? How about seventy-three years old? Bingo!'

Meriwether closed his eyes and sat back in his chair.

'Old enough, I daresay, to be your mother.'

He was quiet before turning to Jeffers.

'You know, doc, you ought to pay me for doing all your work here.'

Jeffers said nothing.

'So,' Meriwether continued, 'tell us, tough guy. How was it?'

Miller's eyes had narrowed. He waited until there was quiet.

'You know, mouth. It was perfect. It always is.'

Miller paused.

'Right, freak?'

Meriwether nodded. 'Right.'

Jeffers stared around the room, halfheartedly hoping that a voice would be raised in opposition, but doubting he would hear one. He had come to realize that there were certain qualities the group could not frustrate, one being the idea of pleasure. He made a note for follow-up in each man's regular individual session. The group, he thought, only serves to reinforce the ideas imparted through the daily therapeutic sessions. Sometimes – he smiled to himself – the magic works. Sometimes it doesn't.

'Miller,' Jeffers said, 'are you telling the group that you considered the beating rape of a seventy-three-year-old woman a satisfactory sexual experience?'

He would not be so blunt with some of the others, he thought.

Miller shook his head.

'No, doc. Not when you put it like that,' he sneered. 'A satisfactory sexual experience, whatever the hell that is. What I was saying is – and freak there knows what I'm saying, don't you, maggot? – is that she was there. I was there. It was just part of the whole scene – nothing special.'

'Don't you think it was something special to her?'

Miller tried to make a joke.

'Well, maybe she'd never had it so good . . .'

There was a smattering of laughter, which faded swiftly.

'Come on, Miller. You savaged an old woman. What kind of person does that?'

Miller glared across the room at Jeffers.

'You're not listening, doc. I keep telling you, she was there. It was no big deal.'

'That's the problem. It was.'

'Well, not to me.'

'So if it wasn't such a big deal, what were you thinking of when you did it?'

'Thinking of?' Miller hesitated. 'Hell, I don't know. I was worried she might be able to make me, you know, so I made sure I crushed her glasses, and I was trying to be careful, didn't want to wake the neighbors . . .'

'Come on, Mr. Miller. You left fingerprints all over the premises and you got caught trying to fence the old woman's jewelry. What were you thinking about?'

'Hell, I don't know.'

He crossed his arms and stared dead ahead.

'Give it another try.'

'Look, doc, all I remember is being angry. You know, just flat-out pissed off. It seemed like nothing had been going any way except wrong. So I was definitely in a bad mood. And all I remember really is being pissed off. So pissed off I wanted to scream. I wanted to hurt somebody, you know?

That's all, just make someone else hurt. I wanted that real bad. I'm sorry the old gal got in the way. But she was there, and that's what I wanted. Got it? That do you okay?'

Jeffers leaned back. He thought to himself: I'm pretty good at this for a newcomer.

'All right,' he said. 'Let's talk about anger. Anyone?'

There was a small silence before Wasserman, who stuttered said, 'S-s-sometimes I think I'm always angry.'

Jeffers leaned back in his chair when he heard one of the men reply, 'Angry at what?' There were only a few minutes left in the session and he knew that the group dynamic would take over; anger was always a fruitful subject. All the Lost Boys were angry. It was something they were intimate with.

He looked about the day room. It was an open, airy place, painted white, with a bank of windows that overlooked the exercise area. The furniture was old and threadbare, but that was to be expected in a state facility. There was a ping-pong table folded up against one wall, rarely used. Once there had been a pool table, but a pool cue in the hands of a psychotic patient one day had put two orderlies in the infirmary, so now there was none. There were magazines that flapped when a breeze found an open window, a television set that seemed possessed only to play soap operas and old movies. There was an out-of-tune upright piano. Periodically someone would step up to it and play a few notes as if hoping through some process of osmosis that it had come into tune. The piano is like the patients, Jeffers thought. We keep pushing at the keys, hoping to find a melody, usually discovering dissonance. Jeffers liked the room; it had a quiet, benign character, and it seemed to him sometimes that the room itself had defused trouble. It would be an incongruous place for a fight.

He could not remember a time he'd ever fought with his brother.

That was unusual: All brothers fight, why would we have been any different? But he was still unable to come up with a single memory of flat-out murderous brother-rage, the kind that suffuses one's entire being one instant then evaporates the next.

He remembered a time when Doug had pinned him to the floor, easily, arms twisted back; but that had been to prevent him from chasing after their mother, who was transporting their report cards to the druggist. He had failed a course for the first time – French – and had been ashamed. He remembered his brother's grip, which he could not break. Doug said nothing, just held him. He had not been certain what he was going to do: seize the report card, destroy it, he did not know. He simply knew that the druggist would be outraged, which he was. Locked for a week in my room each night. But next semester I got a B and the final semester it was an A.

'Hey, Pope!' It was Meriwether speaking. 'Come on, Pope, you're a killer, Pope. Tell us how angry you've got to be to kill someone.'

Jeffers waited, as did all the men in the room. This is a good question, he thought, perhaps not strictly from a therapeutic standpoint, but from curiosity.

Pope snorted. He had narrow black eyes and shoulders that were outsized for his small frame. Jeffers imagined him to be immensely powerful.

'I never killed nobody I was real angry with.'

Meriwether laughed. 'Awwww, come on, Pope. You killed that guy in the bar. You told us about it the other week. A fight, remember?'

'That's not anger. That was just a fight.'

'He died.'

'That happens. A lucky punch.'

'You mean unlucky.'

Pope shrugged. 'I guess from his position.'

'You mean you fought him and he died and you weren't even mad at him?'

'You don't understand so good, do you, wise guy? Sure, the dude and I had a fight. We'd been drinking. One thing came to another and he shouldn'a called me a name. But this ain't anything special. This happens in every bar every night. But I never been so angry at some man that I sat around sober and figured out a way to do him. You'd think you could guess at that.'

138

This made sense to the group and they were quiet.

'I was that angry once,' said Weingarten. He's been silent most of the session, Jeffers noted. He was a greasy-haired exhibitionist who'd gotten carried away with his display in a shopping mall and actually grabbed a young woman. She'd fought loose, easily picked him out of a lineup the next day, and he'd landed in the Lost Boys. Jeffers doubted the program would have much success with him; he had just begun to escalate his deviant behaviour. He probably remains too fascinated with his new vision to cut it out so early. The Lost Boys do not suffer from ordinary diseases. He had a sudden memory of the emphasis in medical school on catching disease early, before it progressed. Not so here, he thought. Here you had to catch the disease after it had formed and manifested itself fully. Then you tried to eradicate it. It was generally a losing proposition, he realized ruefully, despite the inflated rates of success that were created to ensure continued funding of the program.

'I mean I wanted to kill him and everything.'

'What did you do?' Jeffers asked.

'In high school there was this one guy who was always all over my case. You know the type of guy that walks up to you in front of everyone else and punches you real hard on the arm just to make you look bad. 'Cause he knows you can't hit him back? You know what I mean? A real jock. A real head case . . .'

'Look who's talking,' said Meriwether.

Weingarten ignored him and continued.

'I was gonna just kill him, at first. My dad had a hunting rifle, he liked to go deer hunting, which I thought was real gross, but he never bothered to take me anyway. It had a real nice scope on it and I had the guy, one time, right in the crosshatches. Shoulda done it, too. But then I got smart and figured I'd just get him back kinda like he'd been getting me, right? Good and public, too. So I waited, figuring I'd get him back just before the big homecoming game. I'd get him suspended, you see, it was gonna be simple. The coach had a curfew and I knew this creep was always making it with this cheerleader. I just followed them out to the place where all the kids like to park and waited. Wasn't too long before they was going at it. I watched for a bit, then snuck up and bam! Ice pick nice and easy in each tire. I knew they'd never get home in time. Bingo! He'd get suspended. The girl was the coach's daughter, you see. Foolproof.'

'So what happened?'

'They didn't get in till four in the morning.'

'Did the coach suspend the creep?'

Weingarten hesitated.

'He was the fucking fullback. All-county. Had a scholarship to Notre-fucking-Dame. It was the fucking homecoming game. What do you think?'

The Lost Boys all laughed and Jeffers joined in.

Weingarten laughed as well. 'It was a good idea,' he said. 'At least the creep tore up his knee in the second quarter and kissed his scholarship goodbye.'

'Whatever happened to him?' one of the other men asked.

Weingarten smiled. 'Man, he was such a creep. He had to become a cop.'

Laughter from the Lost Boys filled the day room.

His brother, Jeffers thought, could have been a terrific athlete. When he did play, it always seemed as if the ball would follow him. He was quick and co-ordinated and he had that odd strength, not muscle-bound at all, but stronger than the others. Doug always had that extra ability too, to be able to run all day if need be. He had unbelievable stamina. It came from anger. The more their parents encouraged athletics, the less Doug would have to do with them. It was another of his mini-rebellions. He remembered sitting in their room one night, lights out, listening to his brother talk about hatred. It had surprised him to know how deeply his brother felt: 'I won't do anything for them,' he had said. 'Nothing. Nothing that makes them feel good at all. Nothing.'

Now, Jeffers thought, he would say that such an attitude reflected a fundamental self-hatred. But his childhood memory was more powerful. All he recalled was the force of his brother's words in the dark room. He could not see his brother's face, but remembered instead the nighttime view through the window in their room, across the yard and out to the street, moonlight filtering through the trees. It was a modest house in a modest suburb that quietly contained all the anger within.

'The only person I was ever pissed off enough to want to kill was, man, my old lady.' Jeffers looked up and saw Steele talking. 'She complained, man, day and night. Morning, noon, afternoon. Hell, sometimes I thought she was complaining in her sleep . . .'

The others laughed. Jeffers saw heads nod.

'You know, it made no difference where we were or what we were doing. She just made me feel, uh, little, you know? Small.'

There was quiet before Steele continued. Jeffers had a brief flash of the man's dossier. He had preyed on his own neighborhood, leaving his job as a plumber on lunch hours and finding housewives alone.

The room was silent.

'I suppose,' Steele said, 'if I could have figured out a way of getting back at her, I wouldn't be here.'

Jeffers made a notation, thinking: But you did.

He glanced down at his watch. The session was almost over. He wondered for a moment why his brother refused to join him for dinner or overnight or any extended visit at all.

'It's a sentimental journey . . .'

What had he meant? He felt a rush of anger himself. Doug was capable of blistering directness one instant and unfathomable obtuseness the next. He felt a sudden empty feeling inside, wondering: How well do I know my brother? Then adding, as if by rote: How well do I know myself? He had a quick picture of the rest of his day: rounds. Several individual therapy sessions. Dinner alone in his apartment. A ball game on television, a chapter in a book, and bed. More of the same in the morning. A routine is a kind of protection, he thought. He wondered what his brother found to protect himself. And from what? That gets an easy answer, he thought. He looked around the room.

We protect ourselves only from ourselves.

'I follow on the heels of evil . . .' He smiled. That was

Doug. A certain dramatic flair. For an instant he felt a complete jealousy. Then he let it pass, thinking: Well, we are who we are, and then felt embarrassed. Not much insight there, he said to himself. He wondered again: How close are we?

To his right, Simon the orderly stirred. He stretched and got to his feet.

He heard the men start to shuffle in their chairs and he thought of a grade-school classroom in the few moments before the recess bell rings.

'All right,' Martin Jeffers said. 'Enough for today.'

He stood up and thought: Closer than you think.

Martin Jeffers watched the men as they rose and wandered out of the day room singly or in pairs. He heard an occasional laugh echoing down the outside corridor. When he was left alone, he gathered his notes and papers together, made a few entries in his daily log, and walked through the day room, feeling the warmth of the sunshine as it hit his back. The room was silent and he thought the session had been a success: no fights, no irreconcilable arguments, though Miller and Meriwether would bear watching. There had been a little progress, he thought. Perhaps Weingarten's story was something that could be followed up on. He resolved to bring up jealousy at the next session and shut the day-room door behind him.

The hospital corridor was empty and he moved swiftly past the entrance to one of the wards. He glanced in the window of the door and saw the same lethargic picture that he'd seen every day. A few people standing around talking, others talking to themselves. Some read, some played chess or checkers. So much of the time in a mental hospital is spent simply getting from one day to the next. The patients become expert at the practice of elongating time: meals were interminable. Activities were stretched. Time was wasted deliberately, passionately. It was not that unreasonable, he thought, for people to whom time had lost all urgency.

When he arrived at his office he discovered a note taped to the door: CALL DR HARRISON'S OFFICE ASAP. Dr Harrison was the hospital's administrator. Jeffers looked at the note, wondering what it was about. He unlocked his door and set his papers down. For a moment he stared about himself at the tired steel book shelf sagging with papers, files, and textbooks. There was a calendar on the wall with pictorial scenes from Vermont. He had a sudden pleasurable memory: That was fun there, he thought. Fishing, camping. He remembered a trout that Doug had caught and thrown back, only to hear their father laugh. 'It'll die,' the druggist said. 'Once you touch them, you wipe some of the fish slime off their bodies and they get cold and die. Can't throw a trout back, no sir.' And then their father had continued laughing, pointing at his brother. Martin Jeffers wondered for a moment whether it was true. He had never checked. He felt an odd embarrassment as he thought how he had gone through life believing, from that moment on, that you couldn't throw a trout back into the water without killing it simultaneously. Doctor Harrison is a fisherman, he thought. Dammit, I'll ask him.

He picked up the telephone and dialed the administrator's extension. The secretary picked up the phone.

'Hello, Martha. Marty Jeffers here. I got your note. What's on the chief's mind?'

'Oh, Doctor Jeffers,' the secretary said. 'I don't know exactly, but there's a detective here. All the way from Florida. Miami, she says, and she wants to talk to you . . .'

The secretary hesitated and Jeffers pictured palm trees and beaches. 'I've never been to Miami,' he said. 'Always wanted to go.'

'Oh, doctor,' the secretary continued. 'She says it's a murder investigation.'

Jeffers wondered for a moment whether the trout knew, after it had been touched, that it was doomed to die; whether it swam off, searching out some lonely eddy behind a cluster of rocks to shiver itself to death, cruelly confused and betrayed by its own environment.

'I'll be right there,' he said.

5 A singular pursuit

8

The words echoed within her: *trace alcohol*.

At first she wondered whether her cheeks had been scarred by her tears in the same way that she felt her heart had been ripped and torn by her unchecked grief. She looked up at herself in the mirror, half-expecting to see permanent red welts on her skin, marking the paths her misery had flowed. There were none. She rubbed her eyes hard and felt a vast exhaustion enter her body, fatigue pushing aside and storming the barriers of resolve and perseverance and taking over inside her. She breathed out slowly, battling lightheadedness and residual nausea.

Detective Mecedes Barren wanted desperately to organize her thoughts, but was defeated by emotion. She gripped the edges of the sink and held tight for an instant, trying to clear her mind of everything, as though by creating a blank slate she could control what she thought and felt. She took a deep breath, and, moving with exaggerated deliberateness, turned on the faucets. She felt flushed and overheated so she ran cold water over her wrists, remembering it was her husband who had told her that this would cool her down quickly – an athlete's trick. Then she splashed water on her face and looked up again into the mirror, staring at her reflection.

I am old, thought Detective Barren.

I am thin, brittle, and tired and I am unhappy and there are creases in my skin, on my forehead, and in the corners next to my eyes that were not there not so long ago. She looked at her hands, counting the veins on the backs. An old woman's hands, she thought.

Detective Barren turned away from the mirror and walked back into the living room of her small apartment. She glanced momentarily at the stacks of reports and file folders stuffed with statements, analyses of evidence, photographs, transcripts, psychological reports, and lists of items seized that formed into the paper substance of a criminal investigation. It was all piled haphazardly on her small desk. She walked to it and began idly to sort and arrange the documents, trying to impress reason on the mass of material. Susan's legacy, she thought, and again she bit back tears.

She wondered how long she had cried.

She went to the window and looked out at the pale-blue morning sky. It was cloudless and oppressively bright. It seemed to her that the air was filled with the reflection of the sun exploding off the expanse of blue sea so close to the city. It was a day without darkness, without even a taste of disorder, and this angered her. She put her hand against the glass of the window and felt the tropical heat. For an instant she wanted to draw back her fist and thrust it through the window. She wanted to hear the glass shatter and fall. She wanted to feel physical pain. She stopped herself when she became aware that her hand had balled itself into a fist, turned away from the window, and surveyed her apartment.

'Well,' she said to herself out loud, 'that's it, then.'

She felt as though something had finished and something different was beginning, but she was not certain precisely what. She rubbed a tear away from her eye and took a deep breath, then another. There was a picture of her niece in a simple silver frame on top of the bookcase, and she walked slowly over to the picture and looked at it. 'Well,' she said again. 'I guess it's time to start over.' She put the picture down and felt a rush of sadness slip through her body, like a cool wind in the last few seconds before a hard rain. 'I'm sorry,' she said to herself. 'I'm so very, very sorry.' But she was unsure to whom she was apologizing.

*

The woman officer behind the reception desk at the Dade County Sheriff's Office was abrupt:

'Do you have an appointment?'

'No. I don't believe I need one . . .' replied Detective Barren.

'I'm sorry, I can't let you up to homicide unless there's someone expecting you. Who is it you want to see?'

Detective Barren sighed loudly, irritatedly, swiftly fishing her own gold shield out of her purse.

'I want to see Detective Perry. Right now. Pick up your phone, officer, and call his office. Right now.'

The woman held out her hand for the badge. Detective Barren handed it over and the woman carefully noted the shield number on a form. She handed the badge back and, without meeting Detective Barren's eyes, dialed the number for homicide. After a moment she spoke:

'Detective Perry, please.'

There was a momentary pause.

'Detective Perry? There's a Detective Barren from City here to see you.'

Another pause.

The woman officer hung up.

'Third floor,' she said.

'I know,' said Detective Barren.

The elevator ride seemed to take much longer than she remembered. She suddenly wished that there were a mirror available; she wanted to check her make up, to make certain that all the outward signs of grief were properly concealed. She straightened herself self-consciously. She had selected her clothing that morning with far more care than usual, knowing that appearances were important when connected to what she was going to say. She had ruled out her dark blue and gray courtroom suits in favor of a simple, light-coloured cotton blazer and khaki skirt. She wanted to seem loose, easy, and relaxed – informal. The jacket was cut stylishly large. Once upon a time, she had thought as she slipped it on, it would have been called baggy. Now it was oversize. But it was an excellent design to hide the shoulder harness which held her 9-millimeter. It was not her usual choice of weapons. Ordinarily she simply stuffed a short-barreled .38-caliber revolver into her handbag and forgot about it for the remainder of the day. But she felt a wild sense of insecurity after she had dressed, had looked up suddenly at a sound outside her door, feeling the small hairs on the back of her neck stand. She had discovered herself strapping on the large automatic pistol without even thinking, and now she could feel its weight and bulk and she welcomed it.

The elevator doors rolled open with a swooshing sound.

'Hey, Merce! Over here!'

She turned and saw Detective Perry waving to her from a corridor. She walked toward him quickly. He was holding out his hand and she shook it. He gave her a little wave as well and started walking toward his desk.

'Come on – you want coffee? So how're you doing?' he asked, but, hardly pausing for an answer, he launched ahead. 'You know, I was just thinking about you the other day. We had a rape-murder, the kid out in South Miami, right along the canal, you probably saw it in the papers, and all I could think of was that boxer you busted. Intuition won't get you a search warrant, isn't that how you put it? Anyway, I had this feeling, you see, that the killer wasn't really a murderer, right? I mean, it was a straightforward rape all the way, but the kid's skull got fractured. She was unconscious when she died, the coroner says. I got to thinking maybe he didn't realize, you know? Maybe he didn't know how hard he hit her, right? So I got a couple of guys and a policewoman to dress up like a teenager, and we staked the place out last night – the same spot, can you believe, where the first crime took place, and bingo! Who should come walking up to our lady cop but some guy with scratch marks healing up all over his face. Wanna party? the creep asks. I got a party for you, the detective says back. Guy copped out finally after a couple hours of denials. You know something, Merce? We'd all be useless if the bad guys weren't so damn dumb most of the time. So, as you can see, I had a helluva night. Helluva night. Christ, the type of night that makes it seem worthwhile . . .'

He looked at Detective Barren before continuing.

' . . . So here I am, finishing some paperwork before heading home to the wife and kids, and who calls up from the lobby? This I gather is not a social call, huh? Have a seat.'

He motioned across his desktop to a chair and they both sat down.

'You're being real quiet,' he said.

'Sounds like a good bust. A real good bust.' It occurred to her that she liked Detective Perry and she was suddenly sad because she knew that he would not like her after they completed their conversation. 'It helps,' she said.

'What helps?'

'That so many of them are dumb.'

He laughed. 'No kidding.'

He looked over the clutter of papers at Detective Barren.

'Merce,' he said softly, 'why are you here?'

She hesitated for a few seconds before replying in an equally soft voice: 'He didn't do it.'

Detective Perry stared at her as silence surrounded them. Then he got up from his seat and walked about. She watched him carefully.

'Merce,' Detective Perry finally responded, 'let it go.'

'He didn't do it.'

'Let it *go*, Merce.'

'He didn't do it!'

'Okay. Let's say he didn't. How do you know? How can you be sure?'

'Trace alcohol.'

'What?'

'Trace alcohol. The bite mark on Susan's body was swabbed and saliva tests were run. They turned up trace alcohol.'

'Right. I remember. So what?'

'He said he was a Shiite Muslim.'

'Right.'

'Sincere.'

'Yeah, that's what he said. So?'

'Won't touch a drop of alcohol. Not a beer. Not a scotch. Not a glass of wine.'

Detective Perry sat down heavily.

'That's it?'

'That's it for starters.'

'Got anything else?'

'Not yet.'

'Merce, why're you doing this to yourself?'

'What?'

'Why are you punishing yourself?'

'I'm not. I'm merely trying to find Susan's killer.'

'We found him. He's in prison for the rest of eternity. When he dies he'll probably go to hell. He *will* go to hell. Merce, give it up.'

'You're not goddamn listening to me! Trace alcohol!'

'Merce, please . . .' Defeat and sadness crawled into his voice. 'I'm tired. I'm really tired. You know as well as I that this guy picked up half his victims in bars or student unions. You're saying he never had a beer? Bull! He was crazy, Merce! He was sick crazy. He'd have done anything, anything! to get his victims. The rest, all the religious garbage, that was just, I don't know, cover-up crap. Self-justification. Madness, hell, I don't know . . .'

Detective Perry rolled back in his chair.

'I'm tired, Merce. I shouldn't have to tell you of all people that that damn saliva testing will turn up trace alcohol if the creep rinsed his mouth out with mouthwash before committing the crime. Hell, you know that better than I do. You're the expert. You know.'

'He didn't do it.'

'Merce, I'm sorry. He did. He killed her. He killed all of them. You're going to have to learn to live with it. Please, Merce. Please learn to live with it.'

Detective Barren looked at Detective Perry. She wavered for a moment, measuring all the sadness and discouragement in his voice. She thought how crazy she must sound. Then she thought, vaguely, in an undefined, vaporish way, of her niece and she toughened quickly.

'Will you help me?'

'Merce . . .'

'Will you help me, goddammit!'

'Give me a break . . .'

'Will you help me!'

'Merce. Get help. See the department shrink. Talk to your goddamn minister. Take a vacation. Read a book. Hell, I don't know, but don't ask me to help you.'

'Let me have the file then.'

'Christ, Merce, you've already got everything we had. I gave you everything before the guilty plea.'

'You're not holding anything back?'

Anger flashed across Detective Perry's face.

'No! Goddammit! What a fucking question!'

'I needed to know.'

'You knew already!'

They were both quiet, staring at each other. After a moment Detective Perry spoke again. His voice was slow and sad.

'I'm sorry you feel this way, Look, your neice's murder has been cleared by us. If you turn up some hard piece of evidence, well, you can always come on back and we'll take a look at it. But, Merce, it's over. At least it should be. I wish you'd see it that way . . .'

He hesitated before continuing.

' . . . because you'd be much happier if only you'd realize.'

She waited, to be certain he'd finished.

'Thanks . . .'

He shook his head and started to say something but she cut him off.

' . . . No, I mean it. I know that you believe what you've said. And you've always played pretty straight with me and I appreciate that.'

She looked at him hard.

'I know what you're thinking, but you're wrong. I'm not crazy. And a couple of weeks off thinking about it isn't going to change my mind. He's out there.'

'I don't think you're crazy, Merce. Just . . .'

He couldn't find the word.

'It's okay,' she said. 'I understand your position.' She stood up. 'I don't mind,' she said, 'but I'm still going to go find Susan's killer.'

She hesitated a moment.

'I'll let you know when I've got him.'

She was not exactly certain what she was going to say to her own boss. That she didn't believe the Arab had killed Susan; that the killer was still at large; that she wouldn't rest until he'd been uncovered? Whenever she formulated the sentences to describe the situation she found herself in, it all sounded silly, melodramatic, and unconvincing. She thought: There is something ordinary and trite to revenge. It is a common urge that comes from uncommon circumstances. It carries a package of guilt with it, wrapped up and unavoidable. She knew it was wrong to desire it so, but she was unable to say precisely why.

The door to Lieutenant Burns' office was ajar. She knocked hesitantly, then slowly poked her head inside.

He was sitting at his desk. Spread in front of him were two dozen eight-by-ten color photographs. He looked up and smiled when their eyes met.

'Ahh, Merce. Just the person I need. Come in and look at this . . .'

She walked into the office slowly.

' . . . Around here. Look at these pictures.'

She stared down at the array of photographs. She saw a body curled in the fetal position in the trunk of a car. It was a young man who would have seemed to be sleeping save for a huge swatch of blood that covered his chest. Detective Barren stared at the pictures, struck with the odd peace that had fixed itself to the man's face. She picked up different-angled shots of the car trunk, seeing the same quiet, the same blood and tissue. She wondered idly what the young man had done to deserve his death, knowing the answer intuitively: nine times out of ten, in Miami at least, youth and death translated into drugs.

'You know, Peter, what strikes me is he wasn't scared.'

Lieutenant Burns eyed her cautiously.

'I mean, we know enough about the physiology of death to speculate a little. And this fellow seems, well, too comfortable. If you or I had been snatched, thrown into the trunk of a car, and driven out to . . . to where?'

'A rock pit in South Dade . . .'

'Right, some rock pit. And then blasted by a shotgun . . . it was a shotgun, right? I mean, the guy's chest is just about gone . . .'

'Twelve gauge. One shot.'

' . . . Well, what I'm getting at is that we'd see the residue of fear all over him. Eyes would be open, probably. Face rigid. Fingers stiff. Look. The guy's hands aren't even handcuffed or tied. When you pulled him out, how much of him was left behind?'

'Some blood. Some tissue.'

'Not a lot?'

'Medium amounts.'

'And the car. It looks like a brand-new BMW, right?'

'Six months old.'

'I bet,' said Detective Barren, 'that it belongs to some midlevel drug dealer. A ten-to-twenty-keys a month guy, not a real heavyweight.'

'Right again.'

'Did he report it stolen?'

'I'm checking on that.'

'Well, this is off the top of my head, and only a guess of course, but if you were to ask me, I'd say the poor guy was shot somewhere else by someone he didn't expect to be unfriendly, if you know what I mean . . .'

Lieutenant Burns laughed wryly.

' . . . Then he was quickly dumped into the back of the car conveniently stolen a little while earlier, driven out to the rock pit . . . where they knew we'd find him quick, not like out in the Everglades, and left there. It seems to me like some dim-witted Colombian drug dealer's idea on how to frame somebody in the competition. Perhaps someone's looking to start some bad blood between organizations and this is the first trump played. All speculation, mind you.

But I don't know if I'd issue an arrest warrant for the guy whose car it is, either.'

'Merce, you know why I like working with you?'

'No, Peter, why?'

'Because you think like me.'

Detective Barren smiled.

'Everyone likes a yes-man. Or in this case, woman.'

Lieutenant Burns laughed.

'Well, I agree with what you say about the crime. I had forensics do a test on the guy's sneakers. No rock pit sand at all. But there were some fresh grass stains. You see any grass in that rock pit? Didn't think so.'

He stared down at the pictures.

'Merce, do you sometimes think the world belongs to the drug dealers? It makes me laugh, sometimes, when I think that they are the new entrepreneurs of our society. I mean, a hundred years ago, two hundred, people came over to this country, worked hard, put down roots, and bettered themselves. The American Dream. What's the American Dream now, Merce? A hundred-key score and a nice big brand-new BMW.'

He stood up and gathered all the pictures together. 'I'm getting to be too much of a pessimist. Well, anyway, I guess I'll take a little hike to homicide and talk to the detectives. Got to tell them what they're up against. Better call in narcotics, too, I suppose.' He looked at her and sat down. 'But first, what can I do for you?'

Detective Barren thought of the young man in the pictures and wondered why someone so young would be so silly as to get involved in the drug trade. No sillier than John Barren going to war over some foolish principle and dying and leaving her to face getting on alone. She felt a sudden rush of sadness for all the silly young men who died one way or another, followed quickly by a flash of impatient anger. How useless, she thought. How terribly useless and selfish. Someone, she thought, cried hard over this young man's torn body.

'Merce?'

'Peter, I need some time.'

'Because of your niece.'

'Precisely.'

'It might be easier to talk to a counselor and stay on the job. You know, keep busy. Idle hands, they say, are the devil's playground.' He smiled.

'I won't be idle.'

'I mean, I just don't want you to go off and brood about in your apartment. What are you going to be doing?'

Finding Susan's murderer! her mind screamed suddenly. She bit back the words. She forced herself to sound diplomatic.

'You know, Peter, they were always unable to put together a prosecutable case against Rhotzbadegh for killing Susan. I don't want to imply I think the county guys didn't do their part. It's just, well, it makes me angry. I just wanted to poke around, see what I can come up with. Then maybe spend some time with my sister, you know, help her over this. She's still taking it very rough.'

Lieutenant Burns looked carefully at her eyes. She didn't move.

'I don't know what I think about your poking around in the case. I think it's over. The other stuff, well, of course . . .'

'How much time can I have?' she asked. It makes no difference, she thought. I'll take forever. I'll grow old and grey and stiff and keep searching.

Lieutenant Burns opened a desk drawer and shuffled through a folder. He pulled out a sheet with her name written at the top.

'Well, you've got three weeks' vacation time and at least two weeks' compensatory time for overtime work . . . hell, make it three weeks as well. Then the department regs allow for leave under hardship circumstances. I could put you in for a leave, but it would be at reduced pay. Just how long do you think you'll need?'

She had no idea.

'It's hard to tell.'

'Of course. I understand. I think.' He eyed her, a bit warily. 'Why are you wearing the cannon?'

'What?'

He motioned toward her jacket. 'The elephant gun. What is it, a 45 or a 9-millimeter?'

'9-millimeter.'

'You need that to look at pictures?'

'No.'

'So why?'

She didn't reply. Silence enveloped them. Lieutenant Burns looked down at the paper, then up at her.

'Leave it alone, Merce. It's over. He's doing hard time, which is how it should be . . .' He stiffened, his voice taking on a note of officialdom. 'Here's an order: Stay out of the case. It's closed. All you're going to buy is more heartache. You want leave, fine, take it. But not to work. To recover. Got it?'

She didn't reply. He looked at her and his voice softened.

'All right. At least I gave you the official lecture . . .'

She smiled. 'Thanks, Peter.'

'But, Merce, for my sake, please, get yourself straight and get back to work. Okay?'

'That's what I'm trying to do,' she said.

'Okay, take comp time first, then, if you need more, take vacation. After that, call me and we'll work something out. I'll have them send the checks to your house. On one condition.'

'What?'

'See the department shrink first. Look, they're gonna make you see him when you come back, anyway. Trust me. All he's gonna say is take some time, two aspirin, and see him when you come back.'

She nodded.

'Okay. That's it then.' He rose again and picked up the stack of pictures. 'You want to come with me to homicide? Those idiots usually take some persuading, especially when it means they're actually gonna have to go out and scare up some witnesses and evidence all by themselves.'

'No, thanks,' she said. The next time I see homicide, she thought, it will be to bring them a case.

She bit her lip. Or to turn myself in, she thought.

*

The visit with the department psychologist was as perfunctory as Lieutenant Burns had suggested it would be. She decribed to him a certain amount of restlessness, sleeplessness, inability to concentrate, and fits of depression. She told him that she felt guilty over Susan's death. She said that she thought she needed time to adjust to the loss. She listened to herself speak, thinking how easy it was to create a believable lie by mixing in some truth. He asked her whether she wanted sleeping pills. She declined the offer. He told her that she would probably be dogged by depression until she treated the sense of loss with therapy, but that he agreed some time off might be beneficial. He said he would fill out the proper departmental forms to provide her with a leave of absence for medical reasons, which would give her almost full pay. She wondered why everyone was concerned with money. Then he told her that he wanted to see her regularly after a month and scheduled an appointment. He filled out a card and they shook hands. She thanked him and threw the card away after closing his office door behind her.

It was all much easier than she had expected.

It did not take her long to clear out what she needed from her desk, despite the interruptions from the other members of the evidence-analysis section, who stopped and offered condolences, invitations and friendship, which touched her. But she was excited, pleased, and anxious to get finished and out.

The heat was intense when she stepped through the doors of the city police department. The solid red brick of the building seemed to glow like hot coals. She breathed in slowly, as if afraid she would scorch her lungs, lifting her head and peering up into the sky, shading her eyes from the brightness. She felt for an instant as if she had been hit with a spotlight, singled out for observation.

But that sense passed and she felt a sense of anticipation, almost exhilaration. For the first time in months she could sense the depression sliding from her heart. I'm doing something, she thought. One foot in front of the other. One step at a time. She had a sudden memory of herself, rising in the midst of the nighttime darkness in her sister's home at the first mewings of baby pain and hunger. She remembered it as something of a ritual: Throw back the blanket, swing her feet out and into slippers in a single move, pluck the bathrobe from where she had spread it at the foot of the bed. 'I'm coming,' she would say, loud enough for the baby to hear, loud enough for her sister to know she was taking care of the problem and roll back into sleep. 'I'll be right there, now hush, hush, hush,' speaking the last words in a crooning midnight sleep lilt.

'I'm coming,' she said out loud, but there was no one to hear her.

The she hummed herself a tune as she walked down the steps.

9

The first thing she did was purchase three cheap cork bulletin boards and a child's green blackboard. These she took back to her apartment and set them up next to her desk. She wrote SUSAN on a piece of masking tape and stuck it to the top of the first; RHOTZBADEGH on the second and OTHERS on the third. The blackboard she set up in the center. She moved a bookcase out of the way, grunting as she forced it across the room to give her more space. She took push-pins and mounted a group of eight-by-ten color shots of the crime scene in the center of Susan's board. Then she put up the list of evidence seized and the statements of the two gay men who found her body. The Rhotzbadegh board filled swiftly too, with the evidence lists from his house and copies of the newspaper articles he'd clipped. She took a picture of him and placed it on the board, where she could watch it.

She felt an odd release in the activity. Be a detective, she thought. Make a case.

But first destroy the one they've got.

The inside of the student union at the university seemed cavernous and dark. It had not been difficult to find the people Susan had been with the night of her death. It was exam period and they were anxious to talk. To chatter, really. Anything, Detective Barren thought, to break the drudgery of studying, although their tanned faces spoke more of time spent in the sun than in any library.

'How are you certain?' Detective Barren asked one girl, a dark-haired young woman with the nervous habit of looking directly at a person while listening to their question, then letting her eyes wander wildly about the room as she answered. Must drive her professors mad, thought Detective Barren. 'How do you know that Susan disappeared by 11 p.m. that night?'

'Because we'd agreed we were going to leave by eleven. It was important, we each had an early class and we'd promised that no matter how good a time either of us was having, we were going to leave. It was going to be up to me to get her, you see, or her to get me. We were dancing and I lost sight of her. But at ten thirty I started looking hard and by ten forty-five I'd gotten the guys to help. Teddy even went out to the parking lot and all around outside. I mean, we couldn't have missed her, even in the crowd. I mean, Susan, you know, she always stood out, anyway. She couldn't hide, even in this place when it's packed. She was like that.'

I know, thought Detective Barren.

'You didn't see her with anyone special, anyone you didn't know?'

'Well, the problem was, it was the beginning of the semester. Everyone was new. Everyone was a stranger. There were freshmen and new graduate students. There were some of the new faculty members, too, but they got out early. I mean, everything was new and exciting and friendly. But I didn't see her with anyone suspicious, if that's what you mean.'

Detective Barren sighed and turned to another student, a huge, brawny young man wearing a tee-shirt. She wondered why he wasn't cold in the over-air-conditioned room.

'You tell me how come you know Rhotzbadegh was here until midnight.'

'I told the other detectives but I'll go through it again. It's simple, really. I had a date that was going to meet me at midnight . . .'

'Midnight?'

'Yeah. Sounds romantic doesn't it? It was just, well, she was taking this film history course and they had to go see some Russian guy's flick. Long, I mean, real long. She wasn't going to get out until after eleven. So we agreed to meet here. I squirreled down in a corner of the bar where I could keep an eye on the door. She was real pretty and I didn't want, I don't know, I didn't want her to have to be looking for me, you know. Too many single guys would be willing to help, if you get my meaning. Anyway, I get to talking to the dude sitting next to me. I mean, weird, right? Major-league weird. But kind of a goof, too, the way he was talking about girls and how wicked they are. But he'd say that, and I'd look at him, and then he'd laugh, and I'd laugh and I wouldn't take it too seriously. But still, I mean, it wasn't the kind of conversation you'd forget . . .'

Detective Barren looked up from her notepad. 'What were you drinking?'

'Two beers. That's the limit. The team was still doing two-a-days and man, drink too much and you'll puke your guts out at practice.'

The other students hooted. 'More like two six-packs,' said one. Susan's friend added:

'I saw you that night, Tony. You were ripped.'

'Well, maybe a little . . .'

'Two beers is what you told the coaches, right?' Detective Barren said. The young man nodded.

'What happened at practice the next day?'

'I got sick.'

'Right. So how many did you really have?'

He tried to grin but it died quickly. 'A bunch.'

'How are you sure that this happened the night Susan disappeared.'

'Because of the movie. It was only shown once.'

'What was the title?'

He hesitated, then brightened. 'It was about that battle-ship they had the revolution on . . .'

Detective Barren thought suddenly of a baby carriage bouncing down a wide flight of stairs. '*Potemkin?*'

'That's it!'

'But, Tony,' the dark-haired girl interrupted, 'I think that was the one they showed the next night. The night Susan disappeared they showed the war one, you know, with the knights and the ice breaks, that one. I think.'

'I don't know about that one,' he said.

'*Alexander Nevsky,*' Detective Barren said. She sighed.

'Still, you're certain the suspect never moved from his seat.'

'Pretty certain. I mean, I was dancing a bit. And I had to spend some time in the head. And you know, it was a party. You know, when some of the guys from the team came in, I had to get up and greet them . . .'

'So you weren't sitting next to him the whole time?'

'Well, not the whole time.'

Detective Barren glanced at the young man's wrist. Great witness, she thought. Drunk. Willing to lie to his coaches and probably anyone else. Can't remember details. Probably can't remember what day it was. She looked at him again. I hope he makes the pros, she thought. No wonder his story was discounted by the county detectives. A grand jury would have laughed at it.

'Ever wear a watch?'

'Nah. Just get it stolen out of your gym locker.'

'So you can't be certain what time it was.'

'Well, not exactly.'

'Okay, what did the suspect drink?'

'I bought him one. Tonic water. Like I said, weird.'

'Anything else?'

'Just tonic water. With a lime twist.'

'Go on.'

'Well, not that much to it. He and I pretty much sat there, right until the stroke of midnight, when Cinderella popped through the door. And I grabbed her before the

160

wolves jumped on, know what I mean? I mean, this place can get pretty rowdy some nights. What the dude did next, I don't know. The place was really getting down . . .'

Susan's friend smiled. 'Susan knew that, you know. That's why she and I made the pact to split. If we'd stayed till midnight, let me tell you, this place is a zoo. We'd never have made it out alive . . .'

This was a joke and the other students laughed in shared familiarity.

'Susan didn't,' Detective Barren said.

Some two weeks after taking her leave from the department, Detective Mercedes Barren drove through a blistering afternoon down to the park where Susan's body had been uncovered. It was summer and the heat rose off the highway before her, creating a wavy vaporous curtain. She thought to herself that she had reached a decisive position in her investigation. Days spent maneuvering about the University of Miami and reviewing forensic documents had convinced her of two things: Sadegh Rhotzbadegh was the natural, obvious suspect in the murder. He was at the scene of her disappearance, he had clipped the newspaper story of the murder, just as he had the others, the crime itself was performed in his style. All the other victims had been bashed and strangled. She thought to herself that if this had been her case, she would have devoted all her efforts to finding some non-circumstantial link between Susan and Rhotzbadegh. The tiniest of connections would have resulted in a first-degree murder indictment for sure. But Detective Barren was equally certain that he had not perpetrated the crime, primarily, she thought, because of the lack of some evidentiary link.

It's too simple, she thought.

She remembered the slight shake of the head.

Not him, she thought. Too obvious. Trace alcohol.

She frowned and mentally castigated herself: Find something!

She turned down the road to the park, which in the bright daylight seemed to have none of the malevolence she recalled from the night of Susan's murder. She rounded the corner to the main parking area and stared out at the opaque light bay waters that seemed to blend with the pale sky above in an endless enveloping China blue. There was no wind and the wavelets slid up against the shoreline, lapping at the gnarled mangroves, making a slight noise not unlike that of a faucet dripping. Detective Barren could smell cooking; there were families grilling lunch on open barbecue fires. The inevitable sounds of small children playing seemed distant, like background music.

She parked and hesitated, looking across the nearly empty parking area toward the underbrush and trees where the body had been hidden. Then, sighing, she got out of her car, locking the door, and started walking toward the spot. From the edge of the tarmac, she started counting. Susan weighed one hundred and eighteen pounds. She imagined slinging her niece's body over her shoulder. Fireman's carry. Deadweight is more difficult, more unwieldy. She thought how slight the Arab was, but knew that meant nothing; his arms were powerful. He could easily have carried her. But that meant nothing. She counted the distance in her head, one yard, two, up to twenty-two, before stopping and looking down at the sandy dirt. He'd already killed her, the detective thought, she did not feel the rudeness of this dumping.

He, she thought. Whoever *he* is.

But where? she wondered. The Arab's car was clean. Absolutely clean. Microscopic tests has been run on the rugs in the passenger area and on front and rear seat fabrics. Samples from the trunk, too, were put under a spectrograph. No blood. No hair. No skin. No residue of death.

Mentally she added that to her score sheet.

She bent down and felt the dirt where Susan's body had lain. Come on, she thought. Some cosmic message. Some idea. Something.

But she felt nothing.

All she was aware of was that it was hot. Children were playing. And Susan's murderer was outside somewhere.

'Nothing,' she said. 'Nothing at all.'

She looked back down and had a sudden vision of Susan lying before her. She remembered with awful clarity the pantyhose biting into her neck, the swatch of blood behind her head, the violation of the haphazard way she had been flung to the ground, her legs akimbo, her sex exposed.

How cruel, she thought.

Then she shook her head.

There is something, she thought. Think. She considered the blunt trauma to the back of Susan's head. If I could find a weapon, she thought. Or the real location of the murder. Locations almost always speak of personalities. She went over in her mind all the forensic tests done on Susan's body. If I had a subject, she thought, maybe I could find something. She thought again of the pantyhose and an idea struck her.

She stood, turned rapidly, and returned to her car.

She noticed a small girl watching her. She had blond hair and an open, mischievous face. She was wearing a little girl's bathing suit and that made Detective Barren smile. The child was eating a vanilla ice cream cone and it was melting about her, giving her shy grin a white outline. Detective Barren waved and the little girl half-waved back before turning and racing away. Trust no one, Detective Barren thought as she watched the little girl disappear amidst the trees and shadows, heading toward the beach and play area. Grow up and trust no one.

She had always hated visiting the morgue, not because of the bodies that were filleted there but because of the harsh bright lights which filled the rooms with an otherworldly glow. It seemed to her the light blended in some unusual way with the smell of formaldehyde and antiseptics which covered everything in the morgue. She preferred to think of death as something dark and private, which was the opposite of the atmosphere in the morgue, where people wandered in and out in a near constant parade. She watched from a corner of the theater as the medical examiner plucked various organs from a split body while talking into an overhead tape recorder microphone. His voice was monotonal until he found something that interested him, at which point it soared up an octave into a little boy's pitch. She saw the medical examiner root about inside the body, finally scooping a small shape from the bloody mass, and, raising it high into the light, he said in a delighted singsong, 'See, detective, how small death can be?'

She didn't reply and he dropped the shape into a specimen container. ' . . . In left coronary artery, at approximately three centimeters, one bullet fragment, nearly intact, apparently 22- or perhaps 25-caliber. This was the cause of death . . . impact severing artery, causing sudden massive loss of blood, shock, instantaneous heart seizure . . .'

He looked over his shoulder at Detective Barren.

'In other words he took it in the ticker . . . The news boys like the shoot-outs with machine guns and shotguns and all that fancy television stuff. But some things haven't changed in twenty years. You want to kill somebody coolly and professionally? A small-caliber bullet with a magnum load fired into the heart at close range. Or, if you need a variation, right here, at the base of the skull . . .' He tapped the back of his head with his index finger. ' . . . A little pop! and your man's history. Or woman. No fuss. No mess. No people diving for cover. No innocent bystanders gunned down. No explosions. And, from my point of view, a big advantage. A little hole, right here . . .' He thumped his chest and the sound seemed to echo in the small room. 'An Uzi or an Ingram makes a complete mess out of a person. No class. No class at all.'

He looked back down at the shape on the slab before him.

' . . . My kind of murder. No doubt about it. Simple. Direct and to the point, if you please, thank you, ma'am.'

He shook his head and looked at Detective Barren. 'I heard you were on a medical leave. What brings you around here?'

'I need to talk about . . .'

' . . . Your niece. Right?'

'Yes.'

'Well, what's the question?'

The medical examiner looked over at one of the orderlies who was replacing a shrouded body into a refrigerated container. 'Hey, Jesús! Go get me file number eight-six dash one eleven four, huh? Pronto, please. Susan Lewis is the name.

Detective Barren watched the orderly exit.

'He won't take more than a minute or two,' said the medical examiner. 'Still, what is it that's bothering you?'

'Susan was . . .'

'Asphyxiated. Cause of death was strangulation. Method of death was a pair of pantyhose around her neck. She was unconscious when it happened. You know all this. You were there and you saw the report.'

'Knocked out by the blow on the back of the head?'

'Ahhhh, yes. Probably.'

'You're not certain?'

'Well, the trauma to the back of her head was severe. It might have caused her demise in and of itself. But it always made me wonder.' The orderly returned and handed over a manila envelope. 'Right. Here it is . . .' He read momentarily. 'Right. Left hemisphere . . . tissue loss . . . brain matter lost . . . well, what bothered me is that not much of the detritus from that blow was at the scene. I mean, there was just what you would expect from ordinary leakage from a wound that severe.'

'I don't know that I follow . . .'

'Okay, she was hit, then strangled. Well, the theory of the case is that that Arab snatched her from outside the student union over at the university, banged her noggin, dumped her into his car, then took her to the park, raped her, strangled her and abandoned her. But to me that simply didn't make sense.'

'Why not?'

'Well, the blow Susan received on the head would have, as I said, killed her. Probably pretty promptly. There would have been a mess all over his car. A mess he couldn't clean up enough, realistically, to pass the spectrograph examination. And, if she had died while he was driving to the park, well, then the strangulation and the sexual congress would have been postmortem. Would have looked completely different. I mean, to a medical examiner it would have looked different.'

'I think I see . . .'

'There was one other thing. Beneath the circular pattern the pantyhose made around her neck, I found a few slight areas of bruising.'

'That's what I wanted to ask you about,' said Detective Barren. 'You mention those in one of the reports but not another. What were they? Could those have been finger-pressure bruises?'

'Well, yes is the answer to that question. But put me on the stand and ask me under oath whether those bruises were caused by a pair of hands and I couldn't testify to that, not to any degree of medical certainty. I mean, the marks were consistent with manual choking, but not conclusive. And they were just barely visible.'

He hesitated before continuing.

'I hate this, you see. I much prefer things to fit together with the scenario the homicide detectives arrive with. If you add into the picture this manual choking, well, where? When?'

'Were you able to measure the distance between bruises?'

The medical examiner smiled.

'Good question. You always ask good questions, Detective. Yes. But only one possible combination . . .'

He carefully slipped off his surgical gloves and approached Detective Barren. 'The problem, medically, is finding the right finger-and-hand positioning . . .' He put his hands around Detective Barren's throat. The medical examiner was a small, slight man, with mousy features and eye-glasses perennially perched on the end of his nose. But Detective Barren started at the strength in his thin fingers as they closed theatrically around her throat. 'Here is your classic, Hollywood-in-the-nineteen-thirties strangulation, face to face. But see, if I'm a little taller' – he stood up on his tiptoes – 'the angle changes. Or if you struggle, it changes . . .' The medical examiner kept moving his hands about Detective Barren's throat as he spoke. She watched him like a man would watch a barber he didn't quite trust shave him. ' . . . And what about from behind? Changes things, too.'

He dropped his hands.

'Five and one-half inches.'

'From where to where?'

'My guess, and it is only a guess, I'd never, ever testify in court on this, is that the murderer's hands had to be at least five and one-half inches from thumb to index finger.'

The medical examiner snorted.

'I hate this,' he said. 'Really. Sometimes I get so frustrated with questions.'

'Do you think Rhotzbadegh . . .'

He cut her off.

'Of course I do.' He stared at her. 'Who else, tell me? The guy had desire. He was in the location. It pretty much followed his regular pattern. He killed her . . . that's certain, really, I'm sure.'

'But?'

'But not exactly how they think it happened.'

'Did you ever talk this over with them?'

The medical examiner snorted again.

'Of course!'

He turned and walked back to the corpse on the examining table. He looked down into the body before him, then spoke up. 'The trouble is, there's no clear-cut indicator that it *didn't* happen the way they believed it did. And, really, what difference does it make? He did it, just as sure as I'm standing here breathing, and this young fellow is lying there dead . . .' He poked the body several times with his finger, as if testing to be sure he was right.

'But?'

'But. But. But. But I'm a man who likes things in order. This is the way the body works: take something away, and voilà! It no longer functions properly. Sprain the ankle and you'll start to limp. Take a bullet in the heart and you'll die. Things out of whack and out of line. Things twisted and things obscured. Hate it, really. That's why I like a good shooting. Dig around and bingo! There's the bullet. No doubts about it. He's dead. There's the reason. Can't stand loose ends . . .'

He hesitated again.

'You see, it makes no difference. And I may be off my rocker completely. That's what the prosecutor told me, anyway.' He looked back over his shoulder at Detective Barren. 'You know,' he said with a touch of sadness, 'that if you show two different medical examiners the same set of facts they will reach different conclusions? Every time. You can bet on it. We're the most contentious, disagreeing bunch. Everyone likes to think that, because we deal with the dead instead of the quick, we're not subject to the same vagaries of diagnosis, guesswork, what have you. We are.'

He took a deep breath.

'Makes me sad.'

The medical examiner seemed to be staring into the open chest of his subject. Detective Barren waited an instant before speaking.

'Five and one-half inches?'

'Right. For what it's worth.'

She turned and started to leave.

'But it won't prove anything,' he said after her. As she walked through the doors to the operating theater, she turned and saw the man bend over the remains, lost again in his work.

In her apartment that night, Detective Barren poured herself a glass of red wine, remembering the words of the clerk in the liquor store who'd assured her this Californian Cabernet was the equal of those priced twice as high. She had not told him that she could barely taste the difference and liked to slip an ice cube into her glass as well. She had stripped off her clothes after the visit to the morgue and taken a long shower, scrubbing herself fiercely – pathologically, she joked to herself – to remove the lingering stench from the death room. You can't really smell it, she told herself as she had stepped from the shower, and then she had paused, sniffed the air, and finally said out loud, 'Well, the hell you can't.'

She stood in her room naked and sipped the wine, feeling the tinge of alcohol slide through her body. She breathed out deeply. For a moment she felt like staying naked, turning out all the lights and letting the darkness soothe her. The idea made her giggle and think that it had been a long time since she had done anything spontaneous and offbeat, anything that would remind herself that the world was not all murder and death. Then she shook her head and found a pair of shorts and an old Miami Dolphins tee-shirt from one of their Super Bowl years, which she slipped on.

She padded barefoot into the living room, carrying her wine glass and the bottle. She went to her bookcase and picked out a leather-covered photo album, then retreated to an armchair and, perching the glass on her knee, opened the book of pictures. There was one in specific she was searching for.

She flipped past snapshots of herself, of Susan and her parents, lingering momentarily over a few, a picture of a birthday party here, a graduation there. She was suffused with the warmth of memories, comforted. Finally she found the picture she wanted.

It was a simple five-by-seven snapshot of Detective Barren at age twenty-one, standing between John Barren and her father. She thought: The summer before we were married, the summer Dad died. She looked at the background, an expanse of blue-green waves rolling steadily and benignly against the Jersey Shore. In the picture the three were all in bathing suits, and Detective Barren remembered how the two men had teased her mercilessly about her inability to swim, yet her constant attraction to the beach. She thought about how she would lie, hours on end, reading on the sand in the sun, peaceful, relaxed. When it became unbearably hot she would take a child's red plastic water bucket down to the edge of the ocean and plop herself down in the damp sand, waiting for some slightly larger wave to send a small current of water shooting up the beach toward her. The foamy clear cool liquid would rise about her toes, curl around her buttocks, and refresh her. If need be, she would take the bucket, fill it in the shallow water, and unceremoniously dump it over her head. John would laugh and point and plead again for her to learn to swim, but not seriously, for he knew she wouldn't, regardless of how ridiculous she appeared.

She did not swim for the simplest of reasons.

She had been young, barely more than a baby at age five. She closed her eyes in the apartment and felt the familiar anxiety pass through her, just as it always did when this particular recollection came back. Her heart seemed to pick up its pace momentarily, the sweat on the back of her neck grow slightly clammy and uncomfortable, her stomach tense. She thought for an instant of the potency of fear, undiminished even as it traveled over the decades of memory. She had been sitting on the sand with her mother, her father had been in the surf, riding the waves in on the beach, then dashing out again with the little boy's exuberance that he always displayed at the shore. Her mother had glanced at her and said, 'Merce, darling, go get your father and tell him it is time to eat.' It had been the meagerest of requests; even sitting in her apartment room, she thought it easy.

Detective Barren closed her eyes and with absolute sun-drenched clarity remembered every step. She'd jumped up, and turned, and run down to the water, her eyes on her father as he turned and caught a large roller heading swiftly toward the beach. As she opened her mouth to call for him, she looked up, and in a frozen moment of utter terror realized that she had run right beneath a curling wave. The force of the water as it broke over her head knocked her on to her back, loosening all the air within her, stealing it from her little girl's chest. The water suddenly seemed dark green, then black, and it was as if the world had been blotted out. She had struggled hard, searching for the surface, and then suddenly something great and heavy had landed on her, holding her down farther, blocking her from reaching the sunlight. She could still remember with an expected uncomfortableness the sensation of sand scoring her back. Her mind had spun, her eyes clouded, her little lungs seared, her heart been clenched by darkness. She did not know really what death was, but thought in that incredibly brief, interminable moment, that it surrounded her.

And then, suddenly, she had been snatched from the blackness and lifted gasping into the sunlight.

It was her father.

His own ride had carried him directly over her. It had been he that held her down, he that raised her up.

She remembered a few tears, drying quickly in the hot afternoon. She had played safely on the sand that day. But at night, tucked into her bed, as the light had faded from the day and nighttime filled her room, she had cried bitterly and vowed never to trust herself to the waves, never to know the sensation of the ocean closing over her head, and never ever to go into the water again.

Stubborn, she thought. A stubborn little girl who kept her promise to herself.

She laughed. The little girl has not changed a whit in thirty-how-many years. And probably won't.

She looked at the picture again. She smiled. John had a sleek, muscular body which glistened as the ocean water caught the sunlight. She thought of the way her father would tease him about his hairless chest, sticking out his own, with its swatch of curly black hair, puffed up, mocking a beach body-builder.

They were such easy times, she thought.

She looked at her father's face. Sunlight was causing him to squint, just barely, giving his face an elvish look. It made her laugh out loud.

'What,' she said to the man in the picture, 'would you say about this case?'

Mathematics, her father would lecture in his best academic drone, prefers a steady procession of data to reach for an elusive conclusion. But this was not always the case: sometimes you could prove a theorem through an absence of contradictory information.

She suddenly felt a spasm of despair.

There would be no way to prove that Sadegh Rhotzbadegh didn't commit the murder of her niece.

Proving a negative. Her father would shake his head and smile. Now, that, he would say, requires some real intellect, some pure mathematical reasoning.

She felt that she wanted to scream.

Then she took a deep breath and a sip of wine.

She thought angrily about the concept of proof. Legal proof. Proof that stands up and is counted in a courtroom. Proof that clears murder cases. Evidence coupled with opportunity equals supposition of guilt, and finally an absence of alternative hypotheses amounts to a verdict. The hypotenuse squared is equal to the sum of the squares of the two remaining sides. Logic, she thought, is insidious. All logic points to the Arab. We live in a world that insists on accommodation. For every action there is an equal opposite reaction.

All instinct points away.

What did she have? A murder that happens not exactly as the investigators would want. A suspect who fits almost perfectly into the niche required of him – save for one or two critical details.

Start at the source of the dilemma, her father would say.

That was easy enough, she thought. And she knew where she would drive in the morning. She felt a rush of excitement and drained the remainder of her wineglass. She stared a last time down at the picture in the album resting in her lap.

Two weeks after her mother snapped the picture, the summer had ended. They had piled blankets, towels, umbrellas, and all the other traveling paraphernalia into their old bedraggled station wagon. The Labor Day weekend traffic had been horrendous, bumper to bumper at sixty miles per hour. She remembered the way her father had gripped the wheel, cursing mildly, complaining as the other cars swerved and swooped about them. An invitation to slaughter, was what he said. He said it every year when they packed up after the holiday and headed home. No wonder so many people die on the highway, he complained. They leave their brains at the beach. One hour slid into two, then three, and finally they turned up the street to their own home. She remembered her father adopting his best Charles Laughton accent and hunching over the wheel: 'Sanctuary! Sanctuary!' he cried out as the exhausted family cheered. She stared again at the picture and in her mind's eye saw them unloading the car and her mother turning to her father and saying, 'Oh, there's nothing in the house for dinner, just run down to the corner store and pick up some hamburgers.' Her father had nodded, jumped back into the car, waving, be back in fifteen minutes.

But he wasn't, she thought.

She and John had been on the front lawn, hauling the stuff inside, and they'd heard ambulance and police sirens in the distance, looked up, thought nothing, and lifted another load.

Two drunken teenagers had run a stop sign and broadsided his car. He had been knocked clear across the seat and out and crushed as the vehicle rolled over him.

She smiled. He probably appreciated the irony of a mathematician becoming a statistic on Labor Day weekend fatalities. I still miss him, she thought. I still miss all of them. She looked again at the picture. She was standing between the two men in her life and they had each thrown an arm across her back. She remembered the moments before the snapshot had been taken: there had been a mock argument between boyfriend and father as to whose arm was going where on her back. They had loved each other, she thought, and I loved both of them. She felt a pleasurable rush of memory, as if she could feel the weight and pressure of those two arms draped across her shoulders and the warmth flowing from their bodies as she squeezed between them.

Sanctuary, she thought.

She closed the book and went to bed.

She was shading her eyes from the noontime glare and almost missed the small square green sign by the side of the road. It was set back a few yards farther than most roadside signs, which Detective Barren thought reflected a concession to distaste. No one wants a prison as a neighbor. It said: LAKE BUTLER CLASSIFICATION AND EVALUATION CENTER F.S.D.O.C. NEXT RIGHT. There was a dusty black macadam road a hundred yards up from the sign. The road cut between two stands of tall pine trees, their needles turning a brownish green in the unrelenting Florida summer sun. Detective Barren slowly steered her car down the road, passing beneath a huge willow tree that threw shade down defiantly. The road curled around, across a brown field where some cattle grazed idly, contentedly, and Detective Barren caught her first sight of a cluster of low gray buildings that seemed to glow in the midday heat. She stopped the car to read a large black and yellow sign that dominated the side of the road: CAUTION. ANYONE PASSING OVER YELLOW LINE SUBJECT TO SEARCH. ANYONE CARRYING CONTRABAND INTO L.B.C.E.C. WILL BE PROSECUTED TO FULLEST EXTENT OF LAW. Painted across the road surface was a wide strip of yellow. Detective Barren accelerated gently, picking up her first sight of a twelve-foot-tall, barbed-wire-topped chain-link fence that surrounded the clutch of buildings.

Detective Barren parked the car in an area designated VISITORS and walked toward a pair of wide glass doors. Another sign informed her that this building housed the prison administration, although the word 'prison' was not used. This was typical: We live in an enlightened age which is dependent upon euphemism, she thought. Thus, prisons are correctional facilities, manned not by guards but by correction officers, and prisoners are subjects. If we change the designation, somehow we believe the reality to be less evil and distasteful, though in actuality nothing ever changes. She stepped through the doors into the dark, cool interior, where she was blinded by the sudden shift in light.

Her eyes adjusted slowly. Then she walked to a receptionist.

Within a few minutes she had checked her automatic with a uniformed security guard who'd eyed her with suspicion when she produced the heavy pistol and been ushered into a small office with the name and title of Arthur Gonzales, Classification Officer, on the door. It was a cramped space, filled with file cabinets, a small, cluttered desk, and two chairs. A window overlooked the prison's exercise area. Detective Barren stared out, watching a small cluster of men playing basketball. They were stripped to their waists, and sweat made their bodies gleam as they maneuvered about the court. The window was closed to contain the air conditioning and Detective Barren could not hear the men. But she knew the sounds they were making, of sneakers pounding the cement surface and bodies slapping together.

She thought idly of her husband, who'd loved the game.

'There's a zone, Merce, a time, I guess, I don't know, but you get hot. It's like no other sport I can think of, but you just get possessed by this sense that you can throw anything toward the basket and it will fall. Hot. Electric, I suppose. It's hard to describe, but it sometimes seems that you can jump just a little higher, a little faster, and that the basket seems suddenly closer and the rim wider, and you know, you just know, that what you put up will slip in. It just happens, you see, in the course of the game. I don't know why. And then, just as the sensation arrives, it disappears. The ball starts to clank about and fall off. Your feet slow down. The magic evaporates. Maybe it passes on to someone else. You become mortal, suddenly, sadly. But the moments of immortaility, Merce, they're something. It's as if you've been touched. Graced by some god of athletics. And until his mood changes and he plucks someone else out, you're on fire . . .'

She smiled.

He would take her to the outdoor courts on summer mornings and they would play against each other. At first he restricted himself to shooting only left-handed. Then she beat him one morning on a running, giggling jump-shot.

She smiled again, thinking how foolish men were with their games. Foolish but a little bit wonderful, as well. What she had liked about John was that the morning she beat him, he'd been the first to announce the event to her family. Without alibi, as well. Of course, the next day he'd suddenly shifted the ball from left to right and swooped past her. That was how he announced that the rules of their game were changing.

'Cheater!' she'd yelled.

'No, no, no,' he'd replied. 'Just returning to the proper balance between the sexes.'

That night he'd been especially tender and tentative when he touched her.

Detective Barren shook her head and couldn't prevent the memory from making her grin.

She turned when she heard the door open behind her.

A rotund man in a pair of tan double-knit slacks and a white guayabera shirt entered. He stuck out his hand and said, 'Hello, detective, how can I help you?' in a tone that told her that he no more wanted to see her or help her than he wanted to catch a disease. He instantly buried his head in files of paper, as if to indicate that her presence demanded only a portion of his attention. All detectives hate dealing with prison personnel, she thought. Because they always act like this. They are concerned with logistics and containment, who gets sent where and what bed does he occupy. Not issues of guilt or innocence.

She sat down opposite him.

'Sadegh Rhotzbadegh.'

'He is one of my clients, yes . . .'

A new euphemism, thought Detective Barren.

'I would like to interview him, please.'

'Is this another case like the ones he pleaded to?'

'Yes.'

'And this is an official request?'

'No. Not really. Informal.'

'No? Even so, I would probably counsel him to seek legal assistance before talking with you . . .'

Just whose side are you on? thought Detective Barren angrily. She kept her thoughts to herself.

'Mr Gonzales, this is an informal inquiry. I believe Mr Rhotzbadegh has been unfairly linked to a crime, and I think he can swiftly clear the matter up. He does, of course, have the right to an attorney. I will read him his rights if need be . . .'

She looked hard across the table.

' . . . But you sure as hell don't have the right to tell him anything. Much less give him advice. Now, if you want me to talk to your supervisor . . .'

'No, of course, that won't be necessary.'

He shuffled some papers quickly.

'Well?'

'Well, Mr Rhotzbadegh is currently in his activities period. There is a rest time which follows, right before dinner. You can talk then . . . if he'll see you. He has the right, you know, to refuse . . .'

'But you're going to see he doesn't exercise that right.'

'Well, I can't . . .'

'You sure as hell can. I didn't drive three and one-half hours just to have a convicted killer say, "No thanks, not today". You get him and bring him to a room where he and I can talk. If he wants to sit there and not say anything, well, that's his business and mine. Not yours.'

'I can arrange for the room. But . . .'

'But what?'

'Well, we have just finished our evaluation and he's scheduled to be shipped out at the end of the week . . .'

'Yes?'

'Well, he's going to the psychiatric facility at Gainesville. We don't think he'd be safe in the regular population.'

'You don't think he'd be safe!'

'Well, he's decompensated . . .'

'You think he needs to be protected!'

'That's the opinion of the evaluation and classification staff.'

'So you're going to send him to some country club?'

'It's a maximum-security unit.'

'Sure.'

'Well, that's where he's going.'

'I don't get it.'

'Detective, if we send him to the state prison, someone will kill him. He's, well, no other word to describe it, he's obnoxious and near-psychotic. The other men don't like his religious mumblings. Or his conceited postures. Rapists have enough trouble in general population without these, uh, characteristics. What can I say?'

Detective Barren absorbed the news slowly. Her mouth was dry and her stomach churned. She shook her head.

'Just set up the interview room,' she said.

Sadegh Rhotzbadegh's eyes darted about wildly as he entered the small office, almost as if he were trying to print the room's layout in his imagination. After this momentary assessment he brought his glance to bear on Detective Barren, who sat patiently at a small table in the center of the room. The table and two chairs were the only furniture. Rhotzbadegh stared at her, then took a sudden step forward, paused, and a stride backward, his eyes first reflecting anger, then fear, and finally settling on a confused compliance. He stood still, waiting for the detective to make some motion, which she did, waving him toward the empty chair across from her. He's gained weight, Detective Barren thought, and lost some of the wiry strength he had. Prison kitchen starches, she thought. Rhotzbadegh sat, shifting about in the chair, finally perching on the edge, balancing forward and eyeing Detective Barren. She met his glance and held it until he turned away. Then she spoke:

'First I want to inform you of your rights. You have the right to remain silent, the right to an attorney . . .'

He interrupted.

'I know those things. I have heard them many times and do not need to hear them again. Tell me why you have come to see Sadegh Rhotzbadegh! Why have you summoned him from his rest?'

'You know why.'

He laughed.

'No, you must tell me.'

'Susan Lewis. My niece.'

'I remember that name, but it seems to be in a dream. Tell me more so that I may remember better.'

'September. The University of Miami student union.'

'This remains a mystery to me.'

He laughed again, then continued.

'Why should I remember this person?'

He giggled girlishly.

'What reason do I have for remembering this person? Is she someone great, someone remarkable? Someone important, perhaps? I think not. Therefore there is no reason for Sadegh Rhotzbadegh to remember this person.'

Rhotzbadegh leaned backward in his chair, relaxing, folding his arms across his chest and grinning in a self-satisfied fashion.

Detective Barren breathed deeply and locked her eyes onto his. She waited a moment before speaking, talking in a low, even, harsh voice: 'Because if you do not start remembering, I will personally rip your face off, right here, right now.'

Rhotzbadegh stiffened suddenly in his seat, immediately timid.

'You cannot do this!'

'Don't try me.'

He bent forward, flexing his arm and showing Detective Barren the bulge of his arm muscles. 'You think you have the strength . . .'

She interrupted, leaning forward eagerly.

'What do you think?'

She watched his eyes as they tried to measure the depth of her intentions. She narrowed her own glance until she was staring through slits, her face set. Rhotzbadegh suddenly sobbed and covered his face.

'I have nightmares,' he said.

'You damn well ought to,' replied Detective Barren.

'I see faces, people, but I cannot recall their names.'

179

'I know who they are.'

Tears started to form in the corners of his eyes and he rubbed at them.

'God is not with me. No longer, no longer. I am abandoned.'

'Maybe he wasn't so damn pleased with what you were doing.'

'No! He told me!'

'You misunderstood.'

Rhotzbadegh paused. He produced a tattered handkerchief from a pocket and blew his nose three times hard.

'This,' he said, in a tone suffused with despair, 'is a possibility.'

He wiped his nose vigorously.

'Still,' he continued, 'I will search him out again. I will learn his messages and find the true path. Then he will welcome me to his bosom in the garden, where I will reside for eternity.'

'Great. I'm glad for you.'

He didn't catch her sarcasm.

'Thank you,' he said.

Detective Barren reached down into her bag and pulled out a simple child's schoolbox ruler. 'Stick out your hand,' she said. 'Spread the fingers.'

Rhotzbadegh complied. She held the ruler up to his hand. The distance between thumb and index finger was five and three-quarter inches. Damn, she thought. He could have made the marks.

'My hands reach out for God,' he said.

'Let me know if you manage to touch him.' she said.

Rhotzbadegh looked about the room again. Then he pushed back his chair and rose. He walked over and placed his back firmly against one wall of the interview room. Then, counting loudly, he paced the distance across, bumping up against the opposite wall as he said twenty-one. He executed a military-style about-face and returned to his seat.

'Twenty-one paces,' he said, shaking his head as if in surprise. 'Twenty-one full paces.' He jumped up and leaped

180

to the wall across from Detective Barren. Then he stepped off that distance, walking past the detective without glancing down.

'Nineteen paces!'

He returned again to his chair.

'My cell measures only nine paces by eight paces. I feel sometimes as if my heart has been caged.'

He put his head in his hands and sobbed.

'They will not let me into the yard with the other men,' he whined. 'They fear for my safety. They think that I will be executed. I cannot sleep at night. I cannot eat. I think my food tastes of poison. They have put something in the water to make me drowsy and then they will come and kill me. I have to fight them at every step.'

'The girls?'

'They are the worst. They come in my dreams and they help these men who would kill me.'

'Who are they?'

'I do not know . . .'

'The hell you don't! Think! Dammit, I want some answers.'

Rhotzbadegh lifted his nose in mock snobbery.

'These are my dreams. I do not have to share them with you.'

Detective Barren stared hard at the little man but inwardly she sighed. Useless, she thought. His mind goes everywhere but where I want it. She reached down into her purse and took out a simple yearbook picture of her niece.

'Does she come in your dreams?'

Rhotzbadegh eyed the picture. He plucked it from the table and moved it close to his face, then held it out at arm's length. 'This one, not exactly.'

'What do you mean?'

'She comes in the dreams, but all she does is watch the others. She cries alone. It is the others who are my tormentors.'

He leaned across the table conspiratorially, his voice low.

'Sometimes they laugh! But it is I who live and laugh last.'

Detective Barren took the picture and held it up directly in Rhotzbadegh's line of vision. She raised her voice, demanding, insistent, frightening, mustering everything into a single question: 'Did you kill this young woman?'

There was silence.

'Did you snatch her from the parking lot outside the student union at the University of Miami?'

More silence.

'Did you smash her head and take her to Matheson-Hammock Park and leave her there to die?'

He didn't respond.

Detective Barren lowered the picture and stared at Rhotzbadegh. She felt the hatred slip from her heart, emptying her of emotion. His eyes were filling again as he cowered at the anger in her questions. She felt no sympathy, nothing, just a need to fill a great vacuum within her.

She whispered: 'Tell me!'

He lowered his face into his hands momentarily, then raised them. 'I cannot say!' he sobbed. 'I cannot say!'

He took a deep breath and swiveled in his chair as if rooted by agony.

'It seems to be a memory. It sounds like that which I would do. I remember the student union, with all the filth of dancing and alcohol and laughter. An evil place. God will someday cleanse it with a great fire. This I know . . .'

'The girl!' Detective Barren interrupted.

'I was there. The bodies surrounded me. This I know. But the rest . . .'

He shook his head.

'She comes in the dream, but I do not know her, not like the others.'

'Why did you clip the story from the newspaper?'

'I had to keep a record! How else would God know that I had followed his wishes? It was proof!'

'For this one why did you need proof?'

'That is why I am confused,' he cried. 'I had my – my – my prizes from the others. But she I do not remember.'

'When she comes in the dream, what does she say?'

'She says nothing. She stands aside and watches. I do not hate her quite like the others.'

He paused.

'I need to sleep. God grant me sleep. Can you help me, detective, help me sleep? I am so tired. And yet I cannot. I must not. They come and torment my dreams. My enemies plot while my eyes are closed. I will not arise, one day.'

He continued crying gently.

'This frightens you?' Detective Barren asked.

He shifted suddenly, throwing himself out of the chair and standing rigidly before her, his chest puffed out, his muscles flexed. His voice was no longer whining, but bellowing.

'Fear? Nothing frightens Sadegh Rhotzbadegh. I fear nothing!' He pounded on his chest. 'Hear me! Nothing! God is with me. He protects me. I am afraid of nothing!'

Rhotzbadegh stared at Detective Barren. She let the silence lie in the room before replying slowly.

'You ought to be,' she said.

It was late when Detective Barren finally reached her apartment. She had driven back from the classification center at a steady, minimal pace, letting other drivers swoop past her readily as she stuck doggedly to the speed limit. She felt a difficult emptiness inside her, an unruly, awkward sensation, as if the organs inside her body had shifted about somehow, slightly out of position. The thought made her smile when she considered how her friend the medical examiner would react. She easily envisioned his high pitched voice reaching new sopranic levels as he sliced through her: 'What's this, her appendix has moved! Her spleen has wandered! Her stomach has traveled! Her heart has packed up and moved away!' Detective Barren laughed out loud.

It was not so far-fetched, she thought.

She remembered a visit, two years after John Barren's death, from a slender man who stuttered, but just slightly.

He had been a member of John's platoon, and he sat across from her in a restaurant and told her about her husband. He'd been very brave, the man said. Once, pinned down, he'd rushed out to bring back the wounded point man. They always did that, the VC, the man said. Bring down the point man. Then bring down the medic, because the medic always goes. Then bring down the men who owe the medic, which is everybody.

'John was the best of us,' the man said.

She had nodded and said nothing. It was something she had known without being told.

'I just wanted you to know,' the man said. He had risen.

'Thank you,' she said, more for him than herself. 'It helps.'

She'd known it was a lie.

'I hope so,' the man said.

He hesitated.

'I was the p-p-p-p-point man.'

She'd nodded. 'I guessed.'

They had looked at each other.

After a brief silence she had asked, 'What are you going to do now?'

He smiled. 'It's back to the VA hospital for me. More surgery on the old guts. That's the trouble with getting wounded. Bullets tear the hell out of things. Army surgeons are great improvisers. They're like the guy everybody always knew in high school, the guy who could tinker around with any engine, fiddle here, adjust there, until he got the thing running okay. That's what they're doing to me. They've got intestines going north, digestive tract heading south. Pretty soon they'll get it all mapped out the way they want it.'

'Then what?'

He'd shrugged. In her mind's eye, Detective Barren often pictured that young man's shoulders slumping against reality. Whenever she thought of the war, that was what she remembered: a wounded man shrugging at the future.

She wondered sometimes whether John would have been the same. He'd never had the chance to know disappointment. Never known frustration or denial or bad luck. He'd never been fired, never been rejected, never told to get lost, never told to take a hike. Never known loss.

Not like she had.

Detective Barren threw her notepad and briefcase on her small desk, kicked off her shoes, and went into her kitchen. She grabbed some lettuce, cheese, and fruit from the refrigerator. Rabbit food, she thought. She made herself a plate, then left it on her table. She went into her bedroom and dropped her skirt to the floor. She washed her hands and face, then padded out, half naked. She ate, trying not to think of Rhotzbadegh, trying not to fill herself with despair. She barely tasted the food.

He could have been direct, she thought angrily.

Dammit! Dreams! He sees her in a dream, but she doesn't torment him! What the hell does that mean? That he didn't kill her? Probably. Probably.

She smiled sadly, suddenly envisioning herself going to Detective Perry. Great news! she would say. The creep dreams! Clear-cut evidence that he didn't kill Susan.

She shook her head.

What a mess. What a hopeless mess.

She finished the salad and pushed the plate away. All right, she said to herself. Enough. Enough! Stop wasting your time with the Arab.

Clear your mind and start all over again.

She rose from the table and carried her dishes to the sink. She washed them carefully, dipping her hands into near-scalding water, gritting her teeth but making herself do it. She put the dishes away and went into her living room. She looked at the stacks of papers on her desk for what she thought was the millionth time. Maybe the billionth. It's in there, she thought. There is something in there.

'In the morning,' she said out loud, 'go to homicide and start pulling cross-referenced cases. Check out lists of known sex offenders. Go back to the school and find out if Susan had any enemies. Run the modus operandi through

185

the NCIC computers. Maybe the FBI as well. Check for similar crimes after the Arab was arrested . . .'

She stopped and thought. She looked out the window.

'Out there,' she said.

She smiled. You didn't think it would be easy. You didn't really expect to prove the Arab didn't do it and open the official investigation again. You're still on your own, and that's not terrible.

Not terrible at all.

She stared at the picture of Susan in the bookcase. Don't worry, she thought, I'm getting there. I'm getting there.

But her eyes were filling rapidly with tears.

She turned away and stared again out into the blackness of the tropical night. The sky was filled with the constellations, and Detective Barren saw one star burn brightly, shoot quickly across the void, then disappear.

'Oh, damn,' she said. She felt tears flowing freely down her face, but she remained rigid.

After standing empty for minutes, she finally turned. Clear the mind, she thought. She walked to the television set and clicked it on. She was surprised to see a pair of local sports announcers talking animatedly on camera, and in the background she made out the Orange Bowl in downtown Miami.

' . . . Well, this has been a pretty exciting start to the Dolphins' pre-season,' one announcer was saying. 'We're getting ready to start the fourth quarter of the first exhibition game of the year, with the score tied at twenty-four and the Saints with the ball on their own twenty.'

She had forgotten the start of the football exhibition season. 'Not like you,' she said, chastising herself. 'Not like you at all . . .' She grabbed her glass of wine and settled in front of the television set.

'The ultimate in mind erasure,' she said. 'Come on, Fins!'

She watched in oblivious delight, letting the course of the game sweep away her thoughts and tears, comfortable, alone. The start of a new season, she thought. For them and me.

Midway through the fourth quarter the Saints kicked a

field goal to go ahead by three. A minute later, a rookie running back for the Dolphins dropped the ball on his own thirty-yard line. This resulted in another Saints' field goal, and they led by six points as the game started to dwindle away. But as the game hurried toward its conclusion, the Dolphins rallied. Biting off chunks of yardage, they progressed down the field, until with less than a minute to play, they reached the Saints' one-yard line. It was fourth down and the game was in the balance. 'Come on! Dammit! Get the ball in there!' She smashed her fist into her open palm. 'Come on!'

She watched as the quarterback approached the line. 'Over the top, dammit! Just smash it over the top!' Both teams were bunched in, awaiting the blast at the center, strength against strength. She loved it. 'Just bash it in there!' she yelled.

Suddenly the two lines converged and Detective Barren saw the quarterback spin and hand the ball to a halfback flying toward the middle. There was a great crash, and the crowd noise swelled in anticipation. Then the stadium shook with sound as the crowd jumped to its feet, shouting out a great cry. Detective Barren, like the thousands in the stadium, rose up in half-cheer, half-cry, because she, like they, saw the quarterback had not given up the ball, but had only faked the handoff and was now churning desperately, alone, without protection, for the corner of the end zone. Simultaneously, the Saints' outside linebacker, a large, violent man, was bearing down on the quarterback, angling sharply so that they would meet just shy of the goal line, in the very corner of the playing field. 'Go! Go! Go!' shouted Detective Barren, her voice blending with the wall of crowd noise coming through the television set. 'Put your head down!'

And this the quarterback did.

As he flung himself across the goal line, he was slammed by the linebacker. Both men flew into the air, rolling violently into a crowd of photographers assembled on the goal line for pictures. The cameramen dashed out of the way like scurrying geese, trying to avoid the flying bodies. The crowd roared, for the umpire had flung his hands skyward, signaling touchdown, and Detective Barren leaned back, not thinking, just letting the idea of victory fill her.

The annoucers were babbling excitedly.

'That was some collision on the goal line, right, Bob?'

'Well, I think that was a gutsy call by the rookie quarterback and a tough way to learn about life in the National Football League. He took an all-pro shot.'

'I hope those photographers are all right . . .'

'Well, I suspect that linebacker for the Saints probably ate a couple of them . . .'

Both men laughed, then paused.

'Tell you what, let's go down to Chuck on the field. He's with a couple of photographers now. They had a real close-up view of the touchdown, didn't they, Chuck?'

'That's right, Ted. I'm standing here with Pete Cross and Tim Chapman of the Miami *Herald* and Kathy Willens of the Associated Press. Tell us what you saw, guys . . .'

'Well,' said one of the photographers, a sandy-haired man with a beard, 'we were all lined up to get the over-the-top shot, you know. And the next thing we see . . .'

The young woman interrupted. ' . . . The next thing we see is these two fire-breathing players heading our way, and . . .'

'I had to grab Kathy,' said the other, a curly-haired, barrel-chested man. 'She was shooting with the motordrive and I thought they were going to run her over . . .'

'It can be pretty dangerous down here on the sidelines, huh?' asked the announcer.

'No worse than covering your average war or revolution,' said the young woman.

The television picture held then, close-up on the three photographers. Detective Barren was listening idly, wondering whether she had ever met any of the cameramen on any of the crimes she had been assigned to.

And then she sat up sharply.

'Oh, God!' she said abruptly.

She fell to her knees in front of the television.

'Oh, God! My God!'

188

'That's the story from the sidelines. Back to you, Ted . . .' said the announcer.

'Hold it!' screamed Detective Barren. 'Stop!'

She clawed at the sides of the television set.

'No! Stop! I need to see!'

The announcers were continuing to talk and the teams were lining up for the extra point. Detective Barren was unaware of the crowd's cheer as the kick sliced through the uprights. She shook the television set and cried, 'No, no, no! Go back, go back!'

And then she slumped back and thought of what she'd seen.

Three photographers standing in front of a camera.

A slight gust of wind. Just enough to ruffle the hair.

Or to make their press credentials flap around their necks.

A wide, thick, yellow paper tag with the words OFFICIAL PRESS FIELD PASS embossed on it.

Detective Barren scrambled in panic across the floor to her desk. She pawed in desperation at the papers, speeding through her files of evidence until she came to the list of items discovered at the scene of her niece's murder. There were thirty-three items that had been identified, isolated, and seized by the crime-scene technicians. But it was only the last that she was interested in.

' . . . Tag end paper color yellow origin unknown (under body).'

'Yes,' she said out loud. 'I think so.'

She gasped in air.

'Yes,' she said.

She sat down hard on the floor and rocked, holding the paper list in her hands not unlike a woman holding a baby, remembering the piece of paper she'd inspected months earlier.

'I think so,' she said.

In the morning she went to the dirty property office warehouse in downtown Miami. The clerk was reluctant to battle the stacks of boxes gathering dust in the cavernous

189

interior. An angry man, unpleasant, scowling from the moment Detective Barren walked through the door, he first demanded a court order, then a letter from some superior officer. He finally settled for a handwritten authorization by Detective Barren, who kept smiling and acting nonchalantly throughout the man's wheedling complaints. The clerk was a wide man, with the no-neck appearance of a person who spent his free time grunting in a weight room. His shirtsleeves were pushed up high on his arms, revealing a pair of elaborate dragon tattoos, and when he wielded a piece of pencil, snatched from behind his ear, she thought he would break it with the strength in his stubby fingers. She trailed after the clerk, trying not to anticipate, not to prejudge, but with her heart racing and a growing stickiness beneath her arms.

It took nearly an hour to find the right cardboard containers.

'Closed fucking cases, lady,' the clerk complained. 'Closed fucking cases means sealed fucking boxes. I don't have to do this, you know.'

'I know, I know. Officer, I realize this is a special request. I can't tell you how much I appreciate your co-operation.'

'Just so you knows I don't have to be doing this,' he insisted.

'I understand,' she replied.

All the boxes were coded with a simple numerical procession. The first digits represented the year the crime was committed, followed by the case number assigned by the various investigative squads. Robberies, burglaries, rapes, homicides, and other crimes were mingled together in a lazy, haphazard fashion that represented more the distinction of being a closed case than by any design. She ran her eyes up and down the stacks, thinking that if she opened any one, some tragedy would fall out, followed by someone's heartbreak or someone's terror.

'Jesus, I knew it. It's at the fucking top. I'll go get the fucking ladder.'

She waited motionless while he retrieved the box.

'Now, you gotta sign this if you're gonna open it . . .' He

thrust a pre-printed form at her, which she signed without reading. He checked her signature and looked up. 'I'm supposed to watch, even with the closed fucking cases. But screw it. You want something in there? Hey, have at it.'

The clerk stomped away, his belligerence and frustration intact and as mysterious to Detective Barren as it was when she first entered the warehouse. She stared down at the box of evidence. Taped to the top was a disposition sheet listing the items inside and stating the fact of Sadegh Rhotzbadegh's guilty plea and life sentence. There was a large red stamped sign at the top of the sheet of paper: CLOSED/CLEARED.

We'll see, she thought.

She used the penknife from her purse to slit open the tape that held the box together, and, gingerly, as if trying to not disturb the dust collected there, opened the top. She refused to allow herself any excitement, thinking: This is just the first step.

She reached in swiftly and retrieved the yellow tag. It was encased in a plastic cover. As she slid it into her pocketbook, she noted the residue of dust on its surface from fingerprint work. Picking at straws, she thought: Fingerprints rarely come up on paper. She glanced at the box, wondering if there was something else she should steal, then shaking her head and shutting the cardboard flaps.

She breezed past the surly clerk. 'Thanks for your help. If I need anything else I'll be back.'

'Sure,' he said in a voice that implied the opposite.

The late-morning sun caught her as she exited the warehouse. She was not allowing herself to think, to imagine, to process information. One step, two, she said to herself. For a single moment, she felt as if she were winning. She did not think of her niece, then, did not associate the dusty box or the plasticine-covered yellow paper with the memory of the crime scene. Instead her eyes picked out the distant flow of traffic on the expressway. The sunlight glinted off the steel bodies, making it seem like each glowing car was somehow blessed. The movement of the vehicles darting in and out caught her, and she was wrapped in thoughts about commerce and life and progress. Her eyes traveled upward and she fixed on a large, solitary blackbird, flapping purposefully against the morning breeze. She watched the bird's determination outlined against the perfect blue of the tropical sky. The bird brayed raucously once, then seemed to put its beak into the wind and steadily, surely, beat its way across the sky. Detective Barren had smiled and then she walked swiftly to her car to join the flow of people and head downtown.

At the Miami Dolphins team offices on Biscayne Boulevard a secretary made Detective Barren wait. 'You're really lucky that Mr Stark can make time for you,' the secretary said. She was a young woman, equipped with the essential prettiness that all receptionists seem required to have: a breezy smile, a soft voice, and slightly teasing look.

'Why is that?'

'Didn't you read the papers?' the young woman asked.

'Not this morning.'

'Oh. You didn't hear about the new contract?'

As Detective Barren shook her head, she overheard a loud blare of laughter from one of the offices.

'That's the press conference,' the receptionist said.

'Can I see?' she asked.

The secretary hesitated. She looked around quickly. No one else was in sight. 'Are you a fan?'

Detective Barren smiled. 'Never miss a game.'

The woman grinned. 'Come on, then. We'll just poke our heads in the back.'

Detective Barren followed the swishing skirt of the receptionist inside. The young woman gingerly opened an office door and the two women slipped through the crack. Detective Barren recognized the scene instantly, from a hundred sportscasts watched late at night when sleep was elusive. A half-dozen television cameras, mounted on tripods, dominated the center of the room. They had been placed in front of a table, which was raised up on a small dais. Newspaper and television reporters were scattered about; some in chairs, some lounging against the wall, scribbling in notebooks. Sound men and still photographers crept beneath the level of the television cameras. At the table, talking into a stalk of microphones, were the famous jut-jawed coach, the owner, and the tall, curly-headed quarterback. They were all smiling. Occasionally they all shook hands together, and this would prompt a flurry of pictures, all the camera motordrives whirring at once. Detective Barren was instantly mesmerized. She felt like a child who captures Santa Claus in the act of placing presents around the tree. 'He's bigger than I thought,' she whispered in girlish, awestruck tones to the receptionist. 'And better-looking.'

'Yeah,' she replied. 'And richer, too. He's going to get more than a million a year.'

The young woman was quiet a moment. Then she glumly added, 'And wouldn't you know he had to go and marry his college sweetheart, too.'

This was said with such undisguised jealousy and sudden pout that Detective Barren almost burst out laughing. She turned back and watched the figures on the dais. Someone had made a joke and the three men were laughing. This caused another photographic explosion. The motordrives whirred again. In that instant the sound seemed to invade her heart. My God! she thought, looking about her wildly. He might be here. For a panicked instant she reached for her purse to seize the gun installed there. She stopped herself, just as her fingers wrapped around the cold handle. But who?

Her eyes cast desperately about.

She saw a muscular, bearded man fiddling with a wide lens. She stared at his large hands, seeing them suddenly wrapped about her niece's neck; she turned away, fixing on a thickset, balding fellow who was making wisecracks between shots. There was a special hardness about the corners of his mouth that chilled her. Another man, thin, blond, young, almost ascetic-looking, hovered into her line of sight. He seemed almost delicate, then craven, and she saw him mingling freely with the crowds at the student union, his beady eyes picking out her niece's blond hair.

She closed her eyes tightly, trying to dispel the vision.

The noise of the press conference seemed to gain in volume about her; the laughter and gibes filling her head, as if mocking her feelings, her pursuit. She felt dizzy and wondered if she would be sick.

There was a whisper, then, at her side.

'Detective Barren?'

She opened her eyes. A short man in a seersucker sports-coat hung next to her. She nodded.

'Mike Stark here. I'm the guy in charge of this zoo . . .'

He laughed and she gathered herself with a great internal effort and joined him. He looked back at the crowd, then past to the figures washed by the spotlights from the cameras. 'So what d'you think?'

She took a deep breath and forced her nightmare thoughts back into oblivion. She constructed a smile.

'I think a million bucks per year is a lot of money.'

'He's a helluva ballplayer.'

'He sure is . . .'

Stark hesitated. The he clasped his hands before him as if in supplication.

'You're right. A helluva lot of money for a guy with two bum knees. I hope that whatever God there is that looks after football players is paying close attention.' He rolled his eyes skyward. 'Hey, are you listening up there?'

Detective Barren's smile was genuine.

'He doesn't pass with his knees,' she said.

'For what we're paying him, he ought to be able to,' Stark replied.

Their laughter mingled with the general sounds of the room.

The little man looked around. 'I'll wrap this up. Thank God we signed this guy in August, before the season really got under way. I hate to think what he'd be worth if he had another season like the last. Why don't you wait in my office?'

Detective Barren nodded.

She was staring out the large glass window, watching powerboats beat white-plumed wakes on the bay, when

Stark entered. He took his seat behind his desk and she sat in an armchair across from him. 'So?' he asked.

She fished out the tag from her pocket book. For an instant she held it out of his sight, wondering whether she was taking the right approach. Then, wordlessly, she dropped it on the desk in front of him. She saw his brows furrow quizzically for a moment as he picked up the bag and turned it over slowly.

He put it back down.

'I'm sorry . . .' he said, then stopped.

She thought: The silence hurts. It was like being twisted by some great invisible machine.

He picked up the plasticine bag again and her heart seemed to jump within her.

'Well, maybe . . .' he said. He put it down and wheeled about to rummage in a file cabinet. After a moment he came out with a folder. He opened the folder on his desk and Detective Barren saw a small pile of yellow field-passes. 'Last year's model,' Stark said. 'This year we've printed them in aqua and orange, the team colors, for the home opener.' He held one of the tags against the sample in the plasticine.

'Could be,' he said. 'A definite maybe.'

Detective Barren looked at the two slips of paper. They were the same width.

'Right color,' Stark continued. He felt through the plastic. 'Feels like the right thickness, too. Can't say for sure,' he said. 'But a real possibility.'

He hesitated, then looked at Detective Barren.

'Why?'

She hesitated. Why not? she thought.

'Murder,' she replied.

He let out some breath in a long whistle. He looked back down at the two papers.

'I guess it was bound to happen,' he said.

'I beg you pardon?'

'Well we live in Miami, right? This is murder USA, right? I guess everybody rubs against a murder in Miami at some time or another, huh?'

'Maybe.'

'Well,' he said, 'that sure could be what's left from one of our field-pass tags. It could be almost anything else, too, for that matter. I mean, what do I know?'

'Do you know who prints those for you?'

'Sure. That's easy. Biscayne Printing up at Sixty-eighth Street. They can tell you in a minute whether that's theirs.'

So can forensics, she thought quickly.

'And have you got a list of people that they were issued to?'

'Yep. Which game?'

'Last September eighth.'

'Got it right here.' He swiveled to the file cabinet, dug about again, and emerged with another file. She wanted to snatch it out of his hands, but held back. 'Actually, the game was on the ninth. The eighth was the Saturday before.'

An idea struck her. She felt her throat quiver. It was very dry and she had to cough before asking the next question. She felt dizzy again.

'Did anyone request two passes? I mean, did anyone call and ask for an extra because they lost one?'

Stark looked surprised, then nodded. 'I get you,' he said. He looked down at the folder. 'The NFL requires us to keep strict lists of who's shooting the games. Security reasons, partly. But mostly they like to control the photographers, control the publicity. Sometimes I think I'm working for Big Brother.' He picked out a typewritten sheet. 'There were a lot of passes for that game,' he said. 'Everybody wanted pictures of the stud who just got the big contract today. He was a rookie, and nobody had good art.'

'Good art?'

'That's what they call it. God knows why. A good picture is good art. Rembrandt would turn over in his grave if he ever heard one of those animals say that.'

He looked at the list. 'Three guys,' he said. 'Three guys lost their passes. Whoops, sorry. Two guys and a girl. Woman I mean. The local AP gal, a guy from the Miami

News, and a guy shooting for SI. He's a contract guy with Black Star. Usually *Sports Illustrated* uses their own guys, but I guess this time they were strung out too thin. Baseball, college football, the pros — you know.' He flipped the paper across the desk. 'Is a copy all right?' he asked. 'I need to keep the original.'

She nodded. Her head spun, but she thought of another question:

'Did they give any reason for needing another pass?'

'Yeah,' Stark said. 'The NFL is real careful about who gets these things. They don't want the sidelines cluttered with everyobdy's cousin.' He looked at another piece of paper. 'Let's see, ah, yeah. The AP gal had hers in her bag. She was flying Eastern and they lost the bag. That had to be the truth. The guy from the *News* had his eaten by his ten-month-old, and the guy from out of town, let's see, lost his in a fight . . .'

Stark leaned back in his chair. 'You know, I seem to remember when he came in that morning for a new one, he had pretty good welt above his eye. Everybody was kidding him about it. He was pretty good-natured about the whole thing, though.'

Detective Barren felt her stomach plummet. I knew it, she thought. I knew she fought hard. Susan would never let anyone steal her life so easily.

She picked up the list from the desktop, looking down at the names printed on the page.

She tried to steady herself, thinking that she couldn't be sure until she went to the printer. Then she would need to have forensics run tests to make doubly certain. The process could take some time, she cautioned herself. Move slowly. Move carefully. Be certain. Inwardly, she doubted her ability to take her own advice.

She stared again at the names printed on the page, but the letters seemed to jump about, as if teasing her. There he is, she thought. There he is.

The old Cuban gentleman who came out from behind the

counter at Biscayne Printing to assist her was gracious and deferential.

She produced her badge, which caused him to look up in some astonishment, obviously, Detective Barren thought, slightly disturbed by the idea of a female policeman. Still, he took the torn yellow tag gently from its plasticine cover and turned it over, rubbing the paper texture between his fingers.

'This,' he said with a tinged accent, 'is certainly similar to the passes that we print for the Dolphins. But this year, of course, the color has changed.'

'Could it be . . .' she started, but he held up his hand.

'Last year,' he said. 'If I can take this, I could show you the bulk lot we purchased, perhaps make a perfect match for you?'

This was a statement presented as a question. Detective Barren knew that the forensics department of the county police could make the same match easily.

She shook her head. 'No, thank you. I just wanted . . .'

He held up his hand. 'Anything for the beautiful detective.' He smiled with an old man's benign lasciviousness.

She retrieved the paper sample and wondered when the next flight to New York took off.

The droning of the jet engines failed to disturb her preoccupation with a single dominating thought, an inability to focus on anything save the name, which she repeated over and over to herself terrified, in a way, at the ordinariness of it. She gave the taxi driver the address almost unconsciously. When she pulled up in front, the huge office building barely registered. Like an automaton, she punched in the seventeenth floor on the elevator, squeezing into the back with a dozen office workers, riding in swooshing silence to the photo agency.

She waited a few minutes in a lobby while a receptionist went to get an editor. She spotted a series of framed photographs, all of disasters or wars, and she wandered over, staring at the first out of curiosity, then with a frightening interest. It was seeing the name that drove her out of the half-light of consciousness she'd fallen into. There, she said to herself. There he is. It steeled her. Several photos displayed on the wall were Douglas Jeffers', including a shot of a grime-streaked fireman, eyes captured by defeat, as a city block burned in the background. It was Philadelphia.

She turned away as the editor came out to talk to her. Her first thought was to lie. Lie cleverly, lie completely, lie blatantly. Do nothing alarming. Create a diversion, she thought. She did not want the photo agency contacting Jeffers and telling him a policewoman was looking for him. She hesitated only briefly before uttering the first lie. She shook a sense of guilt from her mind and sauntered ahead. She recognized the expediency of her falsehoods, but still considered them a momentary weakness when the forces driving her, she thought, were powered by righteousness and honesty. They had to be.

The assistant dispatch editor was friendly but reluctant. 'I mean, he's not here. I really don't know how to say any more. Sorry, but . . .'

Detective Barren nodded, shaking her head in mock disappointment. 'Boy, you know the old gang is going to be so sorry. Everybody wanted to see old Doug.'

'What do you mean?' The assistant editor asked. He was a middle-aged man, wearing a bow tie. He had an understated lecherous air, the sort of slightly disheveled man constantly on the make, and more often than not able to use his rumpled teddy bear approach successfully. She thought she could use this. Detective Barren smiled generously at him.

'Oh, really, it's nothing. It's just a bunch of us who covered the Move bombing in Philly together and got to know each other have this reunion planned . . . no big deal, really. You know how we all met? Hunkered down a little ways back from where the firemen and cops were getting ready to blow the place up. Old Doug was like a racehorse. He couldn't stand waiting. He just had to get his shot, you know, no matter how much shooting was going on. Isn't that just like old Doug . . .'

'Sounds like the crazy kind of thing he'd do . . .'

'Well, no big deal. It just would have been nice to get Doug involved. Everybody loves hearing war stories, you know. That's why I came up here . . .'

'Gee, sounds like fun . . .'

'Yeah, well, last year it got a bit rowdy . . .' She half-winked and added a coy little blush for the editor's benefit. She hoped he wouldn't ask her anything about the incident in Philadelphia. She busily searched her mind for the few news stories she'd read. 'But it's okay, really.'

'I'm sorry,' the editor said.

'No big deal. It's just, well, you know Doug. He keeps to himself so much. We were kind of hoping to draw him out a bit, you know?'

'You're not kidding. Photographers are an odd bunch . . .'

'Well, old Doug, he's one of the best . . .'

'He sure is.'

'You know, you'd really be surprised how many people he's made into friends, out there in the boonies, on assignment.'

'I always figured he did. Lord knows he keeps to himself around here. But I mean,' the editor said, 'you can't go into some of those places without learning to risk a bit with other people. Flying bullets make for fast friends.'

'Isn't that the truth?' Detective Barren said.

'Where'd you say you were from?' he asked.

'The *Herald*. Just in town for a day or two . . .'

'Well,' he said, 'all I can say is that he's on vacation and he didn't leave any itinerary with us. He's due back at work in three weeks, if that's any help. You can always leave a message here . . .'

She thought of the wait. Impossible.

' . . . Or why don't you try his brother?'

'Doug never mentioned a brother.'

'He's a doctor at a state hospital in New Jersey. In Trenton. Doug always lists him as next of kin before heading into some war zone. Why don't you try him?

Maybe he can get a message to Doug. I'd hate to see him miss a good party . . .'

'Tell you what,' Detective Barren said. 'I'll give the brother a shot. If it doesn't work out, I'll leave a message here, okay?'

'Sure.'

'Boy,' she said in an almost girlish voice, 'you've really been a help. You know, we get this together, maybe you'd want to come for a drink?'

'Love to,' he said.

'I'll call you,' she replied. She smiled. 'I can reach you here pretty easily?'

He smiled the vague smile of the hopeful. 'Anytime.'

But her mind had already closed on the information she'd received, and her heart was tugging her fast toward New Jersey.

6 An easy person
to kill

11

Douglas Jeffers watched the expanse of inky black highway
flow beneath the front wheels of his car and hummed meaningless rhythms to himself. Behind him, morning was
sliding up onto the horizon. Light began to filter gently
through the car, creeping into the corners and filling the
interior. Jeffers glanced over at the sleeping figure next to
him. Anne Hampton's mouth was slightly ajar, her
breathing even and controlled. The morning light seemed
to rest on her features, making them sharp and distinct.
He tried to study her dark eyebrows, long, aquiline nose,
high cheekbones and wide lips, stealing glances from his
concentration on the roadway. He watched the way the
clean early light blended with her straw-colored hair; it
seemed momentarily to be glowing. He wondered again
whether she was beautiful or not. As far as he could tell,
she was, in a clear, simple fashion.

He wanted to run his finger down the side of her face,
where the light was marking the edge of her cheek, to wake
her with a small stroke of tenderness. He saw that she had
a small bruise there and for a moment felt sad. He'd been
extremely lucky that he had not had to kill her.

Jeffers turned away and saw the last wan outline of the
moon in the sky, before it became absorbed by the sweeping
expanse of blue that was building swiftly into daytime. He
liked the mornings, though the light was difficult, sometimes nearly impossible to shoot in. But, when captured, it
touched the picture with a magic that was undeniable. He
thought of a morning in Vietnam when he'd done the
foolhardy thing of going out with a South Vietnamese

Ranger battalion. He had been young and so had the soldiers. The other cameramen he'd been with – a crew from ABC News, another freelance shooting for Magnum, and a guy from the *Australian* – had declined the offer of a chance to see some combat and quietly tried to dissuade him from going. But he had been caught up in the laughter, shouting, and easygoing camaraderie of the men. They had been all posturing and bravado, waving weapons and grinning with confidence as they climbed in the deuce-and-one-half green trucks that would carry them into the field. He had jumped up with them, smiling, snapping off shots, taking names, and enjoying the relaxed mood so intoxicatingly unfamiliar to men at war.

There had been an easy day of tromping through the rice paddies and fields beneath a friendly and familiar sky. They had bivouacked shortly before dark on a small rise, surrounded by trees and high brush. Jeffers remembered that the men had continued their relaxed laughter into the night, but that he'd stared out into the enveloping darkness with apprehension. He'd crawled into this foxhole early after lifting an M-16 and a half-dozen clips from an ammunition pile and putting it next to his sleeping roll. He made a small stack of hand grenades on one side of the bed, and put his Nikon, loaded with fast film, on the other. He tightened his flak jacket around him, ignoring the discomfort. His last thoughts before sleep had been angry, angry with himself mainly, hoping he would survive the night. The goddamn officer in charge had put only a skeleton platoon out on the perimeter and no one deeper in the bush in listening posts and he had wondered idly, without panic, without fear, but with a sense of frustrated foolishness, whether they were all going to die that night. Or just most of them.

Then he had staggered into a light sleep. The encampment had been hit a couple of hours after midnight, and the firefight had lasted through the remaining darkness, until the daylight chased away the enemy, who retreated in victory, fading into the jungles of their success. Jeffers had crawled from his hole, moving slowly and painfully, streaked with dirt and blood, like some primeval beast from its lair. His grenades were gone, his ammunition expended in the frenzy of night. But, he remembered, he still had rolls of film, and he'd stood, as the darkness slid away, loading his cameras, waiting for the light to reveal the night's toll. The first insinuations of morning had landed on the dead, freezing them in grotesque poses. He remembered staring for a single moment, as the mist curled away, a light breeze blowing away the cold and the smell of cordite, revealing the twisted, savaged figures littering the battle-scape. Then he'd seized the Nikon and started shooting, moving crablike through the wreckage of men and matériel, trying to pluck both grace and horror simultaneously from the dead, fighting his own battle after the real battle had passed.

Newsweek had used one of those shots in a prescient story on the questionable capabilities of the South Vietnamese Army. He remembered the picture: a small soldier, probably no older than fourteen, flung backward over a bent ammunition canister, eyes stuck open in death, as if surveying the remainder of the life he would not have. It ran some six months before Saigon fell. That was more than a decade ago, he thought.

I was so much younger then.

He smiled to himself.

Athletes like to talk about young legs, legs that can run all day, then run some more, but photographers need them, too. He remembered just a few months past hiking through scrub hills in Nicaragua with a detachment of Guard when the rebels started to walk mortar fire toward them. He'd stayed in position, listening for the high-pitched whine and thump of the mortar shells as the explosions moved inexorably toward where he and the men had clambered down, seeking shelter. He remembered how he'd heard the sound of his motordrive whirring above the noise of the shells, and thinking then how strange that was and how battle made all one's senses acute.

The men surrounding him had broken, of course, and run. It was infectious, the need to run from fear, and though he couldn't remember actually tasting fright on his own tongue, he'd found his feet just as readily. He'd fled with the young men, a dozen years or more his juniors, but outdistancing them easily, confidently, so that he was able to turn and catch a picture, one of his favorites, f-1.6 shot at 1000. Violent death had not changed much, he thought. In the background there was a spiral of smoke and a violent upheaval of dirt, while in the foreground three men, tossing weapons and web belts aside, were rushing toward the camera. A fourth man was spinning down, caught at the heels by death, pinned by shrapnel. *Life* had used the picture in their World News section. He thought: Fifteen hundred dollars for a millisecond of time, stolen out of weeks of deprivation, some fear, and much boredom. The essence of news photography.

He looked back down at Anne Hampton.

She stirred and he caught her eyes opening to the sunlight.

'Ah, Boswell arises!' he said.

She started and sat up quickly, rubbing her face hard.

'I'm sorry,' she said. 'I didn't mean to doze off.'

'It's all right,' he replied. 'You need your rest. Your beauty sleep.'

She turned and stared out the windows. 'Where are we?' she asked, then she turned back toward him in near-panic. 'I mean, only if you want to tell me, it's not important really, I was just curious, and you don't have to say anything if you don't want to. I'm sorry. I'm sorry.'

'It's not a secret,' he said. 'First stop is the Louisiana coast.'

She nodded and opened the glove compartment, taking out one of the notepads. 'Should I take that down?' she asked.

'Boswell,' he said. 'Be Boswell.'

She nodded and made a notation in the pad.

Then she looked back up at him, pencil poised. She saw that he was watching her as carefully as he could while still eyeing the highway ahead.

'You reminded me of someone,' he said. 'A woman I saw in Guatemala a couple of years back.'

She didn't say anything, but continued to scribble in the book. She wrote: 'Memory of Guatemala, several years old . . .'

'The real story,' Jeffers continued, 'was up on the border, where the military was trying to root out a couple of guerrilla factions. It was one of those little wars that Americans weren't supposed to be involved in, but were, all over. I mean, Army advisers, high-tech weaponry, CIA guys running around in bush jackets and mirror shades on their eyes, and US Navy destroyers on maneuvers off the coast . . .' He laughed a little and continued. 'Remind me to talk about delusions. It's what we're best at . . .'

She underlined the word delusions three times.

'Anyway, lost in all this bang-bang guerrilla-hunting was this little peculiarity about the Guatemalan situation. For years, hell, I suppose centuries, the indigenous Indian population has taken the brunt of the bad times. Both sides, Marxist guerrillas, rightist militarists, shit, even the liberals, what there were of them left after being murdered equally frequently by both sides, uniformly slaughtered the Indians from time to time. I mean, they were just not considered people, follow? Like, if an Indian village lay between the two sides, it was ignored . . .'

'How do you mean "ignored"?' she asked tentatively.

He smiled. 'Good. Very good, Boswell. Questions that help clarify matters are always welcome . . .'

He paused, thinking.

'If the sides were in position for a fight, but the intervening land was some large important estancia, well, things would just be moved. It was as if both sides realized certain places were off limits. Like kids playing touch football. Out of bounds was a state delineated less by boundaries than by a mutually agreed-upon state of mind . . .'

He continued: 'Anyway, not so with an Indian village. They'd just blast away. Anyone who got in the way, well, tough. That was what I was thinking of. We walked through one of those villages after a fight. I think maybe the government troops had killed a couple of guerrillas and the guerrillas managed to kill a couple of government troops. That's it. No big deal. But they sure as hell had torn the shit out of the village.'

He hesitated.

'Baby blood. There's nothing like it. It's almost useless to take pictures of baby blood because no one will run them. Editors look at them, tell you how powerful they are, what a statement they make, but damn, they won't run them. Americans don't want to know about baby blood . . .'

He looked over at her.

'There was one Indian woman, sitting, holding her child. She looked up as I took the picture. Her eyes were like yours. That's what I remembered . . .'

Again he paused.

'I was standing next to this CIA guy named, named, Christ, Jones or Smith or some other lie he told us. He looked down and saw the woman and the child, same as me, and he said to me, "Probably got hit when those rebel rounds fell short." And he looked hard at me and said, "The damn Russians are always short-loading the shit they sell these backwater revolutions. Too bad, huh?" '

Jeffers thought before continuing. 'I remember his words perfectly. He was one of those guys that wasn't there, you know.'

Jeffers was momentarily silent and drove on steadily.

'Do you understand what he was saying?'

'Not exactly,' she replied.

Without hesitation, Jeffers took one hand off the wheel and slapped her hard. 'Wake up! Dammit! Pay attention! Use your mind!'

She cowered back in the seat, fighting the tears that formed instantly in the corners of her eyes. It was not so much the pain of the blow, which on the scale he'd established was relatively low, it was the suddenness of it.

She took a deep breath, struggling for control. She could hear the quaver in her voice as she spoke: 'He was saying we didn't do it . . .'

'Right! Now what else?'

'He was fixing the blame for murder on everyone but . . .'

'Right again!' Jeffers smiled.

'Now,' he said, 'isn't it easier to use your head?'

She nodded.

'Gratuitous cruelty. Delusion. If we had not been there, there would have been no battle and the child would have lived, at least a few more days, weeks, who knows. But we were there. But we didn't cause the death?'

He laughed, but not at a joke or anything humorous.

'Delusions, delusions, delusions.'

She wrote this down.

Anne Hampton thought of a dozen questions and bit back each one.

After a moment he said, 'Death is the easiest thing in the world. People think killing is hard. That's only what they want to believe. In reality it is the simplest thing around. Pick up the newspaper some morning, what do you see? Husbands kill wives. Wives kill husbands. Parents kill children. Children kill each other. Blacks kill whites. Whites kill blacks. We kill in secrecy, we kill in stealth, we kill publicly, we kill with purpose, we kill by accident. We kill with guns, knives, bombs, rifles – the obvious things. But what happens when we cut a federally subsidized grain shipment to Ethiopia? We kill, just as surely as we would had we taken a handgun and put it to the temple of some little kid with a swollen belly. Hell, if you think about it for a moment, our entire national approach to the world, to life itself, is based on the question of who we may or may not kill on any given day. And what weapons we might or might not use. Foreign policy? Hah! We should call it our death policy. Then a spokesman could get up at a nice Washington press briefing and say, "Well, the President and the cabinet and the Congress have decided today that Guatemalan Indian peasants, South African demonstrators, certain elements of the issue in Northern Ireland, both sides, mind you, and a few other sundry peoples about the world are doomed. Once again, just as I said yesterday, and the day before, and the day before that, the Russians are okay. No need for dying there." ' He stared down the highway and laughed.

'I really sound crazy.'

He glanced over at her. 'Do I scare you?'

Her heart sped as she tried to decide what the right answer would be. She shut her eyes and spoke the truth: 'Yes.'

'Well,' he said, 'I suppose that's reasonable.'

He was quiet before continuing. 'Well, politics wasn't how I wanted to start this. I mean, we can talk with more sophistication after you come to know me a little better. That's why we're heading this way.'

'Can I ask a question?' she tried timidly.

'Look,' he answered with a slight tone of irritation. 'You can always ask. I've told you that before. Please don't make me repeat things. Whether you get an answer or' – he balled one fist, then released it – 'some other response really depends on my mood.' He reached down and suddenly grabbed the muscle above her knee, pinching it painfully. She gasped. 'Remember, there are no rules. The game simply progresses, stage by stage, until it ends.'

He released her leg. It continued to burn. She wanted to rub it to try to reduce the pain, but dared not. 'Ask!' he said.

'Are we going someplace where you'll help me know you better?'

He smiled. 'Smart Boswell,' he said. 'Excellent Boswell.'

Jeffers hesitated, just to give his words a bit of impact: 'That should be obvious. That's the whole point of this little trip.' He smiled and aimed the car down the highway.

They drove on in silence.

Anne Hampton daydreamed as they swept past Mobile on the interstate. It was still early and she thought of the pleasant sensation that rising at dawn in the summer brings; a feeling of synchronization with the day. She recalled when she was a child how she enjoyed padding about the house by herself. It was time she spent in special quiet, alone with her things. Sometimes, she remembered, she would crack the door to her parents' room and watch them lie in their bed. When she was sure they wouldn't stir, she would creep across the hallway to her brother's room. He would be flung across the bedclothes, a jumble of sleep, absolutely oblivious to the world. Her brother slept late. Always. Without fail. A bomb blast wouldn't wake the little terror. It was as if her brother's body knew how important it was to store energy for the nonstop way he threw himself into life. Inwardly she smiled. When Tommy died, she thought, the entire world probably slowed, even if just a small amount, an infinitesimal measurement, readable only by the oldest, wisest scientists at the greatest universities with the newest, most exacting instruments. When I die I'll be lucky if there's a ripple on some tiny pond somewhere, or a little gust of breeze in the trees.

She blinked hard several times swiftly, to clear the thoughts from her head. My mind is filled with death, she said to herself. And why shouldn't it be? She glanced over at Jeffers, who was whistling something she couldn't recognize as he steered the car.

'Are you only going to talk about death?' she asked.

He turned toward her momentarily before shifting his gaze down the road. He smiled. 'Good Boswell,' he said. 'Be a reporter.' He paused, then continued. 'No. I'll try to talk about some other things. You raise a valid point. The trouble is' – he laughed before going on – 'a certain preoccupation with morbidity. Fatalism. Ends rather than beginnings.'

He paused again, considering. Anne Hampton scribbled down as many of his words as she could manage, then stared in despair at her handwriting. She didn't trust its legibility, and wondered suddenly, in a moment of fright, whether he would check.

Jeffers broke into a grin and laughed out loud.

'Here's a story for you. The best life-affirming story I can think of off the top of my head. I'll try to come up with some more from time to time, but this one, well, it was when I was with the Dallas paper, the *Times-Herald*, back in the mid-seventies. People used to call it the *Crimes-Herald*, but that's another story . . .

'Anyway, I was working day general-assignment, which usually meant anything from flower shows and business-page shots of captains of industry – what a silly phrase that is – to accidents and cops, and anything else that might come through the window. And we got this call, I mean, it was one of those sublime moments on a newspaper, which of course, no one ever realizes, but happens nonetheless. Guy calls in and says the damnedest thing just happened. What's that? replies the city-desk man, who's bored out of his skull. Well, the guy says, it seems like this couple was having a fight, you know, a domestic. They were getting a divorce and they were arguing over child custody and grab-bing at the baby right and left and screaming at each other, and the dude tries to snatch the baby out of his old lady's hands and whoops! Out the baby goes, right out the fourth-floor window . . .

'Well, the city-desk editor finally wakes up, because this is a helluva story and he starts yelling for me and a reporter to get going, because there's a baby been tossed out of a window and suddenly the editor realizes that the guy on the phone is trying to interrupt. Yeah, yeah, the editor says, just give me the address. You don't understand, the guy on the phone says, starting to get exasperated. What don't I understand? says the editor. The story, says the guy. Well? says the editor. The story, the guy says, after getting his breath back, is that someone caught the baby. What! says the editor. That's right, says the guy, there was this dude walking right underneath, who looks up and sees this baby come out the window . . . and damn if he didn't catch it right on the fly.'

Jeffers looked at Anne Hampton. She smiled.

'Really? I mean, he caught the baby? I can't believe . . .'

'No, no, he did. I promise . . .' Jeffers laughed. 'Fourth story. Just like a football player making a fair catch.'

'What's a fair catch?'

'That's where the guy receiving the ball can raise his arm and signal the other team that he's going to catch the ball without trying to advance it. Then they're not supposed to tackle him. It's the ultimate act of self-preservation.'

'But how . . .'

'I wish I knew.' Jeffers laughed again. 'I mean, the guy must have had incredibile presence of mind. . . . I'd guess that most people would look up and see this shape coming out the window and scurry out of the way as fast as possible. Not this guy.'

'Did you talk to him? I mean, what did he say?'

'He just said he looked up and somehow knew right away, split second, really, that it was a baby, and he circled right under the child. He'd been a center fielder on his high-school baseball team, too, which was really funny, because when he said that, everyone nodded and thought, Sure, that explains it, but of course it didn't explain anything, because baseball players don't usually get much baby-catching practice.'

'But maybe that's where he learned to catch?'

'I guess so. Football, baseball. It was a story that lent itself to sports metaphors.'

Jeffers looked over at Anne Hampton. She caught his eye and shook her head. Then she smiled and the smile widened into a grin. The two of them laughed out loud.

'That's incredible. A bit wonderful, as well . . .'

'In a way, that's what photographers do. They periodically go from one incredible to the next . . .' Jeffers hesitated. 'Better get that down,' he said, then paused while Anne Hampton scrawled some more notes on her pad. When she looked up again, Jeffers continued. 'Anyway, I can tell you that that particular assignment absolutely made my day. Hell, it made everyone's day. Made my week. Made my month, probably. I shot the guy, he had the most, I don't know, delightful, I guess, sheepish grin on his face. We were all of us laughing and giggling, reporters, photographers, television crews, passersby, neighbors, the cop on the beat, everyone. Even the kid's father, standing there in handcuffs, because the cops felt they sure as hell had to arrest *somebody* when a baby gets tossed out of a window. Funny thing was, he didn't seem to mind. Then I got a picture of the mother, too. Have you ever seen a person whose life changes so abruptly, so quickly, so many times? From terror to despair to agony to hope to incredible happiness in a couple of seconds. It was all wrapped in her eyes. An easy picture to take. Just put the baby in her arms, sit her down next to the guy who caught the child, and press the shutter button. Bingo. Instant pathos. Instant joy.'

'Unbelievable,' she said.

'Incredible,' he said.

'You're not kidding me, just trying to make me feel better?'

'No. Not a chance. That's not something I do.'

'What?'

'Try to make people feel better. It's not in the job description at all.'

'I didn't mean . . .'

He interrupted. 'I know what you meant.'

He glanced over at her and smiled. 'But it should make you feel better anyway.'

She felt an odd warmth.

'It's nice,' she said. 'It's a really nice story. It does.'

'Make sure you get it down,' he said.

She scribbed quickly in the notepad.

' . . . And the baby lived,' she wrote.

She stared at the word for a moment: lived. For a moment she wanted to cry, but she was able to stifle it.

They continued down the highway in the first benign silence she'd known for what she sensed was only hours but suddenly seemed to her to be weeks.

Gulfport slid past them as the morning sun took root. Occasionally the roadway would dip toward the Gulf of Mexico and Anne Hampton watched for the insouciant blue of the baywaters. These glimpses comforted her, as did the infrequent sight of a flight of gulls as they floated on the wind currents, just above the waves. She thought they seemed like gray and white sailboats, the way they moved with ease in conjunction with the desires and demands of nature.

It was midmorning when Jeffers said, 'Time to tank up'.

He pulled off the interstate, heading down a narrow ramp toward the first gasoline station he spotted. To Anne Hampton if seemed to be a ramshackle place; the small white clapboard attendant's building seemed to sway in the morning breeze, leaning against the solid square brick garage for assistance. Two lines of red, blue, green, and yellow pennants snapped in the wind above the pumps. They were the old-fashioned kind that gave off a ring as each gallon was pumped, not the newer, computer-driven style that was more familiar to her. It was called Ted's Dixie Gas and was empty save for three cars parked on the side by the garage. Two of the cars seemed to be derelicts, stripped and rusted, barely recognizable. The third was a cherry-red street racer, its tail end jacked up, oversized tires and chromed wheels. Someone's fantasy, she thought. Someone's time and effort and money wrapped up in small-town heroics. She stared at the car as Jeffers crunched up to the pumps, knowing that a slick-haired teenager would emerge momentarily to take their order.

'Hit the head,' Jeffers demanded.

His voice had a sudden roughness in it. She shivered.

'You know the rules, don't you?'

She nodded.

'I don't have to explain anything to you, do I?'

She shook her head. She noticed that he had the short-barreled pistol in his hand, and that he was sticking it in his belt, beneath his shirt. She stared, then turned away.

'Good,' he said. 'Makes things much easier. Now sit still while I come around to open your door.'

She waited.

'Hurry up,' he said as he swung wide the door. She looked up and saw a gangly teenager with straight dark hair sticking haphazardly out from beneath a battered, faded baseball cap, walking across the dusty station toward them.

'Fill 'er up?' he drawled. It took him almost as much

time to speak the words as it had for him to lope across the space between the garage and the pumps.

'To the top,' said Jeffers. 'Where's the ladies' room?'

'Wouldn't y'all want the men's room?' the boy replied, grinning. Anne Hampton thought suddenly that Jeffers would shoot the teenager right there and then. But instead Jeffers laughed. He made his finger into a gun and pointed it at the boy. 'Bang,' he said. 'You got me on that one. No, I meant for the lady, here.' The attendant turned his huge grin on Anne Hampton and she smiled faintly in return.

The boy pointed to the side of the building. 'Key's on the inside of the door there. The old man will show ya.' He waved at the gas station office.

Anne Hampton looked at Jeffers and he nodded.

She felt hot as she crossed the twenty feet to the station. It was as if the wind had suddenly died down, just in the space around her. She stared up at the pennants, which still flapped and twisted above her, and wondered why she could not feel the breeze. She felt dizzy and her stomach churned in quick fashion. She stepped out of the sunlight into the doorway. There was an older man, unshaven, with a greasy striped shirt on, sitting by the register, drinking a can of soda. Her eyes fastened on a sewn name above his shirt pocket. It said Leroy. 'The bathroom key?' she asked.

'Right next to you,' the man replied. 'You okay, miss? You look like yesterday's bacon left in the skillet overnight. Can I get you a cold one?'

'A what?'

'A soda.' He nodded toward a cooler.

'Uh, no. No. Yes, actually. Why, thank you, Leroy.'

'Hell, it's my brother's shirt. That good-for-nothing never did a solid day's work. I put all the grease there. I'm George. Coke?'

'That'd be fine.'

He handed her the cold can of soda and she pressed it against her forehead. He smiled. 'I like to do that, too, when the heat gets to me. Seems to get right inside your head, that way. Better with a bottle of beer, though.'

She smiled. 'How much do I owe you?' Then, suddenly,

she almost choked. She had no money. She turned quickly, searching for Jeffers.

'Hell, it's on me. Don't get to buy nothing for no pretty gals too much no more. Make the boy jealous, too.' He laughed and she joined him, her breath bursting from inside her in relief.

'I appreciate it.' She put the can in her purse.

'No matter. Where you heading?'

She choked again. Where? she asked herself. What does he want me to say?

'Louisiana,' she said. 'Just taking a little holiday.'

'Right time of year,' the attendant said. 'Even if a tad bit warm. We get a lot of folks traveling through. People ought to stay, though. Got a right fine beach and there's fine fishing. Not so famous though, as some other spots. That's the problem. It all boils down to publicity nowadays. You got to get the word out. No two ways about it.'

'Get the word out,' she said. 'That's right.'

'Got to be the right word, though.'

'True enough.'

'Like take this place,' he said. 'The boy's a right fine mechanic. Better'n his old man, for sure, though I don't let on nowdays. Give him a swelled head and all. But got no way to let folks know. They end up taking their cars to those fancy big places near the shopping malls, when, hell, we'd do a better job for half the price.'

'I bet you would.'

He laughed. 'Feeling better?'

'Yes,' she said.

'Got to get the word out. Don't make no matter what you're doing in life, fixing cars or selling burgers or fixing to fly to the moon. Publicity is what makes this nation work. Yes, ma'am. You got to tell folks what it is you got and what it is they're gonna get. You just gotta get the word out.'

He handed her the bathroom key.

'Just cleaned up this morning. Fresh soap and towels on the back of the door. You need something else, just holler.'

216

She nodded and started out the door. She turned and pointed in a quizzical way and he nodded to her and waved her around the corner.

It was cool inside the rest room, but close, and the air seemed old and tired. She quickly used the toilet, then went to the sink and splashed water on her face. She looked up in the mirror and saw herself pale and drawn. I've seen this scene a hundred times, she thought, picking up the soap bar. It's in every movie on television. She remembered Jimmy Cagney and Edmund O'Brien. 'White Heat,' she said out loud. He writes on the mirror in the gas station. She thought of Jeffers and pictured him speaking: I'm on top of the world, Ma! She wrote the word HELP on the mirror. Then she wrote, I'VE BEEN . . . what? She rubbed that out. She felt hot and her hand was shaking. Got to get the word out, she thought, mimicking in her mind the slow Southern accent of the old man. CALL POLICE she scrawled, then rubbed that out when she realized she'd written it too swiftly and it was illegible. And tell them what? She felt nauseated and gripped the sink to control herself. She looked down at her hands and pleaded with them, as if they weren't attached to her body. Be still, she prayed. Be steady.

She looked back up. This is where the heroine gets saved, she thought. The attendant comes in and calls the handsome young policeman, who saves her. It always worked that way. Every time. She rubbed the mirror clean, using quick, panicked strokes. What if it doesn't work that way? she thought. She suddenly felt angry and impatient, and she smeared soap across the mirror. The soap bar had gotten wet, and streaks of white ran down the surface. Like tears, she thought. It never happens like in, what? Fairy tales. The movies. The stories her father used to tell her when she was a child. She looked at her reflection between the soap streaks. She could see redness rimming her eyes. She shook her head in dismay and impotence and clenched her fists in anger and helplessness. No handsome prince through that door. It'll be him. He'll come in. He'll see it.

He'll kill me. And George. And the boy who fixes the cars. He'll kill all of us. One right after the other.

And then maybe the word will get out.

She heard a scraping noise outside.

Bile rose in her throat. Oh, God, she thought. He's there. The door rattled.

It's the wind, she said to herself. But she frantically wiped at the soapy residue on the mirror.

What am I doing? she asked herself. Do you want to die?

Do nothing. Go along. He hasn't hurt you yet.

That was a lie and she knew it. She argued with herself quickly. He will. He has. He's going to use you and kill you, he said it himself.

The door rattled again.

He's everywhere, she thought suddenly. The room was windowless, and she spun about, looking at the white-washed walls. He can see! she said. He knows. He knows. He knows.

Just walk out calmly and apologize, she thought.

She checked herself in the now-clean mirror as if she would see signs of betrayal on her face that he would notice. Then she turned and walked slowly back outside, thinking: I am blank inside. She returned the key to the hook by the door and turned to the gas pumps and froze in sudden and complete terror.

Jeffers was standing next to the car, talking with a state trooper. Both men were wearing large sunglasses and she couldn't see their eyes. She stopped, as if suddenly rooted.

He saw Jeffers look up and smile at her. He gave her a wave.

She couldn't move.

Jeffers waved again.

She screamed commands to her body. Walk! But she was still frozen. She forced herself to push and pull at every muscle and managed to take a step, then another. The walk across the sunlit macadam surface seemed intermi-nable. The heat seemed to build around her, and she had the odd thought that it was burning her. We're all going to die, she thought. She saw Jeffers reach under his shirt and the black revolver jump into his hand. She heard the gun's report. She saw the trooper falling back, dying, but in his own hand was his weapon and it was spitting bullets and fire. She saw the teenager and George the attendant diving for cover as the pumps suddenly exploded into flame.

She took another step and realized none of it was happening.

Jeffers waved again. 'Jump in, Annie, I just want to get these directions straight.' He turned toward the trooper. 'Now, as I get into New Orleans, the road splits and six-ten takes me downtown and four-ten heads to the coastal parks?'

'You got it,' said the trooper. He smiled at Anne Hampton and touched his hat brim. The little motion of politeness seared her insides.

'Great,' said Jeffers. 'Always like to double-check. You've been a big help.'

'My pleasure,' said the trooper. 'Have a nice day.'

He turned toward his own car and Jeffers slid down behind the wheel. At first he was quiet as he slowly accelerated out of the station past the trooper's cruiser. Then he asked in a flat, harsh voice, 'What were you and the old man jawing about?'

'I'm going to be sick,' Anne Hampton said.

'If you're sick,' Jeffers replied, his glance narrowing, but his voice taking on a flat tone better suited to a discussion of the weather or rising prices, 'everyone dies.'

She clenched her teeth and squeezed her eyes shut.

She gulped in air.

'We were talking about publicity,' she said. 'About telling the world when you've got something to sell. Like his boy's mechanical ability.'

'Publicity fuels the world,' Jeffers said. 'Just as much as Arab oil.' He looked quickly at her. She turned away and saw the roadway stretch in front of them. He was steering the car up the ramp, back toward the interstate.

'I'm okay,' she said, and she thought: I must be.

She looked over at Jeffers and saw that he seemed to have relaxed. He was smiling faintly.

'Good Boswell,' he said. 'When you feel good enough, write it all down in the notebook. Exciting, no? Especially the bit with the trooper, huh? Gets the adrenaline flowing.'

Jeffers hummed and gunned the engine. Again, she did not recognize the tune, but she hated it nonetheless.

As Douglas Jeffers drove, he daydreamed half-heartedly. Anne Hampton had grown silent beside him, staring out the window with what he thought was a desirable vacancy. He did not want her imagination moving too swiftly. She was still vulnerable to the strengths she had inside her. That she was unaware of them was typical, he thought. She could still break the spell and make some move for freedom, or perform some act that would jeopardize the trip, but her ability to do this would diminish, he knew. It already had been halved, perhaps quartered. Within a day or so, he considered, it will have evaporated save for a dangerous residue which he must always be aware of. Even the most domesticated, cowed, and docile beast will sometimes, when least expected, slash back at the threat of extinction. He resolved to be on his guard for signs of this. Whether they would ever surface he knew was problematical. For a moment he wondered whether she was aware of any of the literature of possession. Certainly, he thought, she's read John Fowles. Did she remember Rubashov and his interrogators? Should he tell her about the Stockholm Syndrome? He thought he would, perhaps a little later. Knowledge, when wielded properly and dangerously, he considered, can be used to further confuse and obfuscate the truth. It would increasingly underscore her helplessness if he told her that psychologically she was caught in a web from which she was not equipped to free herself. Deepen her despair. He looked over at her, examining her profile as she steadily searched the horizon from the car seat. He tried to see a glow of independence, smell a whiff of resolve. No, he thought, not her.

I've taken it. As I knew I would.

She has given in.

I can do with her what I please.

He almost laughed out loud, stifling the sound before it erupted, like some schoolboy who had been passed a dirty picture behind the teacher's back.

She is like clay now. I can form whatever I want. He wondered idly whether she had any inkling that her life had changed completely, that she would never be the same, nor ever be able to return to what she had once envisioned for herself.

To himself he said: No one's going home again.

He thought of the stricken look on her face when she'd spotted the trooper. It had terrified her, he thought. By tomorrow she will be so wrapped up that she will be more frightened of the police than I am. And I'm not frightened at all.

He smiled, inwardly, but with just a trace on his lips.

She's mine.

Or at least she will be within twenty-four hours.

His mind danced with possibilities. What an education she's about to get, he thought.

No harder than my own.

A memory picture crept quickly into his mind, aggressively, uninvited. He saw himself at age six, being led through the night by the druggist and his wife. He remembered how surprised he'd been at the sight of the house. It seemed to his child's eyes to be huge, imposing, and dominating. He'd been afraid, and remembered how important it had been not to let Marty see how scared he was. It was not at all like the hotel rooms and trailer parks that his mother had dragged them through. His first mother, he thought. For a moment he thought he could smell the battling odors of perfume and alcohol that came back to him whenever she entered his memory. He reached down and cracked the window, letting some air into the car, fearing that he would sicken with all the hatred that churned in his stomach.

The air cleared the memory smell away and he thought of the first look up the flight of stairs to their room. He recalled how tightly Marty had gripped his hand. It had been dark and the few lights the druggist had switched on threw odd shapes on the walls. He could not actually recall climbing the stairs, though they had. But what he remembered next was being half-led, half-pushed into the tiny room. The walls were white-washed and there were two army cots unfolded. There was a single lamp, which had no shade. There was a single window which was open, letting cold air pour into the room.

It had been bleak and sterile, he thought.

He forced himself a smile. It was not a response to pleasure, but an allowance of irony. That had been the first battleground, he thought. Marty had been exhausted and fallen instantly into sleep. But I stared at the walls. In his memory he saw the morning confrontation:

Can we put something on the walls?

No.

Why not?

You'll make a mess.

We won't. We'll be careful.

No.

Please.

Stop whining! I said no! That's it. No!

It's not like a room. It's like a prison.

I will teach you now that you're not to talk to me that way.

It had been his first beating. First of many. He thought it odd that he felt an absence of emotion when he remembered the flailing fists and staggering blows that this new father poured down on him. His mind filled with hatred, though, when he thought of how this new mother sat by so quietly. Damn her eyes! he thought abruptly. She did nothing! She sat and watched. She always sat and watched. She said nothing, did nothing.

He hesitated, as if catching a mental breath.

Damn her eyes to hell!

His memory filled again, like holding a cup beneath a spigot. He'd been shunted off to a new, strange school for the remainder of the day. That had been a horror in itself. But what he remembered best was the morning art class, where he'd seized the biggest sheet of white paper they'd had and quickly, deliberately, smeared great bands of blue and orange, red, yellow, and green across it, swiftly making a great glowing rainbow. Then he'd grabbed another paper and fashioned a steamship tossing on a wild gray sea. Then a third, and a pirate captain, with a red sash, black beard, and Jolly Roger in his hands. He'd left the paintings drying and returned that afternoon to ask the teacher if he might take them. When she approved, he took them and ran to the bathroom. Locking himself in a stall, he dropped his pants and carefully wrapped the paintings around his leg.

He remembered the stiff walk home. Why are you limping, asked his new mother. I fell at school, he said. It's nothing. Feels better already. He'd hopped up the stairs to their room, where he found Marty trying to play on the floor with an empty shoe box. He remembered his brother's smile when he'd pulled out the paintings and stuck them, with stolen school tacks, on the druggist's careful white walls. He remembered Marty's sudden wide smile and it made him grin in pleasure: A boat, his brother had cried, to take us back to Mommy!

That's been a long voyage, Jeffers thought.

One that we're still on.

He eased the car past a large truck with an engine that roared deafeningly, penetrating the silence of the car's cockpit. He saw Anne Hampton flinch at the sudden assault of sound. He swung the car back into the right lane easily as the truck disappeared behind them and continued down the roadway, forcing his mind back to an easy nothingness, as if, he thought, he could make his own mind as blank and horrible as those damned white walls, vacant, forgetting that which he'd seen, that which he'd done, and that which he still planned to do.

They swept past the outskirts of New Orleans as the early-afternoon sky started to darken and Anne Hampton saw great gray storm clouds fill the horizon. She noticed that Jeffers seemed to accelerate as the weather worsened, and when the first large raindrops splattered against the windshield, he reached for the wipers switch with a muffled curse of irritation.

She said nothing, having learned that he would speak when he wanted to. After a moment he broke the silence, proving her prudence justified.

'Damn,' he said. 'This fucking rain's going to make things difficult.'

'Why?'

'Harder to find landmarks in the rain. It's been a long time since I was here.'

'Can you tell me where we're going?'

'Yes.'

He was silent.

'Will you? But only if you want . . .'

'No,' he said, 'I'll tell you. We're heading toward a place called Terrebonne, which is a coastal parish. A little ways past a little town called Ashland. I haven't been here, since, well, since August eight, 1974. This is why anything, like the weather changing, or a new road, and God knows all the roads seem damn new, can screw me up.'

Anne Hampton looked out the car windows at the swampy marshland interspersed with pine stands and an occasional willow tree. It seemed to be a place of prehistoric terrors, and she shivered.

'It looks really wild.'

'It is. It's a fantastic place. Like another planet. Lonely. Forgotten. Isolated. I really liked it when I was here.'

For a moment then she thought that her heart stopped. Her throat closed as if someone had wrapped his hands around her neck. Her mouth went completely dry.

It's where he means to kill me, she thought.

She tried to open her lips to speak but could not.

She knew she had to fill the sudden silence, and she raced through her mind, trying to think of something to say that would fill the cockpit when all she wanted to do was scream. Finally she spoke, instantly regretting the weakness and the vapidity of her words.

'Do we have to go there?' she asked.

She thought she sounded like a whining child.

'Why not?' he replied.

'I don't know, it just seems, I don't know, out of the way.'

'That's why I selected it.'

She saw him glance over at her.

'You're not taking this down,' he said irritatedly.

She reached for the pen and notebook, but her hands were shaking again and the words on the pages were blurred and unreadable.

He hit her then, swiftly, the flat of his hand hardly seeming to move from the rim of the wheel. She gasped, dropped the pen, and using every ounce of presence of mind, instantly reached down and seized the pen again. The pain barely registered.

'I'm ready now,' she said.

'You've got to stop being so stupid,' he said.

'I'm trying.'

'Try harder.'

'I promise. I promise I will.'

'Good. There's still hope for you.'

'Thank you. It's just, just . . .'

She couldn't form the words and she gave in to the quiet that took over. She listened to the engine sounds mingling with the slap, slap of the wipers and wondered what it would feel like when it happened.

'Dumb Boswell,' Jeffers said after a few moments had passed by. He thought idly of reassuring her, letting her know that he still had plans for her. But then he thought better of it. Better to have the occasional tears than to have her gain any confidence. 'You should think less on the longevity of life and more on the quality.'

She nodded.

'Get that down,' he said. 'Aphorisms. The word according to Jeffers. Poor Douglas Jeffers' Almanac. The sayings of Douglas Jeffers. That's your job.'

'Of course,' she said.

They drove on and she felt inundated by the rain, the darkness and fear.

'You know where we're going, Boswell?' Jeffers asked.

Then he answered his own question. 'We're going to visit an old friend. Don't you think sometimes that memories are like old friends? You can summon them up much as you would reach for a telephone. They come into your consciousness and comfort you.'

'What if they're bad memories?' Anne Hampton asked.

'Good question,' he replied. 'But I think, in their own way, bad memories are as helpful as the good. You measure these things on an internal scale, your own set of weights and balances. The nice thing about bad memories is that, well, they're memories, aren't they? You're past them. On to something new . . .

'In a way, I suppose, I don't rate memories. I see them all as part of an overall picture. Like taking a long time-exposure, like one of those fancy *National Geographic* shots, you know, where the camera records the blooming of a flower or the hatching of an egg.'

She wrote that down.

Jeffers laughed coldly.

'We're heading toward where the new Douglas Jeffers hatched.' He craned forward in his seat, peering up into the enveloping gray sky. 'One of the dark places on earth,' he said. He glanced over at Anne Hampton. 'You know who wrote that?'

She shook her head.

'Actually someone wrote it, but a character said it. Who?'

He snorted, almost with humor.

'You're an English lit major, c'mon. Can't let some battered old newshound outquote you. Think!'

She raced through her memory.

'Shakespeare?'

He laughed. 'Too obvious. Modern.'

'Melville?'

'Good guess. Closer.'

'Faulkner? No, too short . . . uh, Hemingway?'

'Think of the sea.'

'Conrad!'

Jeffers laughed and she joined him.

After a minute she asked, 'Why are we going to one of the dark places on earth?'

'Because,' Jeffers said, matter-of-factly, 'that's where I discovered my heart.'

They drove on in quiet. Anne Hampton saw Jeffers' eyes glint when he spotted an exit sign for a rural route. 'I'll be damned,' he said. 'That's the road.' He swung the car from the highway and suddenly she realized they were on a narrow secondary road, lined with large trees that seemed to block the sky and that parted in the wind to let sheets of rain spatter down. They swooped around one twist in the highway and she felt the car slide slightly, the back tires spinning momentarily, squealing for purchase on the rain-slicked highway, an unsettling feeling, reminding her that they were careening down the roadway, just barely under control.

'Love is pain,' Jeffers said.

He waited a moment.

'When I was little, I used to hear my mother's men. They would stumble and clomp about making more noise trying to be careful than they would have if they'd just acted normally. It would be late at night and she would assume I was asleep. I would keep my eyes closed tight. There was a little red light in the room, so I could just crack my lids apart and see. I remember how she would groan and complain and finally cry out in pain. I never forgot . . .

'It seems very simple, doesn't it? The more love. The more hurt. Sounds like some doo-wop song from the fifties, huh?' He crooned, 'You always love the one you hurt . . .'

He looked over at Anne Hampton.

Then he sang again: 'You always kill the one you love . . .'

Then he turned away and concentrated on the road.

'We're getting closer,' he said.

But she could hardly hear him, she was suddenly so wrapped in fear.

They continued cutting between the stands of trees,

heading farther into the swampy darkness. She could see no signs of life save the occasional modest roadside home standing white against the increasing gray of the day. As they drove, she could see more of the sky, filling with even darker clouds, and she knew they were approaching the coast. Jeffers remained silent, concentrating, she hoped, on the highway, staring ahead in a sullen, fixed fashion. She could see great strikes of lightning in the distance, flashes that were flung across the sky, followed by cannon rumbles of thunder that penetrated the car. The rain had increased in volume, pelting the car, flooding the windshield between swipes of the wipers. She prayed they would not have to get out of the car, but knew they would. And then she thought it would probably make no difference, getting wet. Still, she had the odd idea that she didn't want to shiver from the rain onslaught, to seem wet, bedraggled, and pathetic when it happened.

Jeffers turned the car again, and they were on an even smaller road, even more deserted.

She stayed silent, trying to think of home, of her mother, her father, her friends, of the sun and the summer that seemed to have disappeared in the gray flood of rain and wind.

Jeffers turned again, and the road became bumpy. It was unpaved. He swore. 'We'll get stuck if we go down there. Hell, it's only a half mile or so . . .'

He pulled to a grassy spot and stopped the car.

She hated the sudden disappearance of the engine noise. The silence seemed to envelop her.

'Douglas Jeffers thinks of everything,' he said. He reached into the back seat and pulled out a small duffle bag. He unzipped it swiftly, then shoved a bright yellow poncho at her. Then he pulled out a dark-green set of rain pants and coat. 'The best from L. L. Bean,' he said. 'A big part of photography is anticipating future discomfort. I hope that fits. Use the hood.'

He helped her pull the poncho on. Then he slid into the rainsuit. 'All right,' he said. 'Let's go.'

There was a clap of thunder and a new sheet of rain hit

the car. Jeffers smiled and flung himself through the door. In a second Anne Hampton's door was pulled open. She knew better than to hesitate.

The force of the rain seemed to snatch her breath, and for an instant she stood, disoriented, stunned by the strength of the wind. She felt Jeffers' hand grip her arm with familiar strength, and she let herself be pulled along. The road was sandy and infirm, and she slid in her sneakers, half-pushed by Jeffers. For an instant she wished that she could at least die somewhere dry and familiar, that this was especially unfair. She could not see him, it seemed to her that one instant he stood behind her, the next he was at her side, the next pulling her along from in front. She tried to formulate theorems and conclusions in her mind: Why would he give me a poncho and then kill me? she thought. But what frightened her most was the rain-drenched realization that assigning logic to anything that was happening to her was a mistake. She closed her eyes against the lightning and rain and started to mumble snatches of prayers to herself, as each foot hit the ground, trying to find some comfort in long-forgotten rhythms: 'Our Father, who art in heaven, Hallowed be thy Name . . .' Then: 'Forgive us our trepasses, As we forgive those who trespass against us . . .' Jeffers pushed her a bit harder and she gasped. 'Yea, though I walk through the shadow of the valley of death I shall fear no evil . . .'

'Come on!' Jeffers said. 'Should be right ahead.'

'Hail Mary, full of grace, blessed be the fruit of your womb. Hail Mary, full of grace, Hail Mary, full of grace, Hail Mary, full of grace . . .'

'Come on, dammit! Let's go!'

'Hail Mary, hail Mary, hail Mary, fullofgrace, fullofgrace, fullofgrace, Hail Mary . . .' She shut her eyes as she walked forward, trying to think about anything other than the rain, the wind, and the pressure of Douglas Jeffers' grip on her arm. She wondered if he would give her a blindfold and a cigarette like some military execution. Her tears mingled freely with the rain striking her face.

Then, suddenly, she put her right foot down and the

sandy soil beneath it gave way, and she slipped forward, falling. She let out an involuntary 'Ouch!' as she fell, more a sound of some odd indignation than any pain. Then she turned back toward Jeffers, who was standing, shading his eyes as if against the sun, peering about him.

'Damn!' he said.

He kicked the sandy dirt.

'Shit! Shit! Shit!'

He stomped about in a small circle, peering into the distance. He punched the air angrily. 'Damn! Damn! Damn!'

She dared not say anything.

Then he turned and looked at her.

She thought she could not breathe.

Then he laughed. His laughter grew, rising up in the wind currents and seeming to mix with the wind and thunder.

He stood above her, laughing for several moments.

'Well,' he said finally, after rubbing his eyes. 'Well, what a screw-up. We're in the wrong place. I told you it's been years . . . There ought to be a big, I mean a really big, willow down there and there isn't. I must have taken the wrong road.'

He helped her to her feet.

'Back to the car,' he said.

'That's all?' she asked. She regretted it instantly.

But Jeffers seemed not to notice. 'That's it,' he said. He drew an arm around her shoulders and helped walk her back to the vehicle.

The closeness of the car cockpit seemed comforting to her. Jeffers gave her a small towel and both of them tried to dry themselves as best as possible. Jeffers continued laughing, mildly, as if terribly amused. He started the car and they headed back to the highway.

'You wouldn't think a person like me would screw up, would you?'

'No,' she replied.

'I mean,' he said, grinning. 'I pride myself on thinking

of just about every damn thing. Don't leave anything to chance. Just goes to show, the best-laid plans . . .'

He smiled. 'What's funny is that this place is really important to me. At least the memory of it is.'

He smiled and drove the car slowly.

'Well, too many years, I guess. Too many other roads.'

'I still don't know what we were looking for,' she said.

He hesitated, then shrugged. 'My first date,' he said. 'My first real love.'

'A girl?'

'Of course.'

He paused again.

'Down one of these damn dirt roads that all look the same,' he said, 'there's a shady willow tree, set back aways in some scrub brush . . .'

She nodded.

'And that's where I buried her.'

He spoke these words with a sudden, unexpected, total harshness. They plunged into Anne Hampton's heart.

She felt a torrent of nausea overcome her and she clenched her teeth and waved wildly at Jeffers. He stopped the car, understanding instantly, threw open his door, and suddenly dragged her across the center console, across his lap, holding her head in the rain, where she was completely, violently sick.

Night closed around them as they drove back toward New Orleans. They had spent the remainder of the afternoon in damp silence, but Jeffers' mind had filled with memories. He was trying to remember the girl's name. He knew it was Southern, like Billie Jo or Bobbi Jo, and he remembered her silver-spangled dress, cut too short and too tight, and which left little doubt as to what her profession was. He'd picked her up, trying to contain himself, knowing what he was going to do, acting nonchalant and flashing a wad of cash. She had complained, at first, when he started driving toward the outskirts of the city, but he remembered taking the extra twenty-dollar bill and tucking it into her cleavage and telling her he'd make it worth her effort. She had babbled on, the singsong accent and vapidity of her words disrupting the essence of his thoughts, and so, at the first available deserted location, he'd stopped the car, turned to her, and, as she lay back, closing her eyes, cold-cocked her. And then he had headed toward the location picked from a map, with its bastardized French name: the good earth. It had been easy to drive into the swampy darkness alone with his thoughts. It made no difference to him whether she was awake or not. It was the act that intrigued him.

'She was a prostitute,' he said.

Anne Hampton nodded glumly.

'What life had she that she needed so badly?' he asked angrily.

She didn't respond.

'You're filled with silly antiquated ideas about right and wrong and morality,' he said.

'You don't understand,' he continued after a momentary silence. 'She was born to die. I was born to kill. It was simply a matter of finding one another.'

She turned toward him and started to say something but stopped.

He spoke for her: 'You want to say it's wrong to take a life, right?'

She nodded.

'So maybe it is. What difference does it make?'

She couldn't reply.

'I'll tell you: it makes none.'

He looked at her again.

'Governments kill for policy. I kill for pleasure. We're not all that goddamn different.'

'It's not that easy,' she said. 'It can't be.'

'No? You think it's hard to kill? You think it's so damn hard? Okay,' he said. 'Okay, goddammit. Okay.'

The rain had lessened to a drizzle, but it made the headlights from the car streak through the night blackness. New Orleans glowed in front of them, and Jeffers accelerated the car toward the lights. He said nothing as they slid into the city, letting the late-night shadows from the high-intensity vapor lamps crease the darkness. She felt no comfort in the city, no more than she felt in the swamps, and she suddenly realized that to a person like Jeffers they were the same. She looked at Jeffers, at the set to his face and jaw, and felt her stomach churn.

They meandered up and down the city streets. Jeffers peered through the windows, apparently looking for something, but she was unaware what. Suddenly he punched the brakes and steered to the sidewalk.

'You think it's so damn hard,' he said angrily. 'It isn't.'

He searched up and down the street, then reached down into his weapon bag and came up with the short-barreled revolver. He pushed it under her nose. 'Hard? Watch. Roll down your window.' She complied and the car immediately filled with damp, sticky humidity. She shivered. She did not know what was happening. Jeffers exited the car and walked around to her side. He bent down to the window. 'Watch carefully,' he said. She nodded.

He stepped away from the curb and she looked and saw a shape huddled in a dark building entranceway. She saw Jeffers look up and down the street again, then stride across the sidewalk.

Jeffers poked at the derelict with his foot.

'Wake-up, old-timer,' he said.

The man raised a grizzled head, still stuporous.

Jeffers turned and looked back at Anne Hampton. She saw that the man was bearded, with a benign hoary curiosity, not angry at being awakened, only surprised. Her eyes met Jeffers' and he looked hard at her. She felt as if she was caught in an inexplicable downdraft, and that she was tumbling wildly through the air, driven down by some great invisible force. She saw Jeffers turn back to the derelict, who seemed to be trying to find some words from his lost past to form into a question.

'Good night, old fellow. Sorry it had to be like this,' Jeffers said.

He leaned down abruptly and in a single fluid motion stuck the gun barrel into the man's slightly gaping mouth. Jeffers raised his left hand to shield himself from any blowback.

Then he pulled the trigger.

There was a single muffled crack and the man seemed to jump, just once, then slump back as if returning to sleep.

Anne Hampton opened her mouth to scream, but could not.

Jeffers stepped away, glanced down the street again, and returned swiftly to the car. They pulled away from the curb slowly, turning at the corner, then again, and again, and again, weaving their way through the darkness in complete solitude.

'Roll up your window,' Jeffers said.

Her hand shook on the handle. Her breath came in short spasmodic bursts. She let small whimpering noises emerge instead of words.

'You see how easy it is,' Jeffers said.

He looked over at her.

'It's your fault,' he said.

He paused.

'If you hadn't challenged me, then I wouldn't have had to do such a despicable thing.'

He fixed her with a quick, sharp glance.

'It was your fault. Your fault completely. It was just as if you had taken the gun yourself and pulled the trigger. It was just like you murdered that man. Snuffed out a life. See? Now you're just like me. Do you understand that? Do you understand, killer?'

Anne Hampton nodded behind tears.

'How does it feel, killer?'

She could not find words and he did not press her.

They drove into the expanse of night.

Disbelief

12

Martin Jeffers hurried through C ward, white coat-tails flapping behind him. He barely acknowledged the patients who shuffled awkwardly out of his path, parting like innocent animals meandering about a barnyard, making way for one with purpose. He managed to nod at the patients he knew, who greeted him with the usual assortment of stares, smiles, snarls, averted looks and the occasional curse that was the day-to-day standard of the locked wards. He knew that his swift pace would cause some conversation behind his back; it was unavoidable. In a world reflecting the constancy of routine, any behavior that spoke of some external need or force was cause for discussion, debate, and unwavering curiosity.

His own sense of intrigue ran equally unchecked. As he hurried along, he speculated shamelessly about the arrival of the homicide detective; considering as he reviewed the membership of the Lost Boys, trying to think which one might have mentioned being in Miami within the past few years, which member of the group might have been oddly reluctant to talk about some recent event. In a gathering that devoted much of its energies to concealment, Jeffers had become expert at recognizing the hidden or the taboo. He swiftly searched his memory but was unable to come up with an instant answer. He recognized the sense of sudden excitement in himself; there was something compelling about the phrase 'homicide detective' that carried with it a weight of mystery and fascination. He tried to form a mental picture of a woman investigating a murder, and thought she must be someone frumpy, hard-edged, and purposeful. He wondered why he thought the idea of investigating death to be a masculine province; as if the nature of bloodied and shattered bodies was somehow inherently male, a violation belonging, in an odd way, to the arena of poker parties or locker rooms.

His mind filled with images of sudden, violent death. He was struck with the quick portrait of his brother, picturing him in bush jacket and khakis, ready for one of his frequent travels to some war, disaster, or other representation of man's folly.

He thought of his brother's photographs from Saigon, Beirut, and Central America. A photo of his brother's leaped out at him, a shot he'd seen in one of the national newsweeklies. It had been of another photographer, standing in the midst of a group of bodies at Jonestown, Guyana. The jungle greens and rich browns had formed a curtainlike backdrop for the man, who stood out in odd incongruity to the creeping dense growth behind him. The photographer had a red bandanna over his nose and mouth. It took just a moment to stare at the picture and realize that it was protection against the stench from the bodies swollen by sun and death. The photographer looked almost like some child's idea of an old Western desperado, in jeans, boots, and denim shirt. In the photographer's hand, though, instead of a six-gun had been a camera. And in the man's eyes had been confusion and a kind of world-weary sorrow. Douglas Jeffers' shot had caught his competitor at a moment of indecision, as if overwhelmed by the litter of suicide, not quite knowing what horrific image to plunder next. It was a perfect vision, Martin Jeffers had thought when he'd first seen it and now when he recalled it: that of a civilized man, standing in a prehistoric world, trying to comprehend behavior belonging to the world of animals, seeking to capture it for the consumption and fascination of a society that is perhaps less safe from aberration than it likes to think.

Jeffers hurried on, thinking of how many of his brother's pictures were of death. He realized they were all individually fascinating, in their own way. We are forever searching, he thought, to understand people's behavior and the act that frightens all of us the most is murder.

But what is more common? he wondered.

And are we not all capable?

Now he sounded like his brother talking, Jeffers thought. He shook his head and listened to the squeaking sound his shoes made on the corridor's polished linoleum floor. Well, some of us are a hell of a lot more capable than others. The faces of the Lost Boys flashed into his head.

That a detective would come to visit was not unusual. He recalled a number of occasions in the past few years when he'd received a similar summons and been brought face-to-face with some dark-eyed, monosyllabic man who'd asked increasingly pointed questions about one or another of the members of the therapy group. Of course, his ability to assist had been severely limited by medical ethics and the concept of patient confidentiality. He remembered one detective, particularly persistent, who, after a frustrating conversation with Jeffers, had stared at him angrily for a long minute, then asked: Does the man have a roommate? No, Jeffers had replied. Does he hang out with anyone in particular? Well, yes, Jeffers remembered saying, he has one friend. Well, said the detective, let me talk to that man.

Jeffers recalled the way the detective had sat across from the compatriot of this one suspect in some forgotten crime. The detective had been direct, forceful, but never overtly aggressive. Jeffers remembered thinking he should study the detective's approach, that there were some moments in the therapeutic process when it might be effective. He was impressed that within an hour the detective had had all the information he needed from the man, who was all too ready to sell his friend's life for the promise of a reduction in his own term. Jeffers did not resent it. Ultimately, it was the way things worked in the world occupied by the Lost Boys, a place of trade offs, deals and lies.

Treachery as a way of life. Commonplace. Routine. He was struck with the idea that life is no more than a constant series of small betrayals, picayune lies, a constancy of compromise and rationalization.

He wondered again about the woman detective. She complicates things. So much of the work he did with the Lost Boys was to restore some vision of females as individuals, to re-create for them a picture of the opposite sex not dependent on the hatred they all felt. The idea that one of their potential victims would come now to stalk one of their number, that was both explosive and terrifying, as if one of their deepest and most inarticulate fears had risen from some nightmare and knocked on the door to the day room.

It will give us plenty to talk about, he thought. This was part of the challenge of the work: to create some therapeutic value out of the conjunction of memory and day-to-day life.

Maybe I'll ask her to come along to a session, he thought. That'd scare her. She'd want to arrest all of them.

And it would scare the bejesus out of the Lost Boys. They've been all too complacent lately, anyway. She could provide a necessary infusion of reality. It would shake things up, help focus the sessions, help get things back on track.

He grinned at the idea and knocked loudly on the C ward door for the attendant to let him pass. The door creaked as it opened, and Jeffers thought for a moment that everything inside the old hospital creaked and complained at use. He thanked the attendant, who stood sullenly as he swept through. Jeffers hurried down the corridor and was instantly in the administration wing of the hospital. The offices were nicer, the paint fresher, the sunlight unscarred by dirty crosshatched wire bars on the windows.

He opened the door to the administrator's office. Dr Harrison's secretary looked up and pointed at the inner office in the suite, jerking her thumb like a hitchhiker. 'They're in there, waiting for you,' she said. 'Which one do you think she wants?'

'In a way, probably all of them,' Jeffers replied. It was a small joke, and the secretary laughed as she waved him toward the door.

Jeffers entered the inner office. First he saw Dr Harrison, who stood up slowly from his seat behind a great brown desk. He was an older man, gray-haired, too sensitive for the peremptory work of a state mental hospital, too old and tired to try to strike out on his own. Jeffers liked him immensely, despite his shortcomings as an administrator. Dr Harrison nodded at Jeffers, then, with his eyes, motioned toward the other person, who was rising out of a chair.

Jeffers barely had time to assess the woman. That she was close to his own age, he perceived immediately. Then he caught a glimpse of dark brown hair, a conservative but stylish silk dress and slender figure, before he was fixed by the detective's eyes. They seemed to him to be black and staring rigidly at him. The usual male assessment of whether she was attractive or not was obliterated by the singular force of her glare. He had the disquieting sensation that he was being measured by an executioner, who with expert eye was calculating just how hard a blow with the ax would fell his head. He was immediately uncomfortable and stammered:

'I'm Doctor Jeffers. How can I help you, detective . . .'

The words simply froze in the air.

His own hand, extended in greeting, hung momentarily before she raised her own in reluctant acknowledgment. Her grip was firm, perhaps too much so. She released his hand and he let it drop and the room was filled with a solid silence that Jeffers thought was like a fog bank rolling across the ocean. A cold, dampened moment passed, then another, as her eyes held to his, unblinking.

Then she spoke in a voice all the more terrifying for the control he thought she wrapped around every word:

'Where is your brother?'

She damned herself instantly when she saw the mixture of shock and confusion race across his face. It had been unavoidable, she knew. As she had driven toward the hospital earlier that day, she had considered hundreds of approaches, dozens of different opening gambits, knowing all along, however, that when she confronted Susan's murderer's brother that there would be only one question that meant anything to her, and that she would be power-

239

less to contain it. In Detective Mercedes Barren's mind, the question was radioactive, glowing, permanent. She did not doubt that she would get the right reply; when you are willing to spend forever searching for one answer, eventually, inevitably, it arrives.

And when it arrives, she had thought, I will be ready.

A part of her, blissfully optimistic, had hoped it would be obtained easily. She did not trust this optimism, but she knew that a frontal assault often produces a quick, unplanned response, a blurted-out 'Why, he's in . . .' and the name of some city or town, before the forces of caution took over, with the invariable follow: 'Why do you want to know?' She saw the brother's mouth open, and his lips start to form a response, and she leaned forward slightly, expectedly, knowing immediately that she showed too much eagerness. Then, just as quickly, he slapped his mouth shut tight, and her own hard stare was met by an equally cool eye.

Damn, she thought again. It won't be easy.

Damn, damn, damn.

In that moment she hated him almost as much as she hated the man she hunted. Flesh and blood, she thought. He's the smallest step away.

She saw the brother swallow hard and glance over at the hospital director as if to buy a few moments of precious time to sort out what she knew must be a torrent of emotions. She sensed in that brief half-light of time that he used the seconds to order himself, coolly, professionally. She thought: He must be used to the unexpected. It must be part of his daily existence. He knows how to handle it. In a moment he returned his eyes to hers and met her silence with his own. Then, without taking his glance from her, he slowly pulled up a chair, and, carefully, as if unwilling to break the electrical connection formed in the small room, sat down. He deliberately crossed his legs, and with a delicate, easy gesture, as if he had not a care or concern in the entire world, motioned her back to her chair, like a teacher to an overanxious, overeager student.

Damn, she thought again. I almost had him.

And now he's almost got me, she thought.

She sat down across from the murderer's brother.

Martin Jeffers worked hard to affect an air of interested nonchalance, much as he would show when a patient blurted out some confession to one horror or another. Inwardly, however, he felt his throat constrict tightly, as if clutched by another's hands, and the little hairs on the back of his neck rose. He could feel the wretched sudden stickiness of sweat beneath his arms and on his palms, but he dared not rub them on his pants.

He was awash in nightmare.

He would not put image to question in his mind; he focused solely on her request, refusing to engage in any dangerous extrapolation. She wants Doug! he thought. Then: I knew it! Then: But why do you know it? He fought against all the ideas that slid unbidden into his imagination: childhood fears, adult concerns.

He wanted desperately to grab hold of something, as if something solid could help steady the rocking sensation within his mind. But he knew, too, that the detective would notice, and he quickly forced everything, from his terror to his curiosity, aside, thinking: Find out. Give up nothing, but find out.

He took a deep breath. It helped.

He crossed his legs, shifting in the chair to a relaxed, comfortable position.

He reached down and adjusted one of his socks.

He put his hand to his breast pocket and removed a pen and a small notepad. He tapped the pen point against the paper several times in slow succession. Then he looked up, and, mustering all the falseness and lies he could, smiled at the detective.

'I'm sorry, detective, I didn't catch your name . . .'

'Mercedes Barren.'

He wrote that down, feeling the act of scratching word to a page steady him.

'And what organization . . .'

'City of Miami police.'

'Ahh, right,' he continued writing. 'I've never been to

Miami. Always wanted to go, though. Palm trees, you know, sunshine and beaches. Warm all the time. It sounds nice. But I've never made it down there.'

'Your brother has.'

'Really? I don't think so, but then, he's hard to keep up with. And of course there's always a lot of news down in Miami. Riots, boatlifts, refugees, all that sort of thing. So, I guess, maybe. And he's been, well, sometimes it seems like he's been everywhere. Globe-trotter is what they call it.'

'He was there last year. In September for a football game.'

'For a football game? You know, I don't think he cares that much for sports . . .'

'He was assigned to get a picture of a quarterback.'

'Oh, you mean on business? Well, that sounds possible . . .'

Jeffers hesitated. He let his eyes wander about the office for a moment, gathering himself. He thought for a moment that his performance was probably not fooling the detective at all. He looked over at her and saw that she had not moved, not even a muscle. She's wrapped tight, he thought. Very tight. Instantly he wondered why. Most detectives want to schmooze, regardless of how tense the situation is. Concentrate on the question, he thought. He felt better; still wary, still in some undefined and vaporish danger, but better nonetheless.

'But what has a football game got to do with . . .'

'The homicide of a young woman. Susan Lewis.'

'Oh, I see,' Martin Jeffers said, but of course he knew he saw nothing. He wrote down the name and month on his pad. Then he continued:

'You know, detective, you're really getting way ahead of me. What could you possibly want with my brother?'

Revenge! screamed Mercedes Barren's head, but she kept the word to herself. She took her own deep breath, sitting back in her chair and, before replying, she took out her own notebook and her pen. I can play, she thought. And I will win.

'You're quite right, doctor. I'm getting way ahead of myself.' She spoke in a carefully modulated tone, affecting some boredom, trying to rein in her intensity. She even managed a smallish smile and an offhand nod of the head. 'I'm investigating a homicide that occurred last fall. September eighth, to be exact. We have reason to believe your brother may be a material witness. He might even have photographs of the crime which could help us.'

She thought the use of the royal plural particularly effective. She was pleased with the way she'd phrased her response, especially the guess about photos. It would give the impression that Douglas Jeffers could help the police. Perhaps it would appeal to the brother's sense of civic duty. If he had any. She watched the doctor's face for any sign of knowledge or suspicion. He seemed to be weighing every word carefully, she realized. She cursed inwardly again. Try to hit his emotions, she thought. That will open him up. But before she had a chance to continue, he asked a question.

'Well, I still don't understand. Doug never mentioned anything like that to me. Perhaps you could explain a bit more?'

She didn't.

'You're close to your brother?'

'Well, all brothers are close to one degree or another, detective. You must have family and know that.'

A nonanswer, she thought.

'When was the last time you saw him?'

'Well, it's been years since we had what I would call a real visit . . .'

Dr Harrison interrupted: 'Marty, didn't he come to visit just the other week?'

Jeffers wished he could glare at his friend to shut him up, but realized how dangerous that would be. He was trying as hard as possible to understand what the detective was driving at. He trusted nothing she said, not the crocodile smile and sudden easy manner, knowing only with the certitude that comes of a lifetime of fears that his brother was in some kind of trouble and he would be damned if he would add to it.

'Why, that's right, Jim, but he only stopped by for a quick lunch before heading off. It wasn't much of a visit, and it was the first time in years that I'd seen him. Hardly seems to me that that's what the detective is interested in.'

'But he said where he was going?' Detective Barren asked.

Martin Jeffers was filled with machine-gun memories of his brother's cryptic description of his vacation plans. He hesitated, thinking: What did he say? What did he mean? Jeffers looked up and saw that the intensity had returned to the detective's eyes.

'Not that I recall,' Jeffers replied quickly. He was instantly angry with himself for rushing the words out.

The room was briefly silent.

Mercedes Barren smiled. She didn't believe this denial for a second.

There was another pause, then Jeffers added his own question: 'Certainly, detective, you've been to his photo agency? Didn't they provide you with the information you need? I know they try to keep close tabs on the whereabouts of all their staffers. Even when they're tromping about in some jungle somewhere with some guerrilla army . . .'

'They didn't know . . .' Detective Barren started, then stopped in mid-sentence. Idiot! she thought. Give out nothing! She bristled as she saw the murderer's brother absorb the words. She tried to recoup: 'They couldn't be exact. But they suggested I contact you, which is why I'm here.'

She's fishing, thought Martin Jeffers. But how much?

'You know, detective, this is very confusing for me. You come in here asking to see my brother, whom I haven't really had much contact with for .years, to question him about some unspecified crime. You don't describe at all what the crime is, or what you think his knowledge about it might be. You imply that it's important that you contact him right away, but without making an explanation why.

244

I just don't know, detective. I don't think we've gotten this off on the right foot at all. Not at all. I mean, I want to co-operate with the authorities as much as possible, but I just don't understand.'

'I'm sorry, doctor. I can't give out confidential information.'

That was lame and she knew it. She knew what his answer would be.

'No? Well, I'm sorry, too.'

Stonewall me, stonewall you, he thought.

They stared at each other, once again in silence.

Detective Barren suddenly wanted to scream. She was filled with pain. I've blown it, she thought. I'm close, and I've blown it. He's got a passport and money and a brother that's going to protect him without knowing what he's done and is going to tell him that someone's looking for him and he'll be gone, just like that.

Martin Jeffers wanted to get out of the room as quickly as possible. Something is terribly wrong, he thought. He needed to sort it out, and yet realized instantly that he didn't know enough even to begin a process of understanding. He realized then that he would need to talk to the detective and he wondered how to get into a dominant position, receiving information without imparting any. He thought of his friends, the psychoanalysts. They'd know, he thought. Get her on the couch and sit down behind her head. He almost laughed.

'Is something amusing?' asked Detective Barren.

'No, no, just an odd thought,' replied Jeffers.

'I could use a joke,' she said bitterly. 'Why not share it?'

'I'm sorry,' Jeffers replied. 'I didn't mean to make light of . . .'

She interrupted. 'Of course not.'

He could tell she didn't believe him. At that moment Jeffers looked directly at her eyes and realized that there was more at stake. He could not precisely say why he knew this. Perhaps it was the angle of her body, the tilt to her head, the intensity of her eyes. He was almost taken aback by the forcefulness she emanated.

This, he thought, is a dangerous woman.

She was filled with loathing at that moment. He knows something, she thought, something greater than simply where his brother is. He knows something about his brother that he won't put words to. So he hides behind cleverness and all that phony psychiatric technique.

It will do him no good, she thought. None at all.

She saw Jeffers look down at his watch, then up at Dr Harrison. She knew right away what was coming.

'Jim, I've got patients scheduled all afternoon . . .'

She spoke before the hospital administrator could.

'When do you finish?'

'I'm off at five,' he said.

'Shall I meet you in your office or would you prefer to go to your home? Or a restaurant somewhere?'

She presented no other options.

'Do you think it will take long?' he asked.

She smiled, but felt no humor. He's damn clever, she thought.

'Well, that kind of depends on you.'

He smiled. Fencing, he thought. Thrust and parry.

'I still don't see how I can help, but why don't you meet me in my office a little after five and we'll see if we can't straighten all this out quickly.'

'I'll be there.'

They both stood and shook hands.

'Don't be late,' he said.

'I never am,' she replied.

Martin Jeffers closed the thick door tightly behind him and looked about his office, as if expecting to see something that would explain the tangle of feelings in which he was trapped. He felt as if he were on the edge of some moment of panic, about to do something irrational, flooded with visions of his brother. He thought: He has a streak of meanness, that I know. He remembered a neighborhood boy once, filled with taunting and obscenities, who always seemed to get under Doug's skin. It would be a fair fight – they were both about the same size – all the children on the block agreed about that. But it hadn't been. Doug had tripped the boy in a moment, flipping his suddenly helpless adversary onto his back like an upside-down turtle, and proceeded to whale away with his fists at the screaming boy. Jeffers had never seen rage like that, so potent, so unbridled. A killer's anger, he thought. Then he frowned: Don't be ridiculous. He'd rarely seen Doug lose control again. Of course the druggist father had slapped Doug hard, but that was to be expected. A beating for a beating.

He looked about him and thought: Don't be a damn idiot. Don't hypothesize. Don't judge. Don't guess.

Perhaps she was telling the truth: a material witness, that's what she said.

He swiftly pictured the detective's eyes. Not a chance, he thought.

He sat down heavily in his desk chair and swiveled it toward the window. He could see fragments of sunlight as they probed the stands of tall trees that marked the hospital grounds, throwing shadows and light on the well-kept lawns. It was supposed to look more like a campus, as if that would somehow hide the reality of the hospital. He watched as a man in the distance rode across a grassy area on a tractor-mower. For a moment he imagined he could smell the sweetness of new-mown grass. The nice thing about state mental hospitals, Jeffers said to himself, is that externally they are well maintained. It's only inside that one sees the paint peeling, as if steamed away from the walls by unhappy madness. It is the same with people.

He turned away from the window and asked himself: Why are you so quick to believe the worst about your brother? Then he answered the question unscientifically. Because he scares me. He has always scared me. He has always been wonderful and terrifying at the same time.

What has he done?

Jeffers shook the idea from his head. 'All right,' he said out loud. 'All right. Let's see what we can learn.'

He picked up the telephone and dialed the nurse attendants on three different floors. With each, he canceled the afternoon appointments of three patients, directing them to go to each man and tell them that he was called away on urgent personal business. He wished he could come up with some better euphemism at short notice, realizing that rumors and suspicions would fly unchecked about the ward. He shrugged. Then he slipped out of his white hospital coat and seized his tan sportsjacket from a hook on the back of the door.

Martin Jeffers locked the door to his office and quickly headed down a back flight of stairs toward the physician's parking lot.

Detective Mercedes Barren switched the air conditioner in the rental car up to full blast and glanced at her watch. This is not a real surveillance, she thought with irritation. She eyed the front door of the hospital. And even if he did come out, what good would following him do? She answered her own question: You never know until you try. She waited, shifting uncomfortably, trying to get out of the sunlight that poured through the windshield of the car. She shifted her glance to the cars lined up in the physicians' parking lot, which was clearly marked with a large sign. There wasn't a Cadillac among the bunch, she realized, which said something about the difference between the private sector and public health.

She was not totally displeased with the way the initial meeting had gone. What she was mainly concerned about was that the murderer's brother would panic and try to reach Douglas Jeffers immediately. But she guessed he would not. He would certainly wait until after the meeting they'd arranged. He would be coy and evasive, trying to probe her for information. He is the younger brother, she thought to herself. He'll need to be more sure of himself before calling.

She closed her eyes and felt sweat form on her lips. The moist salty taste reminded her of easy summer days. She wondered how many times she and John Barren had driven within a few miles of Trenton Psychiatric Hospital. Often, she thought. It was odd to be so close to home. She remembered driving alongside the Delaware River as the hot sun picked its way through the leafy overhanging branches, heading toward some game or party, lighthearted, surrounded by friends, curled under the expansive right wing of her boyfriend.

The pleasurable memory evaporated in the midday sun. I'm alone now, she thought.

If you need comforting, she said to herself, then do it yourself. She hardened her heart and set her face, staring out through the glare of the sun against the car windshield.

Suddenly she stiffened.

She saw the murderer's brother moving quickly through her line of sight, toward his car. She thought: I'll be damned. He's making a move.

She waited while he crawled behind the wheel, started the engine, and pulled out of the lot. She stifled the desire to hurry, to latch on to him instantly, leechlike. Instead she bided her time, pulling out well after he'd exited, following him carefully, keeping him just at the edge of her vision.

Martin Jeffers figured that the detective was somewhere behind him, but paid it no heed. If she wants to waste her time he thought, she's welcome. He knew he could lose her at any point in the labyrinthine downtown Trenton streets. It was something he planned to do at some moment when it would not seem so obvious.

He paralleled the Delaware River, glancing over at it every so often. It seemed dark and dangerous to him; there were rapids that swept white water over rock points. He turned away, and in the distance caught a glimpse of the shining golden dome of the statehouse. He maneuvered his car through traffic, winding away from the river, cutting between the steady gray block office buildings that housed various branches of state government. He turned onto State Street, which was lined with trees and brownstone buildings on one side, across from the grassy lawns and marble entrance to the statehouse. There was a free meter just down the street from where he wanted to go, and he parked the car quickly. He checked the rearview mirror for some sight of the detective. He did not see her, but again he figured she was back there. He shrugged to himself, locked the car, and headed into the main entrance of the statehouse.

Inside there was a huge state seal inlaid on the floor. It was cool, slightly dark, with a touch of echo gathered about the footsteps of the visitors and office workers who paced through the building. He saw a summer-school class collected in one corner, listening to a teacher recite New Jersey facts. Across the forum he could see the pale-blue-jacketed New Jersey state trooper who guarded the entrance to the governor's suite of offices. The trooper was reading a magazine. Jeffers strode quickly across the center of the entrance forum and ducked down a flight of stairs. There was an underground passageway leading to the New Jersey State Museum. It was empty and quiet and his heels made a snapping sound as he walked swiftly down the corridor. He found the flight of stairs leading up and mounted them rapidly.

There was a librarian at the front. He showed her his state identification card and she whispered, 'How can I help you, doctor?'

'I'd like to check whatever newspapers you have on file for last September,' he whispered back. She was a young woman with dark hair that slid around her shoulders. She nodded.

'We have the Trenton *Times*, the New York *Times*, and *The Trentonian* on microfilm.'

'Can I try them all?'

She smiled, a little wider perhaps than necessary. Jeffers felt a twinge of attraction, then immediately dismissed it. 'Of course. Let me set you up at a machine.'

There was a bank of blue microfilm machines adjacent to the card catalog. The young woman led Jeffers to a seat, then left him momentarily. When she returned, she carried three small boxes. She removed the first roll and showed Jeffers how to load the machine. Their hands touched briefly. He thanked her, nodding, but thinking instead of what he was looking for.

In the New York *Times* he found a three-paragraph Associated Press story in a corner of an inside page:

CAMPUS KILLER IN MIAMI
CLAIMS FIFTH VICTIM

MIAMI, Sept. 9 (AP) – An 18–year-old coed at the University of Miami was discovered murdered here Saturday, the apparent fifth victim of a killer police have dubbed 'The Campus Killer'.

Susan Lewis, daughter of an Ardmore, Pa., accountant, a sophomore majoring in oceanographic studies, was found at Matheson-Hammock Park several hours after disappearing from a party at the University's Student Union. She had been beaten, strangled and assaulted, police said.

Police said she was possibly the fifth victim of a killer who has struck at a number of colleges in the South Florida area.

That was all. Space must be at a premium at the *Times*, Jeffers thought. He read the story twice. Then he took out the roll of microfilm and began searching in the Trenton *Times*. It did not take him long to find an obituary in the Bucks County edition of the newspaper.

He read: '. . . She is survived by her parents, a younger brother, Michael, an aunt, Mercedes Barren of Miami Beach, and numerous cousins. The family requests that in lieu of flowers, donations be made to the Cousteau Society.'

He read that again.

It explains a great deal, he thought.

He had one other idea. He went back to the librarian at the desk and returned the microfilm. 'Is it possible,' he asked, smiling, 'to find out if there were any follow-up stories on a subject? I mean, is there any way I can give you a name and you could check to see if there were any recent stories?'

She shook her head. 'If this was a newspaper library, sure. That's how they file things. It would be easy. But we don't have that kind of computer capacity. The *Times* puts out a yearly index to stories, but this year's isn't out yet. What is it you're interested in?'

He shrugged, suddenly resolved to drive over to one of the local newspapers and see if he could talk his way into their library system. 'Oh, it's not that important,' he said. 'Just a crime down in Florida.'

'Which one?' the librarian asked.

'Someone called the Campus Killer.'

'Oh,' she said, smiling. 'They caught that guy. I remember seeing it on the news.' She made a face. 'A real creep. Almost as bad as that guy Bundy.'

'Caught?'

'Yeah, last fall. I remember because my sister was gonna go to the University of South Florida and then she changed her mind, and then changed her mind back again because the guy was arrested. He went to prison, too.'

It took Martin Jeffers another half hour to find the short story documenting the arrest of Sadegh Rhotzbadegh in the New York *Times*, and slightly expanded versions in both Trenton papers. He read them carefully, printing the information in his mind. Then he made photostats of the stories.

He thanked the librarian profusely. She seemed disappointed he didn't ask for her telephone number. He managed a wan smile, trying, in a look, to say that he never asked anyone for her phone number, which he knew was the truth. Then he let his mind wander elsewhere, instantly forgetting the look of disappointment on the young woman's face. Instead, he was organizing his thoughts, trying to plan his next step, trying to process what he'd learned, trying to create some reasonable picture in his mind that would result in an explanation for why the aunt of a murder victim in a solved crime would suddenly want to talk to him about his brother.

He knew that outrage would be a traditional response. He could scream: Why are you bothering me? What are you doing? What have I got to do with this crime? Who's in charge?

He knew he would not challenge her.

He looked down at the photostats. CAMPUS KILLER ARRESTED IN MIAMI: CHARGED IN SERIES OF MURDERS. They caught the man, he thought. So what does Doug have to do with this?

He refused to answer his own question. Instead his heart filled with fear, an awkward, disquieting sensation. He thought he should be pleased by what he'd discovered in the newspapers, but he wasn't. His nervousness simply grew. He felt encapsulated by danger, as if every step, every action, every movement were riven with chance.

He hurried back to his car, thinking: Time to lose the detective. He knew there was no particular insistence for this feeling other than the massive need to know he was alone with his fears. He did not think he could handle the added pressure of knowing she was watching him. He needed to be completely, utterly, confidently, alone.

He took a quick turn over to Broad Street, then a fast left, and another right, heading down Perry Street, past the Trenton *Times* offices. He accelerated up a rampway onto Route 1, then, just as quickly, took the Olden Avenue exit. At the bottom of the exit ramp he made an illegal U-turn, and headed back the way he'd just come. He thought he saw the detective then, trapped by the traffic, and he quickened his pace.

Martin Jeffers tried to dissect his feelings. In a way, he thought, it is childish to insist on losing the detective. He realized that, but he wanted to digest what he'd learned, and he wanted to do it in a solitude of his own construction. He headed back to the hospital, slowly, trying to compartmentalize his knowledge.

He knew he was no longer being followed. The downtown area of Trenton is an unlikely maze of streets and construction, daunting enough for the regulars, hopeless for the uninitiated. Miami, he thought, is probably all thruways and boulevards, wide, tree-lined streets, not the tangled confusion of an old Northeastern city clinging to life and livelihood. He envisioned the detective, her cool, silken presence melting in the twisted melee of cars, buses, and work crews. He wondered why it did not seem more amusing to him.

And, at the same time, he was still unable to shake the sense of foreboding that followed him even more doggedly than the police detective.

She, of course, was about a hundred yards behind him, her eyes set dead ahead, her mind a blackness of anger.

At five minutes past 5 p.m. Detective Mercedes Barren knocked on Dr Martin Jeffers' office door. He let her in immediately, motioning her to a chair in the cramped office. She sat down, placing her pocketbook on the floor and a small leather briefcase in her lap. She quickly glanced about herself, eyes scanning the rows of books, the stacks of papers, the weak attempt at decoration with a pair of framed posters. She thought to herself: Don't let the clutter fool you; he is likely to be as organized as his brother.

Jeffers chewed on the end of a pencil before speaking.

'So, detective, you've come all the way from Miami, and I'm still confused as to why you need to see my brother with such dispatch.'

She hesitated briefly before replying.

'As I said earlier, he is a material witness in a murder investigation.'

'Could you explain exactly how?'

'Have you been in touch with him today?'

'You didn't answer my question.'

'Answer mine first. Doctor, your evasiveness about this is irritating. I am a police detective investigating a homicide. I do not have to explain myself in order to obtain your co-operation. If need be I can go to your superiors.'

That was a bluff. She knew he knew it.

'Suppose I said, go ahead.'

'I would.'

He nodded. 'Well, that I can believe.'

She thrust forward: 'Did you talk with him today?'

'No.'

They hesitated.

'There's an honest answer for you,' he continued. 'I have not been in touch with him today. Here's another honest answer: I don't know how to get in touch with him.'

'I don't believe that.'

He shrugged. 'Believe what you like.'

Again they were silent.

'All right,' she said after a moment. 'I think your brother has information about a murder. I said that earlier. I do not know the extent of his involvement. That is why I want to speak with him.'

'Is he a suspect?'

'Why do you ask?'

'Detective Barren, if you want me to answer any of your questions, then you damn well better answer a couple of mine.'

Her mind raced, trying to sort out small lies from big ones, trying to chart a course that spoke some truth, enough to gain the brother's assistance.

'I cannot say whether he is or isn't. A piece of evidence that we have traced to him was discovered adjacent to the crime scene. For all I know he may have a perfectly good explanation for this. He may not. That's what I'm here trying to find out.'

Martin Jeffers nodded. He was trying to deduce whether she was at least in part truthful. Sex offenders are easier, he thought wryly.

'What kind of evidence?'

She shook her head.

'All right,' he said. 'The crime is . . .'

'Murder.'

'And your involvement . . .'

'I'm a police detective . . .'

He pulled out one of the photostats of Susan's obituary and slid it across the desk to her. His voice was rigid with distaste. 'I hate lies, detective. My whole business, my whole being, is dedicated to the pursuits of certain kinds of fundamental truths. It is an insult for you to come in here and lie to me.'

He thought he sounded properly pompous and angered. He was unprepared for her response. He had expected her to adopt a polar position, either chastened or outraged. She was neither.

'I insult you?' she asked in a frightening, low voice. She did not wait for an answer before plowing ahead. 'And now you have the audacity to make a speech about truth? And all the time you're sitting there smugly, playing a little head-game and hiding your brother from – from – from questioning. All right. First you tell me that you think your brother is incapable of this.'

She fished about briefly in her briefcase, finally bringing forth one of the crime-scene photographs and tossing it onto his desk.

He pushed it away without looking at it.

'Don't try to shock me,' he said.

'I'm not.'

He realized then that her words had the force of screams, but that she'd not once raised her voice. He picked up the picture and stared at it.

'I'm sorry for you,' he said.

But his imagination was swept into a slippery vortex of fright. The picture seemed like an etching by Goya, each shadow hiding some terror, each line a sense of horror. He saw the young woman stretched in death, savaged. He thought of a moment in medical school when he'd confronted his first corpse. He had expected someone, something, old, tired, mis-shapen with age and disease. But his first cadaver had been that of a sixteen-year-old prostitute who'd overdosed one unfortunate night. He had looked down into the dead eyes of the girl and been unable to touch her. His hands had shaken, his voice quavered. For an instant he'd thought he was going to faint. He'd turned away, heaving air into his lungs, gasping. It had taken him every fiber of strength to go to the anatomy professor and request an exchange. He remembered switching with another student – a loathsome man who'd remarked, 'Nice tits,' as he wielded his scalpel. Jeffers could still see the corpse of the elderly wino he'd been assigned, wanting in some strange way, before plunging his own knife into the man's hairless chest, to embrace this skeletonlike shape and thank him for ridding him of some of his terror.

He stared at the picture again and thought of the girl on the slab.

'I could never do it,' he said softly.

For a moment he did not realize what he'd said.

She did. It seared her. She summoned more control from her heart.

Detective Barren let the silence mount around them before she cracked it ever so gently with a simple question: 'But what about your brother?'

Jeffers felt his insides churn. With difficulty he gathered himself together and retreated into his best clinical tones.

'I don't believe my brother is capable of such a thing, detective. I can't believe it. I won't believe it. I don't believe it. You're talking about savagery, uh, despicable, reprehensible, I don't know. I'm insulted that you'd even ask.'

Detective Barren stared at him.

'Are you really?' she asked gently.

He managed an ineffectual snort and an impotent wave of the hand in response.

'Assume, for the sake of this conversation, that . . .'

He interrupted.

'Assume nothing, detective. I don't want to play with hypotheticals. My brother is a prize-winning photographer. He is one of the most sought after freelancers in journalism today. He travels the world. His work appears in every major publication. He is honored and respected. He is an artist. In every sense of the word, detective. An artist.'

'I didn't ask you about his professional qualifications.'

'No, that's correct. You didn't.'

He hesitated before adding: 'But it's important to realize we're not dealing with some, some . . .'

She cut in: 'Ordinary man?'

He nodded. 'All right.'

Her voice re-formed on the edge of rage: 'You think an ordinary man could do this?'

He reeled.

'You misunderstand me.'

'No, I don't. I don't at all.'

She stared at him and he used the moment to try to regain some distance. Jeffers decided to go on the offensive.

'And this, I suppose, is a routine investigation?'

'Yes. No . . .'

'Well, which?'

'It is not routine.'

'It couldn't be, could it, detective? Not when the victim is your niece.'

'Correct.'

'Then explain to me, detective, if you will, why you are here trying to connect my brother to a crime that has already been solved?'

He reached down and thrust another photostat of a news story across at her. She glanced at it rapidly, then pushed it aside.

'The murder of Susan Lewis was not solved. It was only attributed to that man. I have evidence that indicates he did not commit the crime.'

'Will you share that with me?'

'No.'

'I didn't think so.'

'The evidence is circumstantial.'

'I would imagine so. Because if it were more than mere guesswork, detective, then you would have tried to brow-beat me with it already.'

That was true. She nodded.

'You're correct, doctor.'

He paused before continuing. He felt stronger, more aggressive. He returned to his best clinical approach.

'Please, detective, enlighten me. The aunt of a murder victim arrives here seeking to connect my brother to a crime that's been solved. Now why shouldn't I find that confusing and unusual?'

He looked across the desk at the detective and realized that there was something new in her eyes. They seemed to glow. He realized, too, that all of his pedanticism was useless. There was silence before she replied in a singularly deep, even voice.

'You should,' she said. She paused again before continuing.

'But if it was so goddamned surprising to hear that your brother was sought in connection with a murder, why didn't you toss me out then?'

She looked directly at him, her eyes harsh and unforgiving.

'Why weren't you shocked? Speechless? Astounded?'

She breathed in and out evenly.

'I know why,' she continued quietly, terrifyingly. 'Because you weren't surprised to hear it. Not at all, goddammit.'

She hesitated again while she registered the effect her words had on him.

'Because you've been waiting to hear exactly that for some time, haven't you?'

Her words were like bullets probing for Jeffers' heart. He forced his mind to go blank, not accepting the questions she'd thrust at him, denying his own imagination simultaneously.

He stood and walked to the window.

She sat watching.

The summer evening was closing in. The dusk seemed gray. He thought it was the hour of the day most like the first few moments after a nightmare, when people are not certain whether they are safe, awake in their bed, or still asleep, trapped by their dream.

He took an immense breath. He released it slowly, then took another. To himself he screamed: Get control! Show nothing!

But he knew these were impossible commands.

'Detective, what you say is provocative. I think we had best continue this conversation tomorrow . . .'

It was weak and ineffectual, but he knew he needed time. Insist on it! he said to himself.

She started to speak, but he wheeled away from the window and held up his hand.

'Tomorrow! Tomorrow, goddammit! Tomorrow!'

She nodded.

'After my group session, around noontime.'

'Okay.'

She paused before asking, 'You're not going to cancel that like you did today's appointments?'

He glared at her. He didn't reply.

'All right,' she said. 'I'll take that as a negative.'

She stood and looked at him.

'You won't call him?'

'I told you, detective, I can't.' Jeffers, she saw, was struggling for composure. What a fragile man he was, she thought suddenly. She wondered how she could use this to her advantage.

'Suppose he calls you? Suppose that happens – what're you going to say?'

'He won't.'

'He might.'

'I said he won't.'

'But if he does?'

'He's my brother. I'll talk to him.'

'What will you say?'

Jeffers shook his head angrily. 'He's my brother.'

8 Other dark places

13

They drove north, paralleling the Mississippi River.

Douglas Jeffers called it 'The mighty Miss-sah-sip' and gave Anne Hampton a short course on Mark Twain. He was clearly disappointed to learn that she'd read only *Tom Sawyer*, and that when she had been a senior in high school. She was uneducated, he told her bitterly. If she did not know about Huck, he said, she knew nothing. She certainly would find it more difficult to understand him. 'Huck is America,' Jeffers insisted. 'I am America.' She did not reply, but scribbled down his words in her notepad.

He spoke this in a low voice. Then he adopted a pedantic, lecturing tone and told her that the river had once been the most important route for commerce in the nation, that it had been the signaling point for the jump across the West, that it slid through the heart of America, carrying politics, culture, civilization, and sustenance on the backs of its waters. To understand the river, he said, was to know how America formed. He told her that the same was true of people; one merely had to determine what river coursed through a man, or woman, then follow it to the basin of comprehension. She looked bewildered and he suddenly screamed at her, 'I'm talking about myself, goddammit! Can't you see what I'm saying? I'm trying to teach you things that no one, no one in the world knows! Don't sit there like a slug!' She cowered, waiting for the blow, but he held off, though she saw his hand clench into a fist. Then, after a momentary pause, he continued musing about the river.

Occasionally they would swing close enough in the car

for her to see the gleaming wide surface reflecting the daylight, the waters flowing ceaselessly, steadily onward toward the gulf that lay behind them. He insisted she take down all of his rambling speech, almost word for word, saying that someday she would recognize the value inherent in the phrases and fragments, and she would be thankful that she had managed to copy them down properly.

She did not understand that, but during the past days she had found it comforting when he would talk about the future, no matter how vaguely, as if there were some world extending beyond the windows of the car hurtling through the countryside, a life past Douglas Jeffers' long reach. She obeyed, scratching letters, shaping words as quickly as she could.

When he asked her to reread it to him, she obeyed.

He asked her to make a small correction, then a small addendum. She obeyed.

She obeyed everything. To refuse him anything was utterly alien to her.

Several nights had passed — she had trouble saying to herself precisely how many — since he had shot the derelict. Since I shot the derelict, she thought. Then: No, since *we* shot the derelict. They stayed each night in some forgettable motel near the edge of the highway, the kind of places with neon red vacancy signs blinking in the darkness, where the water-glasses are wrapped in paper and the management puts signs on the toilets to say that they have been properly sanitized.

As they were entering their room in one of the motels she saw a man standing next to a soft-drink machine a short distance away. He wore a cheap brown suit and a tie loosened by the day's heat. She thought of Willy Loman and realized that he was a travelling salesman. He was leering at her as he fed quarters into the machine. She watched as he purchased three cans of orange soda and saw that he had a bottle of vodka in his pocket. She cringed at the man's look, shrinking in fear from the design in his eyes. Jeffers snarled at the man like an animal surprised at the door to its den, and the man shuffled away, protecting his soft drinks and liquor and the evening's oblivion that they held out in promise. Jeffers had said, 'Why kill him unless you're a punk looking for a fifty-buck score? What he's drinking will kill him just as sure as a bullet. Just not quite as quick.'

In bed each night she slept fitfully, if at all, tossing about as much as she dared, but more often lying rigid, listening to his even breathing but not believing that he slept. He never sleeps, she thought. He's always awake and ready. Even when he emitted a snore, she refused to believe that it signaled sleep. When she listened to him, she tried to remain absolutely quiet, as if even the slight whisper of her own breath would rouse him. She thought at those times that she could no longer hear or feel her own body functioning. She would surreptitiously put her hand to her breast and try to sense the heartbeat beneath. It seemed distant, weak; it was as if she were close to death, mortally fragile.

At night he did not try to touch her, though she expected it each minute. She had given up on any idea of privacy, dressing and undressing in front of him, not shutting the bathroom door when she went to the toilet. She accepted these things as part of the arrangement which left her alive. She would have accepted sex as well, but so far it had failed to materialize. She did not expect this hiatus to last.

In the time since the derelict's killing, she had come to realize that she was scared of everything: of strangers, of Jeffers, of herself, of each passing minute of daytime, of each moment of night; of what might happen to her when she was awake or when she slept. When she did manage to fall asleep, her dreams were more often nightmares; she had quickly become accustomed to awakening in terrified flight from some sleep image, only to settle into the constancy of fear that was her waking world. Sometimes she had great difficulty separating the two. She would lie in darkness, remembering the vision of the derelict on the New Orleans street. She saw his mouth circling, puckering in acceptance of the bottle, a safe, familiar act, that gave him a kind of easy joy. Only this time it wasn't the accustomed touch of the wet bottle neck that he felt, but the hard, dry, awful taste of the gun barrel. She could see a glimmer of confusion in his eyes as they looked up in surprise, meeting hers. His eyes were like those of a dog who hears an unusual sound and cocks his head in curiosity. It was a terrible sight; her vision fixing on the derelict's open, accepting mouth, expectant eyes, waiting for all the world as if he were going to be kissed.

And sometimes it would be worse, it would reversed. She would see the derelict, see him lift a bottle to his open lips. And when her own mouth dropped wide in surprise, wondering where the gun had gone, it would be there, in front of her. She would try to snap her mouth shut, but the gun moved too quickly and she could taste the metallic death on her own tongue.

She would see all this, and then scream.

At least she thought she screamed, and more often than not she felt as if she had screamed. But she realized that in reality she had made no sound. Her own mouth had opened, demanding noise, but none had emerged.

That too frightened her.

Outside of Vicksburg, Mississippi, Jeffers slowed the car and pulled to the side of the road. He pointed past her and said, 'See there?' Anne Hampton turned and looked out upon a wide green field with a grassy knoll in the center. At the top of the knoll was a weathered, gray-brown oak tree, an ancient tree with gnarled leafy branches that reached out over the field, throwing shade about with the determination and duty that comes with old age.

'I see a tree,' she replied.

'That's wrong,' he said. 'What you see is the past.'

He took the car out of gear and turned off the engine. 'Come on,' he said. 'History lesson.'

He helped her over a ramshackle wooden fence, and together they walked up to the knoll. Jeffers looked hard at the ground the entire time, as if measuring something. 'It's grown back,' he said. 'I didn't know if it would, but it's been eight years.' He looked pensive. 'I always thought that when gasoline burned the ground, it was scorched, it would take decades to grow back. Do you remember those pictures the German war photographers took in World War Two? From the Ukraine? They were very powerful shots. There would be these immense fields of wheat waving about in the distance, surrounding a huge pillar of black smoke. You always sensed the impotence through the picture, that's what made the pictures so damned good; you knew they couldn't do a fucking thing to stop those fires once the retreating Russians set them. Gasoline and wheat burning. Scorched earth. Damning the future to save the present.' Then he stopped and pointed. 'Look carefully – there! Can you see the way the grass changes color?'

'It seems like a shape,' she said.

'Damn straight. A cross.'

'You were here before?' she asked. Her voice quivered slightly; she saw the tree and remembered the tree lost in the rain and wind along the Louisiana coastline that they'd been unable to find.

'Standing right there.' He pointed down the hill slightly. 'It was a great shot,' he said. 'The fire from the cross framed all the men in their silly little white pointed hats and robes. But that wasn't what made it so good,' he continued, 'it was the way this huge crowd of blacks – spectators, I guess, I don't exactly know why they came out – anyway, they watched in utter silence. All their faces, every eye, was turned up toward this hill. The firelight drifted across them, as well, and I was able to get it all. A fantastic picture. You know why they chose this tree? Because fifty years ago the old Klan hung three men from that single wide branch, the low one.

'Symmetry is important,' he said. 'History. We are a nation of memories. The old Klan hung three men from a tree, and so the new Klan wants to evoke the same terror.

'And so out they march, all bedecked in their robes, all their kleagles and klaxxons and grand dragons in silks and some not so grand dragons waving the stars and bars, to have a rally. Not too many of them, really, but I understand that now their numbers are growing. Anyway, this time there were almost as many reporters and photographers as there were Klansmen. And twice as many blacks.

'That surprised me, you know. I mean, I would have thought that those people would have stayed far away. Ignoring the rally. After all, who wants to go listen to a lot of silly, insulting rhetoric? But they didn't. They showed up in droves. And you know what was really curious about it? These weren't educated people. And they weren't organized. They were farmers and sharecroppers and their wives and children. They came in old trucks and cars and I saw some arrive by cart and mule, too.

'I couldn't get over how quiet they were. The more inflammatory the speeches got, the more outrageous and insulting, the more they stood in silence. It was the strangest thing: you'd think that silence is an absolute, I mean, if someone's not making any noise, they can't get quieter, right? Not that night. Those people stood and never made a sound and the longer they stood there, the more profound their quiet was.'

He shook his head.

'Now, that was strength. They showed that their memories were just as long and heartfelt. A singularity of purpose.'

He looked at Anne Hampton.

'Complete dignity,' he said. He paused.

'You have to understand how much I admire true strength. Because to do what I do requires an absolute dedication. A solidarity with your soul.' He smiled and broke into a grin. 'I like that,' he said. 'Solidarity.' He made a clenched fist.

He looked at her. 'To do what I do,' he said.

She would not let the words form in her mind.

He laughed. She saw that he had a camera in his hand. He lifted it, twisted the lens quickly, and clicked her picture. He bent down, changing the angle, and took another. 'What I do, of course, is take pictures.'

He laughed again, and she stood stiffly in front of him, awaiting a command with a kind of military attention.

'Come on,' he said. 'I will explain more.'

She scrambled after him as he stalked down the hillside.

In the car he said, 'What's the most important thing about America?'

She hesitated, but her mind moved swiftly: She pictured in grainy grays and dark shadows the pictures that Douglas Jeffers had taken the night of that rally, hooded rowdy Klansmen and silent, reproachful farmers. She responded, 'Free speech. The First Amendment, right?'

He glanced away from the highway at her, smiling. 'Boswell learns!' he said. 'Correct.'

She nodded and took out the notebook, oddly pleased with herself for answering one of his cryptic questions properly.

'But can you think of a freedom more frequently abused?'

She recognized it really wasn't a question for her as much as it was the start to some speech he was about to make. 'Think of the evil generated on that hilltop. Think of the wrongs it represented. And protected by what? Our most important freedom. The Nazis want to march in Skokie and who stands up to defend them? The ACLU. A bunch of Jewish lawyers. It's the principle, they say. And they're right. The principle is more important than any individual act. That's what's so silly. We are a nation of hypocrites because we adhere so strongly to rigid concepts. Right. Wrong. Free Speech. Manifest Destiny. What did Superman defend? Truth, Justice, and the American Way. A scout is trustworthy, loyal, helpful, friendly, courteous, kind, obedient, cheerful, thrifty, brave, clean, and reverent. No one ever wants to mention the scoutmaster who likes dressing up in short pants, telling ghost stories around the fire, and diddling the boys beneath the sleeping bags . . .'

He took a deep breath, paused, then added, 'Do you want to truly understand this country? It's simple, really. You just have to understand that on occasion we use our greatest strengths to create the biggest evils. Not always. Just sometimes. Just enough to make it interesting, of course.'

He was speaking in a rush. Not angry, just wired. She was writing as fast as she could.

He stopped.

He giggled.

'From the First Amendment to faggot scoutmasters . . .' He threw back his head and shook it wildly, laughing hard.

He looked at Anne Hampton.

'I must be crazy,' he said, grinning.

'No, no, I mean, I think I understand . . .'

'You're wrong,' he said. His voice abruptly changed back to hard and harsh and the smile on his face evaporated. 'I am crazy. I'm completely, terribly, totally, mad. We all are, in our own way. It's our national pastime, really. My way just happens to be worse than some . . .' He looked at her. 'Worse than most.'

He turned back, staring down the highway.

'Tell me,' Douglas Jeffers asked, 'what you know about death.'

She remembered a time when she was young and visiting her grandparents on their farm. It was before Tommy had died: it had been summer and they had wanted to swim in the pond. But when they got to the edge they had found a mess of gray and black goose feathers strewn about wildly. Her grandfather had nodded and said, 'Snapping turtle. Big one, too, I'll wager, if he took apart that whole bird.' The swim had been canceled and her grandfather had gone back and taken a shotgun from a locked cabinet. He'd let her stick with him, though Tommy had been relegated to the house. Her grandfather set out some leftover chicken by the side of the pond, walked a short ways downwind with her, and then waited.

It had been over twenty pounds. She remembered the explosion of the shotgun, the sound crashing into her ears, deadening them. Her grandfather spread the bloody jaws apart with a stick, saying, 'Turtle that big'd break your leg no problem.' The turtle died, and then Tommy died and two summers after, her grandfather as well. She thought of the neighbor across the street who died of heart failure one humid summer morning, trying to catch up for too many years of indulgence by taking up jogging. Ambulance lights seemed dull, somehow less urgent, in the bright sunshine.

She remembered seeing the man stretched out on the lawn, pasty white, rigid. His shoe had been untied and she'd had the strange thought that it had been fortunate that something had stopped him before he tripped and fell. She'd noticed, too, that his socks didn't match. One had a green stripe, the other blue. She'd thought that terrible. To die was bad enough, but to be embarrassed as well seemed doubly horrible.

She remembered her parents being handed a small white urn containing Tommy's ashes, seeing her mother's hands quake as they reached out. She could still hear the disembodied voices of the guests, mumbling, exhorting under their breath: Be brave. But why? she wondered. What was the point in bravery? Why not simply sob uncontrollably? That made a lot more sense. But she'd seen her mother compose herself, dropping a veil across sorrow. A moment later the urn had been taken away and she had not seen it again. She wondered whether they had burned Tommy's clothes as well. He would probably have preferred seeing the tight blue suit that they'd bought him for church go up in smoke, she thought. All little boys both loved and hated their good clothes. There was a wonderful moment, when they were first dressed, that they looked so grown-up and solemn, handsome and sophisticated. Then, inevitably, they dissolved into the usual *melange* of dirt, grass stains, flying shirt-tails, and ripped knees. The turtle had been female, and she had helped her grandfather find the babies. He'd collected them in a sack, but would not tell her what he was going to do with them.

That's death, she thought. When you're not told. But you know.

'I don't know much,' she answered. 'My grandfather died. A neighbor, too, jogging. I was there. I saw him.' She hesitated before mentioning her brother.

No, she thought, that's enough.

But she could not make herself stop.

'My brother died, too. A skating accident. He drowned.' She was silent, then she added, 'He was just a little boy.'

Jeffers paused before replying.

269

'My brother is drowning, as well. He just doesn't know it.'

She did not know what to say, but she stored the information away. He's got a brother.

'He just doesn't know it yet,' Jeffers continued. 'But he will, soon enough.'

He drove in silence for at least a quarter hour before he spoke again. She had turned, looking out at the other cars that they passed, looking in on families, young men, young women, trying to imagine who they were, where they were going, what they were like. Occasionally her eyes would meet another pair, if only for a second, and she would think how surprised the person would be if they knew of the trip she was on.

Douglas Jeffers only half-concentrated on the task of driving, instead allowing his mind to swing to problems of expression. The countryside that swept around him seemed nondescript, farms and vegetable fields and small towns blending into a constancy of rolling, simple green and brown backdrop. He steered the car back up onto the interstate, still heading north, barely registering speed, distance, destination, traffic. He thought for a while about his brother, then about Anne Hampton, and then about his brother again.

Marty had no passion, he thought. He would never act. He absorbed everything quietly, like those blacks on the hill.

It was odd that they'd never fought. All brothers fight, if not constantly, at least frequently. They struggle over everything, trying to carve out their own fiefdom in the family. It was that tension, he believed, that created the bond between brothers. After enough blood and anger, all that remained was a mutual dedication.

In all the battles with their father, the phony father, he'd maintained a distance. Jeffers grimaced and bit his lip, filling suddenly with a multifaceted anger: rage at the man, rage at the boy, rage at himself.

'I hate neutrality,' he said out loud. 'I despise it.' He saw peripherally that Anne Hampton had been startled.

Well, Jeffers thought to himself, he's not going to be able to remain so damn detached much longer.

He spun a quick glance at Anne Hampton, then turned back to the highway. He pictured her limbs, her body. But his mind wandered quickly back into the past, and instead of his traveling companion, he saw the druggist's wife. When she dressed in the mornings, after her husband left for work, before the boys left for school, she would leave the door ajar. It was a slow, lingering process. She knew he watched her. He knew she knew. When he tried to get Marty to watch as well, his brother had turned away and walked out wordlessly.

'Did you love your brother?' he asked Anne Hampton.

'Yes,' she replied. 'Even though I thought he was, well, I don't know, strange, I guess. Mysterious.'

'What do you mean?'

'Well, I was only three years older than he. And we didn't, I don't know, have much in common. Does that make sense? He was a boy and he did little-boy things and I was a girl and so I did little-girl things. But I loved him.'

'It does make sense. In actuality, I think you share little with your brothers or sisters. A certain shared commonality of memory, because your pasts are the same. But they aren't, really. Everyone remembers the same things differently. So they mean different things to different people.'

'I think I know what you mean,' she said.

He nodded.

They were quiet.

'There,' he said. 'We had an almost normal conversation. Wasn't so terrible, was it?'

She shook her head.

After a moment she asked, 'What about your brother?'

'He's a doctor,' Jeffers replied. 'A head doctor. And he's just as unhappy as the folks he treats. He lives alone and doesn't know why. I live alone but at least I know why.'

She nodded. He noticed that she was taking notes.

'Good,' he said. She didn't reply.

But her unsaid question was the same as the one he'd directed to her, and he answered it: 'No, I don't think I love him,' he said. 'No more than I love anyone. Or anything.'

He shook his head. 'I gave up on love a long time ago. Happiness, too.'

He laughed bitterly. 'I sound like a character in some daytime soap opera. Did you watch them?'

'No,' she replied. 'A lot of the kids at school were devoted to them. It was like a fad, I guess. But I never bothered.'

'I didn't think so.'

She hesitated, then asked, 'But you love your work?'

He smiled.

'I love my work.'

The grin on his face was one that reflected a sudden internal humor, and she felt a rush of panic. What does he think his work is? she said to herself. The thought seemed to punch her insides.

'I mean,' she continued, 'you talk about these pictures with such respect. Both the ones you took and the ones you've seen.'

'I've taken a lot of pictures. A lot of different things.'

She nodded and they sped on in silence.

Douglas Jeffers thought of his pictures.

'Always death,' he said. 'Well, not always. But lately more and more. I shoot death. I did a series, an essay for *Life*, not too long ago. On a twenty-four-hour shift in a big-city emergency room . . .'

'Oh,' Anne Hampton interrupted, 'I saw those. They were good.'

'They were about death. Even the shots of the doctors and nurses and ambulance drivers – the task, you see, was to capture how all that violence and smashed and torn bodies diminished them. Day after day. Night after night. You see, you rub up against something awful for too long and it becomes a part of you. Sticks to your skin.'

He paused before saying, 'That's what's happened to me.'

272

She nodded, and for a moment felt an awkward sympathy.

Then she remembered the rain and wind, the wrong road and the Gulf waters, and she had a sudden horrible vision of what it would be like, lying beneath the earth. She felt instantly suffocated and gulped her next breath of air.

'I've lost track,' said Jeffers matter-of-factly.

She felt her chest contract and air wheezed in and out. She felt asthmatic, feeble.

'Of what?' she moaned her question.

'Of how many deaths I've seen. I used to know, you know. I could count them. But not any longer. They all blend together. When I was in that emergency room, they brought a kid in, a teenager, just a couple of years younger than you. He'd been the passenger in a car driven by a drunk. The other kid, the driver, wouldn't you know it, had a couple of bruises and a fractured forearm. But this kid was going to buy it and the terrible thing was, he wasn't unconscious. He knew it. He knew all the people around him and all the devices and the needles and the machines were all going to be useless. I got a shot of his eyes, right before he went. They didn't use it, though. Not enough clarity in the shot, some sonuvabitch shoved me right as I tripped the shutter . . .'

He shrugged.

'It happens. It's part of the business.'

He paused, then continued.

'I went home that night and wondered just what number that kid was. Was he the thousandth? Or the ten thousandth? I once knew a police reporter who kept a running count, and so I did, too. But the number got out of hand. In Vietnam? Beirut? I was there a couple of times. Talk about cheap life . . . When the charter flight went down outside of New Orleans, it split apart and people were scattered everywhere. The rescue squads were plucking parts of bodies from the trees, just like culling so much rotten fruit . . .'

'It just happened,' Anne Hampton said. 'Things just happen.'

'No, they don't,' Jeffers replied angrily. 'The kid dies because his buddy drinks too much. The flight crashes because the pilot decides to let the copilot try a takeoff and ignores the tower's warning about wind shear. The little kids in Beirut die because they play outside and rocket grenades launched at random have this uncanny way of finding kids in a street . . .

'There are actions and reactions. Death is just the most common.'

He looked at her.

'You see, when I kill someone it's because I want to. It's the only way I have of reminding myself that I'm still alive.'

Her hand shook as she took down his words.

He waited.

Silence surrounded them. She knew, though, that he would fill it.

'More than . . .' But he stopped before adding a number.

She closed her eyes and tried to breathe slowly. When she opened them, she saw he was grinning.

She did not ask him for specificity.

He drove steadily, wordlessly, for two hours. When they needed gasoline he pulled into a station along the interstate, telling the attendant sullenly to fill the tank, paying cash, and accelerating out of the station quickly but nonchalantly, giving to all the world the appearance of a normal couple, not pressed by time, but pushing with routine dispatch toward a known destination and some distinct result.

Finally he spoke:

'Boswell, aren't you filled with wonder? Don't you have hundreds of questions?'

Anne Hampton thought that she was filled with nothing save fear.

'I didn't think I should ask,' she said. 'I figured you'd tell me what you wanted.'

He nodded. 'That seems sensible.'

After a moment he continued.

'Boswell, don't you wonder why we're doing this?'

She nodded.

'I know you've got some plan . . .'

'Yes,' he said. 'Quite a specific one at that.'

He did not volunteer information. Instead he said:

'Do I look old, Boswell? Can you see lines in my face? Do I look tired and frustrated and bilious and cantankerous with age? I feel very old, Boswell. Ancient.'

His voice changed suddenly and he demanded harshly:

'What day did we first meet?'

Her throat closed and she choked.

She could not remember. A part of her wanted to say that she'd been in the car forever, that she'd always been with him. Another part, deeper, as if being awakened from sleep, forced itself into her consciousness, with pictures of her apartment, dried flowers in a vase on the windowsill, bookcases, desk, small bed and table. There were some pictures of her parents and a watercolor on the wall of boats in a harbor that she'd seen on a trip east a few years back. It had been too expensive, but there was something in the picture that captured her, perhaps the peace, the order, the calm of boats at mooring in the late day's sunshine. She remembered her classes, the way the summer heat would wake her in the morning, the sticky sensation of sweat as she walked across the campus. Then, just as swiftly, she saw her parents back home in Colorado, sitting about the house, quietly proceeding with their lives. If they knew, she thought, they would be panicked, crying. In agony. She wondered then whether they were people in a dream.

'I don't know,' she said.

'You understand, no one knows.'

She nodded.

'No one is looking for you.'

She nodded again.

'Even if someone were curious, they wouldn't know where to look. They wouldn't know what direction to start searching. Do you understand? You've left no trail.'

She nodded a third time.

'People walk away from life all the time. Poof! They vanish. Disappear. One minute they're there, the next, well, gone.'

She dipped her head in acquiescent sorrow.

'That's what has happened to you.'

He looked at her harshly.

'I am your past now. I am your future.'

She wanted to cry but dared not. She thought of those funeral voices: Be brave. The memory made her angry.

Jeffers continued.

'It's like those damn milk cartons with the pictures and identifying data of lost children on their sides. Depressing. The children are gone. Stolen away forever. We are a nation of Pied Pipers, you see. Constantly playing a tune to lead others astray. That's what happened to you. Swallowed up.'

He paused.

'That's what happened to all of them.'

How many more? she suddenly wondered.

Oh, God, she said to herself. I'm next. I'm still next. I've always been next. But she didn't have time to let this fear formulate into some panic-stricken scream. And, after a moment she realized that it was the same fear that had dogged her from the start, and when she assigned this degree of familiarity to it, it suddenly seemed less terrifying. She wondered for an instant whether this was some sort of death recognition, whether she was like the people on an airplane that starts to fall precipitously from the sky. She had read of the momentary screams fading into a calmed acceptance, a peaceful, prayerful time. Like the instants before the firing squad. Do you want a cigarette? A blindfold? asks the captain. No, just a momentary look out at the morning.

She stared out the window, shading her eyes from the brightness of the summer sun. She did not know why, but she felt an odd, unfamiliar ease.

Jeffers hummed a tune. 'I wonder what piece the Pied Piper played on his flute. Was it the same for the rats as it was for the children?'

He seemed to consider things briefly.

'I always wondered, even when I was a child, why the parents of Hamelin didn't do anything. You know, they just stood there like a bunch of idiots. I would have . . .'

His voice trailed off for an instant.

'Look,' Jeffers asked. 'What do you know about murder?'

She thought of the derelict and replied, 'Just what I learned the other night.'

Jeffers smiled.

'Good answer,' he said. 'That shows some moxie, huh? Boswell isn't quite as timid as she acts sometimes.'

He punched the accelerator and the car jumped forward. Then, just as swiftly, he eased off and they returned to the same droning modest speed.

'Murder is, as you saw, blissfully easy. It's only in Hollywood that people stare down the barrel of a gun, hesitating, filled with moral conflict and guilt. In reality it happens simply and quickly. An argument and bang! Not that much difference, really, between your standard night-the-welfare-checks-come-out argument in the ghetto and some military operation that requires weeks or months of planning. There's always some fundamentally stupid dispute at the bottom. Even in my case, you know, if I was truly introspective, I could probably find the base, shall I say cause, for what I do. Some unresolved anger. Some out-of-control hatred. That's the kind of phrase my brother would use. But what is an unresolved anger? Just an argument between all the different parts of yourself. Life is always a debate between your good side and your bad side, anyway. The bad side wants you to take that extra dessert, right? Just like those Saturday-morning cartoons they show for kids, where a little devil pops up urging Foghorn Leghorn or Donald Duck or Goofy or whatever cute and furry little animal they use nowadays to do something wrong and then a little angel pops up, insisting they take the true and proper path . . .'

Jeffers laughed shortly, sharply, before going on.

'Anyway, do you know why we committed that crime with impunity? Because it was committed at random. Look at us. Are we the type of people who appear like they would go around blowing out the brains of drunken derelicts? Thrill-seekers? Leopold and Loeb? What? Not a professional photographer. Award-winning, no less. Not an honors college student. You see, we had no connection with that event at all. No one saw us. No one suspects us. It was just a simple, single, random happening, or at least that's what the authorities will think.

'In fact it barely happened at all. Just how much time do you think some overworked and underpaid homicide detective is going to want to spend on a dead derelict who probably has no identification anyway? Ten minutes? An hour? A day? No more. Enough time so that he can fill out some form and file it with his superior and move on to the next case. Something a bit sexier maybe. Something with headlines. Something that our society places some value on. A society killing or a love-triangle murder. And who can blame him? You see, it was really so inconsequential. Unknown drifter dies mysteriously. Put out a memo. Check to see if they have any other unsolved derelict-murder cases that seem similar. End of story. At least that's what the official version will be. The political version . . .

'But of course we know differently, don't we? Too bad, in a way, isn't it? Some poor cop could make his career if only he knew, had some inkling what had really happened. Because it wasn't unimportant, was it? Not to us.'

After a moment she managed a reply.

'But it can't always be so, I don't know, easy . . .'

She hated that word. For him, she realized, it was an absolute truth. For her, she thought, a total lie. I won't, she said suddenly to herself. I won't be him.

She surprised herself with her determination.

'Of course not. Otherwise there would be no challenge. No adventure. Did you ever read *The Most Dangerous Game*?'

'I don't think so.'

He snorted. 'Come on, Boswell, where's your education?'

'I've read a lot,' she replied defensively. 'I've read books you probably don't know about! What do you know about *Middlemarch*?' She heard her own voice speaking and she wanted to clap a hand over her mouth. She shut her eyes, expecting a blow.

Instead he laughed.

'Touché,' he said. 'But on to my question: What is the most dangerous game?'

'Murder isn't a game.'

'Isn't it?'

They were silent.

'All right,' he said after a second had passed, 'I'll be less frivolous. Of course murder isn't a game. But it's not a hobby either. It's a mode of life. My mode of life.'

'I just don't understand how . . .' she started, but he interrupted her.

He was laughing.

'Well, finally. She asks why! She asks how! It's about time.'

His voice darkened.

'And now I'll tell you.'

She felt then as if she had stumbled foolishly into something she was forbidden to see. She remembered once peering through the crack in her parents' bedroom door one restless night and seeing them wrapped together in subdued but noisy love. Her face flushed with the same mixture of fear and embarrassment. She dropped her pencil and had to lean down to pick it up. She was struck with the realization that knowledge was dangerous, that the more she knew the more entwined she was and the more she could never escape. Her mind filled with black sorrow and she wanted to cry like a child, alone, just as she had after that dark and primal vision, some innocence forever abandoned, smothering her tears into her pillow, cut off from any world save that defined by her own personal and exclusive agony.

He waited, filled with confidence and a kind of runaway excitement, until he knew she was riven with the foreboding that the questions were bound to create. He thought: Finally. His words exploded from him in a torrent of enthusiasm.

'I realized after the first that I'd been incredibly lucky.

Picking up a prostitute on the street in a rental car easily traceable to me. Striking her in the car, so that there was her blood type staining the upholstery. Abandoning her in an area that I was unfamiliar with. Why, at any point someone could have seen me. Someone could have latched on to the situation. A passerby. Her pimp. A trucker peering down from twelve feet up in his cab. I left footprints and fingerprints and God knows what else that some forensics lab could trace back to me. Fiber samples, dirt samples, hair samples. Hell, I even used a credit card to buy the shovel I used to bury her. I did everything wrong. Awfully goddamn stupid, you know . . .'

He looked at her briefly but didn't expect her to answer.

'Do you know what I experienced afterwards? The most seductive fear. The sensation that you get when you realize after the fact that you've been in great jeopardy. The kind of fear that takes shape and re-forms in nightmares. I walked around in a kind of twilight, thinking I was becoming paranoid, imagining every minute that any one of these schoolboy errors was going to manifest itself in a detective carrying an arrest warrant. It never happened, of course, but the feeling was like being electrified, constantly.

'My pictures, too. Sharper. Better. Filled with passion. Odd, huh? From fear came art. I was driven to succeed. I remember being unable to sleep one night a couple of days afterwards. I was so filled with excitement. It had just taken me over, you see. I decided I would drive about, just watching the nighttime city glow. Maybe that could help me contain my feelings. I was listening to the police scanner. All photographers keep lots of radios about, this wasn't unusual. You always listen, because you never know. And this was one of those nights.

'I heard this voice come on, a clear channel, excited, near panic: Help, help, officer down, officer down . . . and they gave the address. It was only a couple of blocks away. A state trooper, you see, made a routine traffic stop on a car driving with a taillight out. And for his trouble he'd taken a thirty-eight round in the chest. It had been four guys who'd just done a liquor store. And I got there before anyone. Before any other cops, before rescue. Just me, my camera, and the kid who'd witnessed the shooting from across the highway where he'd been changing a flat and had called in for help. He had the trooper's head in his lap. Click! Click! Help me, the kid said. Click! Help us! he said. What are you doing? Click! Please . . . Click! Thirty seconds maybe. Then I helped him. I took the trooper's hand and felt for a pulse. At first it was there, but then, just like dusk, it faded and disappeared. And then everywhere, lights and sirens. God! Those were fantastic pictures!'

Jeffers paused. His voice became slower, more cautious.

'So I became a student of murder.'

Silence.

'I had to.'

She poised her pencil above the notebook, trying to shed anxiety from her mind and simply concentrate on what he was saying. She told herself to think like she was back in a classroom and that this was just another lecture. She realized that was foolish.

Douglas Jeffers' head filled with images and he wondered idly whether he should start anecdotally. He stole a look at Anne Hampton and saw that she was waiting, pale, shaken, on some rim of terror, but waiting nonetheless. He felt a momentary gratification, thinking: She's mine now.

Then he launched ahead.

'I had been terribly lucky, and I'm not fond of relying on luck. I started spending my spare time in libraries, reading. I read works of literature and works of science. I read legal case histories and medical tracts. I read murderers' confessions and prison reports. I read the memoirs of detectives, pathologists, criminal-defense attorneys, prosecutors, and professional hit men. I purchashed books on weaponry. I studied physiology. I put on a white lab coat and went to anatomy lectures at Columbia Medical School. I needed to know, you see, how exactly, precisely, people died.

'I read newspapers and magazines. I subscribed to *True Detective* and *Police*. I spent hours studying the writings of a number of prominent forensic psychiatrists. I learned about sex murderers, mass murderers, professional murderers, military murderers. I studied massacres and murder conspiracies. I became intimate with de Sade, Bluebeard, Albert DeSalvo and Charles Whitman and My Lai Four or the Shatilla refugee camps. I knew Raskolnikov and Mengele and Kurtz and Idi Amin and William Bonney, whom you probably know as Billy the Kid. I know about the PLO and the Red Brigades. I could tell you about Charles Manson, or Elmer Wayne Henley, or Wayne Gacy or Richard Speck or Jack Abbott or Lucky Luciano and Al Capone. From Saint Valentine's Day to the Freeway Murders. From the Salem Witch Trials to Miami's drug wars to San Francisco's unsolved Zodiac. I know about 007 from fiction and MI-5 in reality. I could explain why Bruno Richard Hauptmann probably wasn't a murderer, although they executed him, or why Gary Gilmore was really just a loser who happened to kill, but he got executed, too. In fact, I studied just about every execution I could. I read everything from Camus' essay on the death penalty to McLendon's novel *Deathwork*, and then I read the Warren Commission Report and congressional testimony exposing the workings of the Phoenix Program in Vietnam . . .

'Did you know,' Douglas Jeffers continued, 'that in some states, court records and police reports become part of the public record? For example: I went down to North Florida not so long ago and read up on the case of one Gerald Stano. Interesting guy. Intelligent. Friendly. Outgoing. Not your reclusive loner by any means. Held a steady job as a mechanic. Did well. Everyone liked him, even the homicide detectives. He had only one small flaw . . .'

Jeffers paused for effect.

'. . . When he went on a date with a woman, he wouldn't settle for a chaste handshake or peck on the cheek to say goodnight.'

Jeffers laughed.

'No, Mr. Stano preferred to kill his dates.'

He glanced at Anne Hampton, assessing the pained look on her face.

'Slicing and dicing them . . .'

Another pause.

'Could have been as many as forty.'

Jeffers waited again before continuing.

'You've got to admire him his consistency, if for no other reason. He treated everyone the same. Every woman, that is . . .'

Anne Hampton remained quiet, waiting for Jeffers to speak. She saw him take a deep breath.

'So you see what I became,' Jeffers said, his voice fairly ringing. 'I became an expert.'

'And then,' he said, after taking a deep breath, 'I was ready to be a killer. Not some lucky jerk who got away with a random murder of a prostitute. But a complete, calculating, professional homicidal machine. But not a hit man, taking orders from some lowlife mobster or Colombian drug dealer. But a murderer completely in business for myself.

'And that's what I am.'

He drove in silence for hours.

Jeffers did not elaborate further. He thought to himself: Well, that's enough for her to absorb for a bit. And what he had in mind next he believed would elevate her to yet another level.

Anne Hampton was grateful for the quiet. She tried to force herself to think of simple things, like the smell of an apple pie baking, or the sensation of slipping on a silk shirt, but they were elusive.

They crossed the river in Memphis in the dead of night. She saw the lights reflecting off the steady black water and Jeffers told her about the time the Cuyahoga River burned in Cleveland. The toxic wastes dumped into the water had caught fire, he said. How do you put out a body of water that's on fire? He described shooting pictures of firemen at night, outlined by the soaring flames. They passed a sign as they crossed, which said, in a cheeriness that contradicted the hour: YOU'RE LEAVING MEMPHIS — COME BACK SOON!

Jeffers sang, 'Ohhhh, momma, can this really be the end? To be stuck inside of Mobile with the Memphis Blues again . . .'

He looked over at her and saw she did not recognize the tune. He shrugged. 'My generation,' he said. He laughed. 'Don't make me feel so old.'

She did not know what to say.

They stayed on the interstate in Arkansas. It was well after midnight when they stopped at a Howard Johnson's. She thought the clash of orange and aqua disturbing late at night, as if the color scheme should be changed as night fell, to something more somber and less jarring.

In the morning they were on the road early, and drove for two hours before stopping for breakfast. Jeffers was ravenous, and he forced her to eat substantially, as well: eggs, pancakes, toast, sausages, several cups of coffee and juice.

'Why so much?' she asked.

'Big day,' he replied between bites. 'Big night. Ball game in St Louis. Game time, eight. Surprises to follow. Eat up.'

She obliged him.

After breakfast, though, he did not drive immediately back to the interstate. Instead he pulled into the parking lot of a large suburban shopping mall. Anne Hampton looked at him.

'Why are we stopping?'

He reached over quickly and grabbed her face, with his thumb and forefinger digging into her cheeks.

'Just stay close, say nothing, and be educated!' he hissed.

She nodded and he released her.

'Watch, listen, and learn,' he said.

He walked quickly through the deepening crowd of people arriving at the mall. She had to hurry to keep pace. Stores flashed about her, and she saw her reflection in the plate glass of one boutique. She heard voices all around, mostly kids yelling and running away from their parents, so she was surrounded by cries: Jennifer or Joseph or Joshua, stop that this minute! Which they never did. She heard couples talking over purchases and teenagers talking

284

over boys, girls, records. These snatches of life around her seemed strangely distant, as if taking place in some other part of history. She quickened her pace at Douglas Jeffers' side. He seemed oblivious to the crowd, striding purposefully ahead.

He escorted her into a sporting goods store, where he plucked out a pair of red St Louis Cardinals baseball hats. He pointed at a plastic snoutlike hat device and laughed mockingly. 'They wear those pig hats to University of Arkansas games. Razorbacks. All I can say is, you damn well better win if your fans are going to wear those.'

He paid cash for the two hats, then headed back through the mall. 'One more stop,' he said.

Inside the large Sears department store, he headed to the office products section. At the counter he purchased a small ream of typewriter paper and a package of business-sized envelopes. Then he walked over to a line of demonstration typewriters. He turned to her and said, 'Watch carefully. Stick very close.'

In a swift motion he produced from a pocket a set of skin-tight surgical gloves. He slid them on and quickly tore open the typewriter paper box. Moving without hesitation, he handed Anne Hampton the box and quickly spun a single sheet into one of the demonstration typewriters. He hesitated for an instant, searching quickly about to ascertain if anyone was close or if anyone was paying attention to them. Certain they were not noticed, he bent down to the typewriter.

Then he typed:

> Yu guyz ar so dum, yu shud bag it,
> Cuz I just naled another faggit
>
> luv an kissies,
> Yu no who

He spun the page out of the typewriter, folded it in three, and placed it inside an envelope. Still wearing the gloves, he put the envelope into his pocket. Then he removed the gloves, glanced about to make certain again that they hadn't been noticed, and without a word to Anne Hampton paced off.

Her mind a jumble, she rushed to his side, breathing hard to keep even with his stride.

He said nothing when they returned to the car, but gestured toward the seat belt. She strapped herself in and kept quiet.

He drove steadily throughout the day and into the evening, doggedly keeping to the speed limit, or driving the prevailing speed, so they were passed by as many cars as they passed themselves. She wondered why it always seemed that Jeffers knew precisely where they were going, and how long it would take. He said to her, 'We should make it by the bottom of the second inning,' but they had to park a little farther from the stadium than he'd anticipated, so that by the time they got to the gate it was the top of the third. They both wore the red caps he'd purchased earlier in the day. Jeffers produced two tickets at the turnstile, whipping them from his wallet with a flourish.

She was taken aback by the gesture, and more by the realization that he'd purchased the tickets far in advance.

'Should be a good one,' he said to the gatetender.

'Yeah, except they're up a couple already and ain't no one figured out how to hit that kid yet.' He was an old man with white hair growing in his earlobes. One ear had a hearing aid attached to it. She saw he'd plugged in a cheap portable radio earphone in the other ear. He ignored them and reached for the tickets of the next set of late arrivals.

They rapidly made their way through the aisles, bumping into people, stepping around vendors.

The huge crowd and constant throb of noise unsettled her. She felt as if she were afloat in space, weightless, and that the swells of sound would sweep her away. She pressed close to Jeffers; at one point, when a rowdy group of teenagers tried to push between them, she reached out for his hand.

In the home half of the fifth, Jeffers announced he was

286

hungry again. 'Listen,' he said to her, 'just run over to the concession stand and get us some hot dogs.'

She stared at him in disbelief.

Around them was a tidal flood of sound: the stately right-hander for the Mets had been throwing in his usual overpowering fashion, and the Cardinals had nothing to show for their efforts but the short end of a 2–0 score. But as Jeffers had made his request, the leadoff man had walked and the next batter promptly lined a base hit to right. The crowd surged in anticipation, and a steady rhythmic clapping of encouragement filled the stadium. She had to yell for him to hear.

'I can't,' she said.

'Why not?'

She felt his hand suddenly on her leg, the fingers biting into the muscle, squeezing it painfully.

'I just can't,' she said, tears forming in her eyes.

He stared at her. He thought: Perfect.

'What's wrong?'

She shook her head. She didn't know. She knew only that she was terrified of the noise, of the people, and of the world that he'd suddenly let into their lives.

'Please,' she said.

He could not hear her; the next batter had singled and the runner had scored from second, avoiding the catcher's lunging tag in a cloud of dust. But he saw her mouth the word and that was enough for him.

'All right,' he said. 'Just this once.'

He released her leg.

She nodded thanks.

'That's what they call a bang-bang play,' he said.

'Bang-bang?'

'Yes. It happens bang! Bang! Bang! Bang! Bang! The runner slides, bang! The catcher tags, bang! He's safe! Bang! Or he's out, bang! I always liked that cliché.'

He spotted a peanut vendor and waved wildly to attract the man's attention. He gave her a bag and after she started cracking the shells and eating, he reached down and from his ever-present camera bag, plucked his Nikon. 'Smile,' he said, pivoting in his chair toward her.

He clicked off a series of pictures.

She felt embarrassed. 'My hair,' she said. 'This silly hat . . .'

But he just gestured toward the playing field. 'Pay attention to the game,' he said. 'You may need to remember some details later.'

This frightened her, and she tried to concentrate on the action in front of her. I understand baseball, she said to herself. I know about squeeze plays and pitchouts and hitting behind the runner. I was the shortstop on my high-school softball team and I learned the rules.

But the figures on the artificial green of the playing surface seemed mysterious to her, no matter how hard she tried to analyse what was happening before her.

She dared to watch Jeffers. He seemed intent on the game and on the action on the field, but she knew that this devotion obscured some other purpose. Her mind would not form concrete possibilities.

She shivered in the sticky humidity.

Her head felt dizzy and she swallowed with difficulty. Once, when she saw him bend toward the bag at his feet, she almost choked in sudden confusion.

Finally, as the teams were changing sides, she asked in a voice that seemed to her hollow, 'Why are we here, please?'

Jeffers turned to her and stared. Then he burst out in a huge laugh. 'We're here because this is America, this is the national pastime, this is the Mets and the Cards and the pennant is on the line. But mostly we're here because I'm a baseball fan.'

He laughed again and looked at her.

'So you see,' he continued, 'right now we're killing nothing. Except time.'

He hesitated. 'Later,' he said.

She did not ask any more questions.

They stayed until the top of the eighth. Jeffers waited until the Mets scored four to blow open the tight game.

Then he grabbed her by the hand and led her, along with the other early and easily disgruntled fans, out of the stadium. As they walked away, a great shout went up from the stadium behind them. He heard a young couple walking a few feet away, listening to a radio, announce to no one and everyone at the same time: 'Jack Clark home run with two on!' And he nodded. 'They should know,' he said softly to Anne Hampton, 'that it's never over until it's over. A great American said that once.'

'Who?' she asked.

'Caryl Chessman,' Jeffers replied.

Jeffers made certain that Anne Hampton was strapped in her seat, then he went to the rear of the car and opened the trunk. He rummaged about for an instant in what he called his miscellany bag, finally coming up with a set of Missouri license plates. To these he'd previously attached metal clips, so he was able to bend down and place them firmly, directly over the car's actual plates. He took a cheap tag frame that he'd acquired in an auto goods store and locked it over the top, so there was no way the telltale yellow of his New York plates would show, but so he would swiftly be able to remove the set from Missouri, stolen sometime before. Then he opened the bag containing the weapons and pulled out a cheap .25-caliber automatic. Taped on the inside of the bag was a specially prepared clip of bullets. He made certain that the soft points were notched, then slid the clip into his camera bag. He searched around for another second before putting his hands on a simple leather briefcase. This he took out before locking the trunk.

Inside the car he switched on the interior light.

She watched as he pulled a small yellow file from the briefcase and opened it on his lap.

The file contained a set of newspaper and magazine clippings beneath a typed checklist. She saw the words: Gun / Typewriter / Access / Egress / Emergency Backup / Lawyer / ID. Each word category had several lesser categories listed beneath it, but she was not quick enough and the light was too shallow for her to see what they said. A number of items had been crossed off, and others had received large check marks next to them. A few had hand-written notes next to them. She saw that the file contained two maps, one hand-drawn, the other a grid map of the city. As she watched, Jeffers seemed to be reviewing the lists and the maps. She glanced at the newspaper clips and saw a half-page article from *Time* Magazine. It was from their Nation section and the headline read: RANDOM MURDER OF GAYS CREATES FUROR IN ST LOUIS. She saw that the other stories were from the St Louis *Post-Dispatch*.

'All right,' Jeffers said with a slightly excited tinge to his voice. 'All right. We're set.'

He looked over at her. 'Ready?'

She did not know how to respond.

'Ready?' he demanded harshly.

She nodded.

'Right,' he said. 'The hunt begins.' He drove into the city darkness.

She was turned around and lost within moments. One second they were up on a thruway, cutting amidst skyscrapers that seemed to leap up into the night-time next to her, then they were circling through shabby, ill-lit streets that glistened with reflected headlights. After what she thought was at least thirty minutes, Jeffers slowed. Anne Hampton stared from the window and saw occasional knots of men standing outside of bars in the warm summer evening air, talking, gesturing. Jeffers was taking it all in wordlessly. But, she thought, he still seems to know where he's heading. She forced her mind into a benign blank. After circling through a ten-block area for another half hour, Jeffers steered the car down a darkened side street, finally pulling to the curb near the end of the block. It seemed a residential neighborhood, not houses, but apartments carved from older buildings, with trees planted in sections cut from the sidewalk. But she saw that they were only a few blocks from the brighter lights of the main thorough-fare. She watched Jeffers slide around the front of the car and open the door for her. She thought his movements spidery, predatory. In an instant she found herself virtually lifted from the vehicle and, arm in arm, walking down the sidewalk. As always, she was taken aback by the taut strength of his hands and arms. She could feel his bunched muscles rigid with excitement.

'Say nothing,' Jeffers said in a low, awful voice. 'Avoid eye contact until I make my choice. But smile and look happy.'

She tried but knew she looked merely pathetic.

She concentrated instead on walking steadily.

She knew what was happening, or, at least, she suddenly knew that she was about to add another nightmare to that possessed by the derelict, but she felt helpless to do anything. Not that anything occurred to her to do, save co-operate.

Look out at the sky, she said to herself. Stare up into the few lights around. She saw the moon hanging above the branches of a tree and suddenly remembered a tune from childhood: The fox went out on a chilly night . . . And he prayed to the moon to give him light . . . For he'd many a mile to go that night . . . Before he reached the town-o, town-o, town-o. The music flowed through her mind like a comforting wave.

They walked around the block three times, each time passing a pair or a threesome of men hurrying through the blackness of the secondary street. On their fourth turn around the block, as they were approaching their car, she felt Jeffers stiffen next to her. She could sense his muscles tightening, and she realized he'd put his hand into his camera bag.

'This could be it,' Jeffers said.

They continued to walk toward the solitary man, who was hurrying in their direction.

'Slow a little,' Jeffers said. 'I want to pass this guy in the shadow of that tree.'

She saw that equidistant between them and the man was a large tree that added shadow to the night.

'Keep smiling,' Jeffers said.

She had a sudden vision of herself being swept out to sea

by a violent undertow. She clung to his arm, suddenly afraid that she would stumble or faint.

Jeffers arranged all his sensations. His eyes darted about the area, taking in all the emptiness. His ears were tuned to noises, searching for some telltale, out-of-the-ordinary sound. He even sniffed the air. He thought he was on fire, or that he was in love, and that every nerve end in his body was on edge, throbbing. Beneath his hand the metal of the pistol seemed glowing hot. He forced himself to measure his pace, slow, so that he would come abreast with the man at the precise moment, the darkest moment. A death march, he thought abruptly.

They moved together.

Jeffers estimated the distance: fifty feet. Then, suddenly, twenty feet. Then ten, and he nodded at the man and smiled.

The man was young, probably no more than twenty-five. Who are you? Jeffers wondered in an instant. Have you loved your life? The man's blond hair was cropped close over his ears and neck. Jeffers noticed that the man had a small gold stud in one ear. He wore a simple open sportshirt and slacks, with a sweater tossed over his shoulders in studied casual appearance.

Jeffers nodded again at the man, and the man returned the look with a small, wan, slightly nervous smile. Jeffers squeezed hard on Anne Hampton's arm and he saw her smile as well.

The man walked abreast, then past.

As the man stepped through Jeffers' peripheral vision, Jeffers slipped the gun from his bag, his finger resting on the trigger.

Jeffers had time only to say to himself: Be calm.

Then he spun around, directly behind the man, dropping Anne Hampton's arm so that he could raise both hands to the pistol grip. When the barrel reached out level with the man's head, Jeffers fired twice.

The cracking sound echoed down the street.

The man pitched forward, slamming to the sidewalk.

Anne Hampton stood frozen. She tried to lift her hands

to her eyes to cover them, then stopped, staring out in terror.

Jeffers leaped over the man, who lay facedown in a growing pool of blood. He was careful not to touch the man or the blood. The man did not move. Jeffers bent down, fired one more shot into the man's back, searching for the heart. Then, in the same fluid, continuous movement, he put the gun back into his bag and came out with the Nikon. He raised it to his eye and she heard the motordrive whir as the film advanced. Just as swiftly, he finished, returning the camera to the bag.

He grabbed Anne Hampton's arm and half-dragged her down toward their car.

He pulled open the door and thrust her swiftly into the seat. In an instant he'd jumped around to the driver's side. He did not squeal the tires, but started the car simply and efficiently, rolling slowly past the body on the sidewalk, down the empty street.

She turned and stared at the inert body as they slid past.

Within a few seconds they were away.

She saw that Jeffers was driving a preset route. She could feel the force of his concentration, as if he were creating a palpable sense out of his intelligence. After fifteen minutes she saw they had reached a deserted spot in a downtown warehouse area. Jeffers stopped the car and exited wordlessly. She waited for him to let her out, but he did not.

At the back of the car, Jeffers removed the Missouri license plate, wiped it with a rag, and threw it into a dark plastic bag. He then tossed the bag into a dumpster, climbing up to make sure that the bag with the plate was well situated amidst other garbage.

He got back into the car and they drove through the city into a suburban area. Jeffers stopped at a convenience store and used the light from the front of the building to see what he was doing. First he replaced his surgical gloves on his hands. Then he took out the envelope with the letter he'd written earlier in the day. Then he opened his file folder and pulled out a small brown manila envelope. He shook it open and Anne Hampton saw that there were several words cut from a newspaper. Jeffers produced a small plastic squeeze container of commonly used glue and fastened the words to the envelope. He used the glue to close the envelope.

Then he spoke.

'Can't be too careful. Now, I know they can't raise fingerprints from paper unless I put ink all over my fingers. But the FBI has all this new spectrographic equipment which I'm just getting familiar with and it can break down enzymes and Lord knows what. That's why no saliva. If I licked that envelope shut, they could come up with my blood type, for example. Hell, for all I know, they could come up with my Social Security number. So, caution is the word.'

He looked at her. His words had spun out in an excited, almost little-boy delight.

'Look,' he said. 'Don't worry. We're finished. We got away. Just a few odds and ends and we're home free.'

He finished with the envelope and put the car back in gear. In a moment he pulled up to the front of a large postal building. He jumped out of the car and put the envelope in one of the mail boxes.

Back in the car he said, 'Now just the gun and bullets, and everything's set. But we won't do those until tomorrow. At our leisure.'

His adrenaline still flowing freely, he maneuvered the car back onto the interstate. Anne Hampton pivoted once in her seat, looking out the rear window toward the fading lights of the city.

He saw her shiver.

'Cold?'

She nodded.

He did nothing.

'Tired?'

She realized she was drained. She nodded again.

'Hungry?'

She thought she would be sick.

'I'm famished,' he said. 'I could eat the proverbial horse.'

She thought: It's endless. It's forever.

After a moment he spoke again. 'It's the strangest thing,' he began evenly. 'The homophobe who has killed all those gays in St Louis, I think seven before tonight, always writes in rhyme. At least according to the *Post-Dispatch*.'

Jeffers shook his head.

'The newspapers haven't given him a nickname, which I think is kinda strange. I mean, usually when you have a series of killings like that, they slap some sobriquet on the poor guy. Like Gay Killer or Homo Homicides or something equally dumb and borderline-offensive.'

He looked at her and saw the weariness in her eyes.

'Do you know what just happened?' he asked.

'Yes,' she said dully.

He reached across the car and slapped her, but not too vigorously, thinking: She's probably pretty tired.

The crack against her cheek aroused Anne Hampton from the sense of lassitude and apathy that had overtaken her since the shots on the street.

'Do you know what really happened?' he asked again.

She shook her head.

'Well, we went in and did a pretty good imitation of a number of other crimes that have taken place in that fair city over the past eighteen or so months. What we performed was what the police call a copycat killing. You see, they always withhold some detail or another from the press so that they are able to tell who's doing what. Copycat killings frustrate the hell out of the police. You have to see it the way they do: While they're all damn busy trying to find some maniac, along comes some other freak to mess up the works. It takes them time, we're talking man-hours here, to sort the killings out. So, by the time whatever task force is assigned to this killer figures out what seems to have happened, we will have disappeared. No evidence. No leads . . .'

She saw that he was smiling, Cheshire Cat-like.

'Oh, not completely without jeopardy, mind you. Someone could have seen us from one of the apartments in the area. Perhaps I dropped something, or you did, that we don't know about. Something that some sullen, dogged detective can latch on to. You see, that's half the excitement. The state of waiting for that knock on the door.'

He rapped the steering wheel with his fingers and the drumming sound startled her.

'You see, that's what I figured out with all my studies. Usually police find killers because murderers and victims have some relationship which predates the murder. The police merely have to ascertain which relationship led to homicide. This is the vast majority of cases. Then there are the serial-type murders, where the crimes adopt a distinct pattern. Those are very difficult to solve, of course, because the killers meander about. Once you get into different jurisdictions, the police hamstring themselves. But I have great respect for the police. They've solved many more of these than you'd think. Often because the poor idiot screws something else up and the cops are on to him like sharks. Never underestimate the intuitive powers of a cop, I say. But, still, the hardest for them to figure out, obviously, are random, patternless killings.

'I thought for a while that that was the type I should engage in. Simply go to a city, pick some poor folk out at random, blow them away. But I realized that that in itself would be a pattern, and eventually, somewhere, some cop would see it. It's the million monkeys, million typewriters theory. Eventually one will type out Shakespeare's complete works.

'So what was I left with?'

She did not really expect that he wanted her to answer.

'I needed to combine this random quality with a pattern. I thought hard. I calculated. I figured. And do you know what I came up with?'

Again she was quiet. His voice was mesmerizing.

'A design with great simplicity, and thus great beauty.'

He smiled.

'I copy things. I continue studying. I find out everything there is to know about a Freeway Killer or a Campus Killer or a Green Mountain Killer. The press is so helpful with these titles. Then I just go out and organize a reasonable facsimile. So the police, who are looking for someone else entirely, have this aberrational killing on their hands in the midst of something bigger and, they think, more important. It gets ignored. Shunted aside. Put in the out basket. Filed.'

He took a deep breath. 'Most killers are caught because, in their arrogance and need, they put some signature on a crime. I am more humble. The act is what is important to me. Not signing it at the bottom. So in, order to murder, I become someone else. I put my mind inside that other person's. I use details I know, and those I can surmise, and I create my own little perfection.

'I arrive. I murder. I leave. And no one, save myself, is anything the wiser.'

He waited an instant before continuing.

'But I've grown so accomplished, too careful. Too clever, too perfect.' He shook his head.

'A knock on the door? A warrant? Never happen. That's not bravado speaking. Just efficiency and confidence.'

She thought she heard sadness in his voice.

'Actually, not much in the way of thrill much more.' He looked over at her. 'It has, to be blunt, become just too damn easy.'

'That's why you're here,' he said matter-of-factly. 'You're here to help me bring all this to a proper, suitable, sufficiently volcanic conclusion.'

He turned away.

'You can go to sleep now,' he said. 'I'm a bit wired. I think I'd rather drive.' He felt, suddenly, a great pleasurable release. He thought to himself: There. I've told somebody. Now the world will know.

'Now we're going home,' Jeffers said. 'The slow route, granted. But home. Good night, Boswell.'

She heard his voice and the word hit her consciousness: home. Try as she might, she couldn't summon up a solid picture of her house and her parents. Instead, what jumped into her mind seemed vaporous and distant, as if hidden behind film, and she had difficulty telling what it was, though she knew it scared her.

She felt the car surge forward and she closed her eyes and welcomed her new nightmare.

9 Another regular session of the Lost Boys

14

Martin Jeffers sat awake and alone.

But his solitude was busy, peopled by memory. Once when they were young and vacationing on Cape Cod, his brother had found a young hawk with a damaged wing. The hawk summer, he thought. The drowning summer. He wondered for a moment why he thought of the bird, when it was the later events that August that had been so much more important. But his mind filled with the images of reflection. Doug had found the bird on a dirt road, hopping about in misery, wing dragging. For two weeks, Jeffers recalled, his brother spent every minute rooting about in the woods, turning over rotten logs, lifting up moss-covered rocks, in a constant search for bugs, beetles, small snakes, and snails, which he dutifully brought home to the bird, which gobbled them down and squawked for more. Martin Jeffers smiled. That's what they named the bird: Squawk. In the little free time they'd had, they'd haunted the local lending library, taking home dozens of books on birds, tracts on falconry, and texts on veterinary medicine. After two weeks the hawk would perch on Doug's shoulder to eat, and Martin Jeffers remembered the triumphant look on his brother's face when he set the bird on the handlebars of his old bicycle and rode the bike and bird to town and back.

Martin Jeffers put his hand to his forehead and shuddered.

The old bastard, he thought. Doug was right to despise him.

Their father had told him to get rid of the bird.

Doug wouldn't put the hawk in a cage and so it defecated all over the storeroom where he kept it. That had infuriated the druggist and he'd presented the two boys with a simple, terrible ultimatum: Cage it, free it, or else. It was the *else* part that was so ominous. If its wing won't work, his brother had complained, it will die when we free it. He remembered his brother's face reddening with anger. And you can't put a wild thing in a cage! Douglas Jeffers had shouted. It will die. It will die surely and stupidly, gnawing desperately at the bars without comprehension. Doug was resolute. He always was. Martin Jeffers remembered trailing after his brother, running hard with his shorter legs, trying to keep up with the pace Douglas Jeffers set out of anger. My brother always moved quickly when enraged, Jeffers thought. Always in control, but fast.

The bird had remained tenaciously on his brother's shoulder, digging his claws into the shirt and muscle, turning his proud hawk face into the wind, while Douglas Jeffers rowed across the pond that separated their house from the path to the ocean. He'd pulled the rowboat onto the shore and set off down a worn route. They'd come to a wide field of sandy dirt, waist high in green seagrass and tangled beach-plum bushes. The ocean was a quarter mile away, just past a ridge of tall sand dunes, and Martin Jeffers remembered the sound of the waves echoing deeply in his memory. The breeze tossed the grass about them, and it seemed as if his brother were swimming through strong currents. The afternoon sun was bright, spiraling down with summer intensity onto their heads. Martin Jeffers saw his brother lift his arm, holding the hawk aloft, like he'd seen in picture books of medieval falconry. Then he tried to toss the bird skyward. Martin Jeffers saw the wings beating in a flurry, trying to lift up into the sky, then failing, falling back onto his brother's arm. 'It's no good,' the older boy had said. 'That wing just won't make it.'

Then he had added, 'I knew it wouldn't.'

He said nothing else. They trudged back to their boat in silence. He'd rowed swiftly, pushing his back into the effort, as if he could make things different by force of strength.

Martin Jeffers' memory skipped ahead to the following morning. Doug had been up before him and had suddenly appeared at the side of his bed, hair tousled, face set, gray, and filled with rage. 'Squawk's dead,' his brother had said.

The old bastard had killed the bird while they'd slept. He'd gone into the storeroom and grabbed the poor trusting brute and wrung its neck.

Martin Jeffers was filled with a rage of his own. His heart swelled with the uncontroverted grief of childhood remembered.

He was just a cruel and heartless man and I was damn glad that he got what was coming to him. I only wish it had hurt him more! He remembered shouting those words out at his own therapist, who had asked in an infuriatingly calm voice whether that was true or not. Of course it was true! He killed the bird! He'd hated us! He'd always hated us. It was the only thing he was ever consistent about. That and getting his own damn way. He would just as quickly have crept into our rooms at night and strangled us the same way! He wanted to!

Martin Jeffers rememberd staring at the dead bird in his brother's hands.

No wonder he hated him so much. You can't be born with a hatred like that. You have to construct it carefully out of cruelty and neglect, first removing any love or affection. That's what he'd told the therapist. He'd asked the woman poised behind his head where he couldn't see her, If you'd had a father like that, wouldn't you want to become someone who cared about people? Someone who tried to help people? Why the hell do you think I'm here?

And, of course, the therapist said nothing.

The layered memories boiled about in Martin Jeffers' mind.

Sonuvabitch, sonuvabitch, sonuvabitch.

No one said a word that night. No one ever said a thing. We all sat at the dinner table and acted like nothing had happened. He remembered his mother looking over at Doug and him and saying, I'm sorry the bird flew away. Both boys had adopted the same disbelieving stare, and she'd finally averted her eyes and nothing more was said. She never knew a damn thing, he'd told the therapist. She just primped and preened and was forever touching them, especially with wet, nerve-racking kisses, and she never knew a damn thing about anything and if you tried to tell her, she just turned away.

Their father just thrust food into his mouth.

Sonuvabitch.

Martin Jeffers rocked back in his seat. He saw himself again that morning as he fell from sleep's pinnacle at the sound of his brother's voice, awakening to the sight of the dead bird in his brother's hands. The bird was stiff and broken.

Then, in his memory, he just saw his brother's hands.

Then he thought: Ohmigod!

He said it out loud though there was no one near to hear him: 'Ohmigod! No!'

He felt the force of memory crushed by his thought, like an exceptionally heavy weight loaded onto his shoulders.

'Oh no. Oh no, oh no,' he said to himself.

In an instant his mind filled with black sadness and horror.

And he realized suddenly, right at that moment, who'd killed the bird.

I am timid, thought Martin Jeffers.

Somehow all these things happened to the two of us and I became quiet and introverted and lonely and passive and he became . . . Jeffers stopped himself before putting a word to it.

He pictured his brother in his mind's eye and saw his loose, flushed, grinning face. He forced himself to see his brother at moments of anger and he remembered the force of Douglas Jeffers' silences. Those had always scared him. He recalled pleading with his brother to speak to him, to talk to him. He thought of the detective and the crime-scene photographs of her niece and he tried to reconcile the two visions.

He shook his head.

Not Doug, he thought.

Then he had a worse thought: Why not?

He could not answer the question.

Martin Jeffers stood up and walked about his apartment. He lived on the ground floor of an old house in Pennington, New Jersey, a tiny town tucked between Hopewell and Trenton's suburbs. Hopewell was just to the west of Princeton, and Martin Jeffers recalled with displeasure that whenever anyone mentioned Hopewell, even when they have been growing up, his brother had always reminded whoever was listening that the little, sleepy town was famous for one thing: It was the place where Lindbergh's baby had been stolen.

The crime of the century, Martin Jeffers thought.

He felt cold and stepped to his window. He put his hand against the screen and felt the late-summer warmth. Still, he shivered, and pushed the window down sharply, leaving only a crack open.

They found the baby in the woods, he thought. Decomposed.

He wondered for an instant whether every state marked its history with crimes. He was taken aback when he realized how much his brother knew. He remembered Doug talking about the Camden Killer, who had walked out on a warm early September day in 1949 and calmly shot and killed thirteen people with a war souvenir Luger. A few years back, Doug had been fascinated to learn that his brother frequently saw this person the papers once described as a mad dog as he peacefully roamed the halls of Trenton Psychiatric Hospital, a model patient for more than twenty-five years, never arguing when the orderlies came about with the daily dosage of Thorazine, Mellaril, or Haldol. Vitamin H, the patients called it. The Camden Killer always took his without complaint. Not even a whimper of protest.

Doug was always interested in that sort of thing.

Martin Jeffers shook his head.

Yeah, but so was that police reporter from the Philadelphia paper who came up to do a story about the hospital.

And you tell it at every stupid seminar or convention you go to. A lot of people remember that crime.

That was the problem, he thought. People are always fascinated by crimes. And it was natural for his brother to be intrigued by them. Hell, he'd spent so much time chasing cops and robbers with his camera, it was natural he was interested.

He paused.

But how interested?

He shook his head again. Denial, he thought.

Ridiculous.

You know your brother, he told himself.

He put his head in his hands.

He could not cry. He could not feel anything save a disjointed confusion.

Do you really? he asked himself.

He thought of the men in his therapy group. He suddenly envisioned his brother sitting among them. Then, just as quickly, he saw himself there as well.

He turned away from the window, as if by walking across the room he could change the view in his mind.

'Dammit!' he said out loud. 'Goddammit to hell!'

He thought of his father and his mother.

'How could you love them?' he said.

He thought of his woman therapist. There had been an abstract painting on one wall of her office, a Kandinsky reproduction, all brightly colored angles and shapes with dots floating about a snow-white background. Across from it had been a Wyeth print, a muted picture of a barn caught in grays and browns in the wan early evening light. American Realism. He had always been struck by the juxtaposition of the two pictures, but never had managed to ask the woman why she had selected them and placed them where they were. 'Well,' she had asked, 'do you think you loved your real mother and father?'

'They worked in a circus! A drunk and a whore!' he had blurted out in angry response. 'They abandoned each other and then they abandoned us! I was only three or four . . .

I did not know them. How can you love something or someone that you don't know?'

She didn't answer that, of course.

And he knew the answer anyway.

It's easy. The mind creates something to love out of the slightest memory of a touch, a sound, a sensation.

He thought then of the corollary.

The mind can also create something to hate.

He stepped over to a small desk in a corner of what passed for his living room, really a room filled with papers, clutter, paperback novels, classic novels, medical texts and reports, magazines, a couple of chairs and a sofa, a television and telephone. He looked around at his things They are cheap. The meager belongings of someone living a meager life. He looked down at the desktop and saw an envelope stuck in the corner of the desk blotter. On it was written in his own handwriting, *Doug's apartment key*.

He remembered his brother tossing the key to him so casually. A sentimental journey, he said.

Nothing is an accident.

Everything is part of some scheme. Conscious or unconscious. He picked up the key in the envelope and held it. He shook his head. Not yet, he said. I'm not convinced. I'm not persuaded. I'm not intruding. Not yet.

He recognized this feeling for the lie it was.

Then he dropped the envelope back on his desk and returned to an easy chair. He glanced at a clock. It was well past midnight. Sleep, he said to himself. He dropped into the chair, knowing that he would not.

He thought of the detective.

Martin Jeffers tried to imagine the forces that drove her. He thought, for an instant, that she was somehow pure; that the only true motivation was justice. If this took the form of war or revenge or anger, it was still honest. Even murder? he wondered to himself. He did not formulate an answer, but he knew: I would not trust anyone who turned the other cheek. Modern psychiatry does not recognize such selfless altruism. Again the detective elbowed her way into his consciousness. He saw her face set, unsmiling, filled with terrifying determination, her hair thrust back severely. What is so frightening, he thought, is that she does not carry herself like a man. A woman detective. She ought to be edged in granite, some middle-aged, bureaucratic type, with farm woman's hands and monocular vision of the world. Detective Barren wears silks and not very sensible shoes and she frightens me all the more. Women do not, as a rule, pursue their quarry all across the United States. They are not motivated by the senseless and stupid egos of insult and outrage like men. They are more worldly, more understanding.

He smiled and thought how silly he was being.

Lesson One, Day One, Medical School: Don't generalize. Don't characterize.

The words obsession and compulsion thrust themselves into his mind, but he was momentarily confused. He considered his brother, the detective, then himself.

It was no wonder, he thought then, that the ancient Greeks invented the Furies and that they were women. His memory tumbled through myth and fantasy. Even if I were blind myself, I would still see.

Martin Jeffers stared across the room, watching the clock, scared of the night, waiting for the morning, desperately wanting to return to the routine of his life: the morning shower, the quick cup of coffee, the drive to the hospital, the first series of daily rounds and the regular sessions of his group and then his patients, knocking in their tentative way at his office door. He wanted everything to return suddenly to normal. The way it was, the way it was before today happened. He realized how childish the wish was and smiled to himself: I wish I were back in Kansas, back in Kansas, Kansas . . . He closed his eyes and laughed half-heartedly at the memory joke, but knew nothing would change when he opened them. There are no magic slippers, he thought. No heels to click together three times. He suddenly remembered his brother's description of his work: on the heels of evil.

He got up, went to a closet, and pulled a winter comforter from a shelf. He wrapped it around his shoulders and sat back down in the chair. He switched off the bright light on a coffee table next to him and sat quietly in the darkness, wanting to be awake, wanting to be asleep, caught between the two, each an equally terrifying prospect.

Outside, in her car, Detective Mercedes Barren saw the light extinguished. She waited fifteen minutes, to be certain that Martin Jeffers did not leave the apartment. Then she put the seat back as far as it would go and tugged a thin blanket appropriated from her hotel room over her. She double-checked to make sure the doors were locked, but the window cracked to the cool night air. Pennington, she thought, is a place of absolute safety, of families and neighbors and backyard barbecues. She remembered visiting the tree-lined streets on high-school football weekends. He doesn't know, she thought. He doesn't know that I am home, too. She loosened the belt to her jeans, and, glancing eagerly once more at the darkened apartment, relaxed, letting her fingers play against the grip of the 9-millimeter that rested on her stomach, beneath the blanket. Its heft, as always, reassured her. She was confident. She dismissed the thought that had troubled her much of the evening. She knew that she was a policewoman and that there was something terribly wrong about her becoming a criminal.

But only briefly, she said to herself. Expediency.

She cleared the thought from her mind.

Then she closed her eyes to the night.

Her dreams, though, were unsettling, flooded with disjointed combinations of people: her husband and Sadegh Rhotzbadegh, the Jeffers brothers and her bosses and her father. When the headlights of a car passing by awakened her, just before dawn, she was relieved. She glanced at the taillights of the car as it slipped through the gray darkness. She could just make out the red and blue light bar on the roof, and for an instant she wondered what sort of sleepy cop could miss someone alone in a car parked on a residential street. What's the purpose in patrolling if you can't see the unusual? But she was glad that she hadn't been spotted, though she knew that her own badge and brusque manner would have been sufficient explanation.

She watched the red lights disappear around a distant corner. They glowed brightly for an instant as the patrolman touched his brakes, then slid from her sight. She stretched and looked about her. She bent the mirror toward herself and straightened her appearance as best she could. Then she bent down and hunted about for the thermos of coffee and half-eaten Danish that she'd brought along. The coffee was lukewarm, but better than nothing, and she sipped it slowly, trying to pretend it was steaming hot.

She saw the branches on the trees around her slowly etch themselves against the morning light. First one bird chirped loudly, then another. The shapes of the houses seemed to stand out stark and bare as morning took hold.

She reached down and felt her stomach where the thick round welt of the bullet scar hid beneath her shirt. The patrol car passing, the pre-dawn quiet, all triggered her own memory. She thought of the experience of being shot; it had still been dark, but close to the end of the graveyard shift. There were aspects of the entire act that remained a mystery to her. The whole event had happened in some other time frame: some parts were speeded up, played out with dizzying quickness; others seemed slowed to a foggy crawl.

She had spotted the two kids.

They had been walking briskly down the opposite street with a hasty purposefulness that was electric to any police officer with more than a few minutes of experience.

'Now that couple has got to be wrong,' she had said to her partner. The teenagers were wearing high-top sneakers. 'They've got their second-story shoes on,' she had added, 'and unless there's some roundball game going on at 5 a.m. that we don't know about . . .' He had looked over at the two boys for a few seconds and nodded his head.

'Can't you just smell the B and E?' he had laughed. 'C'mon. Let's bust them quick and head in.'

She had called it in: 'Dispatch, this is unit fourteen-oh-one, we're fifty-six at the corner of Flagler and Northwest

Twenty-first. We have two suspects in a two-thirteen in view. Request backup.'

She always liked the authority that slipped into her voice speaking the particular codes of the patrol officer. There had been static, momentarily, on the radio, as her partner had steered the car into a U-turn and cruised up behind the two boys. Then the dispatcher had acknowledged their call, telling them that backup was *en route*.

They were only a few feet behind the teenagers, who hadn't turned to notice them, when her partner had hit the flashing lights. 'This'll wake them up,' he had said.

It did. They both had jumped and frozen. She had seen that they were both in their early teens.

'Kids,' her partner had said. 'Christ.'

They had stepped from the car and started to approach the pair.

'I wonder what they stole?' her partner had asked idly.

She thought of those words often: your life.

She had not seen the gun until it was leveled at them. They were only a few feet distant. She remembered struggling, trying to reach her service revolver, while her partner threw his hands out in front of him as if he could ward off the shot. The gun barrel had flashed and his arm had knocked into her as he was thrown back. She remembered seeing the weapon turn, as if it were unattached to anything, and face her. She sometimes believed that she could see the bullet as it was fired and as it had traveled the space between her and the gun.

Then she remembered lying on the ground and looking up and realizing that it would be morning soon and her shift would be ending and she would be able to go home and read the paper over a leisurely breakfast. She had planned to do some shopping that day; perhaps it had been a change in temperature, but she had decided to buy herself something slinky and sexy, even if she never wore it. The names of the stores had flashed into her head. All the time she had thought these things, her hands had been searching for her stomach, and she was able to feel sticky hot blood pumping from her.

Her eyes had focused on the slowly lightening sky, and her breathing had become shallow and she remembered seeing the two teenagers hover into her line of sight. They had stared down at her, meeting her eyes. She had seen one lift the gun and she thought then of her family and friends. But instead of firing, the teenager had dropped the weapon, cursing, and run away. She always remembered the sound of their sneakers slapping away, growing fainter in the distance as the cacophony of sirens had enveloped her, promising her a chance at life.

In the car, she turned away from the memory and watched a paperboy weave his way, first right, then left, up the street on his bicycle, tossing newspapers on to front porches with practiced familiarity and confidence. He spotted Detective Barren and after a momentary look of suprise, smiled and gave her a wave. She rolled down the window and asked, 'Got any extras?'

He stopped the bike. 'Actually, yeah, just today, I've got one. Old Mr Macy down the street's on vacation and I forgot. You wanna buy his?'

She fished a dollar bill from her pocketbook.

'Here,' she said. 'Keep the change.'

'Thanks, lady. Here you go.'

He pedaled off, waving.

The lead headline was more trouble in the Middle East. There was a picture of rescue workers pulling bodies from a wrecked building, victims of a suicide-car bomb. Below that was the national lead, a tax bill in Congress story. There were two crime stories on the front page, opening day in the trial of a reputed mob boss, story and photo of the man walking up courtroom steps, and a local crime story. She read this one first: A homeowner had surprised a burglar breaking into his house and had shot the unarmed man dead with an unregistered and hence illegal weapon. Prosecutors were still undecided whether to indict the homeowner or give him a medal.

She turned to the sports pages. The pennant races were just heating up and football training camps were heading to the last cuts. She turned to an inside page to read the agate and see whether the Dolphins had cut any of her favorite players, but they had not. She saw, though, that the Patriots had released one of their old linemen. He was a steady block of a man from some solid Midwestern state, who'd always played infuriatingly well against the Dolphins and she had come, over the years, to admire him for the constancy of his efforts, carried out in anonymity and pain. She knew he would play hurt, and she respected that, perhaps more than the other fans. She was saddened suddenly by the news, a reminder both of sudden mortality and the changeable nature of life. She thought she would root hard for his replacement to fail.

Everything changes eventually. Everyone passes on to something new, she thought.

She looked back up at Jeffers' apartment and stiffened when she realized that the light had been switched on. She saw a shape move in front of the window and she shrank down in the car seat involuntarily, not really worrying about being spotted, but strongly feeling the need for concealment.

Come on, she said to herself. Come on, doctor. Get the day started.

She was flush with excitement and she rolled the window down, breathing in the damp morning air as if she were scared that her thoughts would suffocate her.

Martin Jeffers moved about the apartment in the weak morning half-light. He had slept, of that he was sure, but he did not know for how long. He felt no sense of refreshment, remaining as exhausted by emotion as he had at the start of the night. He moved into the bathroom and dropped his clothes on the floor. He forced himself into the shower, making certain that it was colder than comfortable. He wanted to shock his system into movement. He wanted alertness and quick wit. He held his face under the cascading cold water, shivering, but feeling vitality creep into his bones and blood.

He stepped from the shower and rubbed himself red with a threadbare towel. Still naked, he shaved with cold water.

310

He padded into his bedroom and put fresh underwear, shirt, tie, and suit onto the bed. Do twenty, he said to himself. He dropped to the floor and managed a fast ten pushups. He laughed out loud. That's good enough. He turned over and did twenty-five sit-ups, with his knees bent, faithfully holding his hands behind his head. He remembered his brother explaining that that was the only way they were effective. Doug never had to worry about exercise. He was always strong, always in shape. He could eat everything in the house and not gain a pound. Martin Jeffers stood and looked at himself in the mirror over the dressing table. Not bad, he thought. Especially considering all the sedentary work you do. Take up running again or find some tennis partners. Back in shape in no time.

He dressed quickly, glancing at the clock.

He thought of Detective Barren. He had not told her when to come to the hospital, but he knew she would be there early. He shook his head.

No, he thought, nothing's been proven. Nothing at all.

It is in the nature of brothers always to exaggerate, both goods and evils. It comes from childhood, from the constancy of love, jealousy, and unrestrained emotion that is inherent in the relationship. So Doug killed a bird when you always thought – no, assumed – that it was your father. You were mistaken. Still, that doesn't make your brother a killer. Not at all.

Martin Jeffers' hands stopped in midair as he was finishing the knot to his tie. He was almost overcome, suddenly, by the force of the self-lie. He closed his eyes, then opened them, as if he could clear the agony of his thoughts from his mind. He said out loud, firmly addressing himself in the third person:

'Well, whatever Doug is, and you damn well don't have any proof, any real proof of one thing or another despite what that goddamn detective says, he's still your goddamn brother and that ought to count for something.'

His words sounding strong in the empty room comforted him momentarily. But he also thought angrily that he'd been a doctor long enough to recognize clinical denial. Even in himself.

Still stretched between the poles of disbelief and realization, not trusting his memory, his feelings, or the knowledge that had grown over the years within him, Martin Jeffers headed off to the hospital. He did not see the detective waiting and watching from her vantage point across the street.

She waited another ten minutes just to be certain.

But she knew from the brisk pace he'd set and the fixed glance he'd worn that he was heading directly to the hospital and to the meeting with her that she assumed he'd spent the night worrying about.

He'll get that meeting, she thought, just not quite as early as he probably expects it. Again, she was mildly troubled about what she was about to do. Part of her argued: You know enough. He will come around and offer to help. But the pessimist within her doubted that the doctor would ever help her to find his brother until she could overwhelm him with necessity. You still need an edge, she told herself, and that apartment is as good a place as any to start looking for something. She was also uncertain about Martin Jeffers. If he's known, she thought, perhaps he's been hiding this knowledge for years. She recalled the look of surprise that Martin Jeffers had so quickly concealed when she'd first blurted out her need. Perhaps he's a killer as well. Perhaps, perhaps. She felt armored by knowledge, weakened by supposition, and realized that she still needed to know more. Facts, she thought. Hard truths. Evidence.

She shut down the mental debate and slid from her car. After glancing about momentarily, she sauntered across the street toward the apartment. But instead of walking up the front steps, she quickened her pace and trotted around the side of the building. Within a minute she spotted the window, cracked to let in fresh air.

Don't hesitate, she said to herself. Just do it.

She grabbed a metal trash can and thrust it against the

side of the house. Then she jumped up on top, throwing the window up in the same moment. She punched in the flimsy screen and jackknifed into the apartment in the same motion, landing like some clumsy waterfowl in a heap on the living room floor.

She scrambled to her feet and quickly closed the window behind her.

She had the odd, slightly humorous thought that she'd accomplished a pretty efficient break-in, for a first time. She pictured several dozen assorted burglars and robbers that she'd arrested in her career, and saw them lined up, a rogues' gallery applauding her. Just one of the guys now, she thought.

She stared around her and felt a momentary distaste at the haphazard arrangement of clothes and furniture. But the sensation passed quickly.

She was reminded of visiting John Barren in his freshman year, before they started sharing quarters. She smiled, remembering the socks festering in the corner, the underwear filed in a gray metal filing cabinet along with reading lists and course outlines. At the very least, she'd told him, you could put it in the drawer marked with a U. He'd lived in clutter as well, as if for him it was important to leave the mind unfettered and the surroundings messy. Then she thought that was her memory just being overly kind: that in reality he was just another man who'd become too accustomed to a mother who picked up after him; as if, even though he was away at college, his mother would mysteriously appear and pluck the socks from the corner, delivering them at a later point freshly laundered and rolled. And – she smiled again – he'd been right: It was almost the first damn thing you did. His damn laundry. You gave him a kiss, then there was a quick roll in the sack while his roommates were out, and then you picked up all his dirty clothes and set out for the local laundromat. Women never learn, she thought. She wanted to laugh out loud.

Then she heard a noise in the hallway and froze in fear.

Her mind swiftly sorted through perceptions: Was it a voice? The sound of a door being opened? Footsteps? She swallowed hard and concentrated her listening, trying to hear above the sudden throbbing within her.

He can't be back! she thought.

She pulled the 9-millimeter from her belt and waited stiffly, thinking: I'm crazy. Put the damn gun away. If it's him, just talk fast. He'll be angry, but he'll know why you're here.

Instead she leveled the gun at the door and waited.

She thought suddenly, terrifyingly: It's the brother!

She felt overcome by an immense, uncontrollable evil, as if its stench had instantly filled the room like smoke from a fire. Oh God! He was hiding him here! They're in it together! It's him!

She crouched, trying to still her noisy heart and quaking hand. She demanded toughness of herself, summoning it from within. Her hands steadied. Her breathing became even and patient. She sighted down the barrel of the gun, just as she had toward hundreds of firing-range targets.

Get him with the first shot, she snarled to herself.

Go for the chest. That will stop him. Then finish him off with a second shot to the head.

She closed one eye and took a deep breath. She held it in.

Then she waited for another noise.

But there was none.

She remained in her shooter's stance. She thought she might be unable to move and that her muscles would never relax. Thirty seconds passed. Then it stretched into a minute. Time seemed elongated by tension.

But the world was precipitously filled with silence.

She would not allow herself to breathe, until finally she could hold it in no longer and she released her pent-up breath in a long, low hiss.

She lowered the gun slowly.

'There's no one there,' she whispered out loud. It was reassuring to hear her own voice.

'You have lost your mind completely,' she continued under her voice. 'Now, stop screwing around and find something and get the hell out of here.'

She gave the bathroom a perfunctory look, then swiftly searched the bedroom. She was not being particularly systematic, she realized, but she also knew that anything Martin Jeffers had that might help her find his brother was not necessarily going to be hidden. Underneath the bed she found two cardboard file boxes filled with personal records. She pulled these out and sat on the floor, reading through them as swiftly as possible. They were mostly income tax forms, loan applications, records from college. She saw that his grades at medical school had been midrange, while in college they had been outstanding. It was as if once he'd arrived at his future, he'd stopped applying himself with the same intensity. That might explain why he was at a state mental hospital, she thought, instead of a Main Street private practice. But that only posed a series of new questions and she threw the papers back into the box, rifling through some more. She came across a certified letter from the state Catholic Charities organization that was a half-dozen years old. Idly, she opened it and read:

. . . We are unable to provide any information about your natural mother. Although the adoption was between family members, we did handle the paperwork. Unfortunately, when St Stephen's Parish burned in 1972, many of the old records that had not been transcribed on microfilm were irretrievably ruined.

Detective Barren stared down at the letter, thinking how interesting a piece of information it was but not knowing precisely why. She thrust it back and flipped through the remaining papers. There was one letter in an unmistakably feminine handwriting. 'Dear Marty,' she read. 'I'm sorry but it's just not going to work between us . . .' And the rest was maudlin self-recriminations by a woman named Joanne. Detective Barren recognized the style. Say you're to blame when you know the opposite is the truth. She'd helped a dozen friends write that letter during her teenage years. Her heart jumped and she remembered her niece at age sixteen once calling her with the same request for help.

She dropped the letter into the box and pulled out a yellowed, brittle copy of a newspaper. It was the *Vineyard*

Gazette from Martha's Vineyard and it carried an August date from nearly twenty years before. She scanned the front page rapidly; the main headline was: STEAMSHIP AUTHORITY REACHES AGREEMENT ON NEW FERRY DOCK. On the other side, above the fold, there was a picture and story: SWORD-FISHING FLEET SETS ONE-DAY RECORD WITH 21 FISH. Next to that, in small type, was: *Swimming Accident Claims Life of Summer Visitor*.

She glanced at the lead paragraph: 'Summer visitor Robert Allen lost his life Tuesday when he was caught in a sudden undertow while swimming off South Beach in the early evening. Police and Coast Guard officials surmised that the businessman from New Jersey struggled against the flood, exhausting himself, and was unable to reach shore after being swept a half mile from the beach.' She was struck by the fact that the man in the story was from New Jersey, but his name was different, and she went on to the next. Butting against that sory was: TISBURY SELECTMAN REJECT BLUE LAW MODIFICATION PROPOSAL.

She stared at the page for a moment and thought: Maybe there's something on the inside, and she started to flip through the pages rapidly. Nothing jumped out at her. It was the usual run of summer stories; she was familiar with the style of small-town resort newspapers. Some marriages, agricultural reports, who's visiting whom, cautious assessments on how many ticks there were in the woods. Warnings about shellfish contamination. Story and pictures of the prizewinning apple pie at the Tisbury Fair. The usual mixture of everyday things. She turned back to the front page and looked at the picture accompanying the sword-fish-capture story. It had no credit line. She stared at the composition of the photograph and wondered: Is that his? The eyes of the fishermen seemed to burn on the page, while the dead eye of one of their catch looked out in eerie contrast. It's his style, she thought. But she was impatient, which she recognized was an awful quality for someone conducting a nonspecific search. She ignored this recognition and dropped the newspaper back into the box. She pushed both cases back under the bed to the locations they'd previously occupied.

So far, nothing.

She went into the living room and saw the comforter tossed onto an easy chair. That's where he slept last night, she thought. If he slept at all.

She noticed that there was a bunch of magazines littering the floor around the chair. So he tried to get his mind off things. Well, I'm sure it didn't work. She started to cross the rooms when something struck her about the pile of magazines. She turned and looked back at them.

'What's wrong?' she whispered. 'What is it?'

She focused on the one magazine dropped in her direction.

She stared, then chided herself: Out of date. Pay attention, dammit!

She stepped across and knelt by the pile. She picked up a six-month-old *Life*. It seemed hot in her hands. She knew what would be inside. She let the magazine waft open and she saw instantly what it was – the by-line leaped out at her: PHOTOGRAPHS BY DOUGLAS JEFFERS. She looked at the page and saw the grainy gray of a picture. It was of an emergency-room physician staring out through the camera in exhaustion. The palpable sense of closeness between the camera and the subject struck her sharply and she had to push the page back.

I know what he was looking for, she thought. She could see the doctor brother sitting in the chair, looking into the pages, trying to see what the pictures could tell him.

She quickly spread the magazines about her, searching each for the pictures inside. People and shapes jumped out of the pages, exploding about her.

But none told her anything she did not know already.

He's good, she thought. But we already knew that. We knew he was one of the best.

But what else is there to see?

For a moment she felt the same frustration she knew the brother had felt hours earlier. There is so much to see, she thought, but it shows so little.

She closed the magazines and arranged them in a close approximation of the positions in which she'd found them.

She complained to herself: Find something!

She crossed to the desk and looked down on it and saw the words: *Doug's apartment key*. It was so obvious that for an instant she did not realize what she was staring at! Then her hand shot out, as if bidden by something other than her conscious mind, and she seized the envelope. She felt the key inside, and put back her head and barely managed to stifle the cheer welling up inside her. She stuffed the envelope into her pocket, then raised her hands above her head, balling them into fists like an athlete at the moment of victory. The exultation dissipated swiftly in the face of a quick demand for discipline: Get ahold of yourself, she thought angrily. Then, with near panic, she started to look about her. Address, address, I need the address. She looked across the room and spotted a small black book next to the telephone. She jumped to it and flipped it open. The Upper West Side of Manhattan address of the brother stared out in black ink. She looked about for a pen and scrap paper and saw none. She ripped the page from the book.

Then, feeling flush with heat, she walked to the front door, opened it, and, after looking back briefly, exited the building. She could think of nothing save the electric feeling that the stolen key in her pocket gave off.

On the street outside the apartment, she passed an elderly lady walking a small dog, carrying an old-fashioned parasol as protection against the rising sun. 'Good morning,' the woman said cheerfully.

'Beautiful day,' replied Detective Barren.

'But hot,' said the lady. She looked down at the Sheltie panting at the end of the leash. 'Dog days,' she said. 'Too hot in the summer. Too cold in the winter. Isn't that the nature of life?'

This was a joke and both women smiled. Detective Barren nodded in farewell and crossed the street. For a moment she was overcome by the bright late summer morning sun and the routine conversation with the woman. Everything is normal, she thought. Everything is simple and ordinary and in its place. Birds singing. Children playing. Light breeze blowing. Temperature soaring. Woman walking her dog. Norman Rockwell America. Simple steady rhythms and melodies.

She shook her head and thought of the dissonance in her pocket. I'm getting closer, she thought.

Pennington faded around her and she envisioned the hard city streets of her destination.

She slid back into her car, and within seconds was heading toward New York.

The tidal flow of argument ebbed around Martin Jeffers.

He had started the session by asking the Lost Boys a simple question: All of you have relations, he'd queried. What do you think they think of your behavior? Do they have any connection with your crimes? There had been a momentary uncomfortable silence, and Jeffers knew he'd struck a nerve within them. He knew, too, that his question, not so innocently posed, came from within his own heart. He had instantly pictured his brother, then forced the image from his mind while he listened to the men's memories unfold. There had been a rush of denial, almost *en masse*, which he had, as always, taken as representing an opposite reality. It was a simple formula: that which the Lost Boys most vigorously denied was closest to the truth.

Now he waited for the voices to subside so he could interject some comment that they would pick up and argue more about. But his attention wandered in and out, and he had trouble concentrating on the progress of the group. Luckily, the Lost Boys were in active form; they needed little input of his. He found himself nervously eyeing his watch, hoping for the end of the session. Where is she? he wondered.

'You know what was funny?' It was Meriwether speaking in his small, reedy voice. 'When I got busted and sent away to this country club, my wife was more upset than I was. I mean' – he breathed through his nostrils with a wheezy laughter – 'I would have thought that she'd divorce me. Shit, I thought she would shoot me herself. Christ, she's twice my size anyway, she coulda just walloped me a couple . . .'

All the men laughed at this.

Jeffers thought: What does she want? Arrest him? He remembered the ice in her eyes.

' . . . But she didn't. She was crying and wringing her hands. And even while I was copping out, she was, you know, denying it. It was like she thought that neighbor's kid I did somehow, you know, seduced me! She had to believe that.'

Meriwether hesitated.

'Hell, the kid was only eleven . . .'

In the momentary pause, Jeffers' mind worked quickly: He has always involved me! I've always been a part of everything he did. Always on the edge, just barely included, but connected nonetheless. He's always wanted it that way. And he's always gotten it the way he wanted. That's the older brother's prerogative. What younger brother ever refuses the older?

'Fucking weird woman. Now she visits twice a week and bothers the parole board.'

He looked out at the group.

'Somebody here explain it to me.'

Jeffers could think only of the words: A sentimental journey. He was suddenly suffused with a complete frustrating anger. What the hell did he mean by that? he asked himself furiously. Where has he gone? What sentiment is there in our lives? Did he visit the old family house? It's right down the fucking road in Princeton. He could have gone and seen the old man's drugstore. A chain owns it now. He didn't have to take off to do that! So where's he gone? What's he visiting? He would never tell me anything!

A thousand dark thoughts flooded Jeffers' mind.

Wasserman spoke quickly in reply to Meriwether's question:

'My mom was the same. I get a package from her every week. She wouldn't believe anything. I coulda fucking killed some gal right under her nose and she would have looked down and said, "Well, honey, it seems you fucked her too hard 'cause now she's had a heart attack and gone to heaven . . ." '

Jeffers noted that Wasserman's usual stutter had deserted him momentarily. My brother, he thought, was always direct and cryptic. He told me only what he thought I needed to know. What he thought! And now when I need to know something, he's left me a void. Empty! Nothing!

But then he said to himself: You do know.

He shook his head. What do you know?

Around him the men were snorting and hooting.

'S-s-s-sometimes I thought M-m-m-Mom was crazier than I am.'

The men nodded in agreement. Jeffers heard the stutter return.

Pope spoke in his solid con-wise tone. 'They never want to believe. They don't want to believe you could do it when you lift a candy bar from a store shelf. When things get worse, they just refuse harder, you know. And when you get busted for fucking, like all of us here, they won't accept it at all. It's easier for them to believe something else. Simpler.'

'Not always,' interjected Miller.

The men turned to the hard-edged professional criminal.

Miller looked about the room as if assessing a stolen jewel. 'Think about it. There's someone for all of us, probably a father, maybe a mother, who knew what we were and hated us for it. Someone you couldn't con. Someone who beat you, maybe, or left you, maybe, because they couldn't beat you. Someone who got out while the going was good . . .'

This comment made him laugh, but the other men had grown silent with their thoughts.

'Maybe someone you wanted to get rid of. Maybe someone you did get rid of, only the good doc there and the proper authorities' – he said this sneering – 'don't have such a good idea about.'

He paused, and Jeffers saw that he was delighting in his opinion and the dampening effect it had on the other men.

'There's always someone who can see just exactly what

we all are inside. It's no big deal, really. You just got to handle that person a bit differently, huh? But they're out there. We all know it.'

The room filled with murmuring, then subsided into silence.

Jeffers tried to prevent himself at that moment of quiet from asking the question that seared across his imagination, but was unable. His words were like his thoughts: runaway, out of control, embodied by a purpose of their own. They frightened him terribly. But he was powerless at that moment. So he asked:

'Well, turn it around for a moment. What would you do if you learned that someone you loved, a family member, was committing crimes? How would you act?'

There was a short hesitation, as if all the Lost Boys had inhaled at the same time. Then he was quickly enveloped in a cacophony of opinion.

Detective Mercedes Barren drove north, passing up the exit on the New Jersey Turnpike for the Holland Tunnel, which would have been a more direct route. She headed toward the George Washington Bridge, with its great gray bulk stretching across the Hudson. She made her decision to avoid the tunnel consciously, despite the press of excitement and the furious sensation that time was growing shorter, compressing around her; she always avoided tunnels as much as possible. Ever since she was a child, she worried about the weight of the water pressing down on the tiles and cement just above her head. She could still see it, with that same child's imaginative vision, cracking and buckling and the dark water suddenly pouring in on top of her. The confinement of the tunnel caused her breath to grow short and her palms to dampen unpleasantly. It's like a kind of little claustrophobia, she thought. It's not that terrible. Indulge it.

As she accelerated across the bridge, she looked back quickly over her shoulder, glancing up at the Palisades. She saw the cliff faces tumbling precipitously into the water. Sunlight glinted on the surface of the river and she caught a glimpse of white sails plying back and forth. She had always understood, especially on bright clear days, why old Henry Hudson was convinced when first he steered up the great river that he had discovered the Northwest Passage. It seemed reasonable to her, when you removed the buildings and boats and saw the river and the cliffs without progress littering them, that anyone would believe that around the first or second bend would be China.

She stared at the city, with its massive phalanx of skyscrapers standing stiffly, like a great army at attention. She clutched the address paper in her hand and wove aggressively in and out of traffic. She stared dead ahead as she entered Manhattan, refusing even to look in the rearview mirror, pointing singularly for her destination.

To her surprise she discovered a legal parking place on the street barely a block from the apartment. But before approaching the apartment, she stopped in a local delicatessen and purchased a haphazard bag of groceries. Carrying the bag and holding the key, she headed toward Douglas Jeffers' home.

He lived in a midsized, older brick building on West End Avenue. There was an ancient doorman who held the door open for her as she breezed through.

'You're going to see?' he asked in a cigarette rasp.

'Just staying at my cousin's while I take in the sights. He's out of town,' she said cheerfully. 'Doug Jeffers. He's the best photographer . . .'

The doorman smiled.

'Four-F,' he said.

'I know,' she replied, tossing him a smile. 'See you.'

She boarded an old elevator, closing the door firmly and punching up four. She saw the doorman had already turned back to his vigil. The elevator creaked as it carried her up slowly. It seemed to bounce into place and she stepped out carefully.

To her great relief, the hallway was empty.

She swiftly found 4-F and set the grocery bag down. She put the key in her left hand and pulled the 9-millimeter from her pocketbook. For an instant she listened, but she could hear no sounds through the thick black door.

She took a deep breath and said: Go!

She thrust the key into the lock and turned it. She heard the deadbolt release and she pushed hard.

The door fell open and she crouched and jumped in.

She swung the pistol up, still bent over, aiming, letting the pistol barrel guide her sight. She swung right, left, center, and saw no one. She waited. No sound. She straightened up and lowered the gun. Then she retrieved the bag of groceries and set them on the floor inside the apartment. She closed and locked the door behind her, putting the chain on as well.

Then she turned and, still holding the gun, truly looked at Douglas Jeffers' apartment.

'I can feel it,' she said out loud. She was flooded suddenly with visions from a hundred crime scenes and bloodied, decomposing corpses that she'd visited over the years. They came back to her as if in some parade from the Grand Guignol. The ghoulish sights and sickly, awful smells filled her imagination and for an instant she thought that there was a body there, in the apartment.

She shook her head as if to clear it and said, 'Well, let's look around.'

She moved from room to room gingerly, still holding the pistol. When she was finally convinced that she was alone, she began to assess what surrounded her. The first thought that struck her was that it was clean and orderly. Everything seemed in its place. Not so organized as to be oppressive, but straightened up and shipshape. The contrast with Martin Jeffers' apartment was striking.

It was not a large apartment. There was a single bedroom and bathroom, a small kitchen and dining alcove, and a wide, rectangular living room. A half-bath off the living room had been transformed into a darkroom. The furniture was comfortable and stylish, but not to the extent that a designer had created a distinctive look. More that it reflected someone who understood quality and purchased an occasional piece. There were a few antiques, and in each room there were knickknacks on shelves and bureau tops. Detective Barren picked up a shell casing from what she took to be a mortar round. There were small artifacts, a statuette from Central America, a fertility statue from Africa. She saw a large shark's tooth encased in plastic and an old rock also encased. It bore a legend: OLDUVAI GORGE, 1977. TWO MILLION YEARS OLD.

She saw that Jeffers had a worktable – a draftsman's bench, situated near the bank of windows which let the room fill with light. She saw the paraphernalia of a photographer: negatives, enlargers, paper, piled neatly about the table.

There was one large bookcase, which covered an entire wall in the living room.

The walls were white. There were two posters, framed: The Art of Photography, an exhibition at the Museum of Modern Art, and a Horn Gallery Exhibit of Ansel Adams.

Everything else was by Douglas Jeffers.

Or, at least, that is what she took them to be.

There were dozens of pictures covering all the walls. They were in all shapes and sizes, framed in different styles. She glanced in their direction, thinking: They are what I saw in the magazines. They'll tell you everything and nothing at the same time.

But her eye was caught by one small frame, in a corner. She walked to it and stared. It was of a man on the near edge of middle age, but with a clearly contradictory youthful vitality. He was dressed in olive fatigues and blue workshirt, draped with cameras and lenses. The background was of some anonymous jungle. She could see tendrils and vines flowing from the twisted branches of a thousand interwoven trees. He was sitting on a stack of boxes marked with ammunition numbers. He was grinning widely out from the picture, his hand cocked in a mock pistol, making a shooting motion toward the camera. In a corner of the frame typed on a small white piece of paper, were the words SELF-PORTRAIT, 1984, NICARAGUA.

'Hello, Mr Jeffers,' she said.

She took the picture from the wall and held it up.

'I am your undoing,' she said.

She replaced the picture and told herself to get started. She cautioned herself to be careful and systematic with this brother's apartment. She turned toward the desk and saw, neatly placed in the center, a large white envelope. On it was written in strong black type: FOR MARTY.

Her hand shot out for it.

There had been much disagreement among the Lost Boys.

Opinions had ranged from Weingarten's whining 'Jeez, what could you do? I mean, ask 'em to stop? But people do what they want anyway. You can't just force them to do anything. I mean, I never could, and nobody could ever get me to stop . . .' to Pope's stolid 'If I knew somebody in my family was doing what I do, I'd shoot the fucker, real fast. Put 'em out of their misery,' to which Steele had interjected, 'Are you in such misery? Dear, dear, you don't act like it . . .' And Pope had replied, 'Watch out, faggot, before I fucking well do you.' This, despite the integrity of the threat, had caused everyone to laugh. Killing a man such as Steele struck most of them as a great waste of time. This opinion was shared among the members of the group with great enthusiasm.

It seemed that they, who should have been experts, did not know what to do any more than anyone would.

Any more than I know what to do, Martin Jeffers spoke to himself.

He despaired inwardly.

He sat alone in his darkened office. Outside, the night had swept up and taken over the hospital grounds, throwing shadows across the stately lawns. He could hear an occasional shout, an infrequent cry, which were the sleeping norms of the hospital. The night awakens our fears, he thought, just as the day calms them.

He thought of all the things the Lost Boys had said. 'You see,' Parker had sputtered in the midst of the argument, 'you got to do the right thing. But what is the right thing? What's right for some cops maybe isn't what's right for your family: You go to the cops and they're gonna want to know everything and they sure as hell aren't gonna be your friend. All they're looking to do is bust somebody. And, man, you're gonna give them your mother or brother or father or sister or anybody. Shit, even your cousin, man? Blood is thicker, you know . . .'

To which Knight had interrupted: 'So you make yourself into an accomplice? You do. By being quiet, don't you become as bad as the person doing the crimes?'

The room had filled with both agreement and disavowal.

He remembered someone saying, 'If you know, and you stay quiet, you're just as guilty. There ought to be a special prison for people like that!'

There is, he thought ruefully.

Acquiescing to the knowledge of crime is almost as bad as the crime itself. He thought of the Holocaust and remembered the particular problems at Nuremberg, dealing with the people who'd merely remained quiet in the face of depravity. It was easy to single out the performers and punish them. But those people who'd turned their backs? Politicians, lawyers, doctors, businessmen . . .

He wondered: What happened to them?

Jeffers considered the enthusiasm with which the group had greeted the issue. He wondered why he'd never posed the question before. What struck him was the idea that virtually everyone in the group seemed to have considered the problem that they themselves posed to their own families. How would they deal with themselves? They didn't know.

He remembered the shouting back and forth through the sunlit day room. They'd run some twenty minutes over the regular end of the session. Finally he'd held up his hand.

'We'll continue this tomorrow. Everyone think over your responses and we'll talk it over some more.'

The men had stood, starting to exit in their usual small knots, when Miller, the man Jeffers thought perhaps the least perceptive, turned and asked, 'Why'd ya ask us? You got some reason?'

The men had stopped, looking back at Jeffers.

He'd shaken his head in negative, swiftly adopting his

usual exterior countenance of mildly amused intellectual curiosity, and the Lost Boys filed out in silence, without further comment. He thought: No one believed that denial. Not for an instant.

He looked out the window into the darkness.

I will not believe, he said to himself angrily, that my brother is a murderer! They arrested a man for the crime this detective hounds me on! Why is she here?

She isn't, he said to himself.

Where is she?

When Detective Barren failed to call by noontime, he'd telephoned her hotel. There had been no answer in the room. He'd rung the desk clerk back and ascertained that she had not checked out.

He tried to toughen himself inwardly. Just wait, he told himself. Wait for the next development. She has a lot of explaining to do. Wait to hear what she has to say.

Then he thought: She's not the only one who owes me an explanation.

He crumpled a paper from his desktop and threw it on the floor. He picked up a pencil and broke it in half. He looked around for something to punch, but saw nothing suitable. He turned to the wall and slapped his open palm against the whitewashed surface until he felt it redden, and he welcomed the pain, a sensation that replaced, if only for a moment, his frustration. He thought of the detective and felt a great, uncontrollable anger. He wanted to scream at her: I want to know!

Where the hell is she? he asked furiously.

And then his anger fled him and he had the awful thought: Where the hell is he?

Detective Mercedes Barren sat cross-legged on the floor of the living room in Douglas Jeffers' apartment, surrounded by the mass of her search. She had turned on every light in the apartment, as if scared to allow any of night's darkness to crawl in beside her. It was late and she was tired. She had systematically searched the entire place; from the toilet in the bathroom to the files of negatives in the darkroom. She had taken apart the couch and the bedding, hunting for weapons, without success. She had pulled everything out of the shelves in the kitchen. Every closet had been emptied. Clothes had been rifled, drawers dumped out, papers read and discarded. There was not even a ticket receipt from the Miami trip. Not even a picture postcard. The detritus of her search lay in piles about her.

Useless, she thought.

She could feel tears of rage and despair in her eyes.

'Nothing. Nothing. Nothing,' she said out loud.

She knew that he must have a safety deposit box, or a locker or a room somewhere else. Some place that collected the residue of crime. Something somewhere that connected him to her niece.

She could barely stand the tension she felt in the room. That she was close to murder, she knew. She could sense it, smell it; it entered her body through every pore and orifice, covering her, absorbed within her. She recognized the sensation from a hundred crime scenes that she'd visited.

That he was the killer was obvious. A glance at the bookcase had told her that. Virtually every book on the shelves was about some aspect of crime. Novels, textbooks, non-fiction accounts – all lined up in row after row. She was familiar with many, but not all, of the titles. That had impressed her deeply. He is a man who knows his business, she thought.

But a literary interest in crime was not evidence.

It was something she could show the brother, and he would just deny that it was anything other than a slightly morbid preoccupation, and certainly nothing out of the norm for someone who'd photographed so much upheaval and death. She looked up from her seat on the floor at the pictures that covered the walls and she wondered angrily how anyone could stand to be surrounded by so many violent and disturbing images.

She had nothing. She pounded her fists on the floor.

Then she picked up the letter from one brother to another and read it for the hundredth time:

Dear Marty:

If you get this note, one of a number of possible scenarios has come to pass. I suppose you will be expecting some kind of explanation.

You don't need one.

You know it already.

Still, I'm sorry for the trouble I've caused you.

But it was unavoidable.

Or maybe inevitable.

See you in hell.

Your loving brother,
Doug

P.S. What do you think of the pictures? Intense, no?

Detective Barren dropped the note to her lap. It told her nothing. She was overcome by a massive, enraged hatred. Her heart seemed to burn in her chest. Her throat filled with vile-tasting bile. She wanted to spit in the face of the murderer. She wanted to get her own hands around his neck, just as he'd done to her niece.

She wanted to say something out loud, but all that emerged from her throat was a growl, animal-like and savage.

Finally words formed: 'It's not over,' she said. 'I'm never finished with you. I will get you. I will get you. I will get you.'

She thought of her niece. 'Oh, Susan,' she moaned. But it was a sound less of sadness than of fury.

Her anger stiffened her and she rose to her knees in the center of the room. Her eyes suddenly fixed on the self-portrait that hung on the wall in the corner. All she could see was the mocking smile, as if it were laughing at the futility of her efforts. Her hand shot out and siezed the plastic-encased stone from the Olduvai Gorge, and, without thinking, without realizing anything save the rage that enveloped her, still kneeling on the floor, she wildly threw the artifact at the photograph.

The sound of the shattering glass instantly composed her.

She shut her eyes, took several deep breaths, and looked at the wall. She saw that the ancient rock had missed the picture of Douglas Jeffers, which still grinned in infuriating elusiveness out at her. Instead it had crashed into one of the other framed photographs, splintering the glass and knocking the picture from the wall to the floor.

She sighed deeply and got to her feet.

Feel better? she asked herself mockingly.

She stepped over to the shattered picture frame.

'Well, just add this to the tab,' she said. She had no intention of cleaning anything up. She poked at it with her foot. It was a full-color shot of a riot on a city street. In the deep background was a pillar of smoke and fire, and in the foreground a melee of policemen, firemen, and their vehicles. The lights seemed to blend hypnotically. She kicked at it. 'A good shot,' she said. 'Not one of your best, but pretty damn good.' As she started to turn away, she noticed that a corner of the picture had peeled back when the frame had buckled and come loose after falling.

She stopped then and looked down.

She did not know exactly what it was that caught her attention. Perhaps it was the odd contrast between the vivid colors of the picture and the muted gray of the paper behind. She still was unsure what she was looking at, but she thought that something was unusual. She tried to remember whether she'd ever heard of someone mounting a photograph on top of another picture, the way some artists paint over earlier images on their canvases. She could not recall hearing of such a thing.

Not allowing herself to hope for anything, she bent down and picked up the broken frame and photograph. She moved over to the desk and put it under the light. She examined the corner that had peeled. She touched the paper and saw that there seemed to be a double thickness. She grasped the top photo and tugged it gently.

It slid back another inch, revealing a black-gray background beneath.

She touched this underneath paper and felt the glossy exterior of a photograph.

She breathed deeply.

Move cautiously, she said to herself.

She pulled at the photo again and it slowly peeled off, like an apple skin.

One inch, then another. The two sheets of photo paper had not been glued solidly together. She worked the paper carefully, making certain that she did not rip the two. When it stuck, she moistened a finger with saliva and gently worked the top loose.

It was only when the entire photograph came free that she dared to look beneath. She thought in that instant of the sensation a child feels when picking off the top of a scab, that it is painful, but there is a great release when it comes off.

She looked down and saw that there was a picture beneath the picture.

She dropped the riot scene to the floor and looked at the other. It was black and white.

The breath rushed out of her suddenly as the image took shape in her eyes.

It was a nearly naked body.

It was a young woman.

Detective Barren's hands shook. She could feel an instant clammy sweat moistening her forehead.

'Susan,' she said.

But then she looked again.

The young woman's legs were chunkier. Her hair was shorter. She was lying in a different position than that her niece had been found in. And the underbrush, illuminated by the flash which cut away the darkness, was different; no Florida fronds and palms. The photograph's subject seemed to be lying amidst Northern forest leaves. Detective Barren's head spun and she felt flushed with a dizziness created by reining in sharply on her imagination. What she could make out of the young woman's features seemed to be all wrong.

'It's not Susan,' she said.

For the briefest of moments she felt defeated. It's just another one of his damn pictures, she thought.

Then she realized: It's a snapshot. She saw none of the composition, the care, the attentiveness and thought that went into Douglas Jeffers' work. It was a picture taken hastily, under duress. Under fire.

She held it up.

'You're not Susan,' she said to the picture.

'Who are you?' she asked.

She looked again and saw a large dark splotch on the young woman's chest. Blood, she thought.

She scanned the pictured quickly for the signs of search, of police presence, of official investigation.

There were none.

And then, creeping unbidden into her imagination, came a thought that she would not contemplate. She dropped the picture to the table and looked up wildly. Around her were dozens of pictures, Jeffers' home gallery. She jumped from the chair and tore from the wall a large photograph of two Far Eastern farmers and their brace of water buffalo, outlined against the changing sky of evening. She threw the picture frame violently to the floor.

From the shattered glass, she picked up the picture. She felt the double thickness of paper. She tried to peel this photo back, but this time it seemed stuck. She bent it and creased it and worried at it swiftly, finally seizing a small X-acto knife from the desk and scraping away a part of the top picture.

Beneath was another black and white image.

She could see a naked leg. Then a naked arm. It was streaked with dark. She had seen too much blood in too many crime-scene photographs not to know what this was.

She stopped and looked in panic at the walls.

'Susan,' she said again, her voice a mirror reflecting agony. 'Susan, oh, my God, Susan. You're here somewhere.'

Again her gaze swept the photo gallery. Suddenly she felt stupid, embarrassingly so.

'Oh, my God, Susan, you're not here alone.'

It was so obvious that it terrified her more.

'Oh, God, you're all here,' she said to all the eyes in all the pictures that stared out at her. 'All of you.'

She felt nauseated. She pictured Douglas Jeffers, sitting casually in his living room, glancing up at the picture in her hands, of the men and the water buffalo. Only he wouldn't see this image, he would see the one concealed beneath it.

She sat back hard on the floor, overcome by the faces that looked down from the walls at her. She slid past despair into a realm of utter agony. She thought: I am a reasonable person. I use logic, precision, science. My life is ordered, routine. I deal in facts that lead to logical deductions. I do my job with effectiveness and devotion. Things are in place.

She shook her head.

I lie poorly, she realized. Especially to myself.

She spoke then, out loud, hoping that the sound of her own voice might chase her sudden runaway fear and comfort her.

It didn't.

'Oh, my God, you're all here. I don't know who you are, or how many of you there are, but I know you're all here. All of you. All of you. Oh, my God. All of you. My God, my God, my God. You're all here. Oh, oh, oh no.'

And then a thought she realized was worse:

It's up to me.

10 Many roadside attractions

15

Anne Hampton sat alone in the car, half-watching Douglas Jeffers as he fiddled under the hood, checking the oil and water. It was early morning and they were outside the Sweet Dreams Motel in Youngstown, Ohio, a short drive from Interstate 80. Jeffers had made a joke shortly after they had first set eyes on it, calling it The Bates Motel. She turned away and her eyes rested on the stack of notepads that she kept near her seat. She lifted up the pile and counted: eleven. She picked one out from the center of the stack and flipped open to the middle. She saw the words from one of Jeffers' frequent history lessons: January 1958. Charles Starkweather and Caril Ann Fugate. Lincoln, Nebraska, and environs: 'Murders without plan, without much rhyme, without thought or care, random pretty much, except for her family. A true American nightmare, when our children turn on us. Charlie styled himself a rebel after James Dean and killed ten people, including her baby sister. He went to the chair in '59.' Below that entry she'd scrawled her synopsis of Jeffers' terse commentary. 'They were in love, but in the end she turned on him. She was fourteen years old.'

When she had to hurry, her handwriting grew large and childlike, she thought, not like the careful, precise notetaking that she remembered from her courses at school. That was a vague and distant memory, as if her time at the university had been years beforehand, not merely weeks.

Anne Hampton considered: ' . . . In the end she turned on him.' Jeffers had said this bitterly, as if this were what

335

was shocking, not the events that preceded it. She spoke the words out loud, under her voice, so that he could not hear her: 'In the end she turned on him.'

She must have wanted to live, thought Anne Hampton.

She must have believed that life was dear and precious and that she could make something special of herself or maybe even just ordinary of herself despite all the blackness and blood and death, and that living was not ruined by what had happend to her. She was only fourteen and she knew there could be more. She must have felt something magical and wonderful and strong and decided to live.

At any cost.

Anne Hampton wondered where she could find this something, too.

She gazed back down at the words on the white, blue-lined pages. Jeffers had once watched her as she wrote furiously and told her that she reminded him of many of the reporters that he'd worked with, men who'd had their own systems of shorthand that resulted in hieroglyphics that not even an expert cryptographer could read, but which to the author were as clear as a printed page.

She shivered and remembered the dizzying sensation she'd felt two nights earlier when he'd announced that he needed to check her notes.

The moment had been terrifying.

He made the demand late, after they'd checked into another forgettable motel, dragging from too many hours on the highway, depleted by noise and speed and headlights that cut through the dark right into them. Jeffers had grabbed their bags and grunted, 'Bring the notebooks'. She had carried them gingerly, agonizingly, as if she were not strong enough to hold anything else. He had opened the door and tossed their bags onto one of the twin beds. 'Let me see,' he'd said. He had sat at a small vanity, poring over the pages. She had shrunk into a chair in the corner, trying to blank her mind. But one thought had flooded her imagination: He won't be able to understand the words and he will realize how useless and ineffectual I've been and, oh God, I'm lost. She'd shut her eyes, trying to shut out fear, but the scratchy sound of the pages turning had seemed deafening. After a few minutes he'd tossed the note-books aside after quickly flipping through the final entries. He then stretched and said, 'Christ, I'm tired. Look, these are okay. Good, actually. I can read them fine. Oh, there's a rough spot occasionally, like when you were trying to write on that road up in Michigan with the frost heaves from last winter. Felt like a roller coaster and the writing kinda goes up and down, up and down, on the page.' He'd smiled. 'But all in all I'd say you were doing a good job. Just fine. Like I knew you would.'

She wished she'd felt less pleased by his praise.

He had handed her back the notepads and then touched the top of her head, almost like patting an animal or bestowing a benediction. The sensation was relaxing to her at first. She'd remained seated, watching him exit into the bathroom.

Then another fear returned.

You are alone, she'd told herself. Don't forget it.

Don't confuse the pleasure of praise with the pain of a blow. She'd tried to toughen her heart, lying awake in the darkness until sleep had captured all her mingled confusion and resolve.

In the morning he'd told her how to use her memory as well as her notes; to take just a word or phrase down and then, through concentration, to recall word for word what was said. To her surprise she had discovered that by using his techniques it seemed her memory had gained a novel precision, which had pleased her, like receiving a gift. He also told her to note situations and times, that it would help her reconstruct the notebooks when he needed her to. She wondered, though, whether that was possible. It seemed to her that everything was disjointed, each location they visited was distinct and apart; the only linkage between the spots was Jeffers' memory. Each stop, like his mood swings, was unexpected and equally frightening and dependent solely on his own rationale and his design.

They'd driven as far north as Hibbing, Minnesota, as far west as Omaha, Nebraska, almost close enough for her to envision the Rockies rising up above the plains, stirring memories of her home and family that seemed as elusive as the sight of the mountains. Kansas City, Iowa City, Chicago, Fort Wayne, Ann Arbor, Cleveland, and Akron. The locations had blended together in her mind in a melange of rural areas and urban streets. Oddly, she thought that she was fortunate that Jeffers had insisted on such careful note-taking, because even with her newfound precision, her memory still jumbled together the details of the trip.

Outside the car she heard Jeffers humming. He did this, she now recognized, when he was pleased as he performed simple tasks.

She closed the notebook and her eyes and tried to remember. She knew that Chicago had been a lecture on Richard Speck and the nurses and the detective-gene theory of murderers. Thin, bony men with acne and arrested sexual development, he'd said. This had been funny to him, and he'd scoffed with laughter. Then they'd driven to the suburbs and a look at Wayne Gacy's house, where the one-time kiddie clown buried the thirty-three boys in the basement. Jeffers had made her get out of the car and stand in front of the unpretentious white clapboard home. Then he'd quickly taken her picture. It had been raining and he'd said 'Smile' and 'Say cheese' as she huddled nervously, miserably, against a tree. But northern Minnesota had been dry and hot and she remembered light brown wheatfields that seemed to wave in invitation like the sea as they drove past That had been a trip to . . . she hesitated, unable to remember the name. But Jeffers had told her that the crazed farmer who'd eviscerated and stuffed his victims had served as the spiritual basis for the film *The Texas Chainsaw Massacre*, which he'd disliked, although he'd said he'd admired the director's sense of expressing fear through visual imagery. She had been unable to understand this, but had not asked him to explain. When Jeffers pontificated, which he frequently did, she knew it wise to let him ramble. It was when he entered more personal areas, that, contradictorily, he allowed her to ask questions.

338

He told her that he'd wanted to drive past the Clutter farm in Kansas, but that it was too far out of the way, though that seemed odd to her, as the trip to Minnesota was farther. But near Madison, Wisconsin, he showed her the shopping mall where he had picked up a young woman named Irene, and said her death had been attributed to a rapist-murderer who had plagued the malls and campuses of Minnesota and Wisconsin for nearly a year in the late seventies. In Ann Arbor, he showed her the road outside the university where a half-dozen hitchhiking young women had, in his portentous words, taken their last ride. He claimed one of those as well, saying it had been particularly easy. He drove some five miles down a secondary road, through some wooded areas, slowing and pointing into the forest at one moment, telling her that he'd left the victim two hundred yards in. 'Campus Killer, they called him. He was in 1982. The papers made up the same name as they did for that guy in Miami.'

When they had headed to South Bend, she thought that it would be another campus murder, but he'd stopped beside a brace of nondescript middle-class houses on a quiet, tree-lined street. She saw for sale signs on each lawn. She did not need to look at her notes to remember the words of his long description: 'Now, this was interesting,' Jeffers had told her. 'I wanted to see this for myself. Just six months ago. Seems like the family on the right was pretty normal. Mother. Father. Five kids and a Saint Bernard. One of the teenagers apparently was pretty heavy into the local drug scene, which screwed the police up for quite a bit. That's the kind of interesting bit of information that someday I figure to use. Anyway, on one side the All-American-apple pie-Boy Scouts-and-let's-run-up-the-flag-on-Memorial-Day family. On the other, well . . . Well, let's just say not quite the same. One child. Abusive parents. Kid grows to be a teenager harboring some pretty legitimate feelings of persecution. Always hated the neighbors. Thought, you know, that they had everything and he had nothing. Do you know much about psychology? Anyway, my brother would tell you that the situation was ripe for a paranoid personality with a psychotic break. This is pretty much what happened.

'All-Americans head out to work and school one day, lunch pails, kiss on the cheek and see-you-laters all said. Twisted neighbor breaks into the house with his old man's forty-five and a couple of clips of bullets. First thing he does is nail the Saint Bernard and drags her body into the basement. Buffy was the dog's name. Then he pops the family one by one as they come home, putting all the bodies into the basement. Then he exits, walks home, puts his dad's gun away, and acts like nothing's happened. You know what really got people upset, I mean, besides the idea that there was some crazy killer in the neighborhood? The dog. The local paper ran three pictures out front, but the biggest, widest, deepest was a shot of the ambulance crew carrying out that dog. The readers went beserk. They wanted to lynch the guy who killed that dog. What kind of monster would shoot a big, lovable, defenseless – you know what I mean . . . that's what all the letters to the editor said. It took the cops weeks to guess that the weirdo living next door did the crime. Finally, when they hauled him in, he told them everything. He was pretty proud of himself. Which is, more or less, what you'd expect. I mean, after all, he had this hatred and this problem and he'd solved it. Why not be satisfied? Didn't like dogs much, either.'

Anne Hampton picked up the notebook numbered 10. Near the back she found her notes on this crime, including much of Jeffers' long soliloquy. She checked her memory against the rapid scrawl which covered a half-dozen pages and found they fairly closely matched. Sitting in the car, she remembered a phrase or two that weren't in the notes, and she wrote these into the margins. She saw that she had taken down verbatim the joke with which he'd ended his speech: 'The paper should have called it the Canine Caper.'

She looked up sharply as Jeffers slammed down the hood.

The car was still quivering when he jumped into the driver's seat and said, 'Time to go. Many a mile before we sleep and all that.'

Then he asked, 'Do you like the races?'

'What kind of races?'

'Cars.'

'I don't know. I've never been to one.'

'They're loud. Engines roaring, tires squealing. Lots of smells, gasoline, oil, suntan lotion, beer and popcorn in the stands. You'll like it.'

She nodded. He glanced at his watch. 'We've got to go now if we want to catch the first heats. Don't you remember driving around in some boy's convertible in the summertime listening to the radio and all of a sudden this mad, frantic advertisement would come on . . .'

He changed his voice into the tinny wild radio sound:

'Sunday! Sunday! At Fabulous Aquasco Speedway! Dragsters! Fuel-injected Funny Cars! Sunday! See the Big Daddy take on the Okie from Fenokee in a three-race eliminator! Sunday! See the Bad Mama with its two-thousand-horsepower jet engine! Sunday! Tickets still available! Sunday!'

She smiled. 'I remember,' she said. 'But the name of the racetrack was different.'

'Aquasco is outside of New York, on Long Island, I believe. In New Jersey we used to hear the same ad for Freehold Raceway. And, in the summers, the family would drive up to Cape Cod and we'd hear it for Seekonk Speedway, just past Providence. My brother and I used to do a fair imitation of the ad together, shouting back and forth, "See Fabulous Funny Cars! Fuel-injected dragsters! Sunday! Sunday! Sunday!" '

She paused.

'I'd forgotten what day it was.'

'Day of leisure for most. But not us. Much work.'

He steered the car onto the interstate.

It was noontime before they approached the exit for the raceway. The interstate was nearly empty through the morning hours, and Jeffers kept up a steady pace, just a little below the average of the eighteen-wheelers that rushed past, the immense diesel noises seeming to threaten to crush everything they found in their path, buffeting the car with wind velocity. Truckers driving Sunday mornings are invariably late, Jeffers thought. They've rammed a broom handle down on the accelerator and popped a couple of black beauties with coffee and they'd just as soon run over you as past you.

He passed a pair of Pennsylvania state troopers with radar who were scanning the road and decided that the next time he took a road trip he would get a fancy radar-detector, the kind that reads several bands of police radar. He also thought that by investing in a portable police scanner he could monitor police radio traffic. He considered flying down to Miami and visiting a store that he'd heard about from a journalist returning from a trip to Colombia on a drug-connection story. The store, the man had told him, was a favorite of the folks in the trade. It specialized in surveillance gear and the latest in high-tech electronics. Devices that let you know if a wiretap was listening to your phone. Devices that turned on your car from fifty yards away. Perfect for those people who might be worried what else would happen when they switched on their car engine. Night-vision binoculars and portable secure-channel radios. Jeffers wasn't exactly certain what the store held that would help him precisely. But, he thought, we're entering a more technical age and it is important to stay abreast. He knew that the police would. Then he realized that in effect this was defeatist thinking. His whole approach, he told himself, was predicated on the supposition that the police would not ever be searching for him.

I am invisible, he thought.

Anonymous. Deadly.

And that is what makes me completely safe.

He glanced over at Anne Hampton and saw that she seemed to be dozing. 'Boswell?' he whispered, but she didn't reply. He decided to let her sleep.

She'll need her strength, he thought. But not for too much longer. He reflected on the road ahead and thought there was something inherently comforting about America's highways. They stretched out in endless lines, looping back and forth, hundreds of thousands of small connections forming a great grid of the country, like the arteries through a body. There is no beginning and no end, he thought.

Anne Hampton stirred beside him.

No end to anything.

He spotted a billboard for the racetrack and felt a rush of excitement. A lesson in acquisition, he thought. To help round off her understanding.

Anne Hampton awoke when Jeffers pulled into the toll booth. She stretched her arms as wide as the confined space inside the car would allow. She pushed her legs against the firewall, trying to reinvigorate the muscles. 'Are we there?' she asked.

'Almost. Couple of miles down the road. Just follow the signs and the hot rods.'

A ten-year-old fire-engine-red Chevrolet with its tail end jacked up blasted past them. She knew it was a Chevrolet because each window in the vehicle was adorned with huge white CHEVY decals.

'How can that guy see out?' she blurted.

Jeffers laughed.

'He can't. But you got to understand that's not the most important consideration. Appearances are crucial; they take precedence over such mundane considerations as safety, any day.'

'But wouldn't a policeman stop him every time for having obscured windows? And no muffler, either.'

'First off, he does have a muffler. Probably a set of glass packs. At least that's what everybody talked about twenty years ago, when I was in high school. Gotta have glass packs and a hemi engine, whatever that is. Or maybe was. And the reason most cops won't stop a kid driving one of those is that it wasn't so long ago that they were the same kid. And they remember how much *they* hassled the local fuzz just a couple of years back, so now that they've got the gun and badge, they're smart enough to leave things alone. The kid would have to be doing eighty to get hauled over. Or the cop would have had to have had an argument with his wife this morning, kids late for school and screaming in the background and the coffee burned and his whole mood just one big jangle of nerves and bad attitude, to flag the kid. It would be like giving a ticket to your entire history.'

Jeffers looked over at Anne Hampton, who grinned and nodded.

'You see,' he said, 'everything comes around.'

They had to wait in line of almost a score of cars at the entranceway to the racetrack. Anne Hampton rolled down the window and absorbed the sounds coming from the stadium. The whining and roaring of the engines seemed to her at first to be like the sounds of animals searching for partners. Then she realized that each engine made a different noise, uniquely its own, and that all together they blended into a wall of different-pitched loudness. It was like an aural quilt of many different patches of fabric.

The parking lot was a dusty field, filled with rows of brightly colored cars and trucks that stood out against the brown dirt of the ground. Jeffers parked close to a telephone pole that was marked with a handwritten sign that designated the area 12A.

'Wait a minute,' he said.

She sat quietly, watching as he exited the car. She saw him jog down the aisle of cars a short ways. She saw him pause behind a pair of sports cars. He wrote something down and then loped back. Before opening her door he paused at the trunk and took out some items which she couldn't see.

She thought: It's part of a plan.

Her heart plummeted and she glanced around at some of the couples and knots of people straggling through the lot toward the racetrack. The flow of people was steady and she imagined there would be a significant crowd.

She felt hot, then cold, and if she could have made herself be sick, she would have. She thought of the derelict and the man on the street in St. Louis.

We're going to do it again.

She shook her head, shivering slightly. Somehow the act

of visiting Jeffers' memories and his landmarks, regardless of how macabre, was at least safe, separate from action.

Jeffers opened the door and she got out.

But her knees buckled as she stood and Jeffers had to catch her.

He stared hard at her for a moment.

'Ahh,' he said finally, slightly amused, but with a horrible calculating flatness to his voice that she had not heard since St Louis. 'You've guessed that we're here not just because we're racing fans . . .'

He didn't complete the sentence. Instead he took her by the arm and directed her to the back of the car.

First he took two khaki photographer's vests from a bag. He slid one onto her, one onto himself. 'Good fit,' he said. He took half a dozen boxes of film from a case and fitted the canisters into the loopholes on her chest. Then he hung a camera bag around her neck. 'This,' he said, picking up a long black lens, 'is obviously the long lens.' He replaced it in the bag. 'This shorter one is the wide-angle. When I ask for one or the other, or for the camera, you just hand them over as if you were an expert.' He hung a pair of cameras around his neck. One rode in a chest harness, just beneath his chin, the other swung loosely.

'All right,' he said. From his bag he produced a stack of small white business cards. He opened the breast pocket on her vest and stuck them inside. 'Hand these out to anyone who asks for one.' He plucked one out and showed her. It read:

JOHN CORONA
PROFESSIONAL PHOTOGRAPHER
Representing *Playboy*, *Penthouse* and
Other Publications
'*Discreet Work Is Our Specialty*'
Office: 1313 Hollywood Boulevard, Beverly Hills
213–555–6646

'The name is an in-joke,' Douglas Jeffers said, 'especially for Californians. Obviously you call me Mr Corona. Or John if it seems appropriate. You are my assistant. I'll introduce you. Listen carefully and you will get the story quickly enough. Ready?'

She nodded.

'Let me hear your voice,' he demanded harshly.

'Ready,' she replied quickly.

'Remove the little-girl scaredy-cat tone and try again.'

She swallowed hard. 'I'm ready,' she said firmly.

'Right.' He looked hard at her. 'I shouldn't have to remind you of these things.'

'I'll be good,' she said.

'Make me believe that.'

This was more a threat than a request. She nodded.

Douglas Jeffers turned swiftly and she hurried after him.

Halfway across the parking field, Jeffers started talking again, but his voice seemed distracted.

'One thing I've always wondered about was why we are so mystified by certain types of animal behavior. We can't understand why lemmings dash into the ocean. Scientists spend years studying why pilot whales suddenly beach themselves and broil to death, which, if you think about it, must be a horrible way to go. Ecologists haul the whales back out to sea, and the silly beasts nine times out of ten just head for the beach again. And these are intelligent animals. Healthy, too. I went and shot a bunch of them once, on a North Carolina coast, for *Geo*, which paid great and promptly went out of business. But the whales were beautiful. They are jet black and wonderfully powerful, with bodies that seem like great blunt bullets. They can communicate across great expanses of ocean with hearing-and-sound capabilities that we mere humans can only emulate electronically. They are an ancient and proud race, related to the greatest beasts. Why, then, would they upon occasion commit mysterious mass suicide? What reason do they have? Sickness? Delusion? Confusion? Mass hysteria? Madness? Boredom? How do they become tired of life? It makes little sense.

'Yet they do it. Often, or at least often enough to cause interest and dismay. It is the same with people.'

He seemed lost in thought.

'Have you any idea how frequently people beach themselves? I'm not talking about the solitary, despondent type, clinically depressed and naturally suicidal. There are enough of them around. But people who acquiesce in their own deaths. How they contribute to the worst things happening to them.

'They marched in orderly fashion into the gas chambers. no one ever seemed to say, "Screw you! I'm not going in there!" and grasp for a moment at their own humanity. Did you know that on the first day of the Battle of the Somme, the British lost sixty thousand men? And, knowing this, on the next day, when the whistles blew, the men still went over the top into a wall of machine guns and fortified positions. This was 1916. The modern world! Impossible!

'On death row in just about every state, prisoners scheduled for execution are watched carefully throughout their last night. The fear is that they will somehow find a way to kill themselves. The state,' he said bitterly, 'doesn't like to be cheated, you see. But what would be the difference, really? Ultimately, I think, suicide is the greatest act of freedom. That's what we can't seem to learn from the goddamn whales. They're sick, with what, we just don't know. AIDS for whales, hell, or something. So they abbreviate the processing of their own deaths. They take charge of their lives, take control, and make their choice. And we wonder why. Inexplicable, the scientists say. They act baffled. What is inexplicable is that we can't understand why they do it when it seems so damn obvious.'

Jeffers picked up the pace. He was shaking his head back and forth.

'Boswell,' he said in a tone that rang of solitude, 'I'm confusing two different issues. It will be up to you to sort things out.'

After hesitating a moment he added:

'Today's lesson is really on acquiescence. Lemmings. Watch carefully how people will embrace the means of their demise. Remarkable. I remember reading about this photographer from Florida. Do you remember? It was only a couple of years ago. His name was Wilder, which I suppose created a good bit of punning in news rooms around the nation. Anyway, the guy snatches a gal from a grand prix race in Miami. Then up in Daytona, I think. Off he goes on a cross-country tour, killing as he goes. Always uses the exact same technique: heads to a sporting event or a shopping mall, pulls out his camera, and starts taking pictures of girls. Before long he has one following after him and the next thing you know they're in his car and . . .'

He looked down at Anne Hampton.

'Fill in the rest yourself.'

'I remember,' she said.

'But you know what was truly fascinating,' Jeffers continued, 'was that everyone knew! The FBI, the local police, the newspapers, the television stations, everybody! Wilder's picture was on every station, every front page, every station house. His *modus operandi* was described, discussed, dissected, you name it. It was everywhere! You could hardly be a part of popular culture and miss it. There wasn't a dinner-table conversation or bull session in a high-school bathroom with the girls having a smoke between classes where it wasn't said: If a guy with a beard wants to take your picture, don't get in the car with him! But you know what happened?'

'He died.'

'But not before another half-dozen women got into his car and got themselves killed. Remarkable. You know something? He never even bothered to shave off his beard, which was the dominating aspect of every description in every paper. Now that's a phenomenon that deserves study.'

'He died in the Northeast, I think.'

'Yeah. New Hampshire. We're going there shortly.'

'He got shot by a trooper and the last girl lived,' she insisted.

'He was stupid and careless,' Jeffers said brusquely.

But the last girl lived, she thought.

They approached the raceway grandstand. 'Stick close,' Jeffers said. 'And watch the magic work.'

*

It did work.

Inside the grandstand area, a blurred melee of people, machines, bright colors, and constant sound, Jeffers worked the sidelines expertly. He maneuvered amidst the crowd of spectators and the car crews, picking out young women, singly or in pairs, starting by taking their picture from afar, then moving closer until he not only had their attention, but they were posing for him. Anne Hampton was almost overcome by the rush of raised shoulders, sucked-in cheeks, turned profiles, and perfect smiles that greeted Douglas Jeffers' camera lens. She heard him give the same story over and over again, and she dished out business cards with a blind enthusiasm that mocked her sickened heart. He told the young women that he was on assignment for *Playboy* and they were going to do a feature called 'Race-track Girls'. He was doing some of the preliminary photography, he explained. He and a couple of other photographers were shooting young women at tracks in various locations. Then the editors back in Chicago would look at the pictures and decide where to head for their photo spread.

He had Anne Hampton take the names and numbers of some of the young women; she did this hestitantly, ill, knowing that it was merely a part of the general playacting. In the background the crowd cheered the cars and drivers, but often the noise from the track was so great that it drowned out the sounds from the stands. She looked up as one particularly immense black dragster filled the air with mechanical tumult, to see the crowd rising to its feet in appreciation. But she was unable to hear their response and she thought suddenly of the appearance of a row of fish in a market, lined up on the white shaved ice, eyes and mouths open, as if with animation, their deaths masked by the lights and sounds.

'Boswell,' she heard his voice fade in as the car noise flew away down the track, 'another roll, please. Ladies, this is my assistant, Anne Boswell. Say hello, Annie . . .'

She nodded her head at a pair of young women, probably close to her own age. One was blonde, the other brunette, and both wore tightly fitting tank tops and cut-off blue jeans. She did not think them particularly pretty, the blonde's teeth seemed to bump about in her mouth haphazardly so that her smile came forth slightly skewed, while the brunette's nose was too pert for real beauty, rising ski-jump from her face. Anne Hampton thought that the young woman probably had a mother who always told her that she was cute, and thus she aspired only toward cuteness, not realizing that it would translate from high-school cheerleader into a simple marriage and family and small home in rural Pennsylvania or Ohio, with the television on every night and a weekly trip to the beauty parlor to keep her looks in check after suffering the ravages of childbearing. She tried to remember her own mother talking to her about beauty. She could hear in her head her mother, speaking calmly but enthusiastically, brushing her hair with long strokes, telling her how pretty she would be when she grew up, which, at age twelve, had seemed such an impossibility. She recalled her mother's look of dismay when she returned home from her first college semester with her hair cropped to her shoulders. I always did so much to distance myself, Anne Hampton thought. Even when it grew out long again, something was different. A loss of trust. A voice intruded on her memory.

'. . . Must be exciting, huh?'

It was one of the young women. The blonde.

'I'm sorry,' Anne Hampton said. 'I didn't catch what you said.'

'Oh,' said the young woman, waving her hands about, 'I just said that I thought being a photographer's assistant must be exciting. A really special job. I mean, I just work in a bank and that's nothing special at all. How did you get the job?'

Douglas Jeffers interjected: 'Oh, I picked her from hundreds of possibilities. And she's worked out pretty good so far, right, Annie?'

She nodded.

'Well,' said the young woman, 'I bet it's real exciting.'

'It's different,' Anne Hampton replied.

The brunette was examining one of Jeffers' cameras. Anne Hampton saw that she'd stuck the business card in her front pocket.

'Well,' she said, 'I think being in *Playboy* would be just too wild. I mean, I'd just love to have *my* picture in that magazine. And so would Vicki.' She gestured at the blonde. 'And my boyfriend would think it was neat! But I bet my folks would just die!'

Anne Hampton saw Jeffers smile.

'Well,' he said, 'like I explained, these are just preliminary shots. But sometimes the really pretty girls like you two get called back for the spread . . .'

'Isn't there any way we could, I don't know, help make sure they choose us?' asked Vicki, the blonde. 'I mean, take some extra pictures of me and Sandi, maybe.'

Jeffers looked at the pair of young women intently.

'Well,' he said, 'I can't guarantee anything. Here, stand together for an instant . . .'

He held his arms wide, then narrowed them, directing the two young women. He raised the camera and Anne Hampton heard the motordrive speed forward as he clicked off a series of pictures, moving about the two young women, dipping up and down, framing them rapidly.

' . . . You certainly have the look,' he said. 'But, you know, they're searching for more than just a look, if you know what I mean . . .'

Anne Hampton saw the two young women put their heads together and giggle. She thought suddenly: I'm not here. This isn't happening. I can't be happening.

Then she heard Jeffers' voice again.

'Look, the best I could do, and I don't want you to count on anything, would be to take a few, uh, slightly more revealing shots. That might impress the editors. It's worked before, but, of course, no guarantees.'

She heard the two women laugh together again, nodding their heads.

'Well,' Jeffers was continuing in his most upbeat and harmless voice, 'if you're really interested, why don't you meet me at my car, section 13A, in half an hour. Please don't tell anyone what you're doing, because I've told all these other women that I wouldn't do anything special for them and I'd hate to have it get around that I was doing you two a favor . . .'

Both women shook their heads rapidly.

'So if you can keep a secret, sneak out and meet me and we'll see what we can do. Boswell, give me the long lens, please.'

Jeffers looked at the women. 'Just got to take a couple of action shots to give the editors the right flavor, if you know what I mean. After all, I want them to come back here for the spread.'

Again the girls nodded. Jeffers gave them a little wave and started to wade away through the crowd. Anne Hampton turned and looked back once, seeing the two girls talking animatedly together. For an instant she was confused: she'd heard Jeffers give them the wrong location number for the car.

'How will they find the car?' she asked.

'They won't. They will go to a spot fifty yards away.'

'But . . .'

'Come on, Boswell, use your head. If they mention it to someone else, or if someone tags along with them, then I, from the position I have the car in, have the capability of exiting without fuss. And without being seen. But,' he added, 'it won't make any difference. This is really an unnecessary precaution if ever I've seen one. Those two are in for the ride. They won't tell anyone, and they'll sneak out just like I asked them. They'll be there, ready, willing and able, don't you think?'

Anne Hampton nodded her head.

'Lemmings,' said Jeffers.

He thought a moment as he plowed through the mass of people.

'Boswell,' he said, 'does it ever seem to strike you as contradictory the way we in America can tolerate the most fundamental, righteous, religious prudery on the one hand, and yet the easiest thing in the world is to talk someone out of their clothes? Watch.'

She followed after Jeffers as he made a simple loop of the field, actually pausing occasionally to take a few shots, then heading back out to the parking lot. She thought of a night in her junior year of high school. She and her date had parked on an empty street. She could still feel the sensation of his fumbling hands exploring her body; his lack of guile and barely contained excitement were what forced her to give in – at least in part. He was not someone that she particularly liked. But he was there, and he was a nice fellow, and she had so wanted to experience some of the things that were forever being talked about at school, and so she let his hands wander, discovering that the benefits were pleasing.

When he tried to pull off her underwear was when she realized the necessity of stopping, a moral necessity, to be certain, one that upon later reflection seemed silly. She remembered a frightening moment when she resisted, and he resisted her and she recognized then how much stronger he was. She could still feel in her memory the sudden sensation of force that gripped her and the awful helplessness that penetrated her at that moment. She shivered at the thought. This had made a great impression, the instantaneous fear and terror that she was weak and that she could be forced. But when she gasped out a panicked 'No!' he'd honored that request, his muscles slackening suddenly. Her gratitude had been boundless. Six weeks later, prepared in her mind, she'd let him continue. It had been alternately painful and exhilarating, and she found that memory oddly comforting. She wondered where he was now. She hoped he was happy.

Jeffers reached the car and opened her door. 'We'll put them in the back,' he said.

Her memory fled and she handed him the equipment bag and her vest, which he stowed in the trunk.

'Get in and wait,' he said. She noted that the iron edge had returned to his voice.

She did as he said. Her mind raced about her, envisioning the two young women and what was about to happen. She shut it down, forcing thoughts from her head.

I can think of nothing, she said to herself. Nothing surrounds me. She sat in the car and closed her eyes, trying to concentrate completely on the distant noises from the racetrack, letting the sounds fill her and exclude all else.

'Hi!'

'Hi!'

She looked up, opening her eyes quickly, and the sunlight blinded her.

'Shall we jump in the back?'

'If you don't mind,' she heard Jeffers' voice. 'It's a bit cramped. Sorry.'

'Oh, no problem. My boyfriend has a Firebird, which is pretty much the same, and I've spent a lot of time in the back seat . . .' Both Vicki and Sandi laughed. 'I didn't mean it quite that way,' said Vicki. 'Anyway, boy, is he gonna be surprised!'

The two women squeezed in the back. They were flushed and excited, giggling and laughing, at the limit of control.

Jeffers swung into his seat. 'I know a little park, almost a forest really, not too far from here. We'll drive over, take a few shots in a nice, idyllic location, then Boswell and I will drop you back here, okay?'

'Sounds great,' said Vicki.

'Okay by me, just as long as we're back by six.'

'No problem,' said Jeffers.

The women laughed again.

Jeffers steered the car out of the raceway area.

Anne Hampton's mind screamed at the two women: Why don't you ask! Ask how he just happens to know of a deserted park! How does he just happen to know exactly where he's going? He's mapped it out before!

She said nothing.

Jeffers broke her silence. 'Keep your notepad handy,' he said softly to her. Her hand shot out instantly for a pad and pen. Then he raised his voice into a gregarious sing-song. 'Now I don't want you gals to be nervous, this will be pretty tame stuff, really. But I got to ask – you're both over eighteen, right?'

'I'm nineteen,' said Sandi, 'and Vicki's twenty.'

'Not till next week!'

'Hey,' said Jeffers. 'Well, happy birthday a week early, then. Let's see if we can't make the birthday something special to celebrate, okay?'

'You bet!'

'Mr Corona,' Sandi asked tentatively, 'I don't want to intrude or, I don't know . . .'

'Go ahead,' said Jeffers in as good-natured a voice as possible. 'What's on your mind?'

'Does *Playboy* pay for the pictures they use?'

Jeffers laughed.

'Of course! You don't think we'd put you through the drudgery of a photo session without paying, do you? A photo session is hard work. There's make-up and posing, and high-intensity lights, and, you know, something always goes wrong. To get one picture suitable for the magazine can sometimes take hours. The usual rate, I think, at least the last time I did this, was a thousand dollars a session . . .'

'Wow! What I could do with that!'

'But this is kinda informal,' Jeffers continued. 'I don't think the magazine will pay more than a couple of hundred bucks for your work this afternoon.'

'We're gonna get paid! Fantastic!'

The two women started talking excitedly between themselves. Anne Hampton sat blindly in front. Jeffers spoke to her quietly: 'Boswell, please make an effort to get this down.' His voice was like blackness crawling over her.

Then, with fake cheer, he said briskly, 'Almost there!'

He was driving into a park.

'I know just the right spot,' he said.

'Boy!' gushed Vicki or Sandi from the back seat, Anne Hampton wasn't certain which, but she got the words down anyway. 'I can't believe this is happening to me.'

Think of nothing, she told herself. Do exactly what you're told. Just stay alive.

'Here we are,' said Jeffers. 'Now, I know this little spot . . .'

Anne Hampton saw they were entering a wooded area, staying on a small roadway that cut between the shadows thrown by the leafy overhanging branches. There was a brown National Parks Service sign which said the park was open only from dawn to dusk. She saw that they passed up a large gravel parking area, continuing on into the center of the forest. They drove what she guessed was another half mile, then turned on to a dirt secondary road which they followed for several bumpy minutes until they reached a bend where the trees dropped back sharply so that a brief space was plunged into bright sunlight. There was a single chain stretched loosely from one side of the dusty brown trail to the other and another small sign that read, AUTHORIZED PERSONS ONLY BEYOND THIS POINT.

'Luckily,' Jeffers said brightly, 'I've got park service authorization. Most professional photographers do. Hang on, ladies, while I deal with this chain.'

Jeffers jumped from the car, leaving the two women laughing in the back seat and Anne Hampton staring out blankly at the forest colors from the front. He felt a twinge of concern. She seems to be lost, he thought. Though his back was to the car, his mind pictured her sitting there, fastened to her seat by the layered fears of knowing what was happening and being unable to say or do anything, caught by the event just as surely as if he'd tied her with rope. He wondered for an instant whether she would be able to control herself. I want her to make it to the end. I don't want to have to leave her here with the others. He considered whether she recognized the danger she was in and thought that she must, for she seemed to have entered a detached state, like a mannequin in a store window or a marionette dancing on the end of a set of strings.

This, he realized, was exactly as it should be.

My strings, he thought. Dance, Boswell, dance. When I jerk the strands holding you, jump.

He smiled.

Keep things in order, he told himself. Boswell represents time and effort and investment.

He heard more laughter from the car.

They don't.

The chain was just as it had been when he visited the

park a month earlier. He reached down and grasped the links a few inches above the spot where it was fastened to a small brown post. With his free hand he flaked wood chips off the post. It had rotted with age. He gave the chain a sharp tug and it came free. Then he walked the chain across the road, clearing it out of the way.

He shuffled his feet in the dusty road surface as he walked back to the car. No sense in leaving an impression of his shoe.

'All set,' he said to the three in the car. 'Just up the road.'

He goosed the car ahead gingerly and they bumped for some two hundred yards until they pulled around a corner. Anne Hampton recognized then that they could not be seen from the main roadway.

'All right, pile out,' Jeffers said with a brisk enthusiasm. 'We don't want to take up too much time, and everybody wants to get back to see that last race, so let's do it.'

Anne Hampton saw that he had thrown his brown photographer's bag over his shoulder. She hesitated for an instant, watching the two young women follow Jeffers into the forest. They are blind, she thought. How can they rush after him so? Then she felt her own feet hurrying her forward, and she ran to keep up with him.

'Boy,' said Vicki or Sandi – she had gotten them confused – 'this sure is exciting.'

'It always is,' replied Douglas Jeffers. 'In more ways than one.' The two women giggled again.

Anne Hampton thought she would be sick if she stopped. Her breath came in short bursts and she felt her head spin. The heat rested on her body like a wool blanket, prickly, uncomfortable, and she felt dizzy. Vicki or Sandi heard her laboring and turned to her.

'Do you smoke? No? Good. But you sound out of shape. A little walk in the woods shouldn't get to you . . .'

'I've been a little sick,' Anne Hampton replied. She heard the words quiver weakly.

'Oh, I'm sorry to hear that. You should take vitamins like I do. Every day. And regular exercise. Have you ever tried aerobic dancing? That's what I like to do. Or maybe do some running to build up that wind. I'd like to quit my job at the bank and get a job teaching dancing at the health club. I think that would be neat. Are you okay?'

Anne Hampton nodded. She didn't trust her voice any further.

'Try doing some running,' the young woman continued. 'Start out slowly, maybe just a mile or so a day. And then gradually build up. It'll make the world of difference.'

Douglas Jeffers suddenly stopped.

'So how do you like it? Pretty, huh?'

He stood under a pine tree at the edge of a small open clearing. Even Anne Hampton, in the midst of her growing terror, thought it a pretty spot. That made her feel worse.

There was a large boulder cropped up in the midst of the clearing. Sunlight spread around it; making the small patch of green grass glow. The entire area was encircled by forbidding pine trees that seemed to stand against the blue sky like so many silent sentinels. When she stepped into the clearing, Anne Hampton had the sensation of striding into a quiet room, the door closing shut behind her.

'All right, ladies, over to the rock if you please. Boswell, next to me.'

She walked over to Jeffers' side and they both watched the two women take up positions on the boulder. Each was affecting what she thought was the freshest come-hither appearance possible. Jeffers stepped out into the sunlight and glanced up at the high sky. 'Bright', he said. 'Harmless, bright sunshiny day.' He quickly approached the two young women and held up a light meter beside them. Anne Hampton saw him adjust his camera, then start clicking off shots. He kept up a steady, hypnotic stream of encouragement: 'That's it, now smile, now pout a little, now throw that head back, good, good, great. Now twist about a bit, keep moving, good again, good . . .'

She watched the performance before her, wondering: Where does he have the gun? Or will it be a knife? It must be in the photo bag. How is it going to happen? Quickly?

Is he going to drag it out? What is he going to do to them? He will take his time. We are alone and it is quiet and he will not be hurried. The heat from the sun caused her to grow dizzy and she feared she would faint. She closed her eyes, squeezing them tightly shut. I remain me, she said to herself. I am alone and apart and I am myself and I will be strong and I will make it. Make it. Make it. Make it. She repeated this over and over, mantralike.

She looked up and saw that Vicki and Sandi were trying to look seductive. 'That's good,' she heard Jeffers say. 'But I think it's a little, I don't know, restrained, maybe . . .'

She saw the two women look at each other and she heard their mingled laughter. They were having a good time. She hated this. It filled her with guilt. She closed her eyes again.

'Now, that's better!' she heard Jeffers exclaim. 'Wait until those editors get a load of this!'

She opened her eyes and saw that both women had stepped out of their clothes. They seemed sleek, animal-like. They were both deeply tanned and she stared at the white skin that brought their breasts and crotches into relief. She watched as they stretched, and, within seconds, lost whatever residual modesty they might have had. They offered their breasts to the camera; they spread their legs when the lens pivoted toward them. Jeffers bounced about before them, bending and twisting, caressing them with the camera. She could hear the motordrive whirring.

She thought it seemed like some hideous ballet.

Jeffers maneuvered around the two women, bringing them closer, until finally they were slapped together, entwined, all legs, arms, buttocks, and breasts on the rock before him. Anne Hampton stared at their bodies, which seemed to her to be strong and full and terribly, horribly, filled with life. She could not continue to look and turned away.

'Hey, Boswell, come here!'

She hesitated one instant, then trotted to his side. She could see that both women were flush and excited.

'Stand there so I can get a shot of the three of you.'

She stepped between the two naked women.

'Boy! I've never felt so free,' said Vicki or Sandi. 'It makes me feel beautiful.'

'It's got me hot,' said the other, a little under her breath. 'I wish my boyfriend were here.'

'I bet,' whispered her friend, 'that Mr Corona gets a lot of extra surprises when he takes pictures.'

Anne Hampton felt an elbow nudging her. She understood suddenly that this last statement was a question.

'He does okay,' she said. 'He likes taking pictures.'

'Fine, Boswell. Step out. Now, Vicki, just put your hand on Sandi's breast, good, good, continue stroking it, right, and now reach down toward her thigh, good, good, that's right, put your hand right there, perfect! Great, great. Exciting, huh?'

Anne Hampton heard both women exclaim in agreement. She stood next to Jeffers and saw that they continued to stroke each other despite the pause in the sound from the motordrive. She could see sweat glisten on their bodies and she knew they were aroused.

'Well, he said, 'it'll be more exciting in just a second. Let me change film . . .'

She saw his hand reach down into the photo bag.

It's now, she thought. Oh, God, it's now.

She wanted to race away, to somehow jump high into the sky and flee like a startled bird.

She was frozen in her spot. Rigid under the sun.

Oh, God, she thought. I'm sorry. I'm so sorry. I wish I were someplace else, suddenly, magically, anywhere, just not here right now, at this moment. Oh, God, I'm sorry, sorry, sorry.

She saw that Jeffers had put his camera into the bag and she could see his hand on the butt of a pistol.

I wish I could do something, she thought. I'm sorry, Vicki and Sandi, whoever you are. I'm so sorry.

She shut her eyes.

She could hear the two women giggling and the sound of their bodies slapping together. She could hear a pair of birds calling out in the darkness of the forest, raucous and harsh. She could hear Douglas Jeffers' breathing beside her. It was even, rapid, but she thought it ice cold, and she believed behind her closed eyes that she would be able to see the vapors of his breath. Then every sound seemed to fade from her and she was enveloped by silence. She awaited the first noise of confusion and panic from the two women. She wondered: Will they gasp? Scream? Cry? Time seemed empty and she waited for the first moment of recognition and terror. But it did not come.

Instead she heard a distant blare.

The sound seemed foreign, unconnected to the clearing. Alien. She could not at first place it. It sounded again.

She opened her eyes.

Jeffers stood beside her. He was listening.

A moment passed.

'Everybody stay right here,' he said. Command had taken over his voice. Anne Hampton saw the two women look up, surprised. 'It's probably nothing,' he said. 'But I need to check.' He looked at Anne Hampton. He spoke quietly to her. 'Get them into their clothes. Act as if nothing is happening. Wait right here for me. Say nothing. Do nothing.'

Jeffers lifted the photo bag and, after giving the two women a smile and a wave, stepped into the pine forest. Anne Hampton thought it was as if he had suddenly been swallowed by the shadows.

She turned to the women. They were looking into the hole in the woods that Jeffers had disappeared into. They were still wrapped together, their arms in casual connection, draped across each other.

Run! thought Anne Hampton. Get away! Can't you see what is happening?

But instead she said, 'Why don't you two get dressed? I think we're just about finished.'

'Oh,' said one, frowning, 'I could do this all day.'

Anne Hampton could say nothing. She sat, enveloped by fear, waiting for Douglas Jeffers to return. She glanced down at her hands and told herself: Make them do something.

But she was unable.

Douglas Jeffers felt the coolness of the forest dry the sweat on the back of his neck as he stepped away from the clearing. He walked slowly for ten feet. When he knew that he couldn't be seen by any of the three women behind him, he picked up his pace. He jogged first, then ran, cutting between the shadows, leaping like a hurdler over the occasional rock or limb in his path. He kept one hand on the bag, to prevent it from bouncing about wildly, the other clearing branches from his eyes. His footsteps made a crunching sound against the pine needles of the forest. He raced the last few yards and emerged from the mottled forest light into the brightness of the road where he'd parked.

A dark-green park service jeep was pulled up next to the car.

A ranger wearing a Smokey the Bear hat sat on the hood.

He's unarmed and alone, Jeffers thought.

Jeffers commanded himself: Be quick. He swiftly searched the scene. There was no one else around. His eyes scanned the jeep. He saw no shortwave radio antenna on the car, no telltale shotgun fastened to a holder on the dashboard. He glanced at the ranger and saw that the man did not have a hand-held radio strapped to his waist. He's isolated and unsuspecting, Jeffers thought. He took a few steps closer and saw that the man was really a boy. A college student, working for the summer. His hand went into the bag and he felt the solid metal barrel of the automatic. You could do it. You could do it and no one would be the wiser.

Inwardly, then, he screamed at himself: Control! What are you? Some punk killer in a convenience store?

He slid his hand from the bag, bringing out his Nikon.

He waved and the ranger waved at him.

'Hi,' Jeffers said. 'I heard your horn. You screwed up my shot good.'

'Oh, sorry,' said the ranger. Jeffers saw that he was an unprepossessing type, wearing wire-rimmed glasses. He was slightly built and Jeffers knew the young man would be no match for him. Not physically or mentally. 'But this is supposed to be a restricted area. You're not allowed to bring a car up here. Didn't you see the sign?'

'Yes, but Ranger Wilkerson told me it was okay after I found the owl's nest.'

'I'm sorry?'

'Ranger Wilkerson. He's at central headquarters in the state capital. He's the guy all the nature photographers talk to when they want to get into the restricted areas. It's no big deal, really. Did you know I found an eagle's nest last year?'

'In here?'

'Yeah, well, not exactly here, but over that way.' Jeffers gestured widely with his arm, pointing off into nowhere. 'Took me by surprise, too. I got the pictures into *Wildlife* Magazine, too, and the Audubon Society came out *en masse*, almost a little parade through the woods, you know. It was a pretty big show, you know. Weren't you here then?'

'No, this is my first year.'

'Well,' said Jeffers, 'I'm surprised you didn't hear about it. I think they put up one of the pictures at your headquarters.'

'Did, uh, you get some kind of pass or something?'

'Sure,' said Jeffers. 'It should be in your photography file back at your office. Probably right under the picture of the eagle.'

'I'll have to check,' said the ranger. 'I didn't know we had a file.'

'No problem. Check under my name: that's Jeff Douglas.'

'Are you a professional?'

'No,' replied Jeffers. 'I wish. I mean, I've sold some shots. Even sold one to *National Geographic*, but they never used it. But it's just a hobby, really. I sell insurance.'

'Well,' said the ranger, 'I'll still have to check.'

'Sure. And what's your name, so I can call Ranger Wilkerson if there's some mixup?'

'Oh, I'm Ted Andrews. Ranger Ted Andrews.' He smiled. 'By the time I get used to saying that, it will be time to head back to school.'

Jeffers smiled. 'Look, I was just about finished for the

day, anyway. I want to just go back and make sure I didn't leave any film boxes or anything laying around. I don't like to make a mess.'

'We appreciate that. You wouldn't believe what some folks just toss away. And I end up cleaning it up.'

'Low man on the totem pole?'

The ranger laughed. 'Right.'

'You don't have to wait for me,' Jeffers said. 'Go check your file, and next time I'll stop by the office and you'll see it's all arranged.'

'That'd be okay,' said the young man. He started back to his jeep and Jeffers looked hard at the man's back. I could do it now, and it would be easy. He measured the distance. A single shot, no one would hear a thing. No one would know. His hand closed on the pistol butt, but then he dropped it back into the bag. He waved instead, watching the jeep pull out past his car, bouncing up the secondary road.

'Damn,' said Jeffers coldly to himself. 'Dammit to hell.'

For a moment he felt flushed with fury and he had an overwhelming urge to crush something with his hands. He took a deep breath. Then another. He spat on the ground, clearing his mouth of a bilious, evil taste. Someone's going to pay for this, he thought.

Out loud, though, he said to no one: 'They get to live.'

11 One trip to New Hampshire

16

Detective Mercedes Barren drove hard through the glowing vapors of gray-green highway lights that beat back the early-morning darkness. It was nearly 3 a.m. and she was almost alone on the turnpike. An occasional tractor-trailer careened past in the distance, wailing like some great heartbroken beast into the edge of roadway lights and night blackness. She pushed the accelerator down, as if she could transform the engine's surge into energy for her own body. She was exhausted, yet powerless to seek sleep. She knew the burning images she carried vividly in her head and sloppily thrust into a paper bag on the seat next to her would preclude sleep for some time.

The car droned around her and she tried to force the sound to fill her and take away the terrors of the past hours. She refused to think of Douglas Jeffers' apartment, though a final vision was imposed on her memory: She could see shattered glass and dozens of broken or twisted picture frames littering the floor. In her panic and horror, she had finally simply torn the pictures apart, seeking the hidden images. The detritus of Jeffers' art lay in piles strewn haphazardly about the apartment's living room, ripped faces and severed moments, staring out at her in violation. She'd taken the bag of groceries that had been part of her ruse dedicated to the inquisitive doorman and dumped them out on the floor. Then she'd refilled the paper sack, stuffing it with the hidden pictures, creased, folded, mangled by her impatience and anxiety. When she closed and locked the door to the apartment, leaving it behind, it had been like pitching from a nightmare into a waking fear;

like arising from an uneasy dream at the midnight sound of an entering burglar breaking glass, or the tiny crackle of fire from another room.

She drove up a rise on the turnpike. To her right, a huge cargo jet whined and powered in takeoff from Newark Airport, while to her left the massive white oil storage tanks to the port of Newark glistened in floodlights. She felt an incongruity, surrounded by technology, in pursuit of something prehistoric. When the highway swept away from the coast and into darker countryside, she felt comforted. She bent down and peered up into the black sky, catching a glimpse of the moon, hanging low over some trees and buildings.

'Good night moon,' she said out loud, the words bursting out from long-held memory, unchecked. 'Good night room and the red balloon and the three little bears sitting on chairs, good night house and good night mouse, good night to the old lady whispering "hush", good night nobody, good night mush . . .'

She tried to remember the other good nights from the book, but she was unsure after so many years. Mittens? Kittens? She saw herself, her niece perched on her lap, head lolled down and eyes closed, bottle drooping from her mouth, welcoming the deep sleep of childhood. She remembered how the words of the book always worked, but she never cut the rhythms short; if Susan fell asleep before the end, I would still read on.

'Good night moon,' she said again.

She had found her niece's picture behind a large full-color portrait profile of three starving African children, whose wide eyes and distended bellies shouted out in agony. It was perhaps the fifteenth or twentieth photograph that she had torn apart in frenzied search. She had reached the limit of self-control when she ripped into the frame, breaking it with her hands. A piece of glass had cracked off, cutting her thumb, not deeply, but enough to streak the picture with fresh blood.

At first she had not recognized her niece. She had seen too many savaged bodies in Jeffers' apartment to instantly draw a distinction. But then the shape of the limbs had suddenly plucked her memory, and the shock of straw-blond hair, clearly visible even in the black and white picture, had touched her familiarity. The features were in some repose, too; the portrait had been taken from a lower angle and from the side, removing some of the horror that was so clear in the crime-scene pictures that she had gazed as so many times. She could see an immediate difference between the caressing portrait that Jeffers, even in his hurry, had taken and the clinical, bright, horrible photos taken by the medical examiner's office and her fellow crime-scene specialists a few short hours after Jeffers had slipped away into the night. In the photo she had held in her hands, Susan seemed merely asleep, and she was thankful for that small touch.

She had stared deeply at the photograph. She did not know for how long. She had not cried, but it seemed to her to drain her soul. Then she had carefully, almost tenderly, put it aside before going on with the terrible task of checking the other frames.

She had thought herself calm and in control, but her hands had shaken wildly when finally she had put her niece's photo in the growing pile along with all the murdered others and had readied herself to leave.

Driving through the darkness, she said to herself: I don't know who you all are, but I'm here for you now.

I'm here. I'm here. I know. Now I know everything.

And I will make things right.

She gripped the steering wheel tightly with her fingers and continued fast toward the morning.

Martin Jeffers could not sleep. Nor did he want to.

He sat in the center of his apartment, the only light coming from a small desktop lamp off in the corner. He debated with himself the single question whether it was better or not to know. He questioned whether, if the detective disappeared, as he supposed she had, and his brother returned, as he knew he would, his usual cryptic, smart-guy self, whether he could simply return to the status quo, the usual uneasy peace between brothers.

He did not know whether he had the strength to reimpose this normality on his life.

He tried to envision facing his brother. In his imagination he saw himself stern, prosecutorial, strong, suddenly invested with the powers that accompanied being firstborn, easily dismissing his brother's weak jests and jousts until Douglas Jeffers finally succumbed to his relentlessness and told the truth.

And then what?

Martin Jeffers plunged his face into his hands, trying to hide himself from the fantasy he'd created. What would he say? He could not envision his brother tearfully confessing to the crime that had brought the detective into their lives. What would he say? I'm sorry, Marty, but I picked up this girl and everything was going great until she said no, and then I got a little carried away, you know, and maybe I used a little too much force. I'm strong, Marty, and sometimes I forget and suddenly she wasn't breathing, and it really wasn't my fault, but hers, and anyway, someone else took the rap for the crime, so why do anything? It's gone, it's past, it really, when you think about it, never happened.

He stood up and paced about the dark room.

I knew it, I knew it, I knew it, he said to himself. He was always wild, he always thought he could do whatever he wanted. He wasn't like me, he wasn't organized, patient, I can't stand it. He never, never, never listened to me.

He killed that girl, dammit!

He should pay.

Martin Jeffers sat back down.

Why?

What good would it do?

Again he stood up, then, just as swiftly, slumped back into his chair.

Why do you jump to these conclusions? He addressed himself in the third person, like a debater.

The detective has disappeared. She was crazy anyway. Why are you so swift to believe the worst about Doug?

You've been too long with the men in the therapy group. You've heard too many lies, too many evasions, too many phony reconstructions. You've heard blame shifted about from one person to the next, never assumed by the guilty. You've heard horror after horror year after year and nothing has ever changed and it has finally skewered your thinking about completely so that now you're willing to leap to the most ridiculous conclusions.

Go to bed. Get some sleep. Things will sort out.

He smiled to himself. That is hardly the kind of attitude that four years of medical school and four more years of internship and residency at the mental hospital should prompt. Where did Freud write: Things will work out? What neo-Jungian approach is that? Did you pick that up from some journal or some scholarly lecture? Perhaps from Dear Abby or Ann Landers? When have you ever known things just to work out? He heard himself laugh, briefly, and the sound echoed emptily in the apartment. Still, it was a tenet of his profession to await events rather than prompt them, and there was nothing wrong with that.

We shall see, he said to himself.

We shall see what Detective Barren has to say – if she ever shows up again.

We shall see what Doug has to say.

And then we shall figure out what to do.

This seemed to him to be like a plan of action, the decision to wait for something to happen. It pleased him and he felt suddenly tired. Christ, he said to himself, how do you expect to ever reach any conclusions about this mess without getting some rest?

He rose again and looked over at a small digital clock that blinked its numerals in red. It was 4 a.m. He stretched and yawned. He ordered himself: Go to bed. His mind answered with a military snap: Yes, sir!

He took three steps toward the bedroom.

Things will sort themselves out.

And the doorbell rang.

It was a high-pitched, irritating sound that struck his heart. It startled him deeply and he jumped involuntarily.

He took a great breath.

Who? he wondered.

My God, he thought.

He took another breath. What the hell? It's 4 a.m.

It rang again, buzzing swiftly and insistently.

His mind twirled in confusion and he walked to the door. There was a small, circular peephole, and he peered through it.

Standing outside was the detective.

His heart plunged and he felt suddenly dizzy and nauseated and he wanted to be sick. He fought off the sensation and he reached for the doorknob.

As soon as she heard a hand start to open the door, Detective Mercedes Barren reached behind her, to where she had stuck her 9-millimeter pistol beneath her shirt, tucked into the belt of her jeans. She freed the weapon and swung it forward, just behind the paper sack she carried in her other arm.

She raised the gun to eye level as the door swung open.

She thrust the barrel forward so that it hovered an inch from Martin Jeffers' nose.

She saw him pale quickly and take a sudden step back in surprise.

'Don't move,' she said, her voice deadly cold and even. 'Is he here? If you lie I will kill you.'

Martin Jeffers shook his head.

Using the gun to gesture, she slipped into the apartment. She glanced around quickly. She could sense they were alone, but she was not willing to put trust in her sensation.

'Please, detective, put the gun away. He's not here and I still don't know where he is.'

'I'll believe you after I take a look around.' She maneuvered so she could see into the other rooms. After a quick inspection, never moving the gun too much, so that it could not instantly be brought to bear on Martin Jeffers, she returned to the living room and gestured for the doctor to sit down.

'I can't believe that . . .' Martin Jeffers started, but she cut him off sharply.

'I don't care what you can or can't believe.'

They were both silent. After an instant he spoke.

'You were supposed to meet me yesterday morning. Not here. Not now. What's going on? And please put that cannon away. It scares the bejesus out of me.'

'It should. And I'll put it away when I want.'

They continued to stare at each other.

'Where is he?' she asked.

'I told you I don't know.'

'Can you find him?'

'I don't know. No. Maybe. I don't know. But certainly not . . .'

'I haven't got too much time. No one does.'

Martin Jeffers managed to compose himself. He ignored her mysterious statement.

'Look, detective, what are you doing here in the middle of the night? We had an agreed-upon appointment and you never show and then suddenly you're at my apartment at four in the morning threatening me with a gun. What the hell is going on?'

Detective Barren sat in a chair across from him. The gun still waved in the air between them. She pulled the envelope containing Douglas Jeffers' apartment key from her pocket and tossed it to the brother.

He looked at it. 'Where the hell did you get this?'

'From your desk.'

'You broke in here? Christ, what kind of cop are you?'

'Would you have given it to me?'

'Not on your life.'

Jeffers started to stand, filled with violation and anger. She raised the gun.

He stared at it and sat back down.

'Threats are childish,' he said.

'I went to your brother's apartment,' she said.

'So?'

She had placed the paper sack at her feet. She reached

371

in and pulled out the photograph of Susan. She tossed it
to Martin Jeffers, who looked at it for several seconds.

'That is my niece,' she said bitterly.

'Yes, but . . .'

'I found it at your brother's apartment.'

Martin Jeffers' head spun suddenly. He breathed
harshly. He blurted out: 'Well, there must be some
explanation . . .'

Her voice was like a frozen morning: 'There is.'

'I mean, he must have . . .'

She interrupted:

'Don't make some fucking stupid excuse.'

'I mean, he could have obtained this picture in any
number of ways . . . I mean, after all, he's a professional.'

She did not reply. She simply reached into the paper bag
and pulled out another photo. She dropped this in front of
Martin Jeffers. Again, he looked deeply at the two
photographs.

'But this isn't the same person,' he said finally.

She threw another photo in front of him.

He spread the three out, looking carefully at the pictures.

'But I don't get it, neither is . . .'

She slammed another picture in front of him.

He glanced at this, then he sat back in his chair.

She was breathing hard, as if near the end of a long run.

She slapped yet another picture down. Then another and
another and another, until finally she dumped the entire
stack on the brother's lap.

'You don't get it? You don't get it? You don't get it?' she
repeated as each flopped in front of him.

Martin Jeffers looked around wildly, as if searching for
something to grasp hold of and steady himself.

'Now,' she said with all the pent-up rage barely leashed,
'where is he? Where is your brother? Where? Where?
Where?'

Martin Jeffers put his head into his hands.

She leaped across to his side, pulling him back sharply
by the shoulder.

'If you cry I will kill you,' she said viciously. She did not know whether or not she meant this; it was that she suddenly couldn't stand the idea of the murderer's brother shedding a tear for himself, for Douglas Jeffers, for anyone other than those people spread about him.

'I don't know!' he said, his voice cracking with stress.

'You know!'

'No!'

She stared at him. He looked at the pictures.

Her voice was filled with controlled fury: 'Will you find him?'

Jeffers hesitated, two answers screaming inside his head.

'Yes,' he said finally. 'Maybe. I can try.'

She slumped into a chair. She wanted to cry, then, herself.

But instead they just sat across from each other, staring into the gap between them.

The dawn light caught the two sitting amidst the pile of photographs, silent. It was Martin Jeffers, his own mind a disaster of crushed emotions, who spoke first:

'I suppose the first step, now, is for you to contact your superiors, tell them what you think you're up against . . .'

'No,' replied Detective Barren.

'Well, maybe we should talk to the FBI,' Jeffers went on, oblivious to her refusal. 'They have a branch office down in Trenton, and I know a couple of the agents. They're equipped to help, I guess . . .'

'No,' she said again.

Jeffers looked over at her. He swiftly filled with rage. He tried to bite back his words, but his tongue was loosened by exhaustion and sorrow.

'Look, detective, if you think I'm going to help you hunt my brother down to satisfy some personal vendetta, you're mistaken! Worse, you're crazy! Forget it and get the hell out of here!'

Detective Mercedes Barren looked at Martin Jeffers.

'You don't understand,' she said quietly.

'Well, detective, it seems to me that you're awfully good at making threats with that big fucking gun . . .' He surprised himself by using an obscenity. 'But you're not too damn forthcoming with details. If my brother has committed crimes, well, then, there's an established procedure for investigating him . . .'

He had the unsettling feeling that he'd said those words before and they had been equally useless then.

'It won't work,' she said. Defeat mocked her.

'Why the hell not?'

'Because of me.'

She sighed deeply and felt fatigue insinuate itself throughout her body and mind. Martin Jeffers watched her, aware suddenly that something was bent, twisted, wrong; he slid effortlessly into his professional posture, waiting, quiet, patient, knowing the explanation would eventually arrive.

The silence filled with weak morning light.

'Because of me,' the detective said again.

She took a deep breath.

'I am the best, you know? I was always the best. I made one mistake, once, and I've got the scar to show for it. But that was all. I lived. I recovered. I made no more mistakes. It didn't matter what kind of case it was, I was always the best. The information I got, the evidence I procured, the arrests I made, everything! It was always right It was always true. It was always accurate. When I got onto a case, there was only one conclusion: the bad guys got busted. Then they went to prison. It didn't matter to me what kind of lawyer they got, what kind of defense they had. Alibi? Forget it. I put them away. All of them . . .

'I was together, you know? I had to be. All my life people stole from me and I was powerless to do anything about it. But not when I became a cop. I was right. Always. I was always right.'

She slung her head back and looked to the heavens. After a moment she looked at Martin Jeffers.

'You have to understand: there is no evidence.'

Martin Jeffers shook his head.

'What do you mean? Look at the pictures.'

'They don't exist.'

'What the hell are you talking about?' He picked up a handful of photographs and shook them at her. 'You come in here and tell me my own brother has committed these, these . . .' He stumbled over the word and finally just raced on ' . . . And now you say they don't exist! What the hell?'

'They don't exist.'

Jeffers sat back and folded his arms in front of his chest angrily. 'I'll listen to your explanation.'

'I always did it right, you see. Until this time. Finally, when I handle something that means something, everything, to me, I screw it up. Ruined.'

She reached out and picked up some of the pictures.

'I broke in here. I stole the key. I broke in there. This goes far beyond the definition of an illegal search . . .'

'A technicality!'

'No!' she screamed. 'It's the rules. Worse: it's the reality!'

'So,' he said, trying hard to remain calm and analytical, 'why don't we go to the FBI? At least show them the pictures.'

'You don't see,' she said. 'We walk into the FBI and I say, look, Mr Agent, I want to show you pictures of homicides which I've obtained in the course of investigation. The first thing they'll ask is what investigation. And I'll say, no, actually I'm on medical leave from my department. That'll ring their bell and then they'll call my boss and he'll say she was distraught and obsessed and, Jesus, I hope she's okay. But he won't say, Believe her, because he doesn't believe that himself. And then they'll call the county homicide people, who'll say, yeah, she hasn't been the same since her niece got killed and sure, we cleared that case and busted the guy, he's doing a trillion years in solitary. And Mr. Agent will learn that I have access to hundreds of photographs, just like these, well, not quite, but close enough, and he'll just conclude I'm crazy. End of story . . .'

'Suppose I say . . .'

'Say what? She's convinced me about my brother? Mr Agent will just figure we're both out of our minds. But even if he does think maybe, just maybe, I better cover my ass, then what he'll do is some sort of computer check on your brother and he'll come up with zero. Well, not zero. He'll find out that your brother has a security clearance into the White House, for starters, approved by the Secret Service, because that's what I found when I did the same damn check. And then you know what he'll do? I'll tell you. He'll write one short little memo and file it under distraught-head cases. In other words: nothing.'

'Well, can't you persuade your own people?'

'They think I'm crazy and distraught.'

Her eyes narrowed.

'They're right of course.'

Martin Jeffers looked about himself, wondering what next.

'So what do you want to do?' he asked.

'Find him.'

'So you can kill him?'

Detective Barren hestitated.

'Yes,' she said.

'Forget it.'

'I could have lied and said no,' she said.

'Right. You could have. One point for your honesty.'

He stared bitterly at her and she returned the look with equal intensity.

'All right,' she said. 'You take a look at those pictures again. A real good look, and think about them for a minute and then you suggest a compromise.'

He answered quickly.

'We find him and arrest him and confront him and he'll confess.'

'Like hell he will.'

'Detective, I have a great deal of experience with people who commit multiple crimes. They almost invariably want to take credit for what they've done . . .'

He stopped suddenly. My God! he thought. I'm talking about Doug!

He stood up and lurched around the room as if drunk on memory.

'This is crazy, you know . . .'

'I think I admitted that,' she said.

'I mean, this is my brother! He's one of the top people in his profession! He's a journalist. He's an artist. He couldn't have done these things! It's just not in him! He's never been violent . . .'

'No?'

They looked across at each other. Both knew the room was filled with denials, disbelief, anxiety, and confusion. Detective Mercedes Barren thought suddenly: This is my only chance. He will never return to that apartment. He will disappear. He will be swallowed up somewhere in the country and be lost forever. If the brother won't provide the link, then there will be no link at all.

She swallowed and forced her face to hide the despair and dismay she felt pumping through her body like blood.

Martin Jeffers looked over at Detective Barren, trying to make his own face a mask to his emotions. He thought: I cannot lose sight of this woman. If I do, she will head off on some murderous tangent of her own.

And then a harder thought crept into his imagination: I must find out for myself what Doug has done.

He felt an almost palpable bond fixing him and the detective, in an equal but vastly different pursuit. He said brusquely:

'If I help to find him, so that we can clear this up intelligently, I must have your promise.'

'Promise what?'

Martin Jeffers stopped short. He wasn't sure. He took a deep breath.

'Promise you won't start shooting. Promise you'll listen. Just goddamn promise you won't kill him! He's my brother, for chrissakes! Otherwise, forget it.'

She did not rush into a hasty agreement. Let him think that you're giving this careful consideration, she said to herself.

'Well, I'll promise this: I'll give you a chance first. After that, well, whatever happens, happens.'

She said this solidly, confidently.

It was, she knew, a complete lie.

'All right,' he said, measured gratitude in his voice. 'That's fair.'

He did not trust her for an instant.

They did not do anything as foolish as shake hands over the deadly business they were about to embark upon. Instead they both settled into their seats and stared ahead, waiting for the next moment to arrive with whatever novel revelations it contained.

The bright morning light enveloped them, imposing some reason, some clarity on their thoughts. Detective Barren finally broke the silence they'd maintained with an orderly question:

'So,' she said directly, 'where do we start? What did he tell you about what he was going to do?'

'He didn't tell me much. He said he was going on a sentimental journey. Those were his exact words. I pointed out that we didn't have much to be sentimental about.'

'He must have said more.'

Martin Jeffers shut his eyes briefly, picturing his brother in the hospital cafeteria, grinning, as always.

'He said he was going to visit some memories. He didn't specify what kind.'

'Well, what do you think?'

'I'm not sure.'

'You don't have to be sure.'

Jeffers paused, considering.

'Well, it would seem to me that, assuming all this is true' – he waved a hand in the direction of the photographs – 'that he could have been talking about two kinds of memories. The first, obviously, are those memories he has from our childhood. The second group, of course, are the memories of these' – he stumbled 'events.'

Jeffers thought his voice sounded reasonable and calm. He hated it.

'Or, most likely, a combination of the two.'

Detective Barren suddenly felt invigorated, as if all the exhaustion slid away abruptly. Her mind raced ahead. She stood up and strode about the room, punching her fist into her palm, thinking.

'Usually,' she said, 'the process of deduction for policemen is to figure out why something happened and how. The two are generally linked . . .' She realized then that she had adopted almost the same lecturing tone that Martin Jeffers had. She ignored this, and continued. 'It is rare that we are asked to anticipate . . .'

'My profession is no different,' Martin Jeffers said.

She nodded.

'But now we have to.'

She could see agreement in his eyes.

'So assume for a moment that it would take us months to figure out which picture belonged in which locale . . .'

'Which is true. Nor do we know what sort of priorities he places on each, which would affect his itinerary,' Jeffers interjected.

'So we look at the other type of memory: personal.'

'Well, the problem there is almost the same. We have no way of telling what priorities he puts on things. Nor do we know the order he might be traveling in.'

'But at least you can make some guesses.'

'But that's all they would be. Guesses.'

'That's enough! At least it's doing something!'

Jeffers nodded.

'Well, for starters, we were abandoned in New Hampshire. That's probably on his list of places to visit.'

'How do you mean, abandoned?'

Martin Jeffers snapped his reply: 'Given up! Kicked out! Let loose! Shown the door! What the hell do you think?'

'I'm sorry,' she said, surprised by his sudden anger. 'I didn't know what you meant.'

'Look,' he said firmly, 'it's nothing that unusual, really. Our mother was the black sheep of the family. She ran away from home with a guy who'd just been discharged from the service. They worked in a carny show – you know, one of those fairs that travel around the country. She never married the guy, as best as we can tell. Anyway, Doug arrived. Then me. I don't think either of them cared too much for children. First he left, then she arranged to have us adopted by some cousins. She was supposed to bring us here to New Jersey, but I guess she got impatient, because she left us in New Hampshire. Manchester, to be exact.'

He hesitated.

'I can still remember everything about that damn police station where we waited. It was dim and the walls were scraped with drawings and grafitti, none of which I could decipher, but which I knew was somehow wrong. And everyone seemed so huge. You know that sense you get when you're little that the entire world is built for big people . . .'

'Your brother?'

'He got me through it. He took care of me.'

'What was his reaction?'

Jeffers took a deep breath.

'He hated her for leaving us. He hated her for not loving us. He hated our new parents just as much. Phony parents, he would say.'

'And you?'

'I hated. But not to the same degree.'

He wondered then if he was lying.

'Where did you end up?'

'Here.'

'No. I mean . . .'

'I know what you mean. Here is correct. The cousins who adopted us lived in Rocky Hill, just on the other side of Princeton. He was a druggist. Actually, though, he was a businessman. A damn good one. He owned a drugstore on Nassau Street which he finally sold to a chain for a helluva lot of money. He invested wisely. He was solid. Middle-class.'

'You don't sound . . .'

'I didn't. Doug hated him worse. The bastard wouldn't even give us his name after the adoption went through. Jeffers is our natural mother's name. Do you know how hard that is, growing up? You feel like you've got to explain things every time you register for school. Or make a new

friend. Or anything. If he gave us anything, we worked for
it.'

'You did okay.'

'You think so?'

She did not know what to say. Jeffer's voice had grown
in bitterness and anger. She wondered how he dealt with
all the rage he had. She knew how his brother did.

'Why don't we try Manchester?' she said.

'What good will it do?' Jeffers fairly spat out the words.

'I don't know,' she said evenly, but her own temper
rising through the words. 'But at least it will be doing
something other than waiting around for him to telephone
you. Which he hasn't done.'

'Not yet.'

'Do you think he will?'

Jeffers paused.

'Yes.'

'Why?'

'Because if he's pursuing shared memories, he's bound
to remember something that he will want to say to me. Or
he'll visit somewhere that prompts some need in him to
express something, and I'm the only logical place to express
it . . . other than that . . .' He gestured toward the photographs. 'That's how the mind works. It's not a guarantee,
but a good guess. An educated guess.'

She thought for a moment.

'I don't want to wait around.'

He nodded.

'It's Saturday,' he said. 'I don't have to be back at the
hospital until Monday.'

She stood.

'New Hampshire,' she said. 'We can show his picture
around, make some inquiries.' She thought for an instant,
then asked:

'Where are your folks now?'

She saw Martin Jeffers take a deep breath, as if marsha-
ling his anger into some military row. When he did speak,
it was in low, barely controlled tones. His voice surprised
Detective Barren, chilling her. She sat down in her chair

and watched as Jeffers struggled with his emotions and his memory, and for a moment she reminded herself instantly: Remember who he is. Remember they are brothers.

'Adoptive parents, both dead,' said Martin Jeffers coldly. 'Natural father? Who knows. Probably dead or in some state home somewhere. Natural mother? The same, unless . . .'

He paused.

' . . . Unless Doug managed to kill her.'

He first drove her past the drugstore, rolling slowly down Nassau Street in Princeton. The university, with its ivy-covered buildings, rested across the street, quiet, as if patiently awaiting the fall with its excitement and bustle from behind a great black iron fence and wide grassy lawns. Martin Jeffers pointed out that it was a few weeks before the semester start, which transformed the entire town. This she knew. She did not tell him how familiar she was with the entire area. She did not want him to know any more than was barely necessary.

She saw the stone classroom buildings and dormitories and thought of her husband. She smiled, remembering how comfortable he'd been at college and how strange it was for him to leave it for the Army. He had loved the internal world of school, she thought. He had been swept up in the false society that placed value on books and ideas and measured achievement through scholarly papers and skilled presentations. On what? On literature, on mathematics, on political theory, on science.

My father's world, too, she thought.

Not mine.

She had showered at her hotel while Martin Jeffers waited in his car outside. She had changed her underclothes and slipped into her jeans, dragged a comb through her hair, and was ready, oblivious to the lack of sleep, wide awake, excited, thinking only that she was getting closer, that she was narrowing down the world of Douglas Jeffers and that she would keep winnowing away at it until his world contained only her and her pistol. This thought had forced a bitter smile to her face.

She had looked in the room's mirror, but instead of checking her appearance, had lifted up her weapon, pointing it at the reflection. She had said, alone, out loud, 'This is what it will look like.'

She froze in the position and absorbed it silently.

Then she had seized a small duffle bag packed with overnight gear and put the 9-millimeter inside. In the top of the bag she had also placed the self-portrait Douglas Jeffers had taken of himself in the jungle, along with two extra clips of bullets.

Martin Jeffers had insisted on using his car, which was fine with her. She thought that he wanted the elusive sense of control that driving his own vehicle gave him, as if in some way he were in charge of the expedition. She acquiesced quickly, thinking that it would allow her to relax, store up energy, even sleep, while he would be burdened with the added fatigue of driving.

After seeing the pharmacy, Martin Jeffers drove out of town and within a few moments was winding through narrow, tree-shaded country roads. After a moment they came to a quiet, small subdivision of houses, plunked incongruously down amidst some farms. He stopped and pointed.

'Third one in. The family homestead. I haven't been here in ten years.'

She saw a modest, trim, three-story, gray and white frame house, with a green, well-kept lawn and a garage and a foreign car parked out in front.

'When we lived there,' Martin Jeffers continued, 'it was painted brown. A dull, ugly, dark brown. The inside reflected the outside; it lacked imagination. It was never friendly, outgoing, open, the way kids' houses ought to be. It was always dark and uncomfortable.'

'But it was a home. You weren't abandoned like some street kids.'

He shrugged. 'People sometimes overestimate the exterior factors. But the interior factors are what are critical for children.'

'What do you mean?'

'Love. Contact. Affection. Pride. Support. With them you can survive, and actually flourish, amidst the most horrendous circumstances. Without them, money and family and education and hired care, whatever, are all relatively useless. The ghetto child who works his way through school and becomes a lawyer. The younger-generation Kennedy kid who dies from a drug overdose. See what I mean?'

'Yes,' she replied. She thought of her niece, and her heart tightened for a single instant. She shook off the sensation by asking a question:

'You said both your adoptive parents are dead?'

'That's right,' Martin Jeffers answered. 'Our adoptive father died in an accident when we were teenagers and our adoptive mother died three years ago of what pathologists like to call natural causes, but which was really the result of too much drinking, too many tranquilizers, fast food, smoking, no exercise, and a heart that was too burdened by all this crap to go on any longer. In reality, totally unnatural causes.'

'Where are they buried?'

'They were both cremated. One doesn't erect monuments to people like them. Not unless one is totally out of . . .' He stopped, thinking that his brother was, in an unusually oblique, psychotic way, doing precisely that.

Detective Barren gathered in the information, mentally filing it, and looked up at the house. There's a monument, she thought, and an idea struck her.

'Wait here for a moment.'

'Not a chance,' he said.

They both exited the car and walked up to the house.

Detective Barren rang the doorbell. After a few seconds she heard footsteps running inside and a young voice crying, 'I'll get it! I'll get it! It's probably Jimmy!' The door was flung open and she looked down at a towheaded child of five or six. He looked at Detective Barren and Martin Jeffers, seemed disappointed, and turned and yelled back into the house, 'Mom! It's adults!' Betrayal tinged his voice. Then he turned and said, 'Hi!'

'Is your mom or dad at home?' she asked.

Before the child answered, Detective Barren heard the quick pace of embarrassment, and a woman about her own age, dressed in jeans and carrying a gardening spade, hove into view.

'I'm sorry,' she said, wiping her forehead. 'I was out back and we're expecting a playmate. What can I do for you?'

'Hello,' said Detective Barren. She held up her gold detective shield. 'My name is Mercedes Barren and I'm a police detective. We're investigating the disappearance of this man . . .' She held out the photograph of Douglas Jeffers. 'We wondered whether you might have seen him?'

The woman looked at the picture, clearly taken aback by the thought that she was talking to a detective in the middle of a hot Saturday morning.

'No,' she said. 'Why? Why would I see him? Is something wrong?'

'It's nothing to be alarmed at,' Detective Barren lied. 'The gentleman, who is related to my partner here, used to live in this neighborhood. We just thought, since he was missing, that he might have come looking at where he grew up, that's all. Nothing to be alarmed at. And this was a real long shot, as well.'

'Oh,' said the woman, as if Detective Barren's mingling of lies and truths answered questions as opposed to raising a thousand new ones. 'Oh,' she said again. She looked at the picture. 'I'm sorry, we haven't seen the man.'

'Let me see,' said the child.

'No,' said the mother. 'Billy, leave us alone.'

'I want to see!' he insisted.

She looked at Detective Barren.

'He needs his playmate,' she said.

The detective bent down and showed the child the picture.

'Ever see him?' she asked.

The child regarded the picture at length.

385

'Yes. Maybe he was here.'

Detective Barren stiffened inwardly and she felt Martin Jeffers take a quick step forward.

'Billy!' said the mother. 'This is serious! It's not game.'

'Maybe I saw him,' said the child. 'Maybe he came here, too.'

'Billy,' said Detective Barren evenly, friendly. 'Where did you see him?'

The child half-waved, half-pointed out toward the road.

'Did he say anything? What did he do?'

The child was instantly shy.

'No. Nothing.'

'Did you see a car? Or anyone else?'

'Nope.'

'When was this?'

'A while ago.'

'So what happened?'

'Nothing. Maybe I saw him, that's all.'

Detective Barren heard a car crunch down the gravel of the driveway behind her. She saw the child's eyes brighten.

'There they are!' he said to his mother. 'There they are! Can I go out, please?'

The mother looked at Detective Barren, who straightened up and nodded. 'Sure,' said the woman. The child burst out of the house, past the detective and Martin Jeffers. His mother stepped out beside them, watching the child and his friend start to play. She waved at the other mother, behind the wheel of the typical large station wagon. 'I'm not sure I'd place too much credence . . .' she started.

'Don't worry,' Detective Barren interrupted. 'I don't. And I don't think he saw anyone.'

'I don't think so either,' she said.

'Thanks for your help,' Detective Barren said. She and Martin Jeffers walked back to his car. She paused and waved at the boy, but he was swept away in excited play and did not see her.

In the car Martin Jeffers asked, 'What do you really think?'

She hesitated for a moment.

'I don't think he was here,' she said.

'Neither do I,' he added.

They both paused.

'Maybe, though,' he said.

'Maybe.'

Another pause.

'I think he was here,' he said.

'So do I,' said Detective Barren.

Martin Jeffers nodded and put the car in gear. It was not lost on him how easily and simply she'd lied to the mother. Then he gently turned the car and drove away from the house and the elusive, hallucinatory vision of their quarry and all their combined, unspoken memories.

Much of the drive to New Hampshire was done in silence, with only the roadway sounds intruding on their individual thoughts. They made a few efforts at small talk. Just past New Haven, Martin Jeffers asked:

'Are you married, detective?'

She thought of lying, of obfuscating, then inwardly shrugged, thinking the effort would be too great.

'No. Widowed.'

'Oh,' he said. 'I'm sorry.' This was convention.

'It was many years ago. I married young and he died in the war.'

'The war seemed to affect everyone one way or another.'

'Did you go?'

'No, they instituted the draft lottery when my time came up and I pulled three hundred and forty-seven. I'm not usually a lucky person, but this time I was. They never came knocking.'

'What about your brother?'

'It's odd, really. He was over there a couple of times, but always on assignment from some magazine or newspaper. And he dropped out of college, too. He should have been a prime target for the draft, but he never was nailed. I don't know why.'

He paused, then asked.

'You seem young. But you never remarried?'

She smiled despite herself.

'High school sweetheart. Hard to find someone who can compete with all those runaway teenage emotions and the way they translate into adult memories.'

Martin Jeffers had laughed a little.

'Quite true,' he said. He continued, asking, 'Why police work?'

'It was an accident, I guess. They had had an equal-opportunity suit down in Miami right about the time I got there. I saw an ad in the paper because they were under a court order to hire more women and minorities, and thought I'd give it a shot . . .' She laughed again. 'Isn't that the American way? Well, I answered the ad, almost on a lark, really. Then I discovered it was something that I did well. Finally, it was something I did best. How about yourself?'

'Psychiatry? Well, two reasons, actually. One, I didn't really like blood, and you've got to be pretty familiar with the stuff to be a successful physician; and two, I couldn't stand the idea of losing patients. That steered me away from a lot of branches of the profession. I guess there's a third, too. It's always interesting. People create infinite variations on several common themes . . .'

'That's true,' she said.

'See,' he replied, 'we sound alike again.'

She nodded. She thought of the Dear John letter she'd read in his files. 'No one to share all this with?'

She saw him order his thoughts before speaking.

'No . . . not really. I'm not sure why, but I have developed a pretty closed life, what with the work at the hospital demanding so much time. And then, in psychiatry as well as any branch of medicine, there's a great deal of self-education and keeping up that requires a lot of time. So, no – no one really.'

She nodded and thought: And you're terrified, too. Terrified of yourself.

The conversation evaporated in the rhythmic thump of tires on macadam and the steady drone of the engine. Detective Barren thought they jousted well. She conceded a significant degree of impressiveness to the doctor; he has been put under a great deal of stress, she thought, yet he still controls his tongue. She had dealt with many sophisticated men, criminals mainly, who, when put under less stress than he'd confronted would open up like flowers in bloom.

She wondered if he was correct about his brother: Confronted with evidence and the truth, perhaps he would confess. She considered this as a problem. A confession, even an egotistical, boasting one, could be sufficient to make him on the crimes. She pictured her niece's body lying beneath the ferns and dark palm shadows. Perhaps not all, but certainly some. Police literature is filled with the confessions of men who, when picked up for jaywalking, suddenly start admitting to serial murders. She remembered the man in Texas, with his claims exceeding two or three hundred. He was a drifter with a peculiarly homicidal bent. Lucas, she recalled. She recollected seeing a picture of him in a news magazine, standing with a detective who wore a ten-gallon hat, in front of a map of the southeastern United States. The hat was white, which she supposed was the way things were done in Texas. Maybe the bad guys were required to wear black. The map on the wall behind the two men was dotted, littered with small colored pushpins, and it had taken her a moment to realize the connection between the map, the pins, and the man grinning obscenely for the camera.

All artists are egotists, she thought. So are all murderers.

She envisioned Douglas Jeffers. Perhaps his brother is correct. Perhaps he will lay claim to his crimes, gaining a degree of satisfaction from the publicity.

She visualized him smiling, posing, accepting that extraordinary and perverse American celebrity that accompanies sensational crimes. He would revel in the attention.

She was flooded with images: Charlie Manson in a courtroom, suddenly holding up the Los Angeles *Times* for the jurors hearing the Tate-LaBianca cases to see, with its massive, screaming headline: MANSON GUILTY, NIXON SAYS; David Berkowitz slipping into his own sentencing hearing, chanting 'Stacy was a whore. Stacy was a whore,' drawing out the *o* sound like some crazed mantra and the poor victim's family frantic and struggling, trying to reach their tormentor. The New York *Times* had carried a remarkable pen-and-ink drawing the following day. She and the other detectives in her unit had stared at it in sad disbelief; Dr Jeffrey McDonald telling an interviewer from *60 Minutes* that he did not kill his wife and two small children at all, certainly not in some near-psychotic fit of rage, and that his murder conviction was all some mistake or worse, some conspiracy.

She envisioned others made into instant celebrities by crime and accusation: She pictured the aristocratic Claus von Bülow, wearing a contented, wry smile, posing for a celebrity photographer from *Vanity Fair* in black leather alongside his lover in the days after he was acquitted of the crime of injecting his wife with insulin and plunging her into an irreversible coma. She could see Bernhard Goetz pausing before a bank of microphones, peering benignly over the rims of his glasses and telling the mass of notepads and flashbulbs and the six o'clock news that he didn't do anything wrong when he shot the four teenagers who accosted him on the subway.

She saw Douglas Jeffers joining the same parade and the thought sickened her.

She rolled down her window and breathed in deeply.

'You all right?' asked Martin Jeffers.

'Yes,' she replied. 'I just needed a little fresh air.'

'Do you want to stop?'

'No,' she said firmly. 'Not until we get there.'

They drove on.

It was well after dark when they reached the outskirts of Manchester. They had stopped once for gasoline and Detective Barren had run into the cafeteria-style restaurant at the thruway rest stop while Martin Jeffers filled up the tank and checked the oil. She had purchased some coffee, a couple of sodas and two sandwiches, tuna fish and ham and cheese. The sandwiches were on soggy white bread and came sealed in see-through plastic containers. When she got back into the car, she had offered them to Jeffers. 'Take your pick,' she said.

'More like pick your poison,' he had replied, eyeing the sandwiches. He had seized the ham and cheese and bitten into it quickly. 'I love tuna fish,' he had said.

She had joined his laughter.

He thought then how long it had been since he'd heard a woman laugh unfettered. He did not think he would hear her laughter again. He reminded himself why she was with him and what she would do if she had the opportunity.

So he cautioned himself to be apprehensive. Not outwardly, he told himself. But question everything inwardly.

Do not mistake some laughter for trust, he said to himself. Or a smile for actual affection.

Trust nothing. Stay alert. He steeled himself against the fatigue of the road and of emotion and drove on into the increasing darkness.

On the outskirts of Manchester he spotted a Holiday Inn sign standing sharply against the blackness of the New Hampshire night. He gestured and asked:

'How's that? We're not going to get anything done tonight anyway. And we've both been up for hours . . .'

She nodded, part of her refusing to accept her exhaustion, another part of her demanding that she acquiesce to it. 'Fine.' Each filled out registration papers and used their own credit cards, which seemed to take the night clerk by surprise. When he handed them their keys, Detective Barren suddenly produced the picture of Douglas Jeffers and thrust it at the man.

'Seen him?' she demanded. 'Has he been here anytime in the past few weeks?'

The man looked at the picture.

'Can't say that I remember the face,' he said.

'Check your register,' said Martin Jeffers. 'Look for Douglas Jeffers. He's my brother.'

'I can't do that . . .' said the clerk.

Detective Barren produced her gold shield.

'Yes, you can,' she said.

He looked at the badge.

'We don't have a register,' he said. 'It's all computer. It cleans out the names every week . . .'

'Try it anyway,' Martin Jeffers said.

The clerk nodded. He punched some letters in on a computer keyboard.

'Nope.' he said.

'Does that tie in with other Holiday Inn computers?' Detective Barren asked.

'Yeah, actually, it does,' said the clerk. 'Just for the three that are in this area.'

'Try them,' she demanded again.

'Well,' he said, 'I'm not sure I know how to do that, but let me try.' He fiddled with the keyboard, making a rapid clicking noise as he tried combinations of letters and numbers. 'Hey!' he said suddenly.

'The name!' said Martin Jeffers.

'No, no, no, sorry,' said the clerk. 'It's just I figured it out. Now let me check names.' Again he punched letters. Then he shook his head. 'Not in the last seven days,' he told them.

'Thanks for trying,' said Detective Barren.

'Is the guy in trouble?' asked the clerk.

'You might say that,' said Detective Barren. 'But at the moment he's just one of the missing.'

The clerk nodded.

Martin Jeffers carried her duffel bag to her room. She let him do this to give it an air of innocence. She knew that if she had insisted on carrying it, he would recognize that was where she kept the gun. She knew he would probably figure it out anyway if he thought about it. But perhaps he wouldn't, and she was always searching for whatever edge she could find.

At the door to their rooms, they looked at each other.

'Do you want to try to find something to eat?' Martin Jeffers asked.

She shook her head.

'Good,' he said.

They stood in silence.

'I need your word,' he said.

'What?'

'Promise that when I go in here, you won't head off without me. '

She almost smiled. That was what she had feared from him.

'If you'll make the same promise.'

He nodded. 'We're agreed then?'

She nodded as well.

'Why don't we start at nine,' he said. 'Leave a wake-up call at the desk.'

'Eight,' she said firmly. 'See you then.'

Moving at the same speed, each opened the door to their room and stepped inside. It seemed an odd ballet, out of sight, but not, thanks to thin motel walls, necessarily out of hearing. They both paused, straining to hear some noise from the other's room. Then each moved into the center of the room and, realizing that the other was next door, and probably listening with the same lack of trust, each bustled about for a moment before falling into bed.

Manchester was once a busy industrial town, and it still retained a sense of blue-collar grime and hard work, with stolid brick buildings and factories that were only partially concealed by the richness of New Hampshire's late-summer green. Detective Mercedes Barren and Martin Jeffers ate a quiet, brief breakfast, then set out amidst the early church-goers and bright sunshine. They spoke little, nor did they have some established plan; they merely cruised the streets, stopping at fast-food restaurants, gas stations, other motels, and hotels – anyplace that Douglas Jeffers might have settled briefly and made just enough of a connection for someone to recall his picture.

She doubted, even if someone remembered him, whether they would have any knowledge that was worthwhile. But, as Martin Jeffers pointed out, if they were to locate him, just once, then they would have some sort of idea what direction he was heading in.

She was skeptical. He was skeptical. But both conceded inwardly that they felt much better doing something – even if it was only creating the illusion of doing something – than it would have been sitting around.

And both longed for the same thing: some slight contact that would bring them within reach of Douglas Jeffers. It was as if by arriving at the same location that their quarry had been, they would gain a scent.

Still, Detective Barren felt slightly foolish. She knew the probabilities of any kind for success were very small. But, she thought to herself, you've never disliked this part of police work. Some detectives hated the drudgery of asking the same questions over and over, trying to sort through the entire haystack, much preferring leaping ahead somehow. She, on the other hand, realized that much of her success was due to her doggedness, and she could be perfectly happy, indeed contented, asking question after question. He felt much the same; much of his work was devoted to going over and over, repetitively, the same memories, the same circumstances, the same facts, until by dint of persistence they were defused.

It was late afternoon when Jeffers asked, 'Why don't we try the police station? Just see if he's gone in there.'

'I was saving it for last,' she replied.

'We're at the end,' he said. 'If he's been there, he certainly hasn't made much of a fuss about it.'

'I don't think he's been here,' she said. 'Which only means that he may show up, anytime.'

Jeffers nodded.

'But I've still got a job, and appointments waiting for me after an eight-hour drive back to New Jersey. If you want to hang around . . .'

'No,' she said. She thought: We're in this together. 'No, we're going to stick together until . . .'

He interrupted. 'Until we get this sorted out.'

'Right.'

'Okay, the police station.'

Martin Jeffers looked up the address of the Central Police Headquarters while Detective Barren showed the picture to one more gas station attendant, unsuccessfully. He got directions from the attendant and they drove through a depressing series of city streets, each seemingly more run-down than the next. The police headquarters was in the grimiest portion of the city. Detective Barren noticed the number of squad cars rolling through the neighborhood and thought they must be close. She spied, to their left, a large red-brick building.

'There,' she said, pointing.

Martin Jeffers hesitated.

'That's not it,' he said. 'That's new. I mean, it's relatively new. The building I remember was old.'

He pulled the car up next to the building. 'Look at the cornerstone,' he said.

She turned and followed his glance and read ERECTED 1973 on a gray slab set on the corner of the building. Martin Jeffers parked the car and said, 'Let's go ask.'

Inside the building was all fluorescent lights and modern design, but slightly scarred with use. They approached a desk sergeant and Detective Barren produced her shield. The sergeant was a corpulent man, probably happy to man the desk, equally as adept at avoiding controversy as he was at dodging a street assignment.

'Miami,' the man said, pleasantly enough. 'My brother-in-law runs a bar in Fort Lauderdale. Once went to visit, but too many kids, if you know what I mean. Whew. And hot! So what can I do for you, detective from Miami? What's in Manchester that you need?'

He pronounced the city's name with a broad *a* that made Detective Barren smile.

'Two things,' she said smiling. 'Have you seen this man? And wasn't there once an old police station in central Manchester?'

The sergeant looked at the picture.

'No, can't say that I've seen him. You want me to make some copies and have them distributed at roll call? If this guy's wanted, we ought to know about it. What d'you think?'

Detective Barren thought hard and fast about the offer. No, she thought. He's mine.

'No,' she said, 'at the moment he's just wanted for questioning and I don't really have enough for you to pull him in on. I'm just making a few inquiries, you know.'

The sergeant nodded. 'Have it your way,' he said. 'Just wanted to offer.'

'And it's appreciated,' she replied.

He smiled.

'Now,' the sergeant added, 'about that old station. There were a couple, actually. Up until the mid-sixties we were like a lot of little cities. We had station houses all over. Then they were consolidated into this new and beautiful spot you see here . . .' He waved his hands about before continuing. 'Most were torn down. One got made into a bunch of lawyers' offices. That's the one that was closest to the courthouse. I think one was made into a condominium. That's in the other part of town, the nice side . . .' He laughed. 'Sometimes I think that's what's gonna happen to all of us when we pass on. We're gonna be made into a condo. Right up in heaven, I guess.' He laughed again and both Jeffers and Detective Barren smiled with him, each recognizing a certain truth to his plaint.

'Which would have been the Central Station? The biggest?' Jeffers asked.

'That'd be the one across from the courthouse.'

'How do we get there?'

'Break the law.'

'I beg your pardon?'

'Just having a little joke. How do you get to the courthouse? Break the law . . . Oh, well, I said it was a little joke. Go straight down this street for six blocks and turn right on Washington Boulevard. That'll take you there.'

They thanked the sergeant and left.

'Let's roll past,' Detective Barren said.

Jeffers nodded in assent. 'Lawyer's offices. Seems appropriate. Kind of like recycling trash.'

She smiled.

'Another little joke,' he said.

They found the building without any trouble. Jeffers was silent for a moment, looking up at it.

'The façade seems the same,' Jeffers said then. She thought his voice had taken on a sudden false determination, as if by sounding strong, he would be. He parked the car in front and stared through the car window. 'It was windy and dark and raining,' he said. 'I remember that night it looked evil and hopeless, like it should have had a sign over the door: Abandon Hope All Ye Who Enter Here . . .'

Not waiting for Detective Barren, he abruptly jumped from the car and then marched up a broad flight of stairs to the front door. He seized the handle and pulled.

'Locked. It's Sunday and the offices are locked.'

She looked at him.

'Thank God,' he said. She saw him shudder slightly. 'Do you know the sensation of being a child and being alone? Children can adapt wonderfully to specific fears, like a pain, a sickness, or a death. It is the unknown which is truly terrifying for them. They have no fund of knowledge in how the world operates, and so they feel completely vulnerable. Do you know what I remember from that night? Oh, everything is vivid and terrible, but I can also remember that my shoes were too tight and I needed a new pair and I thought I would never be able to get them, and how was I going to grow up with no shoes, ever? I remember sitting, having to go to the bathroom so much it hurt but too scared to say anything to anybody. I just knew I wasn't supposed to get off that bench, where they put us to wait. Doug took care of me. He knew, somehow. You know, it always seemed to me, when I was young, that he knew what I was thinking before I even thought it. I suppose all younger brothers ascribe such magical properties to their elder brother. Probably I was squirming around so much. Anyway, he took me to the bathroom. And he told me he would take care of me and not to worry, that he would always be close by. I don't know how much he meant it, but it made me feel safe and wonderful hearing those words. I think I thought I was going to die that night, until he held my hand . . .'

The sun was starting to fade and Martin Jeffers' voice slid into the shadows.

She thought: That's what childhood is, seeking refuge from one fear after another until you become strong enough and old enough and wise enough to battle the fears away. Only some fears can never be defeated.

She looked at Martin Jeffers. He was staring up at the building.

'He's my brother,' he said. 'Now we're grown up and he's doing these terrible things and I have to stop him. But he saved my life that night. I know it.'

Martin Jeffers turned away from the building.

'Let's leave now,' he said. 'Let's just get the hell out of here.'

He grabbed her by the arm and half-pulled her down the flight of steps. She did not resist.

'Let's just go. Go, go back to New Jersey. Now,' he said.

She did not say anything in reply, but nodded. She could see the conflict and agony returning to his face. For an instant she felt a kind of dual sadness, one for the memory of the abandoned child who continued to seek his lost parent throughout his life, one for the adult torn by terrible knowledge. She thought then, oddly, that it was unfortunate that she had met Martin Jeffers in this awful way, that under different circumstances she probably would have come to like him. And this made her feel sad for herself. But she shook the feeling away rapidly and moved to her side of the car. I'm sorry, Martin Jeffers, she said to herself. I'm terribly sorry, but lead on. Lead me to your brother. This, she knew he would do. But she knew too, right at that moment, as Jeffers turned away from the building, holding his head in such a way that he thought she would be unable to see his tears and threw himself behind the wheel of the car, that he would never betray his brother.

It was close to midnight, near the end of another wordless journey, when they crossed the George Washington Bridge, passing New York City with its constancy of light on their left and rapidly leaving it behind. Detective Barren's eyes were closed, and Martin Jeffers assumed she slept in the passenger seat. He maneuvered through the still-thick nighttime traffic. His eyes caught the series of huge green roadway signs directing travelers in a dozen different directions, and he considered the great convergence of people and machines and highways that came together at the bridge: routes 4 and 46 and 9W and the Palisades Parkway and the great ribbon that is Interstate 95 heading north-south and the equally great black rope that is Interstate 80, heading east and west. The lights from oncoming cars blinded him as they sliced through the darkness, a quick rush of brightness, then disappearing. When he looked at the lanes in the opposite roads, he could just barely make out the shapes of the other cars, and the odd thought struck him that his brother was out there. He could be anywhere, he said to himself. He could be anywhere, but I know he's here. He could be any one of the sets of lights passing. That one, or that one or that one, but he's one of them. He wanted to call out to him, but was unable. You're there, he thought. I know it. Please.

Then he shook his head to clear away the idea, and realized he was silly and exhausted and probably hallucinating as well, and drove on, not knowing that he was also right.

12 Another trip to New Hampshire

17

He had tied the ropes too tight and the nylon strands cut into her wrists agonizingly. She had given up struggling against the pain, realizing that when she pulled or twisted, the cord rebelled, chafing away her flesh. She tried to shut away the throbbing in her arms and find sleep, but when she closed her eyes she saw only the redness of hurt, which was impossible to avoid. So, despite having passed some undefined limit of physical and mental exhaustion, she remained wide awake. The gag around her mouth was giving her problems, as well. She could only breathe through her nose, which he'd bloodied, each breath drawn past clogged blood and mucus with immense difficulty. When he'd gagged her, he had pulled her head back sharply, tightening the knot on the kerchief behind her neck, not paying care to what he was doing. Then he'd slapped a piece of gray gaffer's tape over her mouth. The tape stank of glue and she was afraid she would gag. This might kill her, she knew; if she vomited now out of pain and fear and confusion, she might drown. She surprised herself by realizing the danger and despite the cloud created by her restraints was struck by how far she had traveled, how much more she seemed to know. This thought reshaped itself into a fear; she felt a unique vulnerability, having lived so far. She shut her eyes to the idea that he would kill her now.

Anne Hampton did not know why Douglas Jeffers had beaten and tied her this night, but it did not surprise her.

She assumed it had something to do with the failed murder of the two young women earlier in the day. But he had not been his usual specific self. He had reverted to rage alone.

In a way, she had known it was coming.

He had driven fast from the racetrack, sullen, speechless, his silence scaring her more than his usual speechifying. Darkness had crushed them, still he had not stopped until past New York, at midnight, near Bridgeport, Connecticut. He'd found their usual misbegotten accommodations, checking in with a sleepy, unshaven night clerk with hardly a word, paying for the room, as he always did, in cash. Almost as soon as he'd closed the motel door he was on her, pummeling her with open hands, knocking her about the room. She had held up her hands to ward off the first blows, but then had resigned herself and received what he had wanted to dish out. Her passivity may have disappointed him, but the idea had struck her almost as swiftly as his fists that if she were to fight back, she might take the place of the two women. They had lived and she didn't want to pay for their good fortune right then and there.

So she slunk down, barely covering herself and let him flail away.

The beating had been like a spasm, brief, terrifying, yet over quickly. Then he'd shoved her disdainfully into a corner, wedged down past the sagging twin beds of the motel room. She had not seen him grab the rope; suddenly he'd thrown her down and she'd felt the bonds looped tightly around her, constricting her like some horrid snake. The rope was followed with the violence of the gag around her mouth. She had looked up, trying to catch his eyes, trying to discern what was happening, but she'd been unable. He'd pushed her away with a final, irritated thrust, and left the motel without explanation other than a cryptic promise: 'I'll be back'.

She was, by far, most frightened of the rope. He had not used it since the first day and she feared that it signaled some terrible change in their relationship. She was back to being his possession, as opposed to, in some unusual way that she could not quite discern, his partner. She had lost identity, lost importance. If she lost relevance, she knew, he would abandon her. Her mind used the word 'abandon', but she knew that it was a euphemism for something else. She recognized her position as precarious and intensely dangerous. She did not think he would kill Boswell. But he could easily murder some nameless, faceless, bound-and-gagged woman who bothered him with her presence and who reminded him of a failure. She searched about the motel room as best she could. She saw an old dresser and a mirror and two beds with brown corduroy covers that were faded and cheap, and she thought it was a horrid and squalid place to have to die.

She pictured Vicki and Sandi, who'd seemed so reluctant to put on their clothes. She had been confused; Jeffers had emerged from the woods smiling, joking, playful – as if nothing were wrong – yet she knew something had disrupted the plan, which had frightened her even more. He had teased the two about their good looks and promised that they would get a real shot at the mythical photo spread.

She remembered hearing all that as if from a great distance. She had remained rigid with expectation; looking up and seeing the gun in his hands a dozen times, only to blink and realize that it was the camera.

After a few more shots he'd hustled them all back through the woods and into the car. He'd driven to the racetrack, still bantering away with the two giggling women, who had kept saying, 'I can't believe how lucky we are'.

She would have laughed, had she not been so terrified.

She thought that the absence of murder was twice as frightening as the act itself. She did not know what had happened, what accident or stroke of luck had saved the two women's lives. She knew only that he'd dropped them back at the grandstand, given the pair a gay little wave and laugh, then accelerated hard, back to the highway. That false laugh had been the last sign of anything from Douglas Jeffers save building rage.

Anne Hampton relaxed against the rope's pain and considered what had happened.

She determined that when he returned, she would make him free her. She focused on this, saying to herself: Nothing else matters. Nothing else is important. You must make him acknowledge who you are. And he will not do that until he removes the bonds.

She swallowed hard and felt her stomach pitch like a boat in a storm.

She bit back the nausea of fear.

I am closer now to death than anytime since the first minutes.

Make him need you.

Make him.

Make him.

Force him.

She waited for him to return, repeating the words over and over to herself, like some nightmarish lullaby.

Douglas Jeffers drove aimlessly through the dark streets, searching for an outlet for his frustration. For a moment he considered the idea of driving into the inner city and simply assassinating some hard-luck person on the street. He thought of finding a prostitute; they were the easiest of targets, almost accommodating in the creation of their death. The idea of driving into an all-night gas station and simply blowing away the attendant appealed to him as well. That was the occupational hazard associated with taking money for gasoline at night. Every so often, somebody else wanted the money and was quite willing to kill for it. Douglas Jeffers thought all the possibilities had a certain common charm; they were the stuff of every-night police blotters. They would get no more than a couple of paragraphs in the morning paper. They were the urban blighted norm, moments of diminished importance, almost routine. That a life ended was of little consequence, an afterthought of night that faded in the light of morning.

They were not the types of crimes that an expert like himself needed to study for more than a couple of seconds.

He shook his head. Another time, he thought, I'd simply do it. Perhaps a liquor store that stayed open a bit too late.

Get a ski mask and a big handgun. A truly American moment.

He let out his breath in a long, slow whistle.

Not now. Not this close to the end.

Don't screw up.

He alternately wished he'd killed the young ranger, then the two women, but mostly he was angry with himself for not having anticipated all the problems that were associated with the crime. He went back over the details in his head, bitterly castigating himself: I have always properly prepared for every eventuality; I have always foreseen every dilemma. I should have discovered a better hiding place. He berated himself for choosing the glen in the woods. I liked the damn light and background. I thought like a damn photograher. Not like a killer. So all that work was worthless, worthless, damn, damn, damn!

He tried to defuse his anger with the thought that the ranger's arrival had been random, unexpected. But this seemed to him to be the stuff of excuse, which was distasteful. I always get the shot, he said to himself. I always get it.

He pounded his hands against the steering wheel and thrashed about sharply in his seat, barely maintaining control over the car, even at a slow speed. He wanted to scream, but was unable. Then he remembered Anne Hampton tied in the motel room. Let her wait, he told himself angrily. Let her worry. Let her suffer.

Let her die.

He inhaled sharply and held his breath for a moment.

He was surprised that these harsh thoughts left him slightly uncomfortable.

He pulled the car to the side of a deserted street in a warehouse district. He put his head back and suddenly felt tired.

It wasn't her damn fault. It was yours. She did what you asked of her.

He closed his eyes.

Damn. The plan was faulty.

He sighed. Well, it just goes to show: nobody's perfect.

His anger fled him suddenly and he rolled down the window, letting the stale air of the car mingle with the dark cool of the night.

He laughed out loud. The laughter turned to a childish giggle. Nobody's perfect, he thought. Right.

But you're pretty damn close.

He thought of the two women cavorting about in the nude. You didn't have to kill them, he realized. They will probably die quickly from boredom and stupidity and routine lives that promise nothing and deliver less. What was truly hilarious, he imagined at that second, was that they had just experienced the most unique, exciting, and dangerous moment that they would ever have, regardless of how long they lived. For one sublime afternoon they had come into contact with genius and managed to live through it. And the sows didn't know it.

He laughed again. Exhaustion crept inside him and he realized that it was important to get some sleep. Well, he thought, everything is still on track. A nice easy drive to New Hampshire in the morning. He thought of taking her to Mount Monadnock or Lake Winnipesaukee or some other nice spot before settling in for the evening. Something quiet and relaxing. He considered a town he knew in Vermont. Out of the way, but beautiful – and still a quick drive to the appointment in New Hampshire. Then a little bit of business before the drive down to the Cape.

His mind filled suddenly with rolling, thick, swelling electronically synthesized music and a picture of the grinning actor wearing the white jumpsuit, black bowler, parachute boots, and fake proboscis. A little bit of the old ultraviolence, he said to himself. Real horror show.

And then freedom.

He thought of Anne Hampton again. Boswell is probably scared out of her wits. He shrugged. That wasn't terrible; it was wise to keep her off-balance.

But he still felt a twinge of guilt.

Let her up to breathe, he thought. She remains necessary.

That gave him a sense of purpose, and he searched about himself briefly, getting his bearings, ready to head directly back to the motel. He started to consider how he would apologize to her. As he was about to put the car in gear and leave, he spotted the van parked two hundred yards down the street. He knew instantly what it was: Warehouse. Outside of regular police patrol areas. After midnight. Van. It was a simple equation, the sum of which added into breaking and entering. An idea struck him and he smiled.

No, he said to himself.

Then: Why not?

He wanted to burst out laughing, but he cautioned himself: Be careful.

He did not turn the lights on, rolling the car as quietly as possible down toward the van. It was light-colored and suitably battered and nondescript. He could see no movement from the truck, but he kept his pistol in his hand just in case. When he was next to the van, a distant streetlight threw just enough illumination so he was able to make out the license plate number. He paused, noting the doorjamb on the warehouse door that seemed sprung, though it was difficult for him to tell without getting out of the car. This he was wise enough not to do. Not that he feared the man or men inside, but then he would lose the element of surprise. He rolled past, not turning on his headlights until he reached a spot a couple of blocks away.

He stopped at the first gas station with a pay phone and dialed 911.

'Bridgeport police, fire and rescue,' came the flat voice with its studied indifference to emergency.

'I want to report a break-in in progress,' replied Douglas Jeffers.

'Is it happening right now?'

'That's what I said,' Jeffers insisted, with just the right amount of indignation. 'Right now.' He gave the policeman the address and a description of the van and license plate number.

'Thank you. We're rolling. Can I have your name for our files?'

'No,' said Douglas Jeffers. 'Just consider me a concerned citizen.' He hung up the phone. A concerned citizen: he liked that a lot. If they only knew, he thought. He envisioned a pair of robbers, dressed in dark clothes, surprised suddenly by the lights from a police cruiser. He imagined them cursing their luck, rattling their handcuffs in frustration as the police officers passed on those small moments of congratulation and success that accompany a good arrest. If they had any idea who it was that tipped them. Either the good guys or the bad guys. Imagine the looks on their faces.

Then he laughed wildly at the sheer outrage of it all.

Anne Hampton heard the key in the door lock and she stiffened against the ropes. From where she lay, she could not see the door, but she heard it creak as it opened. She made a muffled sound through the gag and tape as the door closed and footsteps approached her. She lifted her head so that her eyes could meet Douglas Jeffers'. She had concentrated hard to remove the weak animal fear that she felt within and replace it with an obstinate, defiant, demanding look. Their eyes met, and Jeffers seemed surprised.

'Well,' he said, 'Boswell seems angry.'

He reached down and tore the tape from her mouth. The ripping sound made her think that her lips and cheeks were cut. She held herself motionless while he loosened the gag.

'Better?' he asked.

'Much. Thank you.' She kept her voice even and slightly irate.

Douglas Jeffers laughed.

'Boswell is angry.'

'No,' she said. 'Just uncomfortable.'

'That's to be expected. Are you hurt?'

She shook her head.

'Just stiff.'

'Well, let's do something about that.'

Douglas Jeffers produced a knife. She could see the blade reflecting the light from the bedside lamp. She breathed in hard, thinking, Boswell, Boswell, he called you Boswell, you have nothing to fear. Not yet, not yet.

He placed the blade flat against her cheek.

'Have you ever noticed how hard it is to tell whether a knife is hot or cold? It depends on what kind of fear you're experiencing. The touch can seem red-hot or ice-cold, just like the feeling in your stomach and around your heart.'

She didn't move. She stared ahead.

After a moment he pulled the blade away.

He started to cut the rope and her hands came free.

'I shouldn't have struck you,' he said matter-of-factly. 'It wasn't your fault.'

She didn't reply.

'Just call it a moment of weakness.' He paused. 'A rare moment.'

He helped her to her feet.

'There you go. A little unsteady, but not so bad. Use the bathroom to clean up.'

She took a few uncertain steps, using the wall to help her maintain her balance. Inside the bathroom she saw that blood had clotted around her lips and nose, but that it washed away with some vigorous scrubbing. She felt all her exhaustion rush back, then, and she had to grip the edges of the sink to keep from collapsing.

When she came out, she saw that Douglas Jeffers had turned down the bed for her. She dropped her jeans to the floor and crawled in gratefully. He disappeared into the bathroom and she heard the water run, then the toilet flush. He came out and hopped into the other bed. He switched off the light and she felt the darkness wash over her like a wave at the beach.

He was silent for a moment, then he spoke:

'Boswell, have you ever thought how fragile life is?'

She didn't reply.

'It's not just the living that's so delicate, but the entirety of, I don't know, life's balance. Think of the mother who turns her back for an instant and whose child wanders into the roadway. Or the father who just doesn't bother, this one time, to fasten his seat belt on the way to work in the family car. Accidents. Disease. Bad luck. Death ends life for some, certainly. But worse, it unsettles. It throws the living off balance, out of whack. It disrupts their centers. Think of all the people you've known and who've loved you. Imagine for an instant what your death will mean to them . . .'

She closed her eyes and suddenly all her brave intentions vanished and she wanted to sob.

' . . . Or what their death would mean to you. Emptiness. A certain vacuum space inside. Some memories that persist. Maybe a photo album, somewhere. A gravestone. Perhaps a once-a-year visit. We are all linked in so many ways, so dependent on the others to maintain our equilibrium. Sons and fathers. Daughters and mothers. Brothers. Sisters. Everything a tenuous relationship. Too many connections. Everything completely, delicately, chinalike fragile.'

He paused, then repeated the word.

'Fragile. Fragile. Fragile.'

Again he hesitated.

'I hate that more than anything,' he said. His voice was filled with the barest of controls, defined by bitterness. 'I hate that you don't choose who you are. I hate that you have no choices. I hate it, I hate it, I hate it, hate, hate, hate . . .'

In the darkness, Anne Hampton could see that Douglas Jeffers was lying on his back, but that both his fists were clenched in the air in front of him.

He exhaled sharply into the night.

'Everyone's a victim,' he said. 'Except me.'

Then she heard him roll over and devote himself to sleep.

In the morning they drove north, finding Route 91 in New Haven, heading past Hartford into Massachusetts. She thought that Jeffers seemed to be acting with control again; he was watching his watch, measuring the distances, careful with his timing. That reassured her, and she relaxed, waiting for something new to happen.

They reached southern Vermont in the early afternoon, continuing north at a steady pace. Anne Hampton wondered, almost idly, whether they were going to Canada. She tried to recall any crimes from that nation, thinking,

What could be up there that he wants to show me? She was unable to remember any, but she was certain that people killed each other there. It's cold, she thought, it's frozen and dark and long winters must mean some horror or another emerges.

Before any other thought took root, Douglas Jeffers said, 'There's a little town up here that you should see . . .'

He did not describe Woodstock further, preferring to drive a few hours in quiet. She will see for herself, he thought. He mentally reviewed the elements of the plan that remained. He wanted to check in his briefcase for the letter from the New Hampshire bank, but he knew that was unnecessary. They are expecting you in the morning, he said to himself. It will be quick and precise and the way things should be.

When he turned off the thruway toward the small town, he said, 'Have you ever noticed that almost every one of these old New England states has a Woodstock? Vermont, New Hampshire, Massachusetts. Probably even Rhode Island, if they can squeeze it in. Rhode Island. They say: Rowdilan. Or NeHampsha. Of course the important Woodstock was New York's Woodstock and the festival that actually was held elsewhere. Do you remember it?'

'I was only a kid,' she said. 'I didn't know.'

'I was there,' Jeffers said.

'Really? Was it as big as the books say?'

He laughed.

'Actually, I wasn't there . . .'

She looked confused.

'There are certain common events that become common memories through popular culture. Woodstock was one of them. I knew a guy, once, in the newspaper business, who was the guy who created the Woodstock myth. He was just starting out, the college stringer for the New York *Daily News*. It was summertime, and so they asked him to go up to the festival, just in case something unusual happened. They had no idea that the crowds were going to be, well, like they were.

'Anyway, he went up the day before, to check on the

410

festival preparations, which was real lucky, because by midmorning the next day, cars had backed up for ten or twenty miles. People were streaming in. Long-hairs. Hippies. Bikers. College kids. You probably saw the movie. Anyway, as you know, it became this massive jam of music and people and suddenly a front-page story. So there was my buddy, sitting behind the stage, on the phone to the city desk at the *News* and there was some editor yelling at him, "How many people are there? How many people?" and of course he had no fucking idea whatsoever. I mean, everywhere he turned there were people and trucks and helicopters buzzing the place and bands turning up the volume and you name it. And the editor yells, "We need an official police estimate of the crowd!" so he runs over to some cop and asks what they're estimating in terms of crowd size, and of course the cop looks at him like he's totally berserk, and how the hell should they know. He goes back to the phone and the editor realizes suddenly it's his ass on the line because here's the biggest story to come down the pike in some time and he was stupid enough to send some college stringer up to cover it and he can't get a real reporter in because the roads are jammed and there aren't any more helicopters for rent because the damn television stations have grabbed them all.

'And my buddy has this inspiration. He decides to lie. He yells into the phone, "Police are estimating more than a half-million people have descended upon this sleepy burg. Suddenly Woodstock is the third-largest city in New York State!" And this the editor loves. Just loves. Because it's the front-page screamer for the next morning. After the *News* put the figure on the front page, the *Times* picked it up and then the AP, and that meant the world. And suddenly my buddy's lie becomes historical fact . . .'

He snapped his fingers.

'Just like that. And everybody got happy and everybody always assumes that's how many people were there. Just because my buddy had the good sense to lie to someone who desperately wanted to hear a lie.'

Douglas Jeffers paused. His voice, as so many times

before, seemed to ratchet between a schoolboyish storytelling delight and some ominous hatred.

'So now I lie as well.'

He grinned, then grimaced.

'I just say I was there. I mean, who's to check?'

Douglas Jeffers paused, and Anne Hampton saw that he'd diluted the lightheartedness of this story with some darker thought. She plucked out a notebook and scraped down a quick series of notes about Woodstock and a half-million people and some fellow her age plucking a figure from midair.

'You see, in a way, that's what we do in the news business. We create a commonality of experience. Who can say they weren't in Vietnam? The pictures invaded us. How about the Watts riot? Or get more current: Beirut. The Mexico City quake. The TWA hijacking. They held a press conference, if you can believe it. The final answer in absurdity. Criminals in the midst of a crime seeking publicity and receiving it. And we were all there, right there, right with them. It depends, it depends.'

He hesitated again.

'The news business is like the old saw about the tree falling in the forest. If no one's around to hear it, did it make a sound? If a thousand Indians die in the rain forest, but we don't report it, did it happen?'

Jeffers laughed out loud. His first burst was one of anger, then followed one of release.

'I am sometimes so boring I'm surprised you haven't killed me.'

He laughed again.

She knew she wore a stricken look.

'Lighten up, Boswell, we're near the end. That was a joke.'

He smiled.

'Or was it? Poor Boswell, sometimes she doesn't think my jokes are at all humorous. And I can't say that I blame her. But indulge me with a smile, a little bit of laughter, please.'

This last was a demand.

She complied instantly. She thought the sound sickening.

'Not much of an effort, Boswell, but appreciated nonetheless.'

He paused.

'Work on it, Boswell. Work on all those little things we do in life that remind us of who we are. Concentrate, Boswell. I think, therefore, I am. I laugh, therefore I am . . .

' . . . If I laugh, I breathe. If I smile, I feel. If I think, I exist.'

He fixed his eyes on the road.

'Boswell lives on,' he said.

She felt her heart tighten with despair.

'But so does Douglas Jeffers.'

He looked down the highway, turning onto a small two-lane road. Evening was sliding up on them; the rich greens and browns of the Vermont hills flowed about the car, the shadowed darkness broken by the occasional wan shaft of late daylight. They passed by the Quechee Gorge, which is on the road to Woodstock, and he saw Anne Hampton crane her head to see the precipitous drop from the car.

He cruised through the quiet streets. Anne Hampton saw trim white clapboard houses behind wide lawns with gazebos that had clinging vines next to small flower gardens.

'You see,' he said, pointing toward a stark white church that rose up against the green darkness of the Vermont night. 'You see how relaxing it all is? Who would think that such terror was abroad at night in such a little safe town?'

He parked the car.

'Well,' he said, 'even terror gets hungry.'

He looked at Anne Hampton.

'Another joke,' he said.

She forced a smile.

'But the best humor is always based on reality.'

He took her hand and led her into a restaurant. It was candlelit and lovely, glowing with a golden warmth. She could smell food cooking, the mingled sensations pouring over her palate. It all made her nauseated.

What is happening? she wondered.

What is going on?

Why are we here?

Why is everything in the world so normal when it isn't?

What is happening to me?

This last thought screamed through her head. She could barely keep from collapsing. I'm standing, waiting to be seated in an elegant restaurant in a beautiful town. Everything is backwards. Everything is wrong. What's going on?

Again she felt sick to her stomach.

'I could eat a horse,' said Douglas Jeffers.

They ate quietly, efficiently, joylessly. Jeffers ordered wine, and he sipped from the goblet, staring over the edge at Anne Hampton. She could see the light reflected in the glass.

After he'd paid, Douglas Jeffers took Anne Hampton's arm and led her through the darkness around the town common. He felt her shiver. The warmth had fled the day, replacing the air with Vermont's promise of autumn.

'Quiet,' he said. 'Peaceful.'

She felt no sense of relaxation. It was all she could do to keep her arm loosely on his. She wanted to grab him and scream: What next?

But she didn't.

He led her back to the car. Within a few moments they were enmeshed by darkness on the backroads of the state, heading toward the interstate. Douglas Jeffers was driving slowly, obviously thinking, his concentration diminished by the wine, a full stomach, and his plans.

He started to say, 'I know a couple of nice inns, down the road a little ways . . .'

A sudden car horn shattered his words and bright lights filled their car.

He pulled abruptly to the gravel shoulder, the car swerving sickeningly as another car roared past. She thought that the other car was somehow inside theirs and she shouted out some sound of half-fear and warning.

She caught her breath sharply and cried, 'Watch out! Oh, my gosh!'

She was aware of the terrifying closeness of the other car. Then she heard a pair of voices yelling in the night and saw the taillights of a jeep roar past. It was a hopped-up model, with fat tires and bright paint, a roll bar, and two kids hanging out the side, gesturing wildly.

Jeffers was cursing uncontrollably.

'Teenagers!' Douglas Jeffers said angrily, his voice a runaway cacophony of rage and relief. 'Must be a week or so before school starts and they're blowing off steam. Christ, I almost dumped the car . . .' He gestured toward the side of the road. 'I know this road. Damn! It drops off sharply over there. Down an embankment and into a little river. Christ, we'd have been killed. The little bastards. Christ. Out joyriding on a Monday night, for crying out loud. They could have killed us.'

He continued driving at his slow pace.

'Are you okay?' he asked.

'Oh, sure,' she replied. 'But they scared the daylights out of me.'

'It was my fault,' he said apologetically. 'I should have seen them coming up behind us so fast. Sorry.'

He smiled. 'They scared me, too.'

He held out his hand, holding it palm down, horizontally.

'Look at that. A little shake. Nerves, I guess.'

He smiled again.

'I suppose it means that regardless of who you are, an auto accident that just barely doesn't happen still gets to you. A moment of complete fear, then life goes back to its own petty pace.'

After a moment he added, 'There is nothing, nothing, as obnoxious as a teenage boy with a car and confidence and a little bit of booze. Christ, they act like they own the world. Immortal. Boy, did that piss me off.'

Then he laughed. 'And it makes me feel old.'

The darkness ahead on the road was interrupted by the luminous presence of a gas station. As they drove past, both Anne Hampton and Douglas Jeffers saw the jeep parked at the pumps.

'Look,' she said, almost inadvertently. 'There they are.' She could see two boys, backs to them, standing by the soft-drink machine. Both were tall and thin and wore base-ball caps and slouched with a natural insouciance and rebellion.

Jeffers drove deliberately past the station. After a quarter mile he accelerated sharply, throwing her back in her seat. She reached out to steady herself.

'I have an idea,' he said. 'The classic highway fantasy.'

His voice was suddenly suffused with excitement.

'There's an interesting spot up ahead,' he said. 'Where the road forks and one side heads down a small ravine, next to the interstate.'

In seconds they'd reached the fork. He took the upper half, and, after a hundred yards, slowed. He found a dark turnout and parked the car.

'Now,' he said. 'We'll see if luck's with us. You don't move.'

Again command entered his voice. She didn't even twitch.

Douglas Jeffers raced to the back of the car and flung open the trunk. His hand reached out and seized the polished steel of the Ruger semiautomatic rifle. He rummaged about amidst the other weapons until he found the clip of nine long shells. He slid the clip into the gun, feeling the satisfying click as it locked into place.

Jeffers left the rifle on top in the open trunk and searched for a moment until he found a long, cylindrical leather case. He grabbed this and turned, jogging back down the road. As he ran, he sharpened his eyes, trying to pluck shapes from the black of the night. He surveyed the area, looking for any sign of life. He peered into the darkness, looking for the telltale sweep of headlights in the distance. He concentrated his hearing, trying to find some sound that might indicate the presence of another person or of a vehicle heading in his direction. All was silent save for a slight rustle of wind in a nearby stand of pine trees. He looked off into the distance, toward the ravine, and tried to hear the sound of the water rushing through the bottom. He suddenly remembered the childhood adage: If you want to be able to see at night, eat lots of carrots. I ate lots of carrots. All the time. And my night vision is fine. But it is a lot finer when I use a night starlight scope.

He opened the leather case and held the cylinder up to his eye. It made the landscape a dirty green, and he swept it about to satisfy himself that his senses had not lied. He was alone. He thought that he must have appeared for all the world to be like some ancient and abandoned mariner, desperately searching for land. He peered down the roadway, into the distance.

'Aha,' he said out loud. 'Company comes calling.'

He saw the fancy jeep moving erratically through the night.

'Well, well, well, will wonders never cease.'

The vista remained deserted save for him and the approaching vehicle. He envisioned the two teenagers in the jeep, laughing, heads thrown back in the rush of wind through the open sides and convertible top. The stereo would be thumping, he thought, and their attention will be stripped by a couple of beers. He turned and rushed back to his own car. He saw Anne Hampton's face through the window, watching him. He could see her shrink into the seat, beaten down by the force of action. He moved quickly, but deliberately, grabbing the rifle and feeling its heft in his hands. Nothing is as comforting in one's arms as a rifle, he thought. He hurried back through the pitch-black night toward his vantage point, slightly hunched over, but assured, like a veteran soldier evading small-arms fire.

He glanced about himself quickly one last time to be certain of his solitude. He thought of Anne Hampton in the car, then shut her away. He lifted the rifle to his cheek and brought the sight to bear between the front headlights of the jeep, tracking it carefully.

'Take the bottom trail,' he commanded.

They did.

He was impressed with the almost electrical connection

417

that linked him, his finger on the trigger, and the target in his sights. He snugged the gun up against his cheek, caressing the trigger with his finger.

'Good night, boys,' he said.

He fired seven shots. The cracking sound seemed to him oddly heavenly, as if the rifle were being held up in the dark sky, sighting down some minuscule shaft of light from a star.

As he lowered the weapon, he saw the jeep start to swerve, battling for purchase on the roadway. He could hear nothing, though, save the echoing of the gunshots. The sound was like the music one hears in one's head from an oft-recalled song. He suddenly remembered a moment in Nicaragua – or was it Vietnam? – when he'd turned at the stolid sound of a rocket-propelled grenade bouncing into a jeep. There had been an explosion and he'd lifted his camera swiftly, firing the shutter as he focused, trying to catch the great ball of fire and shattered bodies pitching through the air. He remembered how little he'd heard then. No screams, no explosions, no cries for help, just the brother noises of the shutter and the autodrive. He started to lift his rifle, then realized that it wasn't a camera and let it rest.

The jeep flipped onto its side. He knew that it was screeching with the sound of twisting metal and complaining tires. He saw it thud toward the edge of the ravine, like some dying dinosaur seeking the refuge of dark waters. He thought of the millisecond of time after touching the first domino before it leans up against the next in line.

Then the jeep rolled over, disappearing into the black.

He could no longer envision the teenagers inside.

He turned away, knowing that it had slammed into the bottom. He felt a complete satisfaction. He did not turn around when he felt the shock wave from the explosion. He saw Anne Hampton's face in the car, horrified, her eyes catching the glow of flames from behind him. He walked toward the car with the steady discipline of Lot.

He dropped the rifle in the trunk and slammed it shut.

Jeffers moved behind the wheel and deliberately put the

car in gear and accelerated away gently. Within a few moments they swept around first one dark turn in the road, then another.

Anne Hampton swiveled in her seat and shivered.

'I told you,' Douglas Jeffers said. 'The ultimate highway fantasy.'

She threw one more quick glance back and thought she could see the glow from the wreck. She turned away and saw the signs for the interstate. Hurry, she thought. Get us away from here. Please.

Jeffers maneuvered the car through the ramps and accelerated on the thruway. 'We are,' he said, 'a nation of assassins and snipers. John Wilkes Booth and Lee Harvey Oswald. Charles Whitman and the Texas Tower. We have a great and storied tradition of ambush.'

'They didn't have a . . .'

'Not really. That's what's important in an assassination. An X-ambush. An L-ambush. Think of it. Bushwacked. Dry-gulched. Nowhere to run. Nowhere to turn. Nowhere to hide. That's the point of the entire exercise.'

She did not reply. Nowhere, she thought. She watched the headlights peel away a sliver of light from the darkness. Sixty miles per hour. A mile a minute. Every second takes us farther.

'Where are we going?' she asked.

She knew the answer: All the way to the end.

'The Granite State,' Jeffers replied. 'Luckily, our little adventure took place in Vermont. And by the time anybody figures out what happened, which they won't, by the way, we'll be history. What a shot,' he said. He seemed suffused with excitement. 'What a shot. Damn! And you know what the cops will think? Nothing. They'll find some beer cans in the jeep and that's that. An accident, until someone thinks twice. Out of sight, out of mind. And who would suspect a nice-looking pair of tourists, anyway?'

He sang: 'We'll be gone, gone, gone . . .'

'Why Vermont?' she asked hesitantly. 'Can't you kill anyone in New Hampshire?'

'Well,' he laughed, 'the Devil had a bit of unpleasantness

in Marshfield a few centuries back. And since then he keeps his works in the neighboring states. As per agreement, of course. And so I follow suit.'

He smiled.

'But that doesn't mean we can't pay a little visit.'

He drove on.

The morning sun was strong and Anne Hampton shielded her eyes. For an instant it reminded her of Florida, and she looked about her for a palm tree clattering in the light breeze. She stared down the main street of Jaffrey, New Hampshire, and wondered whether she had dreamed everything. She tried to pick out specifics from her memory; there was the fear, when they'd almost been driven off the road; there was the darkness on the bend; Jeffers walking with the rifle into the deep black; the cracking sound followed by the nauseating muffled roar of the car exploding. She examined each facet of her recollection like a jeweler assessing a precious stone. Surely, she thought, there was some flaw that would show her that it hadn't happened, something to show that this was a dream, a fake, a piece of cut glass refracting light.

She shook her head and forced order on her memory.

Of course it wasn't a dream, she said to herself. She thought of her night, tossing on sweat-soaked sheets. The dreams are much worse.

She turned and peered through the plate-glass window of the delicatessen. She could see Jeffers at the cash register, paying for coffee and doughnuts. She watched as he pocketed his change and sauntered from the store. As always, she felt amazement. He was whistling, unencumbered by anything so mundane as fear or guilt.

'I got you the jelly kind,' he said as he slipped into the car. 'And coffee and juice.'

He gestured toward the town. 'Pretty, huh? Filled with antiques and outlet stores. *Yankee* magazine always has pictures of Jaffrey. Happy white women standing in front of tables heaped high with freshly baked goods. Calico. This is a calico town. Calico and rag wool in the winter.

Not the kind of place where anyone would notice a visiting couple driving a car with out-of-state plates.'

He rolled down the window.

'It's going to be a scorcher,' he said. 'Late summer up here is completely unpredictable. A little Canadian air tumbles in one day and it'll snow. Then the cross-country currents bring something humid up from the South on the next, and it hits a hundred.' He took sunglasses from his pocket and cleaned them on his shirt-tail. She felt the heat entering the car, penetrating her, almost sensual. She sipped the coffee as Jeffers opened a newspaper. He scanned the pages rapidly.

'No, no, no, see, I told you so, aha! Here's something.'

He paused, reading. Then he read out loud:

'Two killed in Vermont crash. A pair of Lebanon teen-agers were killed Monday night when their four-wheel-drive car failed to negotiate a curve on a back road four miles from Woodstock, Vermont. Police suspect that the youths, Daniel Wilson, seventeen, and Randy Mitchell, eighteen, had been drinking prior to the nine-forty-five crash at the juncture of State Road eighty-two and Ravine Drive . . .'

He looked over at Anne Hampton.

'I could go on. There's a couple more paragraphs.'

She didn't reply. She drank her coffee and savored the bitter taste.

'No? I didn't think so.'

He dropped the paper on her lap. 'Read it for yourself.'

She sat up sharply when she heard the edge in his voice.

'Now, I have business. I want you to wait in the car.'

She nodded rapidly.

'Good. It's almost ten. I should be about an hour.'

Jeffers seized his briefcase and left. She watched him walk across the street and into the New Hampshire National Bank. She felt a momentary panic, looking about wildly, thinking: He's going to rob a bank! Then she recognized that she was being foolish. She settled back in the seat and waited. The idea of escape did not occur to her, even when a police car rolled past. That she could rise up

421

and flag down a patrolman and end it for herself seemed simplistic and impossible. She had no confidence in some obvious and easy dénouement. She knew that she was still powerless; that Douglas Jeffers pulled all the strings for the two of them. So, instead, she thought only of the moment, letting the building heat around her take over her imagination. She wondered what would happen next, and she closed her eyes to the outside world, looking inwardly, thinking: Find some strength. She inspected her heart for bravery, wondering whether there was any there. She knew she would need it to survive.

The bank was cool and dark inside, and Douglas Jeffers removed his sunglasses slowly. It was an old-fashioned building, with high ceilings and polished floors that made shoe heels click. Jeffers walked over to a section of desks where the bank officers worked. A secretary looked up at him, smiling.

'Miss Mansour, please. Douglas Allen. I have an appointment.'

The young woman nodded and picked up her telephone. Jeffers saw a middle-aged, open-faced woman at the rear desk pick up her receiver and listen. In a moment he had shaken hands with the woman and was seated at a chair next to her desk. She pulled out a folder with the name written on the top.

'Now, Mr Allen, we hate to see a longtime customer depart. How many years has it been . . .'

'Ten.'

'Is there any way we can help you? Perhaps at establishing a new account at your . . .' She hesitated.

'Atlanta,' he said. 'Company transfer.'

'I mean, I'd be happy to call someone . . .'

He shook his head. 'So kind of you,' he said. 'But the relocation service with the firm handles most of those things. But I will take your card, and if there's any problem I could have someone call you?'

'That would be fine.' She checked out the forms. 'Now, in your letter you said you wanted the account closed and the funds in traveler's checks. I have those waiting for you. So all you have to do is sign them and then sign this closure statement and then clear out the safety deposit box, hand me the key, and you're all set.'

She handed him a stack of traveler's checks and he started signing. He looked down at the name and mentally rolled it about. For ten years, he thought, here in New Hampshire I've been Douglas Allen. No more limitations. No more pretenses. We shall expand our horizons.

'Please count them,' Miss Mansour said. 'It's over twenty thousand dollars.'

Spare funds from a decade, he thought. Compounded daily.

He followed her into the safety deposit area, and she handed him his key. 'Just bring both keys back after you're finished,' she said. 'I'll be at my desk.'

He nodded thanks and went into a cubicle. A secretary brought him the locked box and then closed the door behind her. He hesitated, reveling inwardly in the ease of the plan.

He opened the box.

'Goodbye, Douglas Jeffers,' he said.

On top was the old copy of the defunct *New Times* magazine that had been the germ of the idea. He flipped the worn pages open to the article. He thought it ironic that the piece had been prompted by the activism of the sixties and seventies. It had seemed such a simple premise: How easy was it to go underground? How hard was it to establish another identity? The answer was: Not very. Particularly in a state such as New Hampshire, with its dogged emphasis on individual freedoms and privacy. He'd followed the article's path religiously, from obtaining a Social Security number, to opening a post office box, to giving himself an address. Then the bank account and a pair of credit cards, used only enough to keep them active. At the same time that he'd established credit, he'd obtained his driver's license under his new name and Social Security number. His greatest triumph, however, had occurred after he'd doctored his own birth certificate into his new name.

The wonders of modern copying machines, he thought. When he'd presented the battered copy, along with all his other documents, at the local post office, no one had raised a word in protest. Six weeks later, in the mail, arrived his most prized possession. He lifted it from the box. A brand new US passport in the name of Douglas Allen. No fake, no forgery.

He stuck it in his briefcase along with the driver's license, credit cards, and Social Security card.

I'm free, he thought.

He laughed to himself. Well, not completely. I can't go to Albania or North Vietnam.

He stuffed his emergency cash reserve, several thousand dollars in twenties and hundreds, into his pants. He checked his ticket, which lay in the bottom of the box. It was a first-class airplane ticket, open date, one-way, New York to Tokyo. He knew that from Tokyo he could easily backtrack to wherever he wanted, instantly losing himself in the Far East. Sydney, he thought, Perth. Melbourne. The names seemed exotic yet oddly familiar. It'll be like going home. The last item in the safety deposit box was a clean, blue-steel .357 Magnum revolver, which also went into his briefcase. He had purchased it in Florida several years beforehand, just weeks prior to the time the state legislature passed a new, slightly restrictive gun law. Then, conveniently, he had reported it stolen. Thank God, he thought, for the NRA. For an instant he stared at the empty safety deposit box and thought how comforting it had been to know everything was there, just in case he'd ever needed it. My emergency outlet.

He sat back in the chair. Australia, he said to himself. A wonderful place to start over. Tie me kangaroo down, sport.

He hummed. 'Waltzing Matilda' to himself as he walked back to Miss Mansour's desk.

'All set?' she asked cheerfully.

'All in order,' he replied.

He signed some papers. He looked down at his signature and felt comfortable with it. Hello, he said to himself. Glad to meet you. And what was it you said you did for a living? Anything you liked. Anything at all.

The sunlight hit him as he exited the darkness of the bank, and it took a moment for his eyes to readjust. He picked out the sight of Anne Hampton sitting in the car, waiting. Not much longer, Boswell.

Humming pleasantly to himself, he crossed the street. He nodded to an elderly lady who walked past him, and said good morning to a pair of young boys, probably no older than six or seven, savoring their final days before school started with a set of chocolate ice cream cones.

Anne Hampton looked up at him as he returned to the car.

'Let's go to the beach,' he said.

Much of the day she dozed as Douglas Jeffers drove across Massachusetts toward Cape Cod. He seemed preoccupied, but in a carefree fashion. He turned on the radio and found a station that played sixties rock and roll, which he told her was the only music worth listening to on the radio. He insisted in a lighthearted way that the only musician he would pay any attention to whatsoever was the guy from New Jersey, and that was because he behaved like a refugee from two decades back. He told her about the one time he'd been assigned to get some pictures at a rock concert. 'Only time I was ever really afraid for my life. They had us down in front of the stage and when these four guys in leotard pants, glitter makeup, and feather boas, for Christ's sake, strutted out, everyone behind the barricades in back of us pushed forward. I thought I was going to be crushed by a phalanx of teary-eyed adolescents. All the cameramen were fighting for air and space and I looked up and saw this one guy with blond hair down to his ass and beady eyes waving his arms, whooping it up, encouraging the crowd. Death by rock and roll . . .' Douglas Jeffers laughed. 'There I was, getting pushed back against the stage, no room to move, screaming kids everywhere, and all I could think about was it was what our parents warned us against. A commie plot. At least it seemed so at the time.'

He drove leisurely, letting the other cars slide past. She thought he seemed in no rush, yet he was clearly keeping to a schedule.

The afternoon was fading when they reached the turnoff for Route 6, which meanders up Cape Cod. She had never seen the Cape before, and looked carefully at the rows of battered antique stores, saltwater-taffy shops, and tee-shirt emporiums that mixed with fast-food restaurants and gas stations by the side of the road.

'I don't understand,' she said. 'I thought Cape Cod was supposed to be beautiful.'

'It is,' Jeffers replied. 'At least where we're headed it is. But no one ever said the road there was beautiful. And it isn't. In fact, it sets some kind of world record for ugliness.'

They passed over the Bourne Bridge in the day's last light. Anne Hampton could see barges far beneath them, moving steadily down the canal. There was a rotary ahead, and Jeffers made jokes about the free-for-all, survival-of-the-fittest element to driving in the state of Massachusetts. They ate a quick dinner at a diner in Falmouth, then proceeded down the road to the Woods Hole Ferry dock. She could see a Coast Guard cutter's bright white paint gleaming in the darkness. The ferry itself was bathed in light from mingled streetlamps and car headlights. There was a row of cars lined up on the street and a teenager in a baseball cap carrying a walkie-talkie. Jeffers rolled down the window.

'I have a reservation on the eight-thirty boat,' he said.

'Great,' said the teenager. Anne Hampton thought he probably looked exactly like the young men they'd seen the night before. 'Just pull in behind the station wagon.'

Jeffers drove down. Another teenager came up and he produced tickets.

'You know what I've always loved about this ferry?' he asked. He didn't wait for her acknowledgment. 'It has this perfectly functional design. The boat has no front, no back. That's to say, the front is like the back. You drive on in Woods Hole, drive off in Vineyard Haven. It has the same big old opening on either end. The boat just yo-yos between the two docks.'

She looked over and watched people stream in and out of the squat ferry office adjacent to the dock. She saw a line of bicyclists with backpacks move to the front of the line of cars. She could see boat handlers waving vehicles into an opening on the ferry, which loomed up stark white and black against the evening sky. She could not see the open water from where she sat, but she sensed the sea in the air that tumbled through Jeffers' window.

'Where . . .'

'The island of Martha's Vineyard,' he said. 'Summer home to the upscale. Old money, new money, all dressed down in jeans and work shirts. It's where they filmed *Jaws* . . .' He started to mimic the ominously familiar music. 'All sorts of Kennedys, too. You remember when Teddy swam from Chappaquiddick to Edgartown? At least he said he did. Jackie O has a place and so does Walter Cronkite, half the staff of the New York *Times*, and more poets and novelists per square foot than you can count. John Belushi owned a house in Chilmark for about five minutes before he managed to get himself killed in LA and now he's buried there. A striking place called Abel's Hill. Kids go to the graveyard all the time. It's a very benign island,' Jeffers said. 'Filled with East Coast elite sophistication. It's quiet, pleasant, beautiful, and relaxed. The islander's idea of controversy would be a shortage of swordfish steaks or too many mopeds on the roads. It's friendly, and filled with appreciation of the nicer things available to anyone with scads of money, wrapped up in this faded-blue-denim approach to day-to-day life. Lots of beautiful people living in intellectual harmony. From June first through Labor Day.'

He hesitated.

'The perfect place for something unspeakably unsettling.'

Jeffers drove the car in a haphazard course around the island, slicing through the narrow, unlit roads. The headlights tore bizarre shapes from the light fog and overhanging trees. Around one corner they came up upon a Great Horned Owl feeding on some muskrat or rabbit that had failed to maneuver the road successfully. The bird's huge white wings spread out abruptly, and it cried in irritation at the unruly interruption. It seemed to rise ghostlike in front of them right over the hood of the car, and for an instant she thought they would collide and she gasped in a sudden fear that penetrated her exhaustion.

She did not know what time it was, but she knew it was past midnight, crawling into morning. Jeffers seemed indefatigable, his adrenaline coursing, his voice alert, bantering.

He drove back and forth across the island several times, thoroughly confusing Anne Hampton, despite the fact that he kept up a running travelogue throughout. He would point at different locations and link them with memories, like any person visiting a favored spot after many years. She tried taking some notes, but found that his attention ricocheted from one mundane recollection to another. None had anything to do with death or dying. Instead, he talked about the best place to find wild blueberries, or the secret paths down to the nicest beaches on the island. He drove her out to the Gay Head cliffs and let her stand up by the edge, looking out toward the ocean. She could see white foam where the waves pounded up onto the beach, and even in the darkness could make out the steady movement of big rollers on the black sea. There was a steady breeze that pushed against her face and she felt it restoring her. But the height made her dizzy and for an instant she fantasized tumbling down over the great red and gray cliffs, spinning into oblivion. She felt his hand on her arm, and she saw he was pointing out into the deep ocean night.

'Out there,' he said, 'is an island called No Man's Land, where the Navy tests weapons. You can see it on a clear day, and if the wind is right occasionally you can hear the thump thump of high explosives. I've always wanted to go there, ever since I was a kid. Not because of the practice runs the Navy makes, which are interesting, sometimes you can see the jet vapors, but to see what it looks like after being bombed so steadily for so many years. Like some vision of the future, I think . . .

'Never went, though. Got pretty close once, when I was a kid and we went out fishing for blues. We were in some pretty good action, when all of a sudden there was this Coast Guard helicopter hovering overhead, telling us to get the hell out of there.'

He laughed.

'We obeyed.'

'Did you come here often?' she asked.

'A bunch of summers when I was a kid. We stopped after, well, when I was a teenager.'

He looked about.

'It's changed. It's the same, yet different. Some new things. Lots of old things. There's steadiness, continuity. But growth, too.'

He laughed again.

'Everything changes. Everything stays the same. Like life.'

He thought of the passport, air ticket, and money waiting in his briefcase. Like me.

They got back into the car and he slowly headed back into the center of the island. She did not dare ask about plans or accommodations.

Jeffers wondered why, instead of his usual rigid delight, he felt a sort of leisurely pleasure, almost a lassitude. He felt a headiness, like having drunk too much of some excellent wine, not stumbling drunk, but giddy. After adhering so strictly to ideas and concepts, having planned right down to the ferry tickets on and off, now he was in no rush. He thought he wanted to savor this last act, draw it out. He felt a rush of blood through his veins, warm, exciting. He listened to his own heart, and thought that it was going to prove to be hard to say goodbye to his old identity. But – he smiled inwardly – thinking of the creation of the new.

They passed through the tiny town of West Tisbury and Jeffers summoned himself to attention. Not far now, he thought. He tightened himself mentally, concentrating on the problems at hand.

Anne Hampton looked over at Jeffers and saw that he was suddenly paying close attention. He had hunched forward in the seat slightly, and she knew that this meant something was going to happen. It caused her body to stiffen and she moved to the edge of her seat. He had said so much about an ending, and, she thought, now it is starting. She could feel her own sleepiness flee her, and she marshaled her emotions like a military reserve being held in check for that critical moment in any battle when victory and defeat are held in balance.

Jeffers turned down a sandy secondary road and immediately they were bumping along a washboard dirt single-line trail. The scrub bushes and gnarled trees of the island seemed to envelop them in a tunnel, and she felt immediately as if they had stepped from civilization into some wilder, prehistoric place. The car pitched and yawed as he steered it slowly down the road. Occasionally the tires spun briefly in sand, and the cockpit was filled with the scratching, screeching noise of bushes rubbing against the car sides. After traveling what she guessed was more than a bumpy mile, deeper into the beech forest, they arrived at a juncture of four tiny roads. There were a few small arrows in various colors pointing down the alternate routes. The dirt roads seemed ever smaller, tighter and darker.

'The arrows are for the different homes,' Jeffers explained. 'It's precious. You have to know the right color to get to the right house. Otherwise you end up on the wrong side of the pond.'

He steered down the left-hand fork.

The yawing and bumping of the car started to make her nauseated. She tried to see through the overhanging branches and she caught a glimpse of the moon, high in the sky.

They traveled another ten minutes. At least a mile, she thought. Perhaps farther.

Then, as if by some stroke of a knife, they passed out of the forest into an open area. Jeffers doused the car lights as they emerged from the trees, steering the car slowly by the moonlight.

She could see off to her right a wide expanse of water.

'That's the pond,' Jeffers said. 'Pond isn't a good word. It's actually as big as a lake and as deep as one.' He stopped the car and rolled down the window. 'Listen,' he said.

She could hear the surf pounding on the shoreline in the distance.

'The pond separates the houses from the beach,' he said. 'We used to have to take a little motorboat or a rowboat over. A lot of people used little sailboats. Canoes, kayaks, windsurfers, too, I guess. Now, look carefully. See across there?'

He pointed over the pond.

'It's all wild land. The only person who lives out there is an old sheep farmer named Johnson. He's crazy. Literally. Steals motorboat engines from the summer pople whose boats he doesn't like. He shoots his shotgun at folks who drive their cars on the sand dunes. Once he made a home-made land mine and tank trap for the kids and tourists who tried to use his road to get to the beach. The old bastard once chased me off his property at gunpoint. That was twenty years ago, but he hasn't changed a bit. He was discharged from the Army with a mental disability and it hasn't gotten any better. He's certifiable, but an old islander, so they let him get away with things. The summer people, of course, think he's quaint.'

Jeffers paused. When he spoke again, it was with complete fury.

'They're going to blame him at first for what we do.'

Then he pointed down the road.

'This land ends in a point that projects into the pond. Finger Point. A half mile down this road is a house. If you look carefully, you can just see the roof line. It's the only place out here. People pay great sums of money for the right kinds of isolation. Anyway, that's where we're going.'

Jeffers abruptly rolled the window up and thrust the car into reverse. The car bumped wildly while he backed it into the forest. He spun the wheel sharply, sliding the car into a small turnoff that she hadn't noticed. Then he shut off the engine.

'All right,' he said. 'We're here. Wait.'

Jeffers walked to the back of the car and seized the duffle bag where he kept the weapons. He opened the zipper and pulled out a pair of black workmen's coveralls and several other items. He slipped one of the set on, then put a pistol in the belt. He reloaded the rifle and chambered a round. Then he slung the duffel over his back.

'All right,' he said. 'Out of the car.'

She complied instantly.

'Put this on.'

She slid on the black coveralls and thought: I am part of the night.

He appraised her.

'Good. Good. You almost look the part. You just need this.'

He handed her a small knit hat. She looked at it quizzically.

'Like this!' he said, his voice suddenly at the edge of rage. He stepped to her and grabbing the hat, thrust it on her head. Then, in a single, violent motion, he pulled the rolled brim down. It was a ski mask. She thought she might suffocate beneath the tight-fitting wool. She saw he'd pulled his down as well.

'Real horror show,' he said. He turned and trotted down the road and she hurried to keep pace.

13 An irregular session of the Lost Boys

18

Detective Mercedes Barren waited impatiently in Martin Jeffers' office, agonizing over lost time. She had trouble sitting; whenever she rested in a chair, she felt as if an angry impulse surged through her, reminding her that the killer wasn't waiting for her somewhere with his feet up on some desk. He's out there, she told herself, just past my reach. He's doing something. Her head flooded with the images she'd stolen from his apartment. She grimaced and thought: I'll never lose them. Those pictures will be with me forever.

She slowly rubbed her hands across her eyes and remembered a lecture from her first days at the police academy, when an FBI agent had come in, arms and pockets and head filled with crime statistics. He had used clock models and a steadily droning voice to demonstrate how often each armed robbery, each burglary, each murder took place in the United States. She thought: 10 p.m., a ghetto crap game turns to knives; 11 p.m., a suburban couple's argument results in gunplay; midnight, Douglas Jeffers sweet-talks another woman into his car. She wanted to grab hold of something and shake it violently. She wanted to see something shatter and break. She wanted crashing noise. But all that surrounded her was a steady, infuriating silence, and she had to console herself by pacing around the room, fiddling with her papers, envisioning moments past and moments to come, trying to prepare herself mentally for confrontation.

It will happen, she told herself.

And I will be ready.

She thought of herself as a warrior preparing for battle.

Mercedes Barren remembered how Achilles had oiled his body before his fight with Hector. He'd known he would win, because that was preordained, but known as well that his own demise was fast approaching, signaled by his victory that day. Then she dismissed the image: He won, but lost. That isn't what you intend. Knights in the Middle Ages would pray before a fight, imploring divine guidance, but you know what you have to do. No one, not even the heavens, needs to tell you. Of course, Roland was obstinate; he would not sound his horn, and it cost him his friend's life and his own, but he gained immortality. She smiled to herself: Bad idea. Then she asked herself: Are you any different? She refused herself an answer. She considered the rituals of the samurai and the ghost-dancing of the Plains Indians. The spirit filled them and they believed that the horse soldiers' bullets would pass right through them. Unfortunately they were right. The only problem was that the bullets took their lives, as well, which wasn't what had been advertised. Sitting Bull was old and wise, and knew this, but fought anyway.

She considered whether John Barren had done anything special before a fight. Had he dressed with any special care, like some superstitious athlete who wears the same socks every game so as not to upset the god that guides victories and prevents injuries? She imagined that he had; he was a romantic, filled with foolish ideas about chivalry and myth that probably penetrated even the muck and swamps of Vietnam. She smiled, recalling that when they had sent home his possessions, weeks after they'd sent back what remained of him, what made her eyes redden and tears flow freely was a dog-eared copy of *The Once and Future King*.

She wondered what he'd failed to do on the day he died. Was there some special charm or amulet that he'd neglected? Did he violate the order of dress in some small yet deadly way? What did he do to upset the delicate equilibrium of life?

She wondered too, whether he knew it, walking along

beneath the sun, eyes wide, senses on edge, but aware in the recess of his mind that something was not right on this day that looked and smelled and sounded like every other day.

He would have shaken it off and marched on, she thought.

March on.

He would say to me: Do what you must. Do what is right.

She thrust her hands out in front of her.

They were steady.

She turned them over, looking at the palms. Dry.

It is time to get ready, she thought.

Then she clenched the hands into two solid, balled fists. Choose the battle ground, she said, directing her mental energies at the ethereal Douglas Jeffers. Do something. Contact your brother.

She envisioned Martin Jeffers. She glanced at the wall clock. He's on his way to that damn group, she thought. I'm stuck here, waiting for him to remember something, or his brother to call, or the mail to arrive with a postcard that says: Hi! Having wonderful time! Wish you were here!

Fury filled her and she struggled around the office for the hundredth time, realizing how tenuous was her grasp on the brother, how dependent she was upon him and thus incapable of doing anything save the hardest, most impossible work of all, which is waiting.

Martin Jeffers stared out at the assembled men and saw that he had always been wrong, pitying them the weakness of their perversions when his acquiescence and unseeing impotence were infinitely more depraved.

Oedipus, at least, looked upon the horror and tore his eyes from his face. His blindness was just. Martin Jeffers forced a smile, reflecting the inward thought that the Oedipal myth was sacred to his profession. But we don't acknowledge what happened after. We don't remember that after the desire and the act, the one-time king was forced by guilt to wander blindly through life in rags, his feet driven step upon step by the depth of his despair.

He wondered if the same emotions were so clear on his own face. He tried to force his usual semi-detached professional gaze out into the center of the room, but he knew he was unsuccessful. He looked across at the men, warily.

The membership of the Lost Boys was restless. They shifted about in their seats, making small, uncomfortable noises. He knew they had noted his fatigue in the previous day's session, knew, as well, that he had spent another sleepless night, and he wore that exhaustion equally obviously. He had sleepwalked through Monday, after returning late from New Hampshire, barely listening to the usual mix of mundane complaints and ills that made up his routine day. He had thought he would embrace a day of regularity, that it would somehow postpone all the difficult feelings, but he discovered that they were too powerful. His mind remained filled only with images of his brother.

He was overcome with a sudden rush of anger.

He saw his brother in a familiar pose, insouciant, grinning. Without a care in the world.

Then the vision grew darker and he pictured his brother with eyes set, deadly: the stalker, all business and bitterness.

A killer.

Why have you done these things? he asked the man in his mind's eye. Why have you become what you are? How can you do it, over and over, and not show it every waking instant?

But the brother in his mind faded, refusing to answer, and Martin Jeffers realized how foolish his questions were. Even if it is ridiculous to ask, he thought, I still must.

He felt his hands tighten on the arms of the chair and his anger redoubled, bursting forth, flowering, and he wanted to scream at the brother in his mind: Why have you done these things? Why? Why?

And then a greater anger still:

Why have you done these things to me?

He took a deep breath and looked out again at the waiting therapy group. He knew he had to say something to get the group started, and then he would be able to lose himself in the steadiness of their conversation. But instead of tossing out a subject or idea for the men to worry and chew, he thought instead of New Hampshire and tried to remember the last moment he'd seen his real mother. She was fixed in a memory, a pale face, framed in a car window, turning back just once before rolling steadily out of his life. He could see it as clearly as on the night it happened. He had never described the sight to anyone, least of all his own therapist. He knew that violated a fundamental trust, one that he hypocritically demanded of his own patients. I am not free, he thought. I don't expect to be. I never will be. He thought again of his real mother. What had we done wrong? He knew the answer: nothing. The ancients had it completely backward, he thought. Psychiatry has proven that it is the sins of the parents that are visited upon the children. We were abandoned, then we were treated cruelly, lovelessly. The twin pillars of despair. Is it any surprise that Doug has risen up, as an adult, to exact a measure of revenge on a world that hated him so?

By why him and not me?

Where is he?

'So, doc, what's bugging you? You look like you've got one foot in the grave.'

'Yeah. You gonna take us with you?'

This prompted nervous laughter from the room.

Martin Jeffers looked up and saw that it was Bryan and Senderling asking the questions. But all the men's faces wore the same impatient inquisitiveness.

His first reaction was to ignore the questions and try to launch the group into another direction. That would have been the proper technique. After all, the group's focus should be on themselves, not on the group leader. But at the same time he was filled with an insistent anger that told him to throw away all the precious tenets of his profession and rely, for a moment, on the street smarts of the men.

437

'Do I look that bad?' he asked the assembly.

There was a momentary silence. The direct question surprised them. After a moment Miller growled from the back of the room:

'Yeah, you look bad. Like something's on your mind . . .'

He laughed cruelly.

' . . . which sure is a change.'

Again quiet dominated the room until Wasserman sputtered:

'If you d-d-d-don't f-f-f-feel so hot, we c-c-c-can come back tomorrow . . .'

Jeffers shook his head. 'I feel fine. Physically.'

'So what is it, doc? You got some kind of emotional flu?' This was Senderling, and Bryan laughed with him. That was a good image: emotional flu. I'll use that, someday, Jeffers thought.

'I'm concerned about a friend,' he said.

There was a pause before Miller jumped back in. 'You're a hell of a lot more than concerned,' he said. 'You're worried sick. Hell, I ain't a doctor, but I can see that. Something a lot more, huh? More than just concern?'

Jeffers didn't answer. He searched the eyes, glowing about him, and thought the twelve men were like some damned jury waiting for him to slip and convict himself from his own words. He fixed his eyes on Miller.

'Tell me,' he said, filling his voice with insistence. 'Tell me how you got started.'

'What do you mean?' Miller replied, shifting in his seat.

Like all sex offenders, he hated a direct question, preferring to be queried in some oblique fashion so that he could control the route of the conversation. Jeffers thought they were all probably taken aback by bluntness.

'I want to know how you got started doing what you do.'

'You mean, the, uh . . .'

'That's right. What you do to women. Tell me.'

The room had gone completely quiet. The forcefulness of Jeffers' demand had stopped all of them. He knew that he was violating established procedures. But suddenly he was tired of rules, tired of waiting, tired of passivity.

'Tell me!' His voice was raised louder than it had ever been within the confines of the day room.

'Hell, I don't know . . .'

'Yes, you do!' Jeffers eyed all the men. 'You all know. Think back! The first time. What went through your mind? What started you?'

He waited.

Pope broke the silence. Jeffers looked at the older man, who stared back with obvious hatred for anyone who probed at his memory. 'Opportunity,' he said.

'Please explain,' Jeffers replied.

'We all knew who we were. Maybe we hadn't quite said it to ourselves yet. Maybe the words hadn't formed in the head, the way they do, but still, we knew, you know. And so it became a matter of waiting for the right opportunity. The demand was there, doc. You know you're gonna do something, you know. It's gonna happen. It just needs the right – I don't know what do you call it – circumstances . . .'

He saw heads start to nod in agreement.

'Sometimes' – it was Knight, interrupting – 'once you make the decision to be what you are, it like takes over. You just start looking. Looking and looking and looking. Nothing's gonna come along and change anything, because it's already all set. You're looking. And when you find what you're looking for . . .'

'I s-s-s-still hated it,' Wasserman interrupted jerkily.

'So did I,' said Weingarten. 'But that didn't mean a thing.'

'Right.' It was Pope again. 'It didn't mean nothing . . .'

Parker: ''Cause once you're started, it's happening, man.'

Meriwether: 'Whether you hate it, or you hate yourself, or hate the person you're going to do it to, it makes little difference.'

Martin Jeffers absorbed the men's words.

'But the first time . . .' he started, only to have Pope jump in.

'You don't understand! The first time is only the first time it happens physically! In your head, man, in your head, you've already done it a hundred times! A million!'

'To whom?' Jeffers asked.

'To everyone!'

Jeffers thought hard.

He saw the men sitting forward, on the edges of their chairs, anticipating his questions. They were alert, interested, excited, more engaged than he'd seen them before. He saw the predatory ridge in their eyes, and thought of all the people who'd seen the same hard look before being smothered, or choked and beaten and then violated.

'But there had to be something,' he asked slowly. 'There had to be some moment, or some word, or something had to happen that allowed you to become what you are . . .'

He stared hard at the men.

'Something allowed you. What?'

Again silence. The men were considering the question.

Wasserman stuttered: 'I r-r-r-remember my m-m-m-mom telling me I'd n-n-n-never be the m-m-m-man my d-d-d-daddy was. I never f-f-f-forgot that, and when I d-d-d-did it the f-f-f-first time, it was all I could t-t-t-think about.'

He looked about the room and his stutter evaporated for an instant:

'And I damn well was!'

'Well, it wasn't anything like that for me,' Senderling said. 'It was just I got tired of waiting, you know. I mean there was this one gal in the office, a real tease, you know, and, man, I guess everybody had a piece of her action, so I just took mine.'

Bryan snorted. 'You mean she wouldn't go out with you.'

'No, no, it wasn't like that.'

The men started to hoot.

Bryan kept at it. 'She turned you down and so you waited for her in her apartment building's garage. You told me about it yourself.'

'She was a bitch,' Senderling said. 'She deserved it.'

'Just because she said no?' Jeffers asked.

'Right!'

'But why did you decide to do it this time? Other women had told you no, certainly,' Jeffers asked.

'Because, because, because . . . well . . .'

He waited.

'Because I was alone. My sister and brother-in-law, that jerk, had finally moved out, and I didn't have to support his lazy ass anymore, or hers, 'cause all they did was lie around fucking like a pair of fucking rabbits while I was doing all the work and bringing home the fucking paycheck so we could at least eat. And so I kicked 'em out. And then the bitch wouldn't go out with me! Christ, she deserved it.'

'So you were free?'

'Yeah! Right. Free. Free to do what I fucking well wanted.'

Jeffers looked around the room again.

'Something freed all you men?'

He saw heads slowly nod in agreement.

'Talk about it.'

He saw hesitation.

Knight said: 'It's different for everyone.'

Weingarten added: 'It can be a big thing, or a little one, but . . .'

Knight repeated: 'It's different for everyone.'

Martin Jeffers took a deep breath. All is lost, he thought. Then he asked:

'Suppose it was more. More than just what you've done, suppose you went a step further.'

The men seemed to rock under the suggestion.

'There's only one more step,' said Pope. 'You know what that is.'

'Why didn't you?'

'Maybe some of us have,' said Meriwether. 'Not me, you know, I'm not admitting anything. But maybe some of us have.'

'What would allow you to do it?'

The men didn't reply.

Jeffers waited. He, too, said nothing.

'Why do you need to know?' Meriwether asked.

He hesitated, trying to choose his words carefully.

'I need to find someone.'

'Someone like us?' Bryan questioned.

'Someone like you.'

'Someone worse?' It was Senderling.

Jeffers shrugged.

'Someone you know well?' Senderling tried again.

'Yes. Someone I know well.'

'And you think he's gone someplace and you can figure it out, is that it?' Parker asked.

'More or less.'

'Someone real close?' Senderling asked again.

Jeffers fixed him with a stare and didn't reply.

'You figure we can help you?' Weingarten said.

'Yes,' Jeffers replied.

Weingarten laughed. 'Well, damned if I don't think you're right.'

'This someone,' Parker questioned, 'he's at it right now?'

'Yes.'

'And you need to get to him to make him stop?'

'Yes.'

'Or something . . .'

'Right,' Jeffers said. 'Stop or something.'

'It's r-r-r-real important?' Wasserman jumped in.

'Yes.'

Miller started to laugh hard. 'Well, fuck you, doc. This puts things in a whole new light.'

'Yes, it does,' Jeffers said. He stared hard at Miller, who instantly stopped laughing.

'Well, tell us some more.'

Jeffers hesitated.

'I think,' he said slowly, 'that he's visiting the scenes of some crimes.'

Miller laughed again, but less maliciously. 'The criminal returns to the scene of the crime?'

'I suppose.'

Miller grinned. 'Maybe it's a cliché, but it's not so stupid. Crimes become memories, you know. And everybody likes to visit their pleasant memories.'

'Pleasant?' Jeffers questioned.

The men in the group laughed and snorted.

'Haven't you learned anything here?' Miller asked. The rapist's voice was rife with sarcasm. Jeffers ignored the question and Miller continued: 'Everything's turned around for men like us! We love what we hate. We hate what we love. Pain is pleasure. Love is hurt. Everything's skewed about and upside down and backwards. Can't you see that? Christ!'

And suddenly he could.

'So,' Miller said, and the men around him joined their heads in nodding agreement, 'look for a memory that's filled with all the worst. And that will be the best.'

Jeffers took a deep breath, scared of the thoughts that started to gather and form, like great storm clouds in his imagination. He looked up as Pope, grizzled, tattooed, filled to completion with anger and hatred and irrevocable in his antipathy to the world, spoke in a low, awful voice:

'Look for a death or departure. They're the same. That's what cuts you loose. Someone dies and you're free to be yourself. It's simple. It's fucking simple. Look for a death.'

The first image that flitted into his head was the darkness trapped in the trees on the night they were abandoned in New Hampshire. I went there, he told himself. I went back to that memory and he was nowhere to be found! That's where he was supposed to be and he wasn't.

But another image forced itself into his mind.

Another night.

And not a departure, but a death.

He slid his head into his hands, ignoring the way the men grew silent in the room around him.

I know, he told himself.

I know where my brother is going.

Jeffers looked up at the ceiling, and the white paint seemed to spin about, dizzyingly, for just an instant. How could you not have seen it? he said to himself. It's clear. It's obvious. How could you be stumbling about so blindly? Anger, sadness, hope, and despair all rushed through his body. He knew he had to get there, he knew he had to leave right away. Time suddenly bore its great weight down

443

on top of him and he felt trapped in its vise grip. He exhaled slowly, gathering himself together. He looked out at the men, whose eyes were alive, expectant.

'Thank you,' he said.

He stood up.

'There will be no more sessions. Not for a few days. Check the ward announcements for their resumption. Thank you again.'

He saw a great surge of angry disappointment in the men. They are curious, he thought. They like to gossip and be in the know as much as anyone. He would not apologize, and, instead, he ignored the murmuring, excited sounds from the group, pitching headlong into the darkest nights of his own memory. I know, he said to himself again. I know.

He thought of the detective waiting for him in his office.

She will be watching. She will be alert for any change.

For an instant he felt a terrible sadness.

Then he turned from the men and walked steadily out. As he closed the door, he heard their excited voices join together. He shut them from his mind, concentrating on the importance of the next hours. He toughened himself inwardly. Be careful. Show nothing, he told himself. Show nothing at all.

Martin Jeffers stepped quickly away from the door, and the voices faded. He picked up his pace as he headed through the wards. His walk became a quick march, and, finally, a jog, his shoes making a slapping sound as they hit the linoleum floor. He ignored the surprised eyes of patients and staff as he broke into a run, his breath coming hard, oblivious to everything save the knowledge that vibrated in his head. I know, he repeated, over and over. I know.

He slowed as he entered the corridor where his office was located. He waited, catching his breath, thinking of the detective again. Then, composed, he slowly walked the last hundred feet, devising his escape.

Detective Mercedes Barren was standing, staring through

the window, when Martin Jeffers entered the room. He beat her to the punch:

'Anything happen? Any news?'

She hesitated. 'That was my question for you.'

He shook his head, avoiding her glance momentarily. He stiffened himself. Meet her eyes, he insisted inwardly. So he raised his head as he took a seat behind his desk.

'No,' he told her. 'I've heard nothing. I told the switchboard operator that I was to be paged for any call, regardless of whether I was in a session or not. So far, nothing.'

Detective Barren dropped into a seat across from him.

'What about at your home?'

'I left the answering machine on.' He picked up his telephone and opened the desk drawer, producing a small black device. 'It's got one of those playback thingamijigs,' he said. 'We can check.' He dialed his home phone number and put the electronic instrument to the receiver. There was a series of squeaks and beeps before the tape started to play.

They listened to a message from a plumber and a tape-recorded sales pitch for a local candidate. Then the tape hissed emptily.

'There was nothing in the mail here,' Jeffers said. 'But it doesn't get delivered at home until about four.'

'Screw the mails,' Detective Barren said blankly. 'He's not sending any postcards.'

'He has before.'

'And so we get one. Then we're only four or five days behind him.'

'But it would tell us, maybe, what direction he was heading.'

She knew this might be true. Still, her frustration gripped her. 'Screw the mails,' she said again. She sighed. 'What about your memory? I have more confidence in that.'

'I thought he would be there,' Martin Jeffers replied. 'I was sure that he'd be there in New Hampshire. It seemed the most logical place to start.'

'So think again.'

He rolled his head back. 'Aren't you exhausted, too?' he

445

asked. 'Christ, we've been pushing. It's getting hard to figure. Don't you want to take a break?'

'I'll rest when it's over.'

Martin Jeffers nodded. He knew she would not stop until his brother was – and then he paused. He would not fill in the remainder with a word, though he realized what she was saying.

'You're right,' he said. 'I'll keep at it.'

He saw her relax, if only slightly.

After a moment she said:

'It's not a difficult proposition, really.'

'What?'

'The idea that at any given time one ought to know where one's brother is. Or sister, for that matter.'

He thought the question provocative. But he droned his answer.

'Maybe as children. When we were growing up I always knew. Even through school I always could have told you where he was. But when we became adults, well, adults head off on their own ways. We become independent. We have our own lives. We become more ourselves, less someone's brother or sister.'

She shook her head irritatedly.

'Don't lecture me. That's not true. Your own profession tells us that the adult only masks with age and responsibility and morality and ethics all the desires of the child. So force yourself back! Think like you used to, not like you do today!'

She glared at him with eyes rimmed with equal parts of exhaustion and tension.

She was completely correct, he realized.

So, instead, he rose from his chair and circled around her nervously. 'I'm trying, I'm trying. My mind is filled with possibilities. But there are a hundred shared moments between brothers growing up. A thousand. Which is the one that triggers him now?'

'You know,' she said. 'You just block it.'

He smiled. 'You sound like me.'

Detective Mercedes Barren lifted her hands to her face

and tried to rub away her fatigue. She smiled faintly. 'You're right,' she said. 'I'm sorry. I push too hard sometimes.'

Her confession surprised her.

'But you're right, too,' he continued. 'I'm probably blocking it.'

His own bare smile joined hers.

Martin Jeffers looked over at the detective. His stomach clenched as he thought how deep her despair must be. For an instant he thought they should embrace and shed tears together, on to each other's shoulders, tears for the living, tears for the dead, tears for all the memories. He wanted to touch her in that moment, both angry and sad at the reason they had been thrust together into this small room, in the ever-changing world created and defined by his brother. He felt his hand start forward to touch her arm, but just as swiftly he ordered the muscles to stop, and he jammed his hand into the white pocket of his laboratory coat. Instead, he spoke:

'Detective, what are you going to do when this is over?' He held up his hand to make her pause before replying. 'Regardless of how it comes out.'

She laughed, but without humour.

'I haven't really thought of it,' she said. She shook her head. 'I suppose I'll go back to work, as before. I enjoyed what I was doing. I liked the people I worked with. No reason to change.'

That was surely a lie, she thought. She expected nothing ever to be the same again.

She looked at him.

'And what about you, doctor?'

He nodded.

'The same.'

We lie well together, she thought wryly to herself.

'Most lives,' she said, 'don't present that many options, do they?'

'No,' he said sadly, 'they don't.'

But both were struck then with the same vision: each knew of one man's life that seemed filled with options.

447

Detective Mercedes Barren looked over at Martin Jeffers and for an instant tried to envision herself in his position. Then, as the first empathetic feelings crowded her heart, she hardened herself. Concentrate! she shouted to herself. Remember! She saw the lines that ridged the doctor's eyes, the gray pallor to his skin, and thought he was indeed filled with remorse. What has happened to me has happened, she told herself. What remains for me is justice, which is not an emotion but a need. He's still living his grief.

She wanted to say something, then, but could not think of anything even vaguely appropriate.

Martin Jeffers was aware of the silence between them, and the suddenly lessened degree of tension. He recognized the moment for what it was, knowing its duration would be short. He leaned back in his chair, stretching. But if he appeared relaxed on the outside, inwardly he was rigid:

Spring the trap, now!

'Look,' he said slowly. 'You're absolutely right. We've got to keep at this until I figure out where he's gone. Someone's life may be at stake – we don't know. Let's just do it, okay?'

Detective Barren nodded in agreement.

'Here's what I think,' he said. He glanced up at the wall clock. 'It's getting late in the afternoon. I'll drop you at your hotel for an hour or so. Just give me long enough to take a shower and get a second wind. Then meet me at my house. We can have a couple of drinks and I'll pull out every old picture and letter I've got, and we'll try to free-associate an answer to all this. We can set up some sort of chronology. You'll have to listen to my life story, but maybe if I start to talk it out something will strike true. And anyway, if the phone rings, we'll both be right there. He's far more likely to call me at home than here.'

Detective Barren considered the plan. The thought of hot water flooding her body was seductive. For an instant a voice within her shouted caution and she forced her eyes to set on Martin Jeffers. She watched as he rocked slightly in his seat. She searched for anxiety, for nervous motion, for anything other than the discouragement and fatigue that she felt insistently within herself. She saw nothing. He's already had a hundred opportunities to run, she thought. He won't. Not until he hears from his brother.

'Start with a clearer head,' he said blandly. 'See what jumps in.'

'All right,' she replied. 'I'll be there at, say, six-thirty.'

'Six would be fine,' he said. 'And we'll keep at it until we've got at least a good idea where to head. And then we'll just go. The hospital can cut me some time.'

'Good,' she said. She felt a sense of body-slackening release at the idea that they would be acting instead of waiting. She felt a hot flood inside her, thinking hard of Douglas Jeffers, feeling once again that she was embarking on his trail. That comforted her, and blinded her to the fact that the murderer's brother had turned his eyes away suddenly, averting his glance.

Martin Jeffers pulled to the curb in front of Detective Barren's hotel in Trenton. He took the car out of gear and turned to her.

'Look, what kind of sandwiches do you like? I'll stop at the deli on the way to my place so we can eat later.'

She opened the car door and put one foot to the sidewalk.

'Anything's okay,' she said. 'Roast beef, ham and cheese, tuna fish.' She smiled. 'Protestant sandwiches. No corned beef or brisket. No mustard, plenty of mayonnaise.'

He laughed.

'And some sort of salad if they've got anything.'

'No problem.'

He glanced at his watch.

'Look,' he said, 'be there by six. Let's get this thing moving.'

She nodded. 'Don't worry. See you then.'

'All right,' he replied.

He watched as she strode across the hotel entranceway and disappeared into the lobby. He thought that the banality of his plan had been its strongest element. She was so focused on her quarry and the evil he represented in her mind that she neglected the more mundane possibility that Martin Jeffers might abandon her. Mingle obsession with exhaustion and one is ripe for the unexpected. For an instant he regretted his betrayal. She's going to kill me, he thought. Then he realized that the colloquialism that had formed in his head was probably not impossible. She might actually kill me.

He argued with himself: Be realistic.

He pulled the car out into the street. Don't stop. Don't go home. Do without a change of clothes, or a toothbrush, or anything. Just go. Now. He exhaled sharply and thought of his destination. If I hurry, he told himself, perhaps I can make the last ferry. His mind started to picture the detective at the moment his disappearance became clear to her. He rationalized: This is about saving lives. My brother's. The detective's. My own.

Still, he thought again, she's going to be angry enough to shoot me when she sees me again. It did not occur to him that his brother might feel the same.

Martin Jeffers cleared his head and drove hard, struggling with the late-afternoon traffic.

Detective Mercedes Barren stepped naked from the shower, toweling herself off slowly. After she had rubbed her body into a gleaming redness, she wrapped the white bath towel around her hair and flopped onto the bed, refreshed in part by the water, but equally by a moment of solitude. She stretched her body, feeling the muscles tense, then slowly relax. She lay back and ran her hands over her figure. She felt sore, as if she'd been in an accident, or in a fight, and her injuries were all concealed beneath the surface of her skin, internal. She closed her eyes and recognized the drowning pull of sleep. She fought against it, opening first one eye, then the other, blinking away the demands of her body. She argued with herself, pleading with all the currents in her body that demanded rest, first cajoling, then negotiating, and finally promising nerves, muscles, and brain that she would rest, surely, soon, and deeply as well.

But not yet.

She summoned some strength from within her and sat

up on the bed. She shouted orders, Prussian-like, to her arms and hands, a drill sergeant for the body: Get the clothes. Put them on. Get going.

Still battling against the rebellious demands of her body, she dressed herself in jeans and sportshirt. She took time to fix her hair and apply some make-up. She had a need to look less bedraggled by events than she actually felt. She refused to let frustration defeat her. After a few moments she looked at herself in the mirror. Well, she insisted, if not refreshed, at least you look ready.

She glanced over at the red digital alarm clock that rested on the bedstand table. So I'll be a little early, she thought. We can just get started sooner.

She drove slowly through the lengthening shadows, leaving the small city behind and maneuvering through the suburban traffic toward the doctor's apartment in Pennington. She was reminded of John Barren's opinion of the state of New Jersey. He had always loved the state, she remembered, because no other place combined so many varieties of life: abject Newark poverty, incredible Princeton wealth, funky Asbury Park, Flemington farmland. It was a state capable of extraordinary beauty in some regions and exceptional ugliness in others. Her eyes roamed about, fixing on the tree-lined road which cut through rolling green hills. This, she thought, is the nice part.

She turned off the primary highway and drove into Pennington. She could see the usual suburban-evening theater: fathers arriving home in business suits, kids playing on the sidewalks or in side yards, mothers fixing dinners. It grated on her somehow. It seemed too normal, too ideal. Detective Barren spotted a pair of teenage girls, giggling on a street corner, heads together in typical teenage conspiracy. But you're not safe! she thought suddenly. Her heart tightened and her breathing constricted. She had an overwhelming urge to stop and shout at all the assembled, happy people: But you don't know! You don't understand! None of you are safe!

She exhaled slowly and turned the car on to Martin Jeffers' street. She halted across the street, barely looking around. She did not want to see any more portraits of unfettered happiness. No more Norman Rockwell, she told herself. Back to Salvador Dali.

She stepped from the car and stopped dead.

Her skin suddenly seemed to crawl.

Something is wrong, she thought. Something is out of place and mistaken. Her head reeled suddenly.

He's here!

She looked wildly about, but saw nothing that wasn't in its proper location. She informed herself that she was being exceptionally paranoid, but she still scoured the windows of the houses on the street, trying to detect a pair of eyes burning into her.

She could see none.

Moving very slowly, she maneuvered her purse around to her right side. Trying to be as unobtrusive as possible, she lowered her hand beneath its brown leather flap. The 9-millimeter took up almost all the pocketbook. She gripped the handle.

She felt a momentary panic: Is a round chambered?

She could not remember. She clicked off the safety and told herself to assume there was no bullet in the firing chamber. Cock the gun first, she told herself. You're being crazy, because there's nothing wrong, but chamber a round anyway. She kept hold of the grip and slid her left hand in on top, slamming the gun's action back, loading it, ready to fire. She could feel the short hairs on her arms standing on edge, she thought of herself as a dog, filled with unusual smells, hackles rising without really understanding what the danger was, but accepting the demands of instinct born of centuries.

She looked at Martin Jeffers' apartment. She felt her mouth go dry.

Where's his car? her brain screamed.

She took a step sideways, then another, peering into the small driveway. No car. She walked out into the street to give herself a better look up and down.

No car.

She told herself: He probably went to the deli. That's it.

452

But every nerve in her body told her that reassurance was wrong. She made certain that the pistol would slip free from her purse when she demanded it.

She walked to the front door and stepped inside.

What she saw made her heart plummet.

Martin Jeffers' mail lay uncollected on the floor in front of his apartment.

No, she said. No!

She stepped to the door and removed the pistol. With her free hand she pounded on the wood frame.

There was no response.

She waited, then pounded again.

Again nothing.

She made no effort to conceal the gun as she walked outdoors and around the side of the building. She stared in the windows, pausing at the one where she'd broken into the apartment what suddenly seemed a very long time before.

She saw no movement. The interior remained dark.

She walked back to the front door and pounded again.

Silence continued to greet her.

She stepped back, staring at the bolted door. She thought it oddly symbolic. I'm locked out. I should have known, I did know, I just refused to acknowledge it, that he would close me out. They are brothers, she thought. Then she slumped down, sitting on the steps that rose to the upper floors of the building.

He's gone, she said to herself matter-of-factly.

He knows and he's gone.

She felt one momentary rush of rage that evaporated as swiftly as it arrived. She remained sitting, feeling nothing save a great, gray, utterly absorbing cloud of defeat that rained despair on her heart.

A tractor-trailer had jackknifed on Route 95, not far from Mystic, Connecticut, backing up traffic for a half-dozen miles. Martin Jeffers shifted impatiently in his seat, his face bathed by the blue and yellow strobes of a rescue crew and the state police cruisers. Every few seconds the red taillights of the car in front of him would flash and he would have to brake hard himself. He hated the jam-up; it intruded on the frantic press of memories which called to him from the recesses of his imagination. He tried to think of good moments they'd shared, instants in time that create the relationship between brothers: a night spent camping, the construction of a tree house, a halting, embarrassed discussion about girls that disintegrated into a conversation about masturbation. That made him smile. Doug never admitted to anything, but was always filled with the advice of a frequent practitioner, regardless of the subject. He remembered a moment when he was six or seven and had been set upon by other neighborhood boys armed to the teeth with snowballs. He'd been unable to outrun the missiles or the gibes of the others. It was a benign challenge, one that stemmed not from competition or animosity but from six new inches of snow falling steadily and the cancellation of classes that day. Doug had listened to his story of ambush and attack, then carefully decked himself in scarf and winter coat and galoshes and led the way out the rear door. His brother had led him around the back, around the block, and finally up from behind, crawling the last fifty yards on their stomachs behind a white-decked hedgerow. Their assault was commandolike and marvelously successful. Two shots crashed in snowy explosion into the faces of a pair of his tormentors before they had any idea where the grenades were coming from.

Even then, Martin Jeffers thought abruptly, Doug knew how to stalk his prey.

He looked ahead and saw a row of flares burning orange into the roadway. A state trooper with a yellow-lensed flashlight was waving the cars through frantically. Still, people slowed to peer at the wreck.

We are always fascinated by disaster, Martin Jeffers knew.

We crane our heads to see nightmare. We slow to investigate misery.

He wished, suddenly that he were above curiosity, but

realized he wasn't. He, too, slowed in passing, catching a glimpse of a single shrouded figure deathly still on the road.

In ancient times, he told himself, a traveler spotting such an inopportune omen would turn back, grateful that the heavens had shown him a sign foretelling the tragedy that awaited him. But I am modern. I am not superstitious.

He drove on. He glanced at his wristwatch and knew that he would miss the last ferry at Woods Hole. Damn, he said to himself. I'll have to catch the first boat in the morning. He hoped the ferry company still scheduled a 6 a.m. boat. He remembered a good motel within walking distance of the dock. For a moment he toyed with the idea of calling the detective once he'd checked in; not to tell her where he was, but to apologize and try to explain that he was doing what he must, what was dictated by flesh and blood. He wanted her to forgive him. He wanted her to forgive herself. She will blame herself for leaving me alone, even if just for a few minutes. She should realize there were a dozen moments that I could have abandoned her. He knew it was the sort of rationalization that would infuriate her. Well, he said to himself, you were wrong about New Hampshire. Maybe you're wrong about Finger Point as well. The head plays a confidence game with the heart.

'Maybe he won't be there,' Martin Jeffers said aloud. 'Maybe I'll just embarrass myself by knocking on the door of some vacationing family who'll think I'm crazy and that will be it.'

Detective Barren slipped from his mind's eye, replaced by his brother. He felt a great swirl within him. He was caught in a perfect pull of emotions: equal parts demanding he confront his brother and equal parts hoping he wouldn't have to.

The night had moved into position and he felt more alone than he ever had since the evening in New Hampshire more than three decades earlier.

Detective Mercedes Barren remained rooted on the hallway steps outside Martin Jeffers' apartment, letting the darkness sweep over her.

She was filled with memories of her own; of her husband, of her niece. A portrait of Susan filled her, but it wasn't the Susan that she'd seen strangled and molested and discarded beneath a few scrub ferns in the park, but the Susan who would come to dinner and play loud music and dance about Detective Barren's home, suffused with sounds, barely able to contain all the life she had. Then this image faded, and Detective Barren saw the little girl, dressed in pinks and bows, running to greet her, making the detective feel, if only for an instant, completely whole, completely loved. She thought of John Barren, rolling over in the middle of the night with demands of affection, and the friendly, familiar sensation of welcoming him to her body. She thought: If only I'd known. If only someone had told me: Make every moment special, for your time is short.

She saw herself as a child, gripping her father's hand.

She looked over at the dark door to Martin Jeffers' apartment. Well, she said to herself, use some of your father's logic. It was the only thing he had to will to you. It's helped you before. What would he do?

Examine the facts. Investigate each element.

All right, she said to herself. Let's take it simply.

He said: Meet you here.

A lie.

She thought what a wondrous lie it was. Simple, benign, especially the touch about the sandwiches. Use the familiarity of the past days against her.

But when did the lying start?

She reviewed their last meeting, in his office. He didn't indicate anything had changed. But something obviously had. He didn't receive any phone calls. There was no mail. He clearly didn't return to his apartment and then decide to leave. The decision had to have been made by the time they were in his office. She reviewed the situation again. No, she thought quickly, there was nothing from Douglas Jeffers.

So it must have been something he remembered.

She sat back in the darkness and thought deeply.

He went to individual sessions and then to that damn

group of perverts. Then he came back to the office and then he began lying and then he disappeared. She sat up and then stood up. She began to pace about the entranceway, concentrating hard. Her exhaustion slid away in the fury of her mind at work. She felt a wealth of adrenaline pumping through her. Back on the case, she thought. You're back on the case. Act like a damn detective. Now, though, you've got two quarries.

'All right,' she said out loud. 'Start at the hospital. Start with the patients he saw. Get the list from his secretary. If she won't give it to you, steal it.'

These last words echoed in the small area.

She breathed in hard. She saw again her niece, her husband, her father. She smiled and dismissed the images from her head. Work, she thought. She replaced the vision with twin portraits of Martin and Douglas Jeffers.

I'm coming, she said to herself. I'm still after you.

Weak dawn light flowed over the ferry bow, and Martin Jeffers felt the chill of morning air surround him. He pulled the lapels of his lab coat tighter and let the breeze wash over him. He could see miles of rolling gray-green ocean glistening in the first light. He turned his back to the wind and watched the island loom up in the distance. He could see the shoreline trimmed with proper summer homes, then, a short ways farther in the distance, the white glow of Vineyard Haven, where the ferry would dock. Sunlight hit upon a row of a half-dozen fuel tanks next to the docks. In the harbor, dozens of sailboats bobbed at moorings. He thought of the small slapping sound that wavelets make against the hull of a sailboat.

The ferry moved fast through the morning seas. As it approached the slip, it blared out a single raucous blast on the air horn. Martin Jeffers saw some of the other passengers jump, startled by the sound.

The ferry bumped to a stop, its huge diesel engines grinding the bow into the dock. There was a momentary pause while gangways were lowered and people started to exit. Martin Jeffers pushed through the early crowd of people. The lines of cars waiting to get on the ferry were already stretched up the street. It reminded Jeffers how close they were to the end of the summer; the boat over had been almost empty. Returning to the mainland, it would be filled.

He looked about briefly as he exited the ferry and walked across the loading area, past the ticket office. He thought: It's all the same, but different. More buildings. New shops. A new parking lot. But it's all the same, still.

I thought I would never come back here.

He started to count the years, then stopped. He knew the house would be there, just the same, next to the pond, across from the ocean. His eyes scanned the crowds of people and cars. It will still be isolated and wild, he said to himself. It will have stayed the same.

He did not base this conclusion on any fact, more an overwhelming sensation of familiarity.

It was, he thought, the best worst place.

He remembered what the Lost Boys had said. And he'd come to that place where they'd told him to look.

Look for a death.

Well, he said to himself, I'm here.

And this is the place for both.

He hurried across the street to Island Rent-A-Car, washing his mind of everything save the insistent fear that he would be right.

The clerk was eating a doughnut and sipping coffee.

'How can I help you?'

'Martin Jeffers. I made a reservation last night with the late guy.'

'Yup. Saw his note this morning. On the early ferry, right? Said you wanted a car for a couple of days, right? A little vacation?'

'A little business. Could be short. Could drag out a bit.'

'Just so's we have the car back Friday. Labor Day weekend, you know. All booked up. Everything is.'

'No problem,' Jeffers lied.

'You got an island address for the form?'

He hesitated. 'Yeah. Chilmark. Out on Quansoo. Sorry, there's no phone.'

'Best beach, though.'

'Right you are.'

'Of course,' the clerk said as he filled out the forms, 'I don't go down there too much. I ain't much of a swimmer and those waves and the undertow and all that stuff scares the daylights out of me. But the surfers, they love it. You ain't a surfer, are you?'

'No.'

'Good. Those kids are always renting the cars and trying to drive them out on the beach and getting them stuck and tearing up the transmissions and all.'

The man picked up a set of keys hanging on the wall behind him. 'You need a map?' he asked.

'No, unless things have changed much in the past couple of years.'

'Things always change. That's the nature of life. But the roads ain't, if that's what you mean.' The clerk shoved a form at Martin Jeffers for his signature. 'All set. It's the white Chevy just outside the door. Return with a tank of gas, okay? Before Friday.'

'See you then.'

Martin Jeffers started up the car and fought his way through the building morning traffic. He realized he had no plan other than simply barging in on the people who were there. What are you going to say? he asked himself. What are you going to tell them? Excuse me, sir or madam, but you wouldn't happen to have seen a man bearing a family resemblance to yours truly dripping blood in the neighborhood?

What can you say other than the truth?

He realized that was impossible. This particular truth was too far removed from reality to absorb at 8 a.m. on a late-summer morning, when eating a leisurely breakfast before heading to the beach.

So, he thought, just tell them he's lost and you're trying to find him. Tell them he's in a fugue state, wandering between poles of memory, disengaged from life, like everyone's crazy Aunt Sadie, who one day simply walked off and took a train to St Louis. Tell them he's harmless. Tell them you're concerned. Tell them anything.

Every construction he tried sounded equally far-fetched.

Just tell them you're looking for your brother and once you lived in this house and you thought he might have come visiting.

Tell them what they want to hear.

This, he admitted to himself, is going to be impossible.

But he realized that embarrassment was by far the least terrible thing that could happen.

He drove through the rising morning, darting between the shadows the green trees tossed so casually across the road. He was driving unconsciously, letting his memory take over and steer the car. Distances seemed strangely different, first longer, then shorter. He saw the houses that he remembered, and new buildings that he didn't. He was pleased, in an odd way, to see that the general store in the tiny town of West Tisbury had not changed. He cruised past, heading toward the turnoff.

He continued following the path of his past. He thought: The hospital is that way. But we didn't have to drive fast, because there was no hope.

He saw the great sand-pit entrance to the road off to his right and slowed. He was surprised that he'd found it, and equally surprised that it looked the same. He hesitated only momentarily before heading down the road. The washboard dirt surface pitched the rental car about, and he heard the paint being scratched on the sides where the bramble bushes bent toward the road. He recalled why the road had never been improved: the people who lived down it wanted to discourage anyone from coming sightseeing. He hit a bump and heard the bottom of the car scrape violently against the rocks and dirt. They were always successful, he thought.

He had driven several miles when he came to the trees with colored arrows. He didn't bother to check; he knew which fork to take, even after so many years. He could feel his pulse quickening as he steered through the overhanging trees.

I never thought I would return, he said to himself for the thousandth time.

He emerged from the trees and caught his first sight of the pond off to the side of the road. In the far distance he could see, just barely, the glint of the sun as it hit the ocean. There were a half-dozen bright triangular sails from small boats already cutting across the pond toward the beach. His eyes focused on a farmhouse several hundred yards across the water. Old man Johnson, he thought, smiling. The old bastard. I wonder if he's still shooting at kids who drive on the sand dunes? He stopped and rolled down the window. He could hear the surf in the distance, and he wondered why such a constant and violent sound was also so soothing.

He looked down the road and caught sight of the house.

The best worst place.

He closed his eyes and tried to think of what he would say and realized that he would simply have to rely on whatever words came to him. The important thing, he thought, is to seem open and friendly and nonthreatening. Just get in the door, he thought, and then see what happens.

He drove the last quarter mile and pulled into a small driveway. He got out of the car and stared up at the house. He could see that it had received some new gray shingles and some of the windows appeared new. It was a low, single-story, old Cape design, with a front door that looked back at the road and a back side of the house that looked out over the pond toward the ocean.

Finger Point, he thought. The spit of land reaches out into the pond, pointing at the ocean. Not a particularly interesting method of naming a piece of property, but accurate. He looked out at sea grass waving in the breeze across the water on the Johnson property and remembered running through the grass, the blades slicing at him, oblivious to the sharpness of the pain, trying to keep up with his brother. He shut his eyes and felt the sun striking his head and shoulders. For a moment he felt completely foolish, then completely terrified. He wanted to get back in the car and drive away. He's not here, he thought. He's somewhere, lost in America, doing terrible things. He's gone forever. Just turn and leave and never think of him again.

He knew that was impossible and he opened his eyes.

You made it this far without turning back. Might as well make a complete ass of yourself.

He walked up to the front door and knocked loudly.

Sorry, he said to himself. I hope I'm not getting anyone out of bed. He heard footsteps from inside and then the front door opened.

It was a young woman, pretty, in her early twenties, Jeffers guessed, with blond hair that was set off by her black mechanic's outfit.

'Excuse me,' Martin Jeffers started. He thought she was dressed unusually for a summer morning, but he did not have time to assess this idea. 'I know it's early and I'm terribly sorry to be bothering you, but . . .'

And then he stopped.

The young woman was staring wide-eyed at him, as if shocked by his appearance. He saw her eyes absorb the details of his features.

'I'm sorry . . .' he started in again.

'But why?' came the terrible, mocking, but totally familiar voice behind him.

The membership of the Lost Boys filed slowly into the sunlit day room and took their customary seats. This they did out of habit and the demands of hospital scheduling, which told them that in this time period they were to be in this room, doing this therapy. Deviations from the normal routine were discouraged. So they went, knowing that the normal routine had already been shattered. But they were all well versed enough in the ways of bureaucracies to understand that, even if there were to be no session, they surely were required to be there until told explicitly to the contrary. They knew that Martin Jeffers would not be there, for he'd told them that himself. They knew that their session would consist of sitting about while some other doctor, thrust by his precipitous departure, filled in. They also knew they'd tell the new doctor nothing.

They waited, smoking, talking quietly amongst themselves, idly curious as to what would happen.

They were, to a man, shocked when Detective Mercedes Barren walked through the door.

In the silence that accompanied her entry, Detective Barren fixed the room with a rock-hard glare. These, she thought, are my natural enemies. She could feel goose-bumps on her skin.

The room was empty of sound.

She waited for an instant, then walked to the front of the group. She could feel their eyes on her. They did not know who she was, of course, but she knew they hated her, instantly, profoundly.

As she did them.

She turned and faced the group.

Slowly, exaggerating her movements, she reached into her bag and brought out her gold shield. She held it high, so they could all see it clearly. It reflected the sunlight, glowing in her hand.

'My name is Mercedes Barren,' she said firmly. 'Detective. City of Miami Police Department.'

She paused.

'If it had been me on your case, you'd be doing hard time.'

This was stated as a blunt fact.

The room remained quiet. She had little doubt that the men absorbed her words carefully. Now, she thought, throw them the curve.

'Your regular group leader is Doctor Martin Jeffers. He left the hospital suddenly yesterday afternoon, not long after meeting with you men . . .'

She paused.

'Where is he?'

The room exploded into a cacophony of conversation; the men had their heads together, everyone talking at once.

She held up her hand, and the twelve pairs of eyes rested back on her.

'Where did he go?'

There was another flurry of talk that faded swiftly into a belligerent silence. Finally one man, a pockmarked, heavyset man with a ready sneer, said, 'Fuck you, lady.'

'What's your name?'

'Miller.'

'You facing a little prison time after this holiday is over, Miller? Maybe you'd like to do it in maximum security?'

'I can do the time,' Miller replied.

'I hope so.'

Again silence took over until a smallish round man waved his hand at Detective Barren. She nodded in his direction and he spoke in a sarcastic, effeminate voice:

'Why, detective, should we bother to help you?'

'What's your name?'

'I'm Steele,' he said. 'But my friends call me Petey.'

'If you had any,' said another voice. She couldn't tell who and she had to force herself not to smile. There was a smattering of laughter in the room.

'All right, Steele, I'll tell you why you should help me. Because you are all criminals. And just who the hell do you think helps the police? That's the way things work, you know. Bad guys know where other bad guys are.'

'You saying the doc's a bad guy?' This was Bryan speaking.

'No. I'm not. But he went after somebody real bad.'

'Who?' It was Senderling and Knight together.

She hesitated. Well, why not?

'You all help me. I'll tell you. I just want an agreement first.'

She looked around the room. She saw the men leaning their heads together. 'All right,' said Knight and Senderling, both. 'We'll help.' They laughed. 'Got nothing to lose.'

'Except maybe the d-d-d-doc's trust,' stuttered Wasserman.

That made the men pause.

'What's in it for us?' Miller asked.

'Nothing solid. You just get to know a little bit. Information is always valuable.'

Miller snorted. 'You're just like every cop, even if you ain't got the right equipment. You want to get something for nothing.'

She didn't reply.

'Look,' said Parker, 'if we help you a little, can you promise that the doc won't get hurt? I mean, legally, too, not just physically.'

'Doctor Jeffers is not the subject of my investigation,' Detective Barren replied. 'But he knows the person who is. I want to keep him from getting himself into more trouble. How's that?'

'I don't trust no cops,' said Miller.

'Well, is the doctor in danger?' asked Bryan.

Maybe. Maybe not. She didn't know. So she lied.

'Yes. Absolutely. But he doesn't know it.'

This made the men start murmuring again.

'Tell you what,' Knight said. 'You tell us what the deal is, who this bad dude is, and we'll see if we can help.'

Detective Barren shrugged. She knew that if she were to get any information out of the group, she would have to keep the conversation flowing. If she stonewalled, so would they.

She took a deep breath and answered:

'His brother.'

There was an instant's silence, then Steele began to whoop and clap his hands. He jumped from his seat and danced about the day room. 'I knew it, I knew it. Pay up! Pay up! You, Bryan, two packs of cigarettes. You, Miller, three packs. All you dumb fuckers who bet against me – I told you it was a relative! It had to be! Pay up! Pay up!'

She saw the men grumbling.

'So,' she demanded, 'where did he go?'

'He d-d-d-didn't say,' Wasserman replied.

'He wasn't specific,' Weingarten jumped in. 'He just said this guy, he didn't say who, was worse than us. He said the guy was visiting memories. I didn't think we said all that much to help him.'

'Yeah, except all of a sudden he jumps up and takes off.' This was Parker.

'He had it all fucking backwards anyway,' Miller grunted. 'He wasn't sure what sort of memory he was looking for. We had to straighten him out. We told him to look for the worst memory, because that would be the best for someone like us.'

'What did you say exactly?' Detective Barren leaned forward.

'Shit, who knows? We said a lot of things.'

'Yes, but one thing you said made him think of something.'

The men all started talking together again.

'We said a lot of things,' Miller insisted.

'Come on, dammit! What was said?'

'He wanted to know what happened so that we became free, you know, free to do what we do.'

'What?'

'He asked us what started us. You know. What got us going.'

She took a deep breath and it made perfect sense to her. He had demanded the key. And they'd given it to him.

'So what was said? What was it?'

The men in the room stared at her angrily. She could sense the strength of hatred that they had for her, not merely as a policeman, but as a woman. She met their eyes, filling her own gaze with all the power she could find within her.

The silence was like oil, spread over everything.

She wanted to scream.

Tell me, she shouted in her mind. Tell me!

'I know,' came a deep voice from the back. It was Pope. She leaned forward and met his eyes. Here, she thought to herself, is a truly terrifying man. She had a sudden horrifying image of the man, grabbing her, ripping at her clothes. She wondered how many women had had that nightmare in reality.

'I know what I said. And it made him think of something.'

'What?'

Pope hesitated. Then he shrugged.

'I hope everyone dies,' he said under his voice.

He looked at Detective Barren. 'I said, "Look for a death or a departure." It always starts with one or the other. Sometimes they're the same.'

She leaned back in a chair. A departure, she thought. We went there. New Hampshire.

'That's it?' she asked. She hid the defeat from her voice.

'That was it. He stood up and took a hike.'

'S-s-s-sorry, d-d-d-detective . . .'

She stared at the men. She wondered how many deaths were spread about the room. How many ruined lives. She shivered inwardly.

Then she thought: A death. A ruined life.

The idea formed slowly, like a cyclone deep in the distance, but gaining power and strength with each passing second. She felt flushed, as if the heat in the room had suddenly spiked, and she thought of something Martin Jeffers had said in passing a few days beforehand: The bastard didn't even give us his name. And he died, in an accident.

She put her hand to her forehead, as if feeling her temperature. She looked out at the glowing eyes of the men around her. She stood up, unaware that she was mimicking Martin Jeffers.

'Thank you,' she said. 'You've been extremely helpful.'

I know, she thought. I know.

Maybe, maybe, maybe. At least it's a place to start.

She pictured the aged newspaper in the box beneath Martin Jeffer's bed. Go! The voice deep within her screamed. Go! It will tell you where he's gone! She had only a moment to berate herself for missing the obvious the first time she broke into Martin Jeffer's apartment. This time, she thought, you know what you're looking for. Go! Go! Go! Go!

She turned abruptly and left the men muttering behind her.

Her heels echoed a staccato, machine-gun sound, as she rushed from the hospital.

14 No man's land

19

Holt Overholser, sixty-three years old, the chief of the West
Tisbury police force, and its only year-round member,
fiddled with the paperwork on his desk, inwardly
complaining about the influx of summer people who paid
his salary every year, but who also neglected to obey the
posted speed limits and were forever trying to toss out their
garbage at the town dump on days it was officially closed.
He had spent much of the afternoon with his radar detector,
ticketing cars. The selectmen had put up a SPEED LIMIT 15
sign a half mile from the center of town, knowing that no
one would slow that much until they at least got past the
Presbyterian Church. This was where Holt parked, waving
every other car over and handing the driver a $25 speeding
ticket, which he'd had the sense to fill out in advance.

This had become a major source of revenue for the town;
the selectmen were pleased and Holt was pleased. Last year
they'd made enough to get him a new Ford Bronco with
four-wheel drive and the special police package. This year,
he thought, they'd get those new walkie-talkies that clip
onto the belt, with the microphone up on the shoulder, like
the ones they wore on *Hill Street Blues* sometimes. That was
Holt's favorite show, and much of his police training had
been acquired from a religious watching of it and other
shows, dating all the way back to *Dragnet*. Every time he
signed off the radio, he said, 'Ten four', in the same gruff
manner that Broderick Crawford had made famous. He
wondered whether there would be any good police shows
in the upcoming television season. He doubted it; cops
seemed to have swung out of favor again and it would

probably be a couple of years before television tried something new. He didn't count *Miami Vice* as a police show.

Holt leafed through the ticket book, making certain everything was legible before sending it over to the town clerk's office. He'd written forty-seven tickets in four hot hours. That was three shy of his record, he thought ruefully. But Labor Day was fast approaching, and he was confident that he would not only break his record but shatter it.

He stretched and stared out the window of the small office. Darkness had insinuated itself onto the warm late-summer night. All that remained of the day was a fast-fading red glow off to the West. Holt had never traveled farther in that direction than his sister's home in Albany at Thanksgiving, but he read avidly, mostly novels and travel books, and he longed to go. He liked to think of himself as a throwback to some earlier era, in the Old West. He saw himself as the peacekeeper in the small town, tough yet likeable, fair, yet the wrong man to cross, a good man to side with in a fight.

Of course he had never had a fight in thirty-three years of police work on Martha's Vineyard. The occasional belligerent drunk had been the worst he'd ever faced.

He closed his eyes and rocked back in his desk chair. There would be fresh bluefish casserole for dinner, cooked with vegetables from his own garden. Holt congratulated himself on eating well, which was actually more the result of his wife's dedication. He thumped his heart: Sixty-three and still going strong, he thought. The selectmen had tried to retire him three years earlier, but Holt had passed the state police physical examination ahead of a half-dozen men a third his age, and that had persuaded the selectmen to keep him on. They were amused, too, the way Holt always relieved a good deal of money from the summer kids whom he hired as temporary police help. Holt could out-arm wrestle all of them with his left hand; forty years earlier he'd worked on a lobster boat out of Menemsha, and hauling crates hand over hand from the bottom had left him with a considerable upper body strength. He'd also learned poker as a young man, which now supplemented his income handsomely. College kids always think they can play the game, he thought. They learn.

He examined the stack of tickets and decided: It can wait until morning. Most things could, even in the summer season. He yawned and lazily picked up the police radio on the corner of his desk.

'Dispatch, this is One Adam One, West Tisbury, I'm ten-thirty-six from HQ. Please put us on emergency link, ten four.'

'Hello, Holt, how are you tonight?'

'Uh, fine, dispatch.'

'Did Sylvia get the recipe I sent her?'

'Uh, dispatch, that's a roger.'

He hated it when Lizzie Barry was doing the late shift on the 911 network for the island. She was older than him and half-senile. She never followed the proper teminology.

'One Adam One, roger, ten-four.'

'Nighty-night.'

He hung up the microphone and started to collect his things, when he saw the woman walk through the door. He smiled.

'Just getting ready to close up, ma'am. What can I do for you?'

'I need some directions,' said Mercedes Barren.

'Well, sure,' replied Holt, sizing the woman up. Despite the blue jeans and sportshirt, she did not seem like a vacationer. She had a big-city air about her, and Holt could smell business. Probably another damn real-estate developer, he said to himself.

'I'm looking for a place where an accident took place about twenty years ago.'

'An accident?' Holt sat down and gestured at the chair opposite him. His curiosity was pricked.

'Some twenty years ago a businessman from New Jersey, guy owned a drugstore, drowned off South Beach. I need to know where that accident took place.'

'Well, hell, South Beach is seventeen miles long, and twenty years is awhile ago. You're gonna have to give me a bit more information.'

'Do you remember the incident?'

'Ma'am, begging your pardon, but we have one or two drownings every summer. After a while they pretty much seem the same. Coast Guard handles 'em, anyway. I just push some paperwork about.'

'I have the newspaper account. Would that help?'

'Can't hurt.'

Holt leaned forward while Mercedes Barren fished the old copy of the *Vineyard Gazette* from her bag. Holt caught just the barest glimpse of the automatic pistol barrel, and without thinking of some clever response he simply blurted out: 'You carrying a weapon, ma'am?'

'Yes,' she said. She reached down into her bag and produced her gold shield. 'I should have introduced myself. I'm Detective Mercedes Barren, City of Miami police.'

Holt was instantly delighted.

'We don't get many big-city police, uh, people, up here. You here on a case?'

'No, no, just visiting friends.'

'Oh,' he said, disappointed. 'Then why the gun?'

'Just habit, sorry.'

'Unh, hunh. You maybe want to leave it with me?'

'Chief, if you don't mind, I've got to leave early and it would be more convenient to keep it. Can't you bend some rule for a fellow cop?'

He gave her a smile and a little wave, signifying that she could keep the weapon. 'Don't like handguns on the island much. They never do anybody no good no how.'

'Chief, that's true in the big city, too.'

She shoved the newspaper copy over at him. He scanned the page quickly. 'Yeah, I remember, but vaguely. Guy got caught in a riptide, I think. Didn't have a chance.' He looked over at Mercedes Barren. 'You don't get riptides on Miami Beach, I bet.'

'No, chief.'

'Well, a rip is caused when the wave motion disturbs a bit of the bottom sand, like opening a new hole. The water pours in, and suddenly it has to go back out. It peters out a couple of hundred yards from shore. Trouble is, most people just fight like crazy when they feel that current pulling them out. They don't know that all you got to do is ride it out, then swim back in. Or, if you got to do something, you swim parallel to the beach. Rip's probably only twenty, thirty yards wide. Nope, people don't keep their heads. They fight hard, get exhausted, and bingo! More paperwork for me, and a body search for the Coast Guard boys. Happens once or twice a year on South Beach.'

'The paper just says South Beach.'

Holt kept reading. 'It says the family was staying in West Tisbury, but it don't say where.'

'I know. I thought you might remember.'

He shook his head. He looked at the newspaper again.

'Say, what's this got to do with visiting friends?'

Mercedes Barren laughed. 'Well, chief, it's a long story, but I'll try to make it quick. My friends are renting the house and they came across this old paper. They knew I was coming up to visit and they thought it would be interesting to me, so they sent it down to Miami, along with directions on how to find the place. Well, wouldn't you know it, I lose the paper with the directions and phone number, but kept the silly old newspaper. So now I'm trying to find them.'

'Unh-hunh.'

'I bet you get a lot of weird ones in here during the summer.'

'Unh-hunh.'

'Well, just file me under your silly-summer people file and help me figure out where to go.'

Holt broke into a smile.

'That'd be a helluva long file, if I kept one.'

They both laughed.

He looked at the story again. 'I suppose we could call around to some of the realty people, see if they handled the rental. But that might take some time. Lots of realtors up here on the island nowadays. Did you try calling the *Gazette?*'

'Yes, but they had gone home for the night.'

Holt thought for an instant.

'Well, I got one idea, might as well give it a shot.'

He picked up the police band microphone and said:

'Dispatch, this is One Adam One, come back.'

'Hello, Holt,' said Lizzie Barry. 'You should be home. That dinner's probably getting cold on the table.'

'Dispatch, I've got a woman here, looking for her friends. It's a long story, but they're staying down at the same place where a guy named Allen was staying the summer he drowned. Twenty years ago. Do you remember that case? Over.'

The radio crackled momentarily.

'Sure, Holt. I remember. He was taking an evening swim. It was that summer we had the hot spell, remember, when it went up to a hundred and five at one time. I remember because the same day my old dog died. Heatstroke. He was a good old dog, Holt, you remember him?'

Holt didn't. 'Sure. Sure. A setter?'

'No, a Golden Retriever.'

'Oh.' Holt waited for the voice to continue, but she didn't. 'So, dispatch . . . Lizzie, do you remember where the guy was living? Over.'

'Think so. Not certain, but seems to me that he was staying on Tisbury Great Pond. On Finger Point. Could be wrong, though.'

'Thanks, Lizzie. Ten-four.'

'Anytime, Holt. Over and out.'

Holt Overholser hung up the microphone. 'How about that,' he said. 'Old Lizzie's like an encyclopedia. She remembers damn well near everything that ever happens up here. Anything exciting, at least. Look, though, it's gonna be real tricky to find your way down there at night. You ought to find a hotel room and stay the night, go down in the morning.'

'Sounds like a good idea. Could you just show me, though, on the map?'

Holt shrugged. He walked over the wall. He showed her the sand pit entrance and where the washboard dirt road curved about. He showed her the fork in the road and which path led down to Finger Point. He couldn't remember the

473

last time he'd been down that road. Probably not in the twenty years since the drowning. He shook his head. 'Got to remember,' he said. 'No lights down there at all. All looks the same. You could get real lost down there. Wait until morning.'

'That's good advice, chief. I appreciate it. I think I'll just head into Vineyard Haven and find a hotel room. But I appreciate your taking the effort.'

'No problem.'

Holt Overholser walked Mercedes Barren outside into the night. 'It's right warm tonight,' he said. 'Dropped down to forty-five three nights ago, so these old bones still say we're gonna have an early fall, and a tough winter. Course, you get to be my age, all the winters are tough.'

Mercedes Barren laughed. 'Chief, you look like you could handle anything that winter sends your way.'

'Well, I guess you don't worry about the cold too much down there in Miami.'

'That's right.' She smiled. 'You want to recommend a hotel?'

'They're all pretty good.'

'Thanks again.'

'Anytime. Drop by and we'll talk police work.'

'Maybe I'll just do that,' Mercedes Barren said.

He watched as she got back into her car. He did not see the instant disappearance of her friendly, outgoing demeanor, replaced immediately by a rigid, hard-eyed concentration. She pulled out of the driveway to the small police station. Holt then started to anticipate his waiting bluefish, although he noticed that Detective Barren had taken the road which led not to town, but into the island's dark core, which made him pause briefly, filled with vague concern, before heading home.

Detective Mercedes Barren drove carefully through the thickness of the night, thinking: The darkness will make finding the house more difficult, but it will allow me to approach Douglas Jeffers under concealment, which would give me an advantage. She had no real plan other than to not give him a chance. I will shoot him in the back if I have to, if I can. I will take the shot that's open. Don't hesitate. Don't wait. Just seize the shot when it is there. One shot, make it count. That's all I'll get. It's all I'll need. She watched the road, peering ahead of the weak light thrown by the car headlights, looking for the turnoff that would lead her down toward Finger Point.

Images from the day seemed distant, yet intrusive on her concentration: She could see the Lost Boys, circled around her, poised on the edge of their perversion, watching her. She thought that she'd handled them well. She was struck, momentarily, by the power of suggestion, how the right words spoken in the right context can trigger almost any conclusion. She'd walked away from that session completely convinced that Martin Jeffers had gone to find his brother at the location where their adoptive father had died. That persuasion had remained firm, unshakable, as she'd taken a tire iron to the doctor's window, jackknifing into the apartment as she'd done before, only this time she was oblivious to any noise she made and she made no pretense toward stealth.

She had gone directly into the bedroom for what she needed: the faded old newspaper. She had been filled with a momentary anger when she scanned the story for details, only to learn that it was less specific than she needed.

But, she thought, that old country cop was perfect.

She remembered how she'd driven hard out of New Jersey, battling the afternoon traffic around Manhattan, screaming with frustration at the delays on the road.

She had had to wait what seemed an interminable time in Woods Hole, pacing about the ferry office, clenching her hands together. The ferry ride itself had been tedious, the picture-postcard images of the setting sun and sailboats cutting through the green waters had been lost on her.

But she'd had singular success when she'd gone to the rental-car location closest to the ferry landing. She thought of the smallish man who'd taken her credit card and handed her the keys, and who had also informed her that she was absolutely correct, a Martin Jeffers had come in on the morning ferry.

'Said he had business down island. Friend of yours?'

'Well, competitors, really.'

'Must be real estate. All you guys are always hustling about, trying to beat out the next guy. Or gal.'

She had not corrected him. 'Well, it's a tough buck.'

'Not here. Everybody's making out like bandits.'

He had looked at her license. 'Don't get too many from Florida here. Mainly New York, Washington, Boston. Not Miami.'

'I work for a large firm,' she had lied. 'Lots of offices.'

'Well,' the clerk had continued, 'I think there's too much damn development up here, anyway.'

She had sensed a touch of anger in his voice.

'Really?' she had replied. 'I work for a company that specializes in antique-property restoration. Not like my buddy Jeffers. He does motels and condo complexes.'

'Damn,' the clerk had said. 'Wish I hadn't given him the car.'

'What sort of car was that?'

'A white Chevy Celebrity. Tag number eight-one-seven triple J. Keep your eyes open for it.'

'Thanks,' she had replied. 'I will. Did he say where he was going exactly?'

'Nope.'

'Well, I'll run him to ground.'

'Good luck. Bring that car back by 8 p.m. tomorrow to avoid the extra charge.'

She clicked on the high beams and went down a small dip in the highway. Every hundred yards she saw another dirt road leading off to her right, and she swore angrily to herself, thinking each one looked the same. Keep going. Keep going. Look for the sand pit, like the chief said. Another car came toward her, lights blinking, signaling her to lower hers. She finally complied, and the other car slid by on the narrow roadway with a whooshing sound. It seemed to Detective Barren to have passed only inches from her and she felt a momentary panic. She watched the red

476

tail-lights disappear and was suddenly surrounded by blackness again.

She stared into the night.

'It's here,' she said out loud, the sound of her voice in the car comforting. 'I know it is.'

She drove on, slowing the car to a crawl.

'Come on, come on, where are you?'

She was alone and adrift, the island's dark like the ocean. She stared up at the skyline, barely able to distinguish where the trees ended and the heavens started. She felt unsettled, as if she were dangling above the water, holding on to the slimmest strand of rope. She could feel tension racing unchecked through her body. I'm close, she thought. I'm close. She felt a smothering sensation, as though there were no air inside the car whatsoever. He's here, I know it. Where? Where? She gritted her teeth together, grinding them. She squeezed her hands on the steering wheel until her knuckles were white. She raised her voice to herself, almost shouting against the solitude of the car and the night: 'Come on, come on!'

And then she saw the turnoff.

Anne Hampton sat at the table, staring at the open notebook in front of her. She saw the words: I do what I do because I have to, because I want to. Because something within all of us tells us what to do, and if we ignore it, it will crush us with desire.

She had scribbled the younger brother's reply beneath: You can get help. It doesn't have to be.

She shook her head. That was the completely wrong tack to take with Douglas Jeffers. She looked at the notes again. This part of the conversation was several hours old. Perhaps he's figured out another approach. But she doubted it. She thought the brother seemed lost, unable to comprehend, driven to confrontation, then barely able to articulate a sentence, much less persuade the older brother to set down his gun. She closed her eyes. I could have told him that, she said to herself. I could have told him that it was all set, now, there was no way out, no end to the script other than the one Douglas Jeffers had invented sometime earlier, in some other era, deep in the past, when I was still just a student and someone's daughter and eons before I became the murderer's biographer.

Anne Hampton wondered idly what would happen to them all now. She felt detached, almost as if she were someone else, standing outside her body, invisible to all the others, watching the events unfold on a stage. She remembered that she had felt this way before, during some of the murders, during the first moments in the motel. How long ago was that? She could not tell. She thought that was always what memory was like; it seems like so many snapshots in the mind, film clips with ragged edges and blinking, jerky motions. I can see myself running through the snow, she thought. I can see the hurt and cold in my face, but I cannot recall how the sensation felt anymore. I couldn't save him, she thought. She saw the derelict and the lone man on the street and the two lucky women – what were their names? – then the teenagers in the car. I can't save anybody. I can't, I can't. I wasn't allowed. I wanted to, oh God, I wanted to save him, he was my brother, but I couldn't, I couldn't. I can't.

She wanted to weep, but knew it would not be permitted.

'Boswell!'

She looked up sharply at the sound of Douglas Jeffers' voice. She jumped from her chair.

'Take some water in to our guests.'

She nodded and ran to the kitchen. She found a pitcher in the cabinet above the stove and filled it with water. Walking quickly, but careful not to spill any, she maneuvered past the living room, where the two brothers sat opposite each other, now wordless, after a day of talk. She opened the door to the downstairs bedroom and entered softly. She thought they might be asleep and didn't want to wake anyone. But at the scraping of her feet on the wood floor, she saw four sets of eyebrows soar in panicked anticipation.

She felt wretched.

'It's all right, it's all right,' she said. She knew how silly her words sounded, how foolish it was to try to comfort them. She knew they would die, and soon. That had been the plan all along.

That they were nobodies didn't matter to him, this she knew. What was important was that they were there, in this location, which she knew was important to him. She remembered his words, spoken under his breath, seconds before breaking in through a sliding porch door, left benignly unlocked, open to summer breezes:

'I need to fill this house with ghosts.'

She put her hand on the woman's arm gently, reassuringly. 'I've brought you some water,' she said. 'Just nod if you want a drink. You first, Mrs Simmons?'

The woman nodded, and Anne Hampton loosened the gag from the woman's mouth. She held the jug up to the woman's lips. 'Don't take too much,' she said. 'I don't know if he'll let me take you to the bathroom.' The woman stopped in midgulp and nodded again.

'I'm scared,' the woman said, taking advantage of the loosened gag. 'Can't you help us? You seem like such a nice girl. You're not much older than the twins, please, please . . .'

Anne Hampton was about to respond when she heard a voice from the living room. 'No talking. Just one drink. Don't make me enforce the rules.'

'Please,' the woman whispered.

'I'm sorry,' Anne Hampton whispered back. She replaced the gag, but not so tightly. The woman nodded gratefully.

Anne Hampton moved first to one of the twins, then the other. 'Don't talk,' she whispered to each. When she reached the father she hesitated. 'Please,' she said, 'don't try anything. Don't force him.' The man nodded and she loosened the gag. He drank and then she replaced the handkerchief. For a moment he strained against the rope that bound all of them together. She heard the man say, despite the gag in his mouth, 'Help us, please,' but she could not respond.

'I'm sorry,' she said.

She closed the door on the family and went back into the main room.

'How're they doing?' Douglas Jeffers asked.

'They're scared.'

'They should be.'

'Doug, please,' Martin Jeffers said. 'At least let them go. What have they done . . .'

The older brother cut the younger one off abruptly.

'Haven't you learned anything all day? Christ, Marty, I've explained and explained. It is important that they haven't done anything. That's crucial. Can't you see? The guilty never get punished, only the innocent. That's the way the world works. The innocent and the powerless. They make up the victim class.'

Douglas Jeffers shook his head.

'It can't be that hard for you to understand.'

'I'm trying, Doug, believe me, I'm trying.'

Douglas Jeffers looked harshly at his brother.

'Try harder.'

They lapsed into silence. Douglas Jeffers toyed with his automatic pistol while Martin Jeffers sat quietly. Anne Hampton moved across the room and took up her seat, opening a new notepad.

'Get it all down, Boswell.'

She nodded and waited. She thought: It is all madness. Everywhere. There is no normalcy left in the world, only hurt and death and insanity. And I'm part of it. Completely.

She took the pen and wrote: No one gets out alive.

She surprised herself. It was the first time she'd written any thought of her own in the notebooks. She stared down at the phrase. It terrified her.

The words on the pages shimmered and wavered like heat above one of the black highways they'd traveled. She fought off the exhaustion and the deadly thought and reconstructed the day in her head, blocking fear with memory.

She did not know why Douglas Jeffers had postponed killing the Simmons family, only that they had herded them all from their beds, tied, blindfolded, and gagged, into the side room. He'd left them there while he'd relaxed, feet up on the couch, savoring the rising sun. He'd then fixed a leisurely breakfast. He had only said that keeping them caged for a day heightened the game. She had been surprised; it had seemed almost as if he did not want to hurry himself, that he was luxuriating in the situation, not wanting to rush on to the next. The jeopardy of their circumstances seemed not to affect him. She did not know what it was that was causing him to pause and greet things with such studied delay, but it scared her.

We're at the end, she had thought.

It's the last scene, and he wants to play it for what it's worth. Two thoughts had intruded in the maze of her fears:

What will he do to them?

What will he do to me?

Douglas Jeffers had made eggs and bacon, but she had been unable to swallow anything. They were just finishing when the car came down the driveway. She had been horrifed at the thought of somebody stumbling in on Douglas Jeffers. Then her terror had redoubled at the sight of the brother. She had instantly assumed he would be the same. When he wasn't, it had confused and disturbed her more.

She looked at the two men again.

They were only a few feet apart, but she wondered how distant they really were. She had the vague understanding that it was important to her, but she could not guess why.

She wanted to scream at them: I want to live!

But, instead, she sat patiently, quietly, awaiting instructions.

So far they had spent the day just as one would expect any pair of brothers. They'd talked of old things, of memories. They had laughed a bit. But by the early afternoon the conversation had disintegrated, wilting under the inexorable pressure of the situation, and now they sat apart, waiting.

She looked back a half-dozen pages in her notebook and saw some of what she had written down. Martin Jeffers had said, 'Doug, I can't believe why we're here. Can we talk about it?'

And Douglas Jeffers' reply: 'Believe it.'

She looked up at the pair and saw Martin Jeffers shift in his seat. She did not know what to think of him. Will he save me? She wondered suddenly.

'Doug, why are you doing this?'

'Asked and answered. That's what the attorneys say in a court case when they're trying to protect their witness from cross-examination. Asked and answered. Go on to the next question.'

'There is only one question.'

'Not true, Marty, not true. Certainly there's why, I'll grant you that. But there's also how and when, and what are you going to do now. That seems most relevant.'

'All right,' Martin Jeffers agreed, 'What are you going to do now?'

'Don't ask.'

Douglas Jeffers burst out laughing. The sound seemed alien, impossible, in the small room. Anne Hampton recognized the laugh from all the worst moments. She hoped the younger brother would have the sense to back down.

He did. He sat quietly. After a few moments the older brother waved his hand in the air as if clearing the space between them.

'Tell me,' said Douglas Jeffers. 'How much do you know?'

'I know everything.'

The older brother paused.

'Well, that's not good. Not good at all.'

He hesitated before continuing.

'So that means you went to my place. I thought you would wait until it was over. You were supposed to wait.'

'No, actually, someone else did.'

'Who?'

Martin Jeffers stopped. He suddenly had no idea what to say. He thought of all the times he'd been in intense conversation with one criminal or another. He'd always know what gestures to make, how to act. This time he drew a complete blank. He stared across at his brother, and at the gun waving about in his hands. But he saw the child behind the man and realized: I am one, too. The younger brother. A massive, burning resentment started to grow within him. Always last to know. Always the last to get anything. He always did exactly what he wanted, regardless of what I thought. He never listened to me. He always treated me like some unwanted appendage. He was always in charge. He was always important. I was always nothing. The afterthought. Always, always. He suddenly hated everything and wanted to hurt his brother.

'A detective.'

The word was out of his mouth swiftly. He regretted it immediately.

'He knows, too?'

Martin Jeffers saw his brother stiffen, struggling but maintaining composure. But in the same moment whatever lilt and relaxation emptied from his voice, was replaced with an instant harsh noise. It was a tone Martin Jeffers had never heard before, but which he knew with a familiarity born of years. He thought: Killing tones.

'Yes,' he said. 'Actually, it's a she.'

Douglas Jeffers waited, then said.

'Well, that brings dying time a bit closer.'

Detective Mercedes Barren had trouble controlling the large American car, with its mushy suspension that bounced and yawed back and forth, trying to take the bumps in the dirt road. A high-pitched scratching sound filled the interior as a tree branch scraped paint from the side of the automobile. She heard the tailpipe slap the ground, but she continued on, doggedly, ignoring the difficulty.

She would not acknowledge that she was lost. But the enveloping black of the night and the forest created a sense of despair within her, as if reason and responsibility had been abandoned back on the main highway, and she was descending into some netherworld where the rules were created by death. The shadows seemed to leap from the headlights, each one a bansheelike wraith with the face of Douglas Jeffers. She gasped in fear and drove on, her heavy gun now clutched in her right hand, balanced on top of the steering wheel.

When she arrived at the multiple fork in the road, her headlights picking out the four different-colored arrows, she stopped the car and got out.

She stood, looking at the four different paths.

Her heart was filled with frustration. She remembered the police chief's description, and she formed a mental picture of the map that hung in his office. But it had no correlation to the dark choices that faced her now. She thought of the lady and the tiger, but knew that she wanted to open the door that contained the beast.

'It must be that one,' she said, pointing down one black path. 'I'm certain,' she added in defiance of the fear of her actual uncertainty. The disjointed idea that she would arrive, gun in hand, at some other summer vacationer's house, floated about for an instant in the back of her mind. Then she dismissed it.

'Let's go,' she said, the sound of her own voice seeming small and puny against the forest. She got back behind the wheel of the car and drove ahead.

Two hundred yards down the road, it forked again and she followed her instincts to the left. She knew that she was searching for the pond, and that the point of land where she would find her quarry waiting was long and narrow. She rolled down the window, trying to get a sense of where the water was, but only the night penetrated into the car. She kept driving, rolling through an open wooden fence and a large KEEP OUT THIS MEANS YOU sign. She ignored it, pushing deeper and deeper into the scrub brush and pines, until the forest seemed to envelop her. She was afraid of being smothered and she sucked in air, hyperventilating.

She would not allow herself even to think for an instant that she might be heading in some completely wrong direction.

'Keep going,' she said.

She saw a break in the trees ahead and she punched

down on the accelerator gratefully. The car jumped forward, then crunched down, seeming to fall, like an athlete tripped just short of the finish line. She shouted out in sudden fear. She heard a snapping sound, followed by a grinding noise.

She stopped the car and stepped out.

Both front wheels were driven into a small yet unfortunately effective pit. The car's front axle was ground into the sand.

She sighed and closed her eyes. Keep going, she told herself again. She opened her eyes and got back into the car. The rear wheels spun furiously when she tried to back out of the pit. She pounded the wheel in momentary frustration, then swallowed hard and looked about her. She shut off the engine and switched off the lights. All right, she told herself. You can go the rest of the way on foot. This isn't terrible; you planned on abandoning the car soon anyway. Just keep going, keep going.

She headed toward the break in the trees, her eyes adjusting rapidly to the night light. She kept her pistol in her hand and started to jog, just gently, afraid that she would do to her ankle what the pit had done to the rental car. But the hurried movement encouraged her, and she pressed farther, listening to the thudding sound her feet made as they hit the sandy road surface.

The road seemed like a tunnel to her, and she could see the end. She picked up her pace and suddenly shot out of the overhanging trees into a wide grassy field awash with moonlight. She dizzily stared up into the skies, overwhelmed by the thousands of star lights that blinked and shone in the endless expanse. She felt minuscule and alone, but comforted by being out from under the trees. For an instant she thought she would be blinded by the moonlight, and she stopped, breathing hard, to get her bearings.

She saw a great glistening reflection off to her left and she stared out at the pond. She could clearly see the strip of sand that stood between the edge of the field and the start of the pond water. She held her breath for a moment and realized that she could hear the steady rhythmic pounding of surf against the shore. She looked toward the sound and could easily make out the black line of South Beach a half mile distant.

I found it, she thought.

I'm there.

She looked ahead, expecting the see the house, but could not. She turned and looked to her right, expecting to see the pond, also, but all she could see was the dark forest stretching back into the island.

'That's not right,' she said out loud, hesitant, suddenly worried. 'That's not right at all. Finger Point is supposed to be narrow, with water on both sides.'

She moved forward ten feet, as if by looking at it from a slightly different angle the topography would change.

'This isn't right at all,' she said.

Dozens of conflicting emotions reverberated like so much dissonance within her.

'Please,' she said. 'It must be.'

She walked down to the edge of the water and stared out across the pond. The moonlight shimmered on the light, choppy waves. She stared into the night, across the water.

Then she sank down to her knees in the sand.

'No,' she said softly. 'Please, no. No, no, no.'

In front of her was the pond water, stretching out in one direction across to the rolling sandy dunes of South Beach. But back, just across from where she knelt, she could see a single long, black spit of land that pointed out into the center of the pond.

'No,' she said, under her voice. 'It's not fair.'

She could see the house on the end of the point and knew then that she was looking at the place where the Jeffers brothers waited. She concentrated her eyes in the darkness and saw the moonlight catch what she guessed was the white shape of the rental car checked out to Martin Jeffers.

She pitched forward at the waist and pounded her fist on the sand. 'No, no, no, no, no,' she moaned. Still kneeling, she turned and looked back at the forest. The wrong road, she thought, the wrong damn road. I've come down the wrong edge of the pond. All this way, just to take the wrong damn turn. Dismay filled her precipitously. She battled within herself against herself.

Finally, breathing hard, as if she'd just run a race, not was about to start one, she gained control.

She stood.

'I will not be defeated,' she said out loud. She raised her fist at the house. 'I'm coming. I'm coming.'

Holt Overholser pushed himself back from the table, staring at the few remains of his second helping of bluefish casserole that were left on his plate, and said, 'Damn, damn.'

'What is it, dear?' his wife asked. 'Something wrong with the fish?'

He shook his head. 'Just something happened that's kinda bugging me,' he said.

'Well, don't keep it to yourself,' his wife replied, clearing the dinner dishes. 'What's on your mind? Worries just get in the way of digestion, you know.'

He thought for an instant that his wife had the world figured out pretty squarely: everything was digestion. If the Arabs and the Jews ate more grains, they wouldn't always be fighting. If the Russians were more balanced in their diet and cut their caloric intake, they wouldn't forever be thumping their chests and threatening world peace. If terrorists would stop eating red meat and partake of more fish, they wouldn't need to seize airliners. Republicans ate too many fatty foods, which gave them bad hearts and conservative outlooks, so she always voted the Democratic ticket. He'd once tried to ask her about some of the more substantial members of the Massachusetts congressional delegation, like Tip and Teddy, but she wouldn't listen to him.

'Well, right before closing shop, I had this visit from a detective. She came all the way from Miami.'

'Was she on a case, dear? It must have been exciting.'

'She said she wasn't.'

'Why didn't you bring her home for dinner?'

'But she was armed. And she had a funny story that makes less and less sense the more I think about it.'

'Well, dear, what are you going to do?'

Holt Overholser thought hard for a moment. Maybe he wasn't any Sherlock Holmes, but he sure could match Mike Hammer.

'I think I'm gonna take a little ride,' he said. 'Don't worry none. I'll be back in time for *Magnum P.I.*'

He slung his Sam Browne belt over his shoulder and headed out to the big four-wheel-drive police truck.

Martin Jeffers remained frozen in his seat, watching his brother pace angrily about the room. He tried once to catch Anne Hampton's eyes, but she was rigid, at the table, pen poised. He wondered for an instant what she must have been through; he could not guess, but knew that it must have been severe to bring about the state of near-catatonia she seemed trapped within.

His observation surprised him. It was the first reflection he'd had since arriving at Finger Point that at least displayed some rudimentary psychological knowledge. He tried to give himself commands: Use what you know!

Then he shook his head slightly, just the barest of acknowledgments, signaling to himself that it was hopeless. At this moment, he thought, I am nothing except the younger brother.

He looked up at Douglas Jeffers and thought: With him, it is all I will ever be.

He fixed his eyes on his brother, who seemed filled with excitement. He seemed to be assessing the situation with every step about the room.

'Isn't it funny,' said Douglas Jeffers in a voice devoid of any semblance of humor, 'how one enters into a situation so emotionally complex it cries out, yet there is little, if anything, actually to say to one another? What are you going to do? Tell me I can't be the way I am?'

The comment brought forth a short explosive laugh.

'So,' said the older brother, 'tell me something relevant, something important. Tell me about this lady cop.'

'What do you want to know?'

His brother stopped and pointed the gun at him.

'Do you think that I would hesitate for an instant? Do you think that your status as my brother gives you some special dispensation? You came here! You knew! So you knew the risks as well . . .'

He paused.

'So don't screw around with me.'

Martin Jeffers nodded.

'She comes from Miami. She believes you killed her niece . . .' He couldn't state what he knew, and what his mind insisted: You did kill her niece! You killed all of them!

' . . . She was the one that broke into your apartment and found the pictures.'

'Where is she now?'

'I left her in New Jersey.'

'Why?'

'Because she means to kill you.'

Douglas Jeffers laughed.

'Well, that seems sensible from her point of view.'

'Doug, please, can't we . . .'

'Can't we what? Marty, you were always such a dreamer. Don't you remember? All those books I used to read to you when you were little. Always fantasies, adventures, filled with heroes and battling for just causes against insurmountable odds. You always liked reading about soldiers who fought desperate fights, about knights that charged dragons. You always liked the ones where goodness triumphs . . .

'You know what? It doesn't. It never does. Because even when goodness wins, it lowers itself and has to beat evil at its own game. And that, dear brother, is a far worse defeat.'

'That's not true.'

Douglas Jeffers shrugged. 'Believe what you want, Marty. It makes no difference.' He paused, then continued. 'Tell me more. Is she a good detective? What's her name?'

'Mercedes Barren. I suppose she is. She found me . . .'

Douglas Jeffers snarled. 'You think she'll find me, too?'

Martin Jeffers nodded.

'No fucking chance. Not unless you told her where to come. You didn't, did you, brother?'

Martin Jeffers shook his head.

Douglas Jeffers scowled. 'I don't fucking believe you.' He paused. 'Oh, you probably didn't know you were telling her, but you did. I know you, Marty. I know you as well as I know myself. That's part of what being older means: the older brother is burdened with understanding, the younger brother is filled only with equal parts awe and jealousy. So, even if you think you left her behind, you probably didn't. You said something, probably didn't even know what it was. But you said it and now she's on her way. Especially if she was smart enough to get to you in the first place. But how close is she? There, dear brother, that's the real question. Is she outside the door?'

Martin Jeffers' eyes involuntarily flicked to the sliding glass doors. His brother laughed again, menacingly.

'. . . Or is she a little ways behind? Maybe a few hours.'

He smiled, not with any enjoyment that belonged on the earth.

'You see,' Douglas Jeffers continued, 'after tonight I will be long gone. I thought coming to Finger Point an excellent place to be born again. And not in some silly fundamentalist religious sense. We've got a lot of memories, shall I say, floating about around here. That's a joke. Anyway, here is where it all begins again for me. Starting over. Back to square one, free as the proverbial bird.'

'How?'

Douglas Jeffers gestured towards his photo satchel. 'Details, details. Suffice it to say, inside the bag is the new me.'

'I still don't understand,' Martin Jeffers said.

'There's only one thing you need to know,' Douglas Jeffers said abruptly. 'The new me doesn't have a brother.'

The words punched Martin Jeffers in the core. He thought he would be nauseated and he tried to steady himself by grasping the arms of the chair.

'You won't,' he said. 'I don't believe you could.'

'Don't be ridiculous,' Douglas Jeffers said irritatedly. 'Boswell can reassure you: I;ve never had any qualms about killing anybody, have I, Boswell?'

They both turned and looked at Anne Hampton. She shook her head.

' . . . So why should I hesitate to kill my brother? Come on! Cain slew Abel, didn't he? Isn't that the deepest secret all brothers harbor? We all want to murder each other. You should know that, you're the shrink. Anyway, what better route to complete and total freedom could there be? With you alive, I would always know you were out there, one solid, unshakable link to the past. Suppose we bumped together on the street one day? Or maybe you saw my picture somewhere. I could never be certain, you know, never be really sure. You know what the silly thing is? I was willing to take that chance. Right up to the moment you showed up here. Then, as soon as I saw you, I realized how wrong that was. If I wanted to live, well . . . you see, don't you? With you gone, well . . .' He shrugged. 'Seems reasonable to me.'

'Doug, you're not, don't be, what do you . . .' His voice trailed off. He was confused and astonished. Martin Jeffers kept thinking: But I came here to save him!

In a single terrifying leap, Douglas Jeffers crossed the room, thrusting the barrel of the automatic up under his brother's throat. 'Can you feel death? Can you smell it? Can you taste it on your lips? They all could, all of them, if only for an instant, but they could.'

'Doug, please, please . . .'

Douglas Jeffers stepped back. 'Weakness is disgusting.' He looked at his brother. 'I should have let you go, then you would have died, too.'

Martin Jeffers shook his head. He knew immediately what his brother was talking about. 'I was a strong swimmer. As good as you. Much better than he was. I would have saved him.'

'He didn't deserve to be saved.'

Their eyes locked and both men's minds filled with the same memory.

'It was just like tonight,' Martin Jeffers said.

'I remember,' his brother joined in, some of his menace sliding away in recollection.

491

'It was hot and he wanted to swim. He took us to the beach, but you said not to go in. You could see the water tossing about. I remember.'

'There'd been a storm a few days earlier, remember? Storms always knock the hell out of the beach. That's why. I thought there might be a rip and you couldn't see it coming at night . . .'

'That's why you wouldn't let me go in.'

Douglas Jeffers nodded. 'But that old bastard called us chicken. He got what he deserved.'

Martin Jeffers hesitated.

'We could have saved him, Doug. It wasn't a bad rip, but he fought it. We were much stronger than he was. Much. We could have saved him, but you wouldn't. You held me on the beach and said let him swim in his own shit, I remember. You held me and I heard him call for help. You kept holding me until he stopped calling.'

Douglas Jeffers smiled.

'I guess it was my first killing. God, it was so easy.'

He looked at his brother.

'In their own way they've all been easy.'

Martin Jeffers asked. 'Is that what started you?'

Douglas Jeffers shrugged. 'Ask Boswell. It's all in the notes.'

'You tell me!'

'Why?'

'I need to know.'

'No, you don't.'

Martin Jeffers paused. That was true.

After a moment he asked, 'So what are you going to do?'

Douglas Jeffers stepped back, rising, 'I told you, Marty, I should have let you go that night. Then you both would have drowned. That was what should have happened. Do you know that was the last time I ever showed anyone pity? No, I don't suppose you know that. I took care of you that night. It didn't matter how hard you fought or how hard he screamed. I wasn't letting you go into the water to save that bastard. I saved your life that night. I gave you all these good, bad, sad years. Now I'm calling in my marker.

Time's up. Game's over. All-y-all-y-in-come-free. Don't you see? All I'm really going to do is what has been delayed all these years: I'm going to let you rush to your own death.'

He paused. 'Maybe you would have saved him. He didn't deserve it. But maybe you would have. It would have been nice for you to do something brave . . .

'But you didn't get the chance.'

Douglas Jeffers took a deep breath.

'You'll never get the chance.'

He raised the gun, pointing at his brother.

'You probably have some romantic idea that this is difficult,' Douglas Jeffers said blankly.

'Well, it isn't.'

He fired the gun.

The echo of the gunshot fled across the black waters and rushed up into the starry sky. Detective Mercedes Barren raced back to the edge of the water, peering into the ink-dark night, knowing that the shot came from the house directly across from where she stood. She could feel the gentle pond wavelets slapping at the toes of her sneakers. Her insides were churning and her head was screaming: No time! No time! It's happening now! I know it!

She stared at the water, filled with impotent rage. I can't swim! Oh, God, I can't, I can't.

Maybe it's shallow, she tried to persuade herself.

She knew that was a lie.

She took a single tentative step into the water. It chilled her heart and she could feel the suffocating darkness start to close on her. She felt dizzy and stepped back. She turned and peered behind her, at the long road back through the woods.

No time.

She thought: I am a hundred yards from success. It might as well be a million miles.

Her half-determination, half-panic swirled within her, filling her with despair and devotion. I will get there, she said to herself, gritting her teeth. I will. I will.

But she did not know how.

She turned and looked up the beach. The moonlight caught the water, spinning wan light about into odd figures and shadows. She saw a dark, oblong shape perhaps fifty yards away at the lip of the water. She took one hesitant step toward it, then another. Her mind would not form the word: boat. But her heart shouted orders and she found herself suddenly running, racing across the sandy beach, toward the shape. With each step it took greater and greater form, until, finally, she could see that it was a small skiff.

I'm coming, she thought. Thank you, thank you. She rushed to the side of the boat and grasped it.

Then she stopped dead.

There was no engine. No oars. Just a single mast, without sail.

Not allowing disappointment to move within her, she slid to the front of the boat. It was chained to a post sunk into the sand. The chain had been padlocked.

She slipped to the sand, frustration and dismay unleashed within her. She breathed out hard, fighting tears. She thought she could not deal with the capriciousness of life anymore. It's all wrong, she told herself. Everything's been all wrong. All along.

I'm sorry. I'm sorry. Oh, God, I tried. I tried so hard.

She stared back at the lights across the water.

He'll get away, she said to herself. I was never any closer than I am now. There was always something that would keep me from him.

I've lost.

She put her head down on her arms, leaning against the gunnel of the boat.

I'm sorry, she said again.

The moonlight seemed to make the boat glow in the darkness. It caught the ridge of something white, stuck in the corner of the hull.

She sat up, instantly curious, a vague sense of reprieve filling her. She reached out her hand and seized a plastic-coated cushion. It had two looped handles on either end. Her hands twitched: a floatation cushion.

She looked across to the house, where she knew Douglas Jeffers was getting ready to leave, to disappear forever from her grasp. This is it, she told herself. This is your only chance. Then she stared at the water, curling black and bottomless in front of her. She thought of her niece and she remembered the effortless way Susan slipped through the opaque blue pool, graceful, at ease, fearless. 'Oh, God,' she said again. She remembered the crushing green fury that boiled around her and slammed her down, tearing her breath away, trying to rip the life from her little-girl lungs. She thought of the promise she'd made as a child and kept as an adult. Her mind filled then with the sum of every nightmare she'd ever had and her entire body revolted, shaking.

'I can't,' she said.

She remembered her father coming padding through the dark house to the side of her bed, comforting her when nightmare awakened her. He would take his big hands and gently rub her temples, saying to her that he was going to coax the bad dream out of her head. After a moment he would hold his palm up, as if he held the frightening thought in the air before her. She remembered he would say: Goodbye, bad dreams; begone, nightmare. And then he would take a deep breath and blow the unsettling thoughts into some childhood oblivion. She remembered stroking her niece's forehead the same way so that Susan could settle back into the easy sleep of youth. She took a deep breath and exhaled slowly. She said to herself, Begone, nightmare!

She took a step toward the water.

'I can't,' she repeated.

But she slipped the loops on the cushion over her arms. She dug her pistol into her belt.

'I can't swim.'

She felt the water curl around her ankles. It seemed to be grasping for her, trying to pull her into its dark void.

'I can't,' she said a last time.

Then she pushed herself gently into the water.

For the first twenty yards her toes bounced against the bottom and she felt confident. It was in the twenty-first yard, when her legs bounced down, expecting to touch the mushy bottom and found nothing save more fluid, that panic started to grip her. She shouted to herself: Keep going, keep moving.

She paddled gently with her arms and kicked steadily with her feet.

You can make it, she told herself with false bravado.

A wavelet rose up and slapped her in the face.

It caused her to lose her equilibrium, and she teetered as if on some pinnacle. She twitched, then thrashed, trying to regain control. Another wavelet punched her and she spun about, feeling herself slipping. Black panic started to explode within her, and she struggled to regain her balance. But each movement, no matter how little, only pitched her back and forth harder. She squeezed the cushion, but it bucked and fought her.

She wanted to scream but could not.

A small wave broke against her, and she could feel everything sliding away from her.

No! No! No! she screamed inwardly.

Then she rolled, turtlelike, the black water suddenly slamming over her head like a closet door shut around her.

Oh, God! I'm dying!

It was as if the water were tugging her down. She battled against the flood pulling her to the bottom.

The water held her, embracing her like some demon lover, squeezing the breath from her, twisting her into its darkness. She could no longer tell which was up and which was down. The night had been ripped away, replaced by the thick grasp of the pond.

Where's the air!

Help, me! Help, me! Oh, God! Please! Don't let me drown!

She thrashed and fought like a tigress alone in the blackness against death.

I won't, I won't, I won't let it happen like this! Susan! God! Help me! Susan, no!

She suddenly thought that it was all wrong to die so close to victory. And in some microsecond of reason that penetrated the fear that gripped her, she thought: Do not give in.

And so she didn't.

Within the vacuum of panic, she knew to clutch the flotation cushion. She seized it with a fury, screaming to herself her desire to live. She wrestled it around, so that it was suddenly riding beneath her chest. She could feel, abruptly, the cushion pushing her up, and in a second her head broke the surface of the water.

She did not understand exactly how it had happened, but she gratefully gulped in great gasps of air, resting.

Her eyes remained on the house. It was closer.

'I'm still coming,' she said between gritted teeth.

As she started to work herself forward, she saw an extraordinary sight: a flight of six ghost-white swans soaring three feet above the pond surface flew directly over her as if pointing the way. She watched as the birds, their wings glowing in the moonlight, pivoted above the house and then disappeared into the night sky. 'Susan,' she said out loud in near delirium. 'I'm coming.'

She realized then that she had lost her mind.

Perhaps I did die, she thought. Perhaps I'm dreaming this.

I'm really dead, beneath the water, and this is all the last fantasy before entering the void.

She paddled on, stretching with every fiber for the mixed safety and danger of the waiting shore.

'Well,' Douglas Jeffers said rigidly, 'that proves something.'

Martin Jeffers stared wide-eyed, on the promontory of panic. He could smell cordite and powder, and the gunshot still rang in his ears, deafening him. He did not dare to turn and inspect the wall where the bullet had slammed in, a foot, perhaps two, above his head.

'Now you know,' said Douglas Jeffers. 'Now you know.'

Know what? Martin Jeffers thought. He did not speak.

Douglas Jeffers turned and stepped to the sliding glass doors, standing, looking out over the water. He paused, seeming to absorb all the night sensations.

Martin Jeffers blinked his eyes and took a deep breath, as if double-checking to be certain he remained alive. He watched his brother. He's right. He has no choice.

'I would never tell,' Martin Jeffers said.

'Yes, you would.' Douglas Jeffers snorted, a small laugh. 'You'd have to, Marty. They'd make you. Hell, you'd make you.'

'I keep confidences – in my profession . . .'

The older brother interrupted. 'This isn't part of your profession.'

'Well, there are lots of families with great dark secrets that they never tell anyone. It's in all the literature. It's in dozens of novels and plays. Why not . . .'

Douglas Jeffers interrupted, a weak smile flitting across his troubled face. 'Awww, come on, Marty.'

He paused before continuing.

'And, anyway, it would ruin your life. Think about it. No one could carry that kind of knowledge about their brother forever. It would eat away at you, gnawing like some determined rat at your guts. No, you'd tell. And then she'd find me.'

'How?'

'She just would. Never underestimate what madness and revenge can drive someone to.'

Martin Jeffers said nothing. He knew his brother was right.

A silence filled the room.

'So?' said Martin Jeffers. He was filled with confusion. He heard his own voice speaking in the room, but it was as if it were someone else giving the commands to talk. What are you saying? he said to himself. What are you doing? Stop, for Christ's sake! But his voice continued, unchecked: 'I guess you're just going to have to kill me.'

Douglas Jeffers continued to look out the door. His silence was his answer.

'What about Boswell?' Martin Jeffers asked.

Again Douglas Jeffers didn't reply.

Anne Hampton stared at the two brothers and thought:

This is the end. He does not need anyone. He has the notebooks. He has a new life.

She tried to will her body to move. Run, she thought. Escape! she was unable to. I know I can, she said to herself. I know I can. She gritted her teeth together and squeezed her hands. She looked down and saw that her knuckles were white around the edge of the pen and started to push it against her other hand. Pain filled her. You're still alive! she screamed to herself. It hurts and you're alive. She looked at the two brothers and slowly, she said to herself: My name is Anne Hampton. Anne with an *e*. I am twenty years old and I attend Florida State University. I have a home in Colorado and I am a literature major because I love books. I am me.

She repeated this over and over to herself.

I am me. You are you. We are we. I am me.

Martin Jeffers watched his brother, filling with dread at what he might do, despair at what he was.

'Doug, why did you become you? Why not me, too?'

Douglas Jeffers shrugged.

'Now who the hell knows? Maybe it was the difference in years. A few months can mean you see things differently, feel things differently. It's like asking ten people to recall the same event that they witnessed. They'll all come up with slightly skewed versions of the same thing. Why is it any different with people?' He laughed. 'I'm just a slightly skewed version.'

'I'm sorry,' Martin Jeffers said.

'Fuck you, little brother,' Douglas Jeffers responded. 'Do you think I don't want to be the way I am?'

He turned and eyed his brother.

'I am one of the greats of all time.'

He gestured at Anne Hampton. 'She can tell you.'

Douglas Jeffers looked back at his brother.

'You will be forgotten. Me? Never.'

Douglas Jeffers warred within himself. He refused to let his brother see the raging factions of his heart, masking the internal battle with all the savage words he could muster. It's all gotten screwed up, he thought. And it was all moving so perfectly before he showed up. He was supposed to learn after I disappeared. Damn! Damn that damn detective! He kept his back to his brother for fear that the younger would see the indecision that had crept into his eyes. Hundreds of images from their childhood swept him. He remembered the night in New Hampshire. He remembered all the nights that he'd crept to his younger brother's side, to comfort as best he could the little boy's tears. Does he remember? Douglas Jeffers wondered. Does he recall all the lullabies and stories, all the times I rocked him to sleep? Does he remember how I pinned him to the sand so that he wouldn't rush out into the water to his death? That man would have killed us both if he could. But I protected him. I always protected him. Even when I teased him or mocked him. Even when I knew what I was becoming. I always took care of him because he was always the good part of me. He laughed inwardly: They're wrong, he thought. Even psychopaths have some emotions if you dig deep enough.

Then he thought: Maybe we don't.

He measured, on the balance scale within him, his life against his brother's.

One of us starts over tonight.

One of us dies.

He could see no other options.

He turned away, staring back out across the night waters. 'You know, all those summers we were here, I always loved it,' he said. 'It was always so damn wild and beautiful at the same time.'

His eyes caught a flashing shape of white, and he watched a flight of swans skim the surface of the pond.

'Have you noticed?' he said. 'Everything is the same. Even the swan family that lives on the pond.'

'Nothing is the same,' said Martin Jeffers.

But his brother didn't hear him, his attention suddenly riveted elsewhere.

It was as if someone had sent a red-hot stake through his core. Douglas Jeffers stiffened, his eyes burning into the darkness, directly at the shape he saw struggling in the water. For an instant he was confused. What the hell is that? he asked himself. Then, immediately, he knew.

She's here!

He pivoted and abruptly brought the automatic to bear on his brother.

'Boswell! The rope and the tape!'

Anne Hampton was incapable of refusing the summons. She grabbed the satchel with the equipment in it and rushed it to Douglas Jeffers.

'Marty, don't screw around. Don't try anything. Just reach out your hands and let me tie them.'

Martin Jeffers, suddenly filled with apprehension, complied unwittingly, as any younger brother would do. He felt the loops of rope encase his wrists tightly. He wanted to complain, but before he had a chance, his brother had slapped a piece of tape across his lips. He looked up, trying to say, I don't want to die tied like some animal, but his brother was moving too quickly to stop and meet his glance.

'Boswell! Stand there. Don't move. Regardless of what happens, don't move.'

Anne Hampton froze in position and waited.

Douglas Jeffers took one quick look about and slid through the open porch door, disappearing into the blackness that pressed against the weak light of the living room.

For a moment he stood on the porch, peering down toward the water where he'd seen the shape. Then he cast about quickly. An idea struck him and he moved into position.

Relief flooded her as her toes and knees scraped against the bottom.

Detective Mercedes Barren pushed forward, suddenly realizing that the water had grown shallow. She stood, liquid dripping from her like great tears, her eyes lifted upward as if in gratitude. She strode through the water, trying to make as little noise as possible, then threw herself on the beach. She dug her hands in, feeling the dry solid sand slip like wealth through her fingers. She allowed herself one totally unbridled moment of relief and joy.

Then she breathed in and whispered to herself, 'That was the easy part.'

She climbed to her knees and retrieved her bearings.

She got up, crouching over, and moved to the edge of the sand, hiding behind gnarled and tangled beach scrub brush. She could see the lights of the house, but she couldn't see anyone inside from her position. She removed her weapon from her belt and started to maneuver forward.

She crawled through the brush.

It seemed as if the night were alive about her. She could hear the scurrying sound of a small animal, perhaps a skunk or muskrat, that dashed away. The steady hum of cicadas filled her, almost deafening, though she knew that it would not mask the sound of her movements.

She remained in a half-crouch, half-crawl, as she approached the house. She stopped once to make certain her weapon was ready, safety off, round chambered. Don't hesitate, she told herself for the millionth time. Take the shot when it is there.

She longed for some sound from the house, but it remained quiet. She kept moving, steadily, patiently. Death never hurries, she thought. It moves at its own pace.

She reached the edge of a wooden deck and slowly raised her eyes above it. She could see past a set of lounge chairs to the living room. She saw that the sliding glass door was wide open, as if in invitation. Well, she said to herself, here we go.

She crawled up onto the deck, thinking that every squeaking sound she made was like a bell pealing in the night. She got to her feet gingerly, maintaining her crouch. But now she put both hands on her pistol and steadied herself. She was surprised that she didn't feel more anxiety. I am calm. I am deadly.

She slid to the edge of the doorway.

She took a deep breath.

Then, slowly, she peered around the edge.

Confusion struck her. She saw Martin Jeffers, tied and trussed, sittting directly across from the door. She saw a young woman standing stock-still, a few feet away from him. She could not see the brother anywhere. She took a tentative step toward the opening.

And then she heard the voice.

'Behind you, detective.'

She didn't even have the time to fill with panic.

I'm dead, she thought.

But she pivoted, bringing her weapon up, trying to get it into position to fire at the sound of the voice. She caught one small glimpse of a shape, stretched out on one of the outdoor lounges, and then everything exploded before her, as Douglas Jeffers fired his gun.

Pain impacted on her entire being.

The force of the shot ripping into her right knee spun her like a child's top, throwing her back into the living room, where she sprawled desperately on the floor, writhing in agony. Her own weapon had slipped from her fingers, flung violently across the room as she spun in helpless agony.

She squeezed her eyes shut and thought: I failed.

She opened them when she heard the voice above her.

'Is that her, Marty? Boswell, rip that tape off my dear brother's mouth so he can respond.'

Douglas Jeffers stood over Mercedes Barren.

'My hat's off to you, detective. At least it would be if I had one.'

Holt Overholser swore as the big Ford bucked and scraped its way down the dirt road. He had paused, almost giving up, when he reached the multiple fork in the path. Damn, he said to himself. Which damn road is it? Got to be the blue arrow. He made a mental note to contact all the homeowners on Tisbury Great Pond and inform them that for security reasons all roads had to be clearly marked with names and addresses and all sorts of identifying material. Damn! he thought again.

Every ten yards he changed his mind.

'What the hell are you doing, Holt?' he swore.

'Have you really got some damn good reason for being out here in rich people's heaven in the middle of the night?

Jesus H. Christ, I hope the selectmen don't hear about this little escapade. You ought to turn around now and get out of here before you make more of an ass out of yourself.'

His speech made him feel better. He kept on driving.

When he broke out of the forest into the clear, he felt better still.

'Well, it ain't all that late, and if nothing's up, why, she'll probably appreciate your concern. Hell, she's a cop, she'll understand.'

He laughed. 'Well, maybe.'

He stopped the truck, switching off the engine and stepping outside into the starry night.

'This better be the right place, Holt, old boy, or you're gonna look pretty damn stupid.'

He was about to get back into the truck when he heard the shot.

'Now what was that?' he asked himself.

'Just what the hell was that?'

He answered his own questions out loud:

'That sounded to me like a handgun. Damn. Damn. What the hell's going on?'

He got back into his truck and quickly drove ahead.

Martin Jeffers did not ask how she'd found them. He simply said what jumped into his mind: 'I'm sorry, Merce.' He realized it was the first time he'd used her first name. 'I'm sorry you found us . . .'

'But clever, very clever. Tell me, quickly, what was it? How did you guess?' Douglas Jeffers interjected.

'It was something one of them said,' she moaned.

'One of who?'

Martin Jeffers answered. 'She must have talked to my group. They were the ones who gave me the idea of coming here.'

Douglas Jeffers looked at his brother. 'We are all Lost Boys,' he said. He stared at the detective. 'Clever. Very clever.'

She twisted in pain on the floor. She wished that she could look defiantly at him, but the pain surging like some runaway electrical impulse within her prevented any brave looks. She realized that her eyes were filled with tears, and she thought again: I tried. I'm sorry. I did my best.

Douglas Jeffers aimed his automatic at her head.

'This is like shooting a horse with a broken leg.'

He hesitated.

'I'll give you a few seconds, detective. Welcome death.'

She closed her eyes and thought of Susan, of her father, of John Barren. I'm sorry, she said, I'm terribly sorry. I would like to say goodbye to all of you but I haven't the time. She hoped there was a heaven, suddenly, and that she would be pitched by pain into their waiting arms. She squeezed her arms tight and said to herself: I'm ready.

The explosion filled her.

Her head spun in red and black, dizzy, out of control. I'm dying, she thought.

And then she realized she wasn't.

She opened her eyes and saw Douglas Jeffers standing over her, pistol still poised but unfired.

As she watched, he seemed to step back in slow motion.

Her eyes searched about madly and she saw the young woman standing a few feet away. In her outstretched hands was Detective Barren's large handgun.

'Boswell,' Douglas Jeffers said, genuine surprise covering his voice. 'I'll be damned.'

He looked down and saw a streak of red on his shirt.

The shot had torn through his side, ripping the flesh of the waist, then spinning off into the night. He knew instantly that it was not a killing wound, that it would be painful, but he could live.

And in the same thought he knew it had killed him.

He was rapidly flooded with emotions. I can't go to a hospital, he thought. Walk into an emergency room and say, here, fix this gunshot wound without asking any questions. He was struck with a simple, almost silly realization: It's over. Ended by an unlucky shot from a confused child.

'Boswell,' he said gently, 'you've killed me.'

He raised his own weapon, bringing it to bear on Anne Hampton.

She gasped and her fingers let slide Detective Barren's gun. It crashed to the floor. She stood rigid, expecting her own death to storm from the pistol. I tried, she thought. I tried.

Detective Barren saw the young woman drop her hands to her sides, giving in to stunned acquiescence. She saw Douglas Jeffers sight down his weapon, ready to fire. It was as if everything that had happened to her coalesced in that second, and memory and strength combined to defeat pain. She dragged herself toward the murderer, screaming, 'No! No! No! Susan! Run! I'll save you!' and knowing that this time she could, she could, she could. She thrashed across the floor with every fiber of residual strength she could find. She reached out for the murderer's leg, to pull him off-balance, to bring him down on her. 'Run!' she cried again, her mind now oblivious to anything except all the agonies that had dogged her for so many months. 'Susan,' she moaned, as she flung her hands forward, nails scratching, in a desperate effort to seize the man she had chased for so long.

Martin Jeffers threw himself out of the chair, still bound by the rope. He was screaming 'No! No! No!' as he stumbled, falling to one knee, then rising, pushing himself forward as his brother paused so curiously in the deadly business at hand. Martin Jeffers thrust himself in front of the young woman.

Then he turned to his brother.

'No, Doug,' he said. 'No more.'

The two brothers' eyes met. Martin Jeffers saw his brother's leap first with flame, then suddenly subside.

'Please,' he said.

Douglas Jeffers stepped back, still aiming at Anne Hampton, and now at Martin Jeffers as well. He glanced down at the detective writhing on the floor.

'Please.' He heard the voice and thought of his brother in all the lost moments of childhood, when Marty called out and needed him at his side.

Douglas Jeffers hestitated again. He put his hand to his

waist and it came up bloody. He heard the word 'Please' one more time.

Then he turned and disappeared through the door.

Holt Overholser came sailing down the driveway to the house on Finger Point and spotted the man rushing from the front porch. He flipped on the switch that turned on the red and blue strobes on the truck's roof. As Holt braked the truck violently, he saw the man turn and carefully assume a shooter's stance.

'Sweet Jesus!' Holt shouted, ducking as the windshield exploded. 'Holy Mother of Christ!'

He scrambled for his own service revolver, the terrible thought jumping unbidden into his mind that he just might have forgotten to load the damn thing this year.

He didn't bother to check. Brandishing the pistol, he slid from the car and fired four shots in the direction of the fleeing man. The first shot struck the hood of the Ford, making a sound like a cat in heat. The second shot exploded into the ground about ten feet in front of the truck. The third crashed into the house filled with the people he was unwittingly trying to save, and the fourth sped off into night's oblivion.

'Jesus H. Christ,' Holt said. He tried to force himself to remember what he'd been taught, and he finally assumed a proper stance, feet spread, both hands on the weapon, slightly crouched, ready for action.

But there was none to be had.

The night opened endlessly before him.

'Holy Christ,' Holt said. He rushed toward the house. If the West Tisbury police department had any procedure for events such as these, Holt surely would have written it. But he hadn't, and they didn't, so he just barged ahead blithely into the house, gun held ready.

What he saw simply confused him more.

Anne Hampton had loosened Martin Jeffer's hands, and the two of them were helping Detective Barren on to a couch.

'Jesus Crutch on a Christ,' Holt said loudly.

Anne Hampton gestured toward the back room.

'The Simmons family is in there,' she said. 'Help them.'

Holt raced to the door and saw the family tied and gagged. He bent down and tore the bonds off Mr Simmons. 'Get your family free,' he said. Then he ran back out into the main room. Anne Hampton and Martin Jeffers were trying to treat Detective Barren's bleeding leg.

Holt saw the telephone and picked it up. He dialed 911 and waited until he heard Lizzie Barry's voice. She seemed infuriatingly calm to him.

'Police, Fire, Emergency,' she said.

'Jesus, Lizzie, it's Holt. I've got some kinda situation here, I don't know, Jesus, I mean, he was shooting at me!'

'Holt,' replied Lizzie Barry with utter control, 'what is your location exactly?'

'Jesus, I mean, gunshots! I coulda been killed. I'm down at Finger Point, Jesus!'

'All right, Holt, stay calm. Is this an emergency?'

'Jesus Crutch on a Christ,' Holt misspoke again. 'You bet it is!'

'All right,' she said. 'State police will be moving within minutes. Do you need an ambulance?'

'Jesus, we need an ambulance, we need everybody! The Coast Guard, the state cops, Christ! We need the Marines!'

'All right, Holt, help is on the way.'

Lizzie Barry began making the proper calls and sirens started up throughout the night.

Martin Jeffers and Anne Hampton sat on either side of Detective Barren. Anne Hampton asked, 'Can you take it? Help is coming.'

Detective Mercedes Barren leaned her head on the young woman's shoulder. She nodded. Martin Jeffers looked confused for an instant. 'Did you get that, Boswell?' he asked. 'Did you hear what he said? He said, "Jesus Crutch . . . " ' Anne Hampton smiled. 'I got it,' she said. Martin Jeffers laughed and put his arm around both women.

The three of them looked at each other. 'It's over, I guess,' Anne Hampton said. The others nodded, and they all bent their heads together. Tears started to run down Martin Jeffers' face, and he was joined then by Detective Barren and Anne Hampton, neither of whom cried from pain, but from some great, unfathomable release that moved within all of them.

Holt Overholser looked upon the three people sitting on the couch and thought first they must be crazy and then that the detective would be crippled forever with a wound like that. He did not realize that the same was equally true for all three.

Douglas Jeffers ignored the shots fired by the policeman who'd blocked his route to the car and raced across the sandy spit of land to the spot where he knew whoever lived at Finger Point would leave their boats. He saw two Sailfish pulled up on the beach and a dark inflatable dinghy with a small outboard engine next to them. He grabbed the anchor rope to the inflatable and within seconds had the boat pointed toward the crashing surf sounds of South Beach. He pumped the small bulb on the gas line twice, then pulled the starter cord. The little engine coughed once, then caught, and he thrust it into gear.

He was aware of the engine noise interrupting the night solitude. He thought: It cannot be helped.

He steered the boat out of the absolute confidence of memory, for the spot where the pond came closest to the ocean and where he knew the rolling surf was only fifty yards of flat sand away from the calm pond waters.

I could have killed them all.

He smiled. They know it.

As he drove, he checked the clip in his pistol. There were seven shots remaining in the 9-millimeter. She was using the same weapon, he thought idly. Probably says something.

He saw the beach looming ahead, a strip of vague blond light drawn across the endlessness of night. The sound of the waves on the ocean side seemed redoubled. He pointed the dinghy into the beach and felt the sand grab at the underside, scraping at the thick rubber.

509

He cut off the engine and pivoted it up so to not lose the prop in the sand. He stood and stepped from the inflatable onto the beach.

It's just the way it always was.

He stayed motionless, almost entranced by the steady explosion of waves against the sandy beach. It is so constant, so powerful, he thought. It makes us small.

He bent and grasped the inflatable by the bow, pulling it from the water. The effort made his side ache and he was suddenly aware of the pain created by Anne Hampton's shot.

He shrugged it off.

Struggling, he pulled the boat ten feet across the sand.

I never would have thought she had it in her. I never would have thought she could do it. He was oddly proud of her. I always knew she had strength. She just didn't know where to look for it.

He forced the boat across the beach. It made a swishing sound as he tugged at it.

Images surrounded him, from all the places he'd been and all the photos he'd taken. No one could touch me, he thought.

He leaned against the weight of the sand, moving the inflatable inexorably toward the surf.

My pictures were always the best. Color, black and white. Made no difference. I always caught the moment just right. They spoke. They cried out. They told stories.

He sank to his knees in the water wash, grasping his side, his head spinning.

It hurts, Marty, it hurts.

He shook himself upright. Keep going.

He started to sing then: 'Row, row, row your boat, gently down the stream . . .'

He lunged forward with each word, pulling the inflatable into the shallow water that ran away from him, back to the ocean. He dropped his grip on the bow and moved to the side as the rubber boat started to bob in the thin water. He could see a steady, thick roller heading toward the beach and he pushed forward to meet it.

White-green water crashed about him, swirling, as he thrust the boat into the waves.

He grabbed the side and flung one leg over as the inflatable spun about. With his one leg, he straightened the dinghy and shoved hard against the mushy sand, meeting the next wave bow-first.

He rode up, dizzyingly, catching a glimpse of the moon hanging just above the waters, so close he thought he could grab it. Then he was swept down the back side of the wave, into the trough. The surf exploded around him, and in the bottom of the dinghy he was awash. He spun about and jammed down the motor, pulling the starter cord simultaneously. The engine started right up, and he goosed it, just catching the next wave as it rose up in front of him, threatening to dash him back on the beach. The dinghy shot forward, riding past the crash of boiling white water.

He jammed the accelerator handle, and the inflatable surged again.

In a second, as if touched by some mystery, he was out of the surf action, riding on the deep black water, bobbing about, the engine noise steadily driving him from shore.

No Man's Land, he said to himself.

I've always wanted to go to No Man's Land.

He steered away from the beach, leaving the dark mass of the island behind, heading toward the open sea. He guessed at the direction of the target range and pointed the dinghy that way.

He saw the moon again, and it comforted him.

He whispered to himself: 'Oh, the Owl and the Pussycat went to sea in a beautiful pea-green boat . . .'

He smiled to himself and skipped ahead. He sang out blissfully: 'So hand in hand, they danced on the sand by the light of the moon, the moon, the moon . . .'

He thought of his brother. Marty always liked rhymes. He pictured his mother and wondered what had become of her. He realized that she had looked out upon the night when she left them, just as he did this. And it swallowed her up forever, he told himself.

His adoptive father jumped into his imagination. He

scowled but understood. 'I'm coming, you bastard!' he shouted. 'I'm coming!' The words raced across the swells, devoured by the night. He thought of the end of the fight against the rip that pulled so terrifyingly. He must have been exhausted and defeated. It must have been like falling into a deep and painless sleep.

He felt the blood again, and torn flesh.

'It hurts,' he said.

Then he comforted himself. 'It'll be all right.'

The land had dropped far away by now, and he shut his eyes. The engine lulled him, and the steady, gentle pushing of the waves was like rocking a baby, beckoning, urging him to sleep. I'm tired, he said to himself. So tired.

It was wondrously peaceful and he remembered the snatch of another rhyme. He whispered: 'Weary wee flipperling, curl at they ease . . .' He rolled his head back and felt a great and final exhaustion within him. He sang low to himself: ' . . . asleep in the arms of the slow-swinging seas.'

The idea filled him with a satisfied defiance.

'They never caught me,' he said. 'They couldn't.'

It seemed terribly right to him.

He shut off the engine and sat listening to the ocean flowing about him. Then he took his pistol and aimed it down between his feet. He fired all seven shots.

The dinghy shuddered.

Black water boiled up around him.

It's warm, he thought with childish pleasure. It's warm.

He reached out and embraced the coal-dark sea.